League of Elder

The House of Bloodstein

Mentralysis

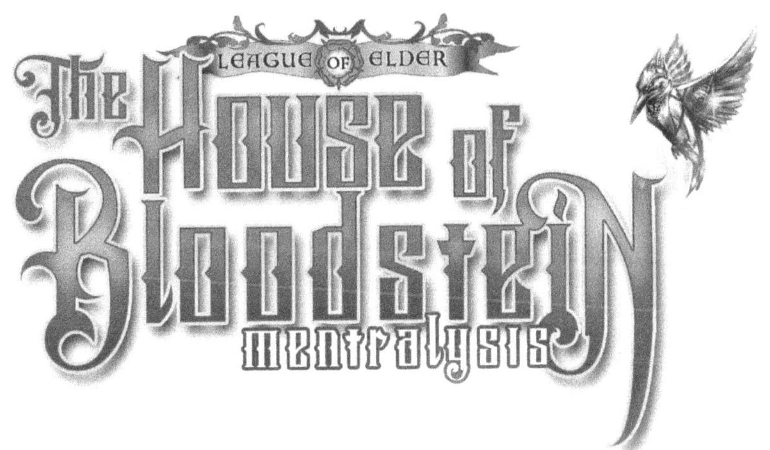

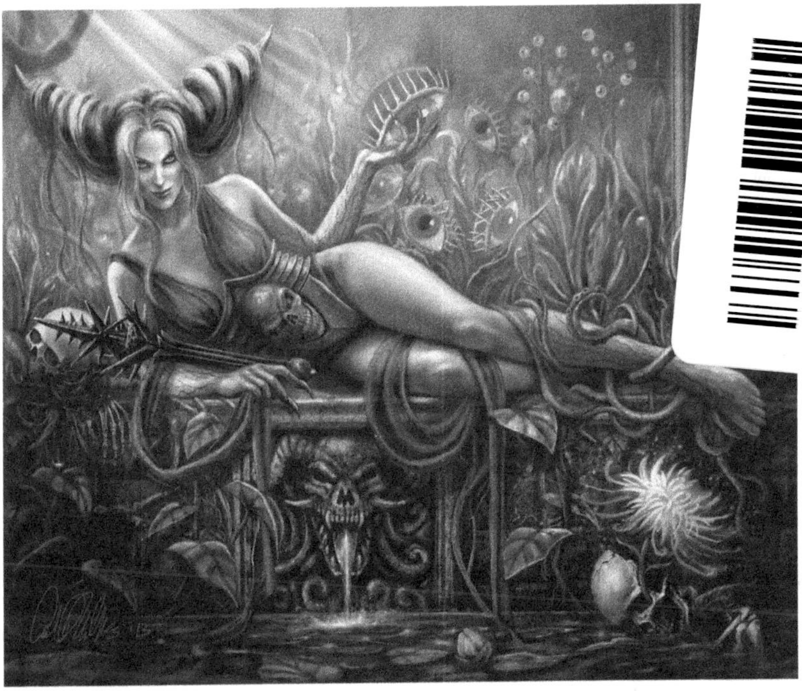

REN GARCIA

The House of Bloodstein: Mentralysis

Copyright © 2017, 2020 by Ren Garcia
Cover Art by © 2017, 2020 by Carol Phillips
Listed copyrighted interior image art is
provided in the 'List of Illustrations'

ISBN: 978-1-937979-93-5

Edited by Cas Peace

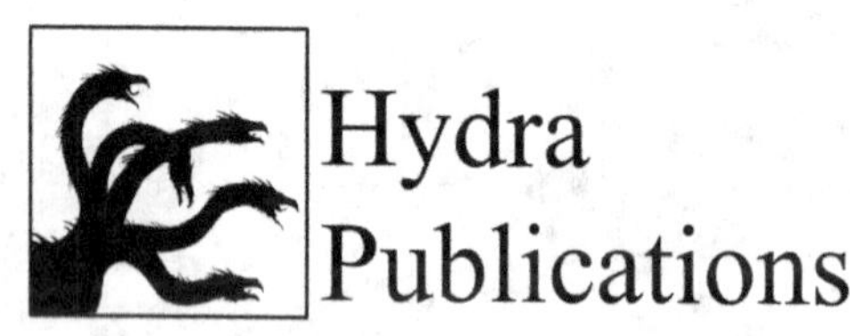

Published by Hydra Publications
Printed in the United States of America
First Hydra edition: February 2020
Visit our website: www.hydrapublications.com

Also by Ren Garcia

The League of Elder Series:
Sygillis of Metatron
The Hazards of the Old Ones

The Temple of the Exploding Head Trilogy:
The Dead Held Hands
The Machine
The Temple of the Exploding Head

The Belmont Saga
Sands of the Solar Empire
Against the Druries

Turns of the Shadow tech Goddess
The Shadow tech Goddess
Stenibelle
Kat
Melazarr (coming soon)
Taara (coming soon)
The Tempus Findal (coming soon)
The All-In-One (coming soon)

The House of Bloodstein
Perlamum
Mentralysis

Non-Fiction by Ren Garcia
10 Weeks at Chanute

For more please visit: www.thetempleoftheexplodinghead.com

Table of Contents

Part 1: Dreams in the Wailing Room

Part 2: The Immortal

Part 3: The Chadburn

List of Illustrations

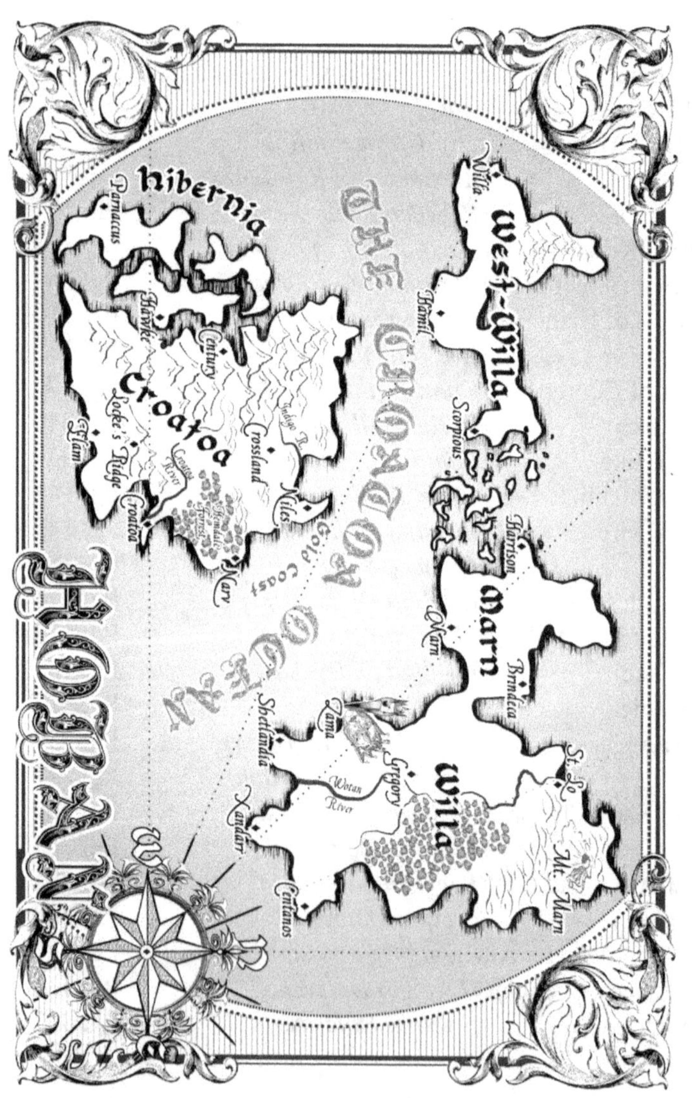
HOBAN
THE CROATOA OCEAN
Gold Coast
hibernia
Parnassus
Croatoa
Hawke
Century
Indigo I.
Crossland
Niles
Locke's Ridge
Crooks River
Elam
Croatoa
Ferndale Marr
Forrest
West-Willa
Willa
Hamil
Scorpious
Harrison
Marn
Brindlea
Zama
St. Lo
Shetlandia
Gregory
Willa
Wotan River
Xandarr
Mt. Marn
Centanos

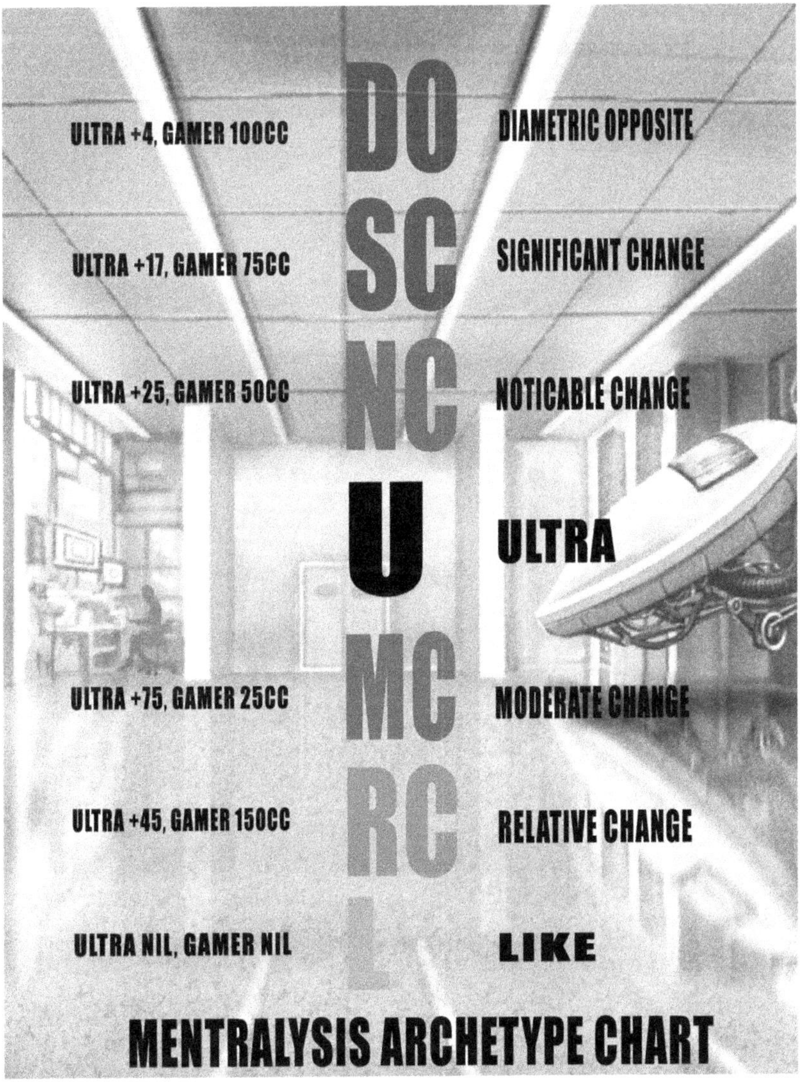

ULTRA +4, GAMER 100CC — **DO** — DIAMETRIC OPPOSITE

ULTRA +17, GAMER 75CC — **SC** — SIGNIFICANT CHANGE

ULTRA +25, GAMER 50CC — **NC** — NOTICABLE CHANGE

U — **ULTRA**

ULTRA +75, GAMER 25CC — **MC** — MODERATE CHANGE

ULTRA +45, GAMER 150CC — **RC** — RELATIVE CHANGE

ULTRA NIL, GAMER NIL — **LIKE**

MENTRALYSIS ARCHETYPE CHART

Part 1

Dreams in the Wailing Room

1—Alone

Rrrrrrriiiiiiiinnnnggggg ...

Sam awoke to bright sunshine coming in through her giant terrace window. She stretched and probed about, searching for Kay's familiar form that was always in bed next to her, regular as the sunrise.

The events of the last week had been truly tiring. Sarah and her bloody adventures. Sarah had dragged them all out into the wilds of space: to Xandarr, a place Sam hated because #6 was there, and then to Waam where they ended up in the temple of a demented Black Hat named Wilhella Cormand-Grande.

There were those hateful Wunderlucks from Remnath and the piece of her heritage that they had stolen; the Mourning Wall sacred to her Astralon people. Had Kay and her friends not calmed her, Sam's anger would have been deadly.

She felt the back of her neck. It felt smooth and blemish-free. Ennez had repaired the gaping hole that had been there. One of the Wunderlucks had attempted to murder her, placing an illegal Xaphan Hemolizer on her neck. She recalled, with a bit of terror, the odd, rushing feeling of her blood coming out in a pressurized cloud. The Hemolizer should have killed her in just a minute or two.

Kay, along with the little Silver tech familiar, King, had saved her, and then Ennez flawlessly healed her wound. She had been bled out by the Hemolizer. Ennez gave her a Malik to keep her out for a few days and a caloric to provide her with nourishment while she slept and healed.

How long had she been asleep? It couldn't have been more than a day or two.

What a terrible nightmare she'd had as she slept. She relived the feeling of the Hemolizer killing her: the rushing of blood, the fruitless gulps for breath, the fall into freezing cold. Kay's terrified eyes looking down on her as she died.

And then there was something else. She dreamt of strangers in her room, going through her things, pawing at her helpless Maliked body and carrying her from bed. She recalled an odd sound, a bell-like ringing and of being in a terrible presence; there was a creature, ancient and bereft of goodness, looking down on her. Cold

hands touching her Maliked body. Red eyes. She recalled seeing the face of #6 of the Xandarr 44, a past rival for Kay's love and her perpetual nemesis. The mere sight of #6 was enough to drive Sam into a killing frenzy.

But in the dream she couldn't move, and then there was the smothering, the horrid feeling of losing one's senses and being buried alive; all replaced with a pervasive, thrumming ringing sound. It was like swimming down into the depths of Lake Monama, like she would often do with her brothers and sisters, competing to see who could dive the deepest, unable to hear or see anything in the deep water, the pressure of her own heartbeat surging through her ears.

She took a deep breath of clean air. It felt so good to cast aside the darkness and smothering of her dreams.

She reached out for Kay again. He wasn't there. His side of the bed was rumpled and empty.

Sam burst with new energy. She sat up. "Kay?" she called out. He must be in the closet getting dressed for the day. She stepped out of her nightgown and kicked it aside. Nude, she slinked into the closet, which comprised three adjoining rooms and a second level opening up into a previously unused bell tower deep within the heart of the castle. It didn't used to be so large, Kay's boyhood closet had simply been one very large room, but Sam had wanted it expanded. She admired Lady Kilos' massive three-story closet over in Harkness

Tower and wanted something similar for herself. Their new multi-level closet was exactly what she had wanted: cavernous, inviting, full of delights, and she loved wandering around in it surrounded by all her things, rather like Lady Kilos did in hers. Whenever some of her sisters from the south came to visit, she immediately showed them her closet and they marveled at it in envy, giving Sam great satisfaction.

She moved through the closet, past the dreamlike racks of Kay's clothes and the multi-tiered sections where her gowns, shoes, dresses, jewelry and other trinkets were located. In all her life she had never possessed so many clothes. So many colors—no black garments to be found. There was so much. A full-formed Snugs hummingbird she had named "Paul" fluttered about, keeping her area nicely warm, so she didn't need her medallion when inside. "Kay, love, are you in here? I feel so much better this morning. Kay?"

No answer. No Kay. Standing there nude under her veil of black hair, she guessed he must be downstairs already, eating. Odd; they always dined together. Perhaps he was going to bring her breakfast in bed.

Breakfast! She was so hungry. She wanted to run down and surprise him.

At the end of the closet under the lofty inlaid dome of the bell tower high above was an illuminated pedestal supporting her unfinished jar of rock and orange clay; the Anuian Jar. The making of the jar was a very exacting and tradition-laden process. Every month when the moons were in the correct phase, they went south to Sam's ancestral home of Castle Astralon and continued its making, Sam sitting on the lakeshore turning the jar with her knees as Monama women before her had done for ages while Kay wandered the shore looking for the correct type of clay. It should be ready in about a year; until then they had to be careful not to allow the fecund Sam to become pregnant as their male children, badly underdeveloped, would die without the jar. The jar, filled with brine and other minerals, would serve as an "external uterus," sustaining them until they came to term.

Standing under the Bronta-covered dome high overhead, she dressed quickly, eager to get downstairs and join Kay. She slipped on her knickers, followed by a comfortable blue dress and stepped into a pair of sandals from Hoban that he had bought for her. Sam loved Vith footwear. After a lifetime of confining her feet in uncomfortable Monama shoes, wearing Elder-made flats and sandals was a joy.

Seeing herself in her expensive mirror, she scoffed at her reflection.

"Pft!" Her black hair was a tangled forest hanging to the ground. She would have to call for her favorite setter later and have it corrected. Perhaps a change might be in order—cut her hair down to a shorter length, like the Vith ladies wore. She had never worn her hair short, that wasn't the Monama way, but she was a Vith lady now, and Vith ladies wore their hair much shorter. She fancied a change might be nice. But Kay said he loved her hair as it was in the Monama style: long and thick, down to her ankles, a curling carpet.

She would discuss it with him later. She ran a brush across her head several times and gave up. She had become used to letting the setters deal with it. That seemed to be something Vith women did, and she was Vith now.

Fully dressed, she emerged from the closet and checked the terrace, just in case Kay was out there enjoying the morning. Their comfortable wicker chairs where they often held hands and watched the sunset were unoccupied. Stepping back inside, she took several deep whiffs—her powerful Monama nose should be able to sniff him out without error.

What was this? She found she couldn't smell much of anything. She should be smelling powders, oils, creams, perfumes and other such things that she painted her face with coming from the closet. She should be smelling a collage of mold in the stone and traces of menthol smoke locked in the fabric of the tapestries from long ago; someone who lived here once smoked quite a bit. She also should be picking up the wafting notes of food being prepared in the kitchens far below and, from the bathroom, the faint smells of urine, scat, hair and water mixed with soap, lotions and cleaning agents.

Mixed in with all those other sundry smells should be Kay's smell; the ghost of his scent, the faint wafting of his presence was stamped in the past like an indelible painting only she could appreciate. Kay could see into the past, which she couldn't do—but her nose told a similar story, the near past locked in the surroundings in a tapestry of telling breezes. Sam liked smelling Kay almost as much as she enjoyed looking at him.

But today, she got nothing. She took in a deep breath; her nose wasn't stopped up like that time they went to Fazo to enjoy the seaside and she was miserable with allergies, she was breathing normally. Her Snugs medallion fouled her ability to smell, but she wasn't wearing it at the moment. She felt the first few fingers of panic stretch out and wrap around her throat.

Can't smell!

Why can't I smell?

Where is Kay?

Kay!

She tried to compose herself and think rationally. She must be sick, possibly a hold-over side-effect from the Hemolizer.

That must be it.

Feeling a bit lost without her nose and without Kay, Sam checked the various sitting rooms and alcoves they frequented.

Nothing. No Kay.

She soothed herself with reassuring excuses. He must have gone down to the Capricos Hall to eat and get a good start on the day.

Perhaps he was out in the Grove getting some air.

Or down in the village getting her a nice surprise.

Yes, yes, that must be it.

She went down and came out of their tower, gliding across the polished castle tiles.

From somewhere down the great central corridor came a peculiar sound.

Rrrrrriiiiiiinnnnnnnggggggg ...

What was that, Sam wondered? She recalled hearing it in her sleep. It was an unpleasant and distracting sound. It was a sound that made her angry.

She moved down the corridor, checking the nooks and crannies for the source of the sound. She listened. Heard nothing. Her nerves must be playing tricks on her; time to find Kay and move on from this odd start to the morning. She headed down the corridor to the Capricos Hall where they always took their breakfast.

Sam went down the corridor, rounded a few corners and there was the Capricos Hall, lined with colorful hanging House banners.

The long table that could seat hundreds was empty.

What was this? Where was Kay?

Frustrated, she went to Xyotel Tower to locate Kay's cousin, Sarah.

The tower was locked tight. Odd, Sarah only locked her tower when she wasn't there for extended periods of time.

With growing confusion, she went to find Sarah's brother Phillip and his love, Thomasina the 19th of Waam.

Gone. Makara Tower was locked up as well. She checked a monitor—Phillip's ship the *Goshawk* was gone from its spot in the Grove.

Ki?

Gone. The Professor too and their son Sebastian.

Her life with Kay and her friends suddenly seemed like a pleasant dream she had woken up from, with the stark realities of a scentless, lonely life setting in on her. She felt a tantrum coming on—a real shouting, castle-damaging rage like those she had been known for as a child. For Kay's sake, she had always managed to keep her fits under control and act like a regal Vith lady, but without Kay and her friends, she was lapsing fast. She desperately wanted to break something. With her vast Monama strength, she was capable of breaking quite a lot.

Sam stormed into the staff area of the kitchen. It was rather surreal to see living people again, to hear the clatter of dishes and steady rumble of the stoves. The staff was a motley collection of Cyan ladies from the village: tall, short, skinny, chubby, all a happy, apron-wearing group. The kitchens always smelled so good with the notes of baking bread and fresh coffee lingering on the air, though Sam could smell none of that at the moment. The staff stopped what they were doing, delighted to see her.

"Ne-Countess, it's so good to see you up and around."

"Where is my husband?"

"Out of the province, my Countess."

"What?"

"He was called away," they said.

"Called away? During the night?"

"Well..."

"Where has he gone?" Sam demanded.

"My Countess, I don't know."

Sam whirled around and was ready to fly into a frothing rage right there in the kitchen in front of the staff.

Riiiiinnnnnggggggggg ...

That sound again. Sam covered her ears.

"What is that bloody sound?" Sam cried.

The kitchen staff uneasily exchanged glances. "My Countess?" one of them said.

Riiinnnnngggggggg ...

"That noise! Don't any of you hear that? That ringing sound!"

"No, my Countess. I'm sorry."

Sam was ready to explode. How could they not hear that?

"Should we call for a Hospitaler, Ne-Countess?" another asked.

Sam wanted to refuse, to say she was fine, but ... something was not right. Not right at all. "Um ... yes, I ... I think that might be in order. Thank you."

Another staff member came in. It was Countess Sygillis' personal assistant, Andorra. "Ne-Countess, welcome awake," she said. "This is most convenient as there is a pending message for you. It came in on the Countess' private terminal. The sender claims it is most urgent."

Sam struggled to compose herself. "An urgent message? In the Countess' study? For me?"

"You are the ranking Household member in residence at this time, with Lord Blanchefort and Countess Sygillis out of the League for the time being."

Sam noticed the kitchen staff standing there with their pins and ladles, blinking at her.

"Thank you," she said, feeling embarrassed and on the spot. "I shall take the message at once. Please, everyone, carry on."

"My Countess?" one of the staff asked as she exited. "Shall we make your favorite breakfast?"

"Yes, yes, thank you. I would like that."

Andorra escorted her to Countess Sygillis' personal study in the northern wing of the castle near the Palantine Courtyard, locked up tight as usual in her absence. Countess Sygillis was out of the League along with Captain Davage, Kay's younger sister, Hathaline, and his younger brother, Maser. They were not expected to return for several months. Sam made a note to go to the Grove every day to pray for their safe return.

Andorra unlocked the door and invited Sam in. Inside was Countess Sygillis' study, three floors high, full of light, ringed with balconies. Giant windows facing the wooded passes of the Palantine admitted an abundance of natural light, giving the room a healthy greenish glow. The countess' somewhat unassuming desk sat in the center of the room; just a blotter and a glyph-controlled terminal adorned its surface. A sketching board where she dreamed up her latest fabric patterns and fashions sat near the desk. A single bench on dragon-ball feet, upholstered in striking crushed velvet, sat opposite the desk. Sam had sat on that bench many times, just never without Countess Sygillis there. Her memory calmed Sam a bit.

The study was splendid and Sam liked the room very much.

"Just there, Ne-Countess," Andorra said. "At the desk."

The Countess' holo terminal blinked innocently with a single tiny red light.

Sam seated herself behind the desk, taking in the surroundings from the unfamiliar vantage point. "Thank you, Andorra. Please give me this room. I shall lock up once I'm finished."

"As you wish, my Countess." Andorra bowed and left the room on hollow footsteps, shutting the door behind her. Sam adjusted her messy black hair and took a deep breath. When she was ready, she accepted the message. "Kay? Is that you?" she asked hopefully.

On the Com screen appeared a handsome man with short sandy hair, wearing a pristine Hospitaler uniform. He was thin and studious seated with formal grace, wearing his black and silver uniform with flawless wrinkle-free care. Unlike the smiling and familiar Ennez and Bethrael of Moane, who were the only Hospitalers Sam had much acquaintance with, this man was stern and businesslike.

"Ne-Countess Sammidoran of Blanchefort?" the man asked. Accent, he had an odd accent. Sam couldn't place it. He certainly wasn't a Vith. It was somewhat shocking to Sam to hear her own name spoken out loud, it had been such a strange morning. "Yes," she said. "May I help you, please, sir?"

The man answered in a workmanlike manner. "My name is Raal, Lord of Niles. I am a member of the Grand Order of Hospitalers."

"I see," Sam said. "Well, this is fast, I must say. We just placed the Com to have someone come and check me over. Where is Niles, please?"

Raal smiled slightly. "Hoban, Ne-Countess, near the Gold Coast. I am a Hobanite."

"Ah, Hoban."

"I have a message from your husband waiting."

Sam jumped out of her seat. "Kay! My husband?" Sam placed her hand over her heart. At last...

"Quite. I have him standing by. However, before I can connect you to him I must ask you a series of questions. These questions might seem a bit odd, but I can assure you they are very pertinent and I urge you to answer them thoughtfully."

Sam had no idea what to make of this, but the promise of speaking to Kay was all-important to her. She would answer as many of Raal's silly questions as he cared to offer. "Yes, yes, of course," she said, re-seating herself. "Please, I am most eager to speak to my husband."

Raal began. "Thank you. What time is it, please?"

"What? What time is it? I ..." Sam looked around for a clock but saw none. "I'm not certain, sir. Morning, perhaps."

Raal noted it down. "I see, and how are you feeling this morning?"

"How am I feeling? Um, fine. I'm having difficulties smelling. I can't smell anything."

Raal didn't react. "I see. That's not unexpected, please bear it no mind."

"Not unexpected? I don't understand. The sense of smell is critical to my people."

Raal was unmoved. "Ah yes, Monamas, our baseline data on Monamas are poor."

Sam was confused. "Your what?"

"We will account for it in the future, rest assured. Do you have any other maladies to report?"

"Well, yes, frankly. I'm feeling a bit confused this morning, and I'm seeing and hearing things."

That seemed to get Raal's attention. He lifted his gaze and cocked his brow. "You are? You're seeing and hearing things?" he asked in his droll accent. "Impossible."

"I tell you, sir, I'm hallucinating a bit and I'm hearing strange sounds."

Raal checked his screens. "Your stagger charts are all within acceptable parameters. All is running as it should be; your hearing should be just fine and you are certainly not hallucinating. Your RDP is running as normal."

"My what? Lord Niles, I don't understand."

"Tell me what you are hearing," Raal said in a slightly annoyed voice. "Please answer accurately. Correct data are critical."

"A ringing sound. I don't like it. It gets in my head, makes me confused and uneasy. It's a frustrating sound to have to hear."

Raal appeared puzzled. He checked his screens once or twice more. "Ringing? Are you sure?"

Sam was close to hysterics. "Of course I'm sure!"

Raal noted it down. "Ne-Countess Sammidoran, I'll ask you to remain calm, that is of key importance. I'm sorry you are hearing things. We'll look into it," he announced. "We are monitoring the situation. Please don't be concerned."

Sam was quite confused. "You will? Are you going to send someone, or prescribe some medication for me?"

Raal didn't offer much of an answer. "We'll take care of it, Ne-Countess. Meanwhile, your husband awaits. I'm certain you're eager to speak to him."

Sam shuffled in her seat. "Yes, I am."

"Before I can connect you, I need for you to follow my next set of instructions exactly. Are you ready?"

Sam was full of all sorts of questions. Why couldn't he simply connect her to Kay? What was all of this—was it some sort of odd Hoban ritual she was unaware of? She thought it best simply to comply and get to Kay as quickly as possible. "Yes," she said, "I'm ready."

"Please repeat after me. About ..."

Sam hesitated. "About what, please?"

Raal was rather impatient. "Ne-Countess, I need you to repeat the word exactly, nothing more, nothing less." He pressed a few buttons at his end. "Are you ready?"

"Yes."

"Are you certain?"

"Yes, yes."

"About," he said again.

"About," she repeated.

"Continue."

"Continue."

Sam noticed a change in the intensity of light coming from outside. She maintained her focus.

"Aftermath," Raal said.

"Aftermath," Sam repeated.

"Melancholy."

"Melancholy."

"Thank you," Raal said, closing his screens out and flipping a few switches. "Well done. Now, my prescription for your issue with seeing things and hearing unusual sounds is to relax. I detect you are unsettled, full of anxiety, heart rate and brain scans elevated significantly. You should ease your mind, Ne-Countess."

Sam heard something coming from the Palantine.

Rrrrrrriiiiiiiinnnnnnnnggggg.

"There it is! The ringing! I just heard it!" she cried.

Raal checked his screens again. "Hmmmm. Something does seem to be amiss. Yes, I see it here. Ne-Countess, I will ask, where is your favorite place to be in the castle?"

"My favorite place? I ... I have many."

"Choose one, please."

"There is a reading room in our tower where Kay and I like

to spend our evenings. It's a place we go to relax. I am working on embroidering a pillow there. Countess Sygillis taught me."

Raal only appeared to be half-listening. "I see," he said. "Go there now, please."

"But what about Kay? Lord Niles, I demand to speak to my husband!"

"I will send his communication to the reading room. It is very important you remain calm and be at rest. Go there now, please. I insist. You shall speak to your husband the moment you arrive, and do not stray. Go there directly."

The screen went dead before Sam could protest further. Frustrated and a bit confused, she decided to Blink to the reading room to get there as quickly as possible. As usual, she reached up to remove her Snugs medallion as it impeded her ability to Blink, but the medallion was not there.

Odd. She never went anywhere without Snugs, the north was too frigid for her to survive, and even safe inside the castle she found it too drafty and cold for her liking. Snugs corrected all of that. It was a wonder in Silver tech that Aunt Poe, in her genius, had created just for Sam.

No Snugs. She didn't feel cold, though. She felt perfectly comfortable, which could not be. Feeling herself on the confused outskirts of a nightmare, Sam needed to speak to Kay at once, to hear his reassuring voice.

She tried to Blink. It failed, she really didn't expect it to work—why should it? The Malik, the Hemolizer had addled her in any number of ways; can't smell, can't blink, not cold ... hearing things. Seeing ghosts.

She ran from the study, forgetting to lock the door behind her as promised. Moving like a deer, she ran down the corridor and soon reached the entrance to their tower.

She heard continuous ringing the entire way.

Rrrrrriiiiiiiiiiiiiiiinnnnnnnnnnnnnnnnnnnnnnnnnggggggggggggg gggggggg ...

She ignored the sound.

Rrrrriiiiiinnnnnnnnnggggggg ...

She covered her ears as she bolted up the stairs of her tower, taking the twenty floors like nothing; at least her Monama speed and constitution never failed her.

At last, the correct floor. She flew down the hallway and entered the reading room, and at once the familiar comfort of the room soothed and eased her mind. Always eager to incorporate things that she liked into her own spaces, she had attempted to reproduce Sarah's Mystery Library into this reading room, moving the furniture around and stocking the shelves full of books. Kay had taken her to Bern and she bought dozens to fill the shelves, though she mostly picked ones she thought were pretty and paid no attention to subject matter, so she had a wild mash-up of books, none of which she had read yet. She also had a custom-made sofa added and a Nadine-wood table with full-cone terminal and glyph controller. Sam loved sitting in the room with Kay and their friends. She picked up the glyph and powered-on the terminal.

It came to life. "Sam?" came Kay's voice.

"Kay?" she called out, her voice flecked with a tinge of panic. "Kay, is that you?" She honestly hadn't expected a reply.

But: "It's me, Sam," came Kay's voice.

Sam's heart burst from its melancholy cage and she sat up on the sofa, smiling from ear to ear. "I can't see you."

"I'm sorry. There's naught but an old Com terminal here. No video."

"It's all right. I have been so worried! I woke up this morning and everybody was gone. It was like a bad dream. I should be very angry, but I cannot be cross with you, Kay, I love you so. Hearing your voice is just what I needed. Where are you?"

"I ... was called away. I'm sorry, I had immediate business to attend to. Such things happen."

Sam was hurt. "And you didn't get me? I would have liked to come with you."

"I'm sorry. You were under the influence of the Malik ... you needed your rest after all that had happened. I didn't want to disturb you. How are you feeling?"

"I'm all right. Just a little unsettled. I also can't smell any-thing."

Kay hesitated before answering. "It must be from the Malik. I'm certain it will come back on its own."

"When are you coming home?"

"Soon. This very day. I'm nearly finished. Would you like me to bring you a present?"

"You're all I want. Come home to me."

"Where are you right now, Sam?" Kay asked. His voice sounded markedly strained. Sam was concerned.

"I'm in our favorite reading room snuggled up on the couch.

I'll not leave until you return. You know, I see many flaws on this pillow I embroidered. I need to make another one and do it better."

"It … was your first attempt. Mistakes are to be expected. I cherish it … because you made it."

"Are you coming home soon, Kay? By dinner, perhaps? May I expect you?"

"I'll try, darling, I'll try …"

"And may we head south to the lake this month's end? The moon phases are correct. I'd like to continue working on our jar. I cannot wait to be pregnant with our children, to feel them grow in my belly. I long for it."

There was no reply over the Com. Sam was fearful the connection had been lost. "Kay?" she asked. "Are you still there?"

He replied. "I … Yes, yes, I'm sorry. I must away, darling, and conclude my business. There is much to do and I wish to be home as soon as possible to share dinner with my … beloved wife."

Sam felt refreshed and invigorated. Kay would be home by dinnertime. *"I love you, Kay,"* she said in Anuie.

"And I love you too."

✶ ✶ ✶ ✶ ✶

Sam sat in the reading room all day working on her pillow as promised. She felt cozy and comfortable there. Countess Sygillis had her study, Sarah her library, and Sam had her closet and reading room, her "office," her home inside of home. Sitting on the couch, her sandals parked at the foot of the couch, legs tucked up underneath her, she called down to the staff and had her breakfast and then lunch brought up to her.

She couldn't wait until Kay got home. She also couldn't wait until her nose started working again. She would ask Kay to take her to see Ennez or Bethrael of Moane as soon as possible. She didn't feel comfortable with that Raal fellow at all. He seemed to have something up his sleeve, and he was from Hoban. Kay and his family often talked about Hoban in a somewhat condescending fashion, so Sam's view of Hobanites was somewhat skewed.

Raal was from Hoban. Hobanites are shifty and unreliable; therefore this Raal fellow must be shifty and unreliable as well.

The Com flashed. A message was pending. Sam put her pillow aside and picked up her glyph controller, giving it a wave. Perhaps it was Kay again. It must be Kay.

The Com connected.

"Sam!" came Sarah's loud voice.

Sam was elated. She loved Sarah, even though the exuberant blue-haired girl, Kay's cousin, often annoyed her.

"Sarah! I can't believe I'm saying this, but it's so good to hear your voice. Where are you?"

"Never mind, Sam, the question is, where are you?"

"Me? I'm in our reading room in Zorn Tower working on my pillow. I'm waiting for Kay to come home. Are you coming as well?"

"Sewing? You're *sewing*," Sarah said in dismay. "That just takes the cake. How do you say 'sewing' in Anuie?"

"What? The word is *beval*—it's not quite a direct translation. It means to weave with yarn."

"Ok, whatever. Stop bevaling! They've got you all messed up, Sam. I'm trying to get things sorted out here for you."

Sam was confused. "They? Who's 'they'?"

"These nutty Hospitalers on Hoban—looks like they're trying to run a standard engine on you, but that simply will not do. It's ok, I'm fixing it now because I love you. You know I love you, right, Sam? Even though we're always out fighting in the Grove."

"Sarah, what are you talking about?"

"Never mind. First off, you need your Snugs medallion."

Sam instinctively placed her hand on her chest between her breasts. No Snugs.

"You're not wearing your medallion, right?" Sarah said.

"I'm not, but I'm not feeling cold at the moment."

"Oh yeah?" Sarah said. "How about now?"

All at once, Sam felt the frosty killing hand of the north wrap around her, giving her gooseflesh, nearly taking her breath away. Cold was the bane of the Monamas and was quickly fatal for them if shelter was unavailable.

"Your Snugs is sitting on the shelf, Sam, go get it."

Sam got up and the floor felt like solid ice under her feet. Hugging herself for warmth, shivering, shuffling about, she found her medallion sitting nearby. She put it on and felt the immediate comforting glow of warmth form around her. The hummingbird's wings flapped across the face of the medallion as usual. She sighed in relief. "Thanks, Sarah," she said, returning to the couch. "How did you know it was there?"

"Come on, Sam," Sarah replied over the Com, "I saw you leave it the other day."

"You did?"

"Yep."

Sam honestly couldn't remember leaving her medallion here in the reading room, but Sarah sometimes had an amazing eye for detail; Sam had to give her that. She was just glad to have it back.

"So, what are they making in the kitchens right now?" Sarah asked.

"I don't know, I can't smell anything right now."

"Really? Are you sure? Go ahead, take a whiff. Don't worry about taking off your medallion, just take a whiff."

Sam took a deep breath in through her nose. Sure enough, the numb nothingness that had been there only moments before was gone. When she wore her medallion, she could usually detect only the strongest of smells. But now she took in a vast array of scents, the flood of information filling in the empty spots in her mind that was thirsting for input. She smelled the frost in the air; the piney-earthy smells from the trees in the Grove; the briny salt from the nearby bay; the rich sugars in the Nadine trees' sap; the vellum pages of her books; the dust in the carpeting; and the pleasant aromas of yeast, breads and sauces from the kitchens: they were making "RibCat" stew again in the vats, and a honey ham or two, some fried onions and hash, thick chewy bread Onaris-style, and a rich fruit tart smothered in homemade whipped cream. Kay's father, Lord Davage, after having been nearly starved as a child, had a standing rule that food should always be available in the castle for those who were hungry, so the kitchens were always going, day or night. Sam had developed a hearty appetite for Vith food, so tasty and filling. Her mouth watered. She had never told Kay, but she had gained twenty pounds since their wedding and was having issues fitting into some of her older clothes. Luckily, she was so tall and wiry that her extra weight was evenly distributed across her frame and didn't show too much.

She burst into a smile. "Oh yes! I can smell once more, even with my medallion on! It's wonderful, Sarah! Wonderful!"

"Great! See, those guys are a bunch of amateurs."

"Who are?"

"The damn Hospitalers!" Sarah responded. "Now, one more thing; this situation they've got set up for you is completely unacceptable, right? And I'm going to fix it for you. Why am I doing this? It's because I love you."

"What? Sarah, are you drunk? I'm just sitting here quietly waiting for Kay to get home, and I intend to stay in here until he does. Shouldn't be more than a few hours. I want you to be here as well.

Wherever you are, come home, please. I love you too."

"Ah, I'm all over the place, Sam. Listen, you are stronger than a dozen men, you can see the future and you can take a person's head off with one swipe of those awesome claws I love so much; you need not be sitting there with your shoes off working on a pillow. You should be out and about kicking butt!"

"Well perhaps, Sarah, the first person whose butt I kick will be yours for instigating the whole Perlamum incident with the Wunderlucks; how about that?"

Sarah laughed. "Oh yeah? Tell you what, come to the window."

"Why?"

"Just take a peek out the window. Trust me."

Sam stood and went to the window.

She was in for the shock of her life.

2—Ennez and Tellerran

Floating on air in her boots and duster over the mountain precipice was Sarah, blue ponytail bouncing on the wind.

"Hi, Sam!" she cried, floating in space. "Look at me, I'm flying! Still think you could kick my butt?"

Sam was open-mouthed. "Sarah, what in the Name of Creation are you doing out there?"

"I'm flying, can't you see?" She whirled around in a grand flourish.

"Get in here at once!"

Sarah laughed. "What for? Hey, don't worry about Raal and his goons, I fixed their wagon for 'em but good just now!"

"You mean the Hospitaler on Hoban?"

"Yep. I knocked out their crappy RDP and put my own better one in, and he's not going to be able to get it out."

"What is an RDP?" Sam asked. Raal had used the term 'RDP' and now Sarah was also using it.

"Never mind, just know they had you in a really poopy one and I saved you from it. You can smell in mine nice as you please. Thank me later."

"Sarah, what are you talking about?"

From the east, a small private yacht came in and softly landed in the castle ship park. Sarah watched it with interest. "Looks like you have a visitor, Sam," she said. "Right on time, too."

Two people came out of the yacht. "Look, Sam!" Sarah cried, pointing. "It's Ennez!"

Sam looked down. She was elated. Far below, there was Ennez of Innari, a close friend of the family and a Hospitaler Samaritan of the Knickerbaum order. He had repaired the hole in her neck made by the Wunderluck Hemolizer and given her the Malik meant to restore her. He was probably here sent by Raal to examine her and explain all these odd goings on. Ennez was the Hospitaler Sam trusted most; she considered him a dear friend.

Walking with Ennez was a Monama woman, no mistaking the ankle-length coal black hair flowing at her back and the chalky-white skin of her face and arms. The two of them were greeted by the staff and led across the Dragontooth bridge into the castle proper.

"See that chick with him?" Sarah asked. "That's his squeeze, Lady Tellerran. You met her briefly before Ennez put you out, but I think you were out of your head with medications, so you might not recall her. She's from the Fphenook tribe. I think I'm saying that right."

"Dear lord," Sam said with disgust. A Fphenook? Sam, coming from the stately Astralon tribe, considered the Fphenooks rubes and peasants, barbarians from the south shore of the lake. "In any event it's good to see him. Come on in, Sarah, and we'll see him together."

Sarah hovered in mid-air. "I'll be along. Go on, Sam, you never want to keep a Hospitaler waiting, except for that Raal guy, and he gets to piss off from now on."

Sam considered that. "I see," she said. "Well, hurry up, I need you with me, Sarah. It's been a trying day so far."

Sarah waved as Sam pulled back inside. "Remember, Sam; Castle Bloodstein. I think you'll find your answers there. Don't forget!"

"What answers?"

"Castle Bloodstein!" With that, Sarah joyously flew away into the distance, swooping about like an insane bird. Sam was puzzled, but that wasn't an unusual thing with Sarah—she was quite unfathomable sometimes. She turned and went down to the ground floor.

Ennez was here! He was an old family friend and had sailed with Kay's father, Captain Davage, for over forty years, though she only knew him in passing. Sarah had just said he had taken up with a Monama girl. She wondered if, perhaps, he could have done himself better—the Fphenooks were not highly regarded by Sam's Astralon tribe. Fphenooks tended to be crass and barbaric, and they spoke that ugly Conox language from the south of the lake. If Ennez had wanted to court a Monama girl, Sam could have introduced him to any number of her available sisters; they would have loved his blond hair, blue eyes, and that Elder belly button they all found so provocative. Her sisters would have fought over an Elder man like Ennez. All he needed to do was ask.

She exited Zorn Tower and went out into the main area of the castle. Andorra was waiting for her.

"Ah, Ne-Countess. It has been a busy morning so far. We have guests and they are requesting to see you specifically. They have been accommodated in the Firth House and properly refreshed."

"Thank you. I will see Hospitaler Ennez at once. Please ask Lady Sarah to join me as soon as she can."

"Aye, Ne-Countess."

Sam went out into the sun-bathed Palantine courtyard. The great black stone mass of the Firth House sat at the northern end, dwarfed all around by the bulk of the surrounding castle. Sam swung open the great oaken door and went in, never failing to be startled by the life-sized statue of Kay's grandfather, Lord Sadric, which greeted everyone entering the Firth House.

Across the rare hardwood floor, seated on a couch of Hoban silks, were Ennez and the Monama woman, their pinkies locked together in a Monama tradition from the southern shores of the lake. Sam, hailing from the northern parts, didn't think much of the south tribe Monamas—the Cardinals, the Derathons, and least of all, the insipid Fphenooks; they were all peasants in her mind.

Ennez, an odd skinny fellow with puffy blond hair, was wearing his usual black and silver Hospitaler uniform and shiny silver helmet hammered with elegant wings. Very unlike that Raal fellow from Hoban, Ennez was loose and casual with the wear of his uniform; as informal as one could get. The Monama woman with him was dressed in a red leather Marine flight jacket festooned with pins and fancy insignia, a white blouse with a string tie clipped at her throat, a tight-fitting pair of black pants and a pair of tall leather boots with long, spiky heels. A Snugs medallion hung around her neck, nestled in the frilly folds of her blouse. Like Sam, her thick hair went down to her ankles in a carpet of coal-black Monama curls.

Though Sam tried to suppress it, she felt she already disliked this Monama woman without her having uttered a word. She seemed like a barbarian to Sam.

"Samaritan Ennez!" Sam said warmly, arms open wide. "It is always a pleasure to see you, sir." She turned to the woman. "And who is this, please?"

Ennez stood. "Lady Sammidoran, I'd like you to meet Lady Tellerran of the Fphenook tribe. She was there when I treated your neck, but you probably don't remember her. She's been dying to properly meet you."

Fphenook ... rabble.

"I see," Sam said.

Tellerran stood up. She was a typical Conox, or Lesser Monama, standing much shorter and slighter than Sam. She was wearing a pair of boots with a healthy three inch heel; Sam herself wore a pair of flat sandals but even so, Sam was taller than Tellerran by several inches. Tellerran's bone white skin stood out from her black and red clothing. Sam, living in the sunny north, had developed a slight but definite rose hue to her skin tone. She found Tellerran's fog-bound, bone-dead pallor distasteful. Her figure lacked curves and her bosom was slight. Her hips were workmanlike and solid, made for birthing a great many children. Her nails were also long and black. Sam once wore her nails in a similar fashion, but she had learned the Vith found them rather aggressive and intimidating to look at, so she cut them down to a much shorter length, requiring two attendants and a power file every day. Sam now considered herself Vith, well beyond her Monama roots; all she had to do was learn to speak Vith and her transformation would be complete. Seeing Tellerran's scythelike nails reminded her of the many barbaric habits her people indulged in that she now found distasteful. Also, as a final slight—in Sam's rather biased opinion—Tellerran was not really a beautiful girl. Ennez could do much better. "A great pleasure, madam," Sam said.

Tellerran smiled and nodded.

"Does she speak?" Sam asked Ennez.

"She doesn't speak League Common, Sam, only Conox," he replied. "I often wonder what she utters during some of our more adult encounters when she's squeezing the life out of me with those legs of hers, but I don't speak a word of her native tongue. Do you speak Conox, Sam? It might make her feel more at home to hear some familiar words."

Sam spoke Anuie, which was similar to Conox in many ways; still ...

"No, I do not."

"Pity." Ennez gave Sam a long, appraising look. Then he turned to Lady Tellerran and did the same.

"Wow, I'd read about the differences between the Conox Monamas and the Anuians, like yourself, Sam. There really is quite a difference in size and topical anatomy."

Sam nodded. "Anuians are much larger than the Conox, that is true."

"Well, there is the size. I also notice you have a very different cranial shape, your lips have those distinctive notches that Tells' doesn't have, your eyes and your orbitals are also of an entirely different configuration. You're much more heavily constructed. Remarkable. I should like to fully document these differences and add to our knowledge. However, the reason for our visit today is to give you a check-up. I'd heard you were having some unusual symptoms. I'm glad I was available to come back on short notice."

"I'm grateful for your presence, Ennez."

He pulled several small scanners out of his uniform pockets. "So, if you would be so kind, take a seat and I'll check you over."

"Thank you." Sam seated herself. "I've been having trouble with my nose today as well. Trouble smelling, and I've been hallucinating."

"Your nose?"

"Yes."

"Hmmmm, I'll take a look at it. Hallucinations too?"

"Yes."

Lady Tellerran smiled at her. "*Purty mornin'*," she said in Conox as Ennez worked. The language sounded broken and pitched to Sam's ear. She pretended she didn't understand, as she frankly had nothing to say to the woman. Tellerran reached into the pocket of her flight jacket and pulled out a small endecar to translate for her. She turned it on and held it up in the flat of her palm, her long black nails glistening.

"I really am a poor linguist. I'm afraid I can't make much out of League Common, though Ennez has tried to teach me," came her synthesized voice from the endecar.

"I'm certain you'll get the hang of it one day, darling," Ennez added.

"Darling?" Sam asked.

"Yep. The two of us recently decided to give married life a try. I took her back to Onaris and we got hitched."

Though Sam already knew that, she was appalled. "Really? Congratulations, I hadn't heard. I didn't know you fancied Monama girls, Ennez. You should have said something, for I have many sisters."

Ennez laughed as he scanned her. "It just sort of happened. Tells is the girl for me, I like her spirit. She just happens to be a Monama."

"How is your neck, my lady?" Tellerran asked through the endecar.

Sam had to remember herself. Though this tiny woman was Fphenook trash, she had to behave like a Vith Ne-Countess. To ignore a guest and possibly offend Ennez and embarrass Kay would not do. "It's fine, thank you."

Tellerran winked at her. "I've never seen an Anuian before," she said. "So big. So different. You're very beautiful. Astralons are said to be so pretty."

Sam felt like grabbing the endecar from her hand and hitting her with it. Why did she feel so hostile? That wasn't like her, even though this woman was a miserable Fphenook. "Thank you," she replied, choking back scorn.

Tellerran reached out and pinched Sam's bicep. "So solid," she said. "I've heard how strong Anuians are."

She moved her endecar aside and spoke in Conox. "*Lookie you picked up a little weight eatin' all that nice Vith food. I pick'd up some weight too. Ennez likes a little padding while we're screwin'. Said my Monama bones hurt him a lot. I'm ... interest'd in determinin' just how tuff'd' up you be. Would you care to wrassle? Lake Rules.*"

Sam responded in Anuie. "*I'm sorry, what did you say?*"

"*I wanna' wrassle. Fight. Tussle. Lake Rules say we gotta' wrassle in the water o' the lake, but anywhere in th' vi-cin-ty will do. We's likes ta fight in Fphenook. I always wanted to scrap with an Anuian, and here you be ... all Anuianlike.*"

Fight this tiny Fphenook woman? She would hardly be worth the effort. Kay on his worst day was probably stronger than she was and much more skilled. What a bunch of heathens the Fphenooks were—even though Sam's own Astralon tribe had similar sports. Impromptu contests of speed and strength were a common event in her tribe, and the fact that the barbaric Fphenooks did the same thing was galling. Being an Anuian, Sam was used to being challenged by the smaller Conox who wanted to test their strength against hers; it happened all the time. She once had beaten two brothers and a sister from the Derathon tribe all at once during a challenge.

She ignored Tellerran.

Ennez ran his scanner down Sam's neck, inspecting the area that had been damaged. "Well, your neck looks to be fully healed, and with no scarring, thanks to me. Your blood levels are back to normal. How does your neck feel?"

"A little sore, nothing to bother about."

"Good, good. Now, what's this about your nose?" He moved his scanner near her face.

"I was having issues smelling earlier today. I smelled nothing, in fact."

"But you can smell now?"

"Yes."

"I'm seeing some inflammation. Probably a reaction from

the Hemolizer's hydraulic fluids. Very caustic. I must say, your nasal cavity and sinus arrangement are magnificent. Look at all those scent receptors. You can probably out-scent a hound dog."

"Is this hydraulic fluid dangerous?"

"Probably. It might have made you seriously ill. It might have even killed you. I'm still collecting data. It got into your synapses. That was some bad stuff. A Hemolizer isn't meant to be very healthy for a person."

He got out a small pouch containing several injectors. He pushed back Sam's sleeve and gave her a shot in the arm.

"What is that?" she asked.

"Antidote."

"To what?"

"To the magga-toxin from the Hemolizer. We had it run at our sanctum on Minz. I'm certain it was reacting with your brain. Soon it would have taken full effect. You would have become emotionally unstable to the point of being psychotic. Are you feeling unsettled? Do you feel moody?"

Was it her exposure to the Hemolizer that was making her feel so angry and giving her wild, vivid dreams? "I feel a little moody, yes. I've had an unpleasant morning to say the least."

"I'm reading all sorts of toxic neuro-chemicals floating around in your head, along with a whole cocktail of hormones, all extremely elevated. The antidote I gave you will fully arrest its effects and you should start to come down, but it might take a few days before you're feeling yourself again."

He looked around. "I was hoping to locate Kay, Sarah and the rest, as they were exposed to the Hemolizer as well."

"They were?"

"Your Hemolized blood, Sam, it probably had the same chemicals in it, and everybody, including Kay, breathed it in. I want to administer the antidote to them as a precaution."

"Sarah's about someplace, so you can administer the medication to her, but Kay, Phillip and Thomasina are not here. They're out, I don't know where. I was hoping you'd know."

He scanned her head. "I heard they were all at Castle Bloodstein checking up on Lady Chrysania. Where's Sarah?"

"I saw her just a few minutes ago. She was flying around outside my tower window."

"Flying? Sarah doesn't know how to fly a ripcar."

"She didn't have a ripcar, she was hovering in the air on her own like a bird."

Ennez scanned her head again. "I think you must have been hallucinating."

"No, no, Ennez, I know I saw her. I spoke to her not ten minutes ago. She told me you had arrived."

"You saw Sarah flying outside your window on her own without a ripcar or any other means of flight?"

"I did. She was saying that Raal and his people, whoever they are, were amateurs and she was going to fix it."

"Fix what?"

"I have no idea," Sam said.

"And Raal? Who is 'Raal'?"

"He's a Hospitaler on Hoban. Lord Raal of Niles, he said."

Ennez checked his scanner and punched up data. "Hmmm, Raal of Niles is in fact a Hospitaler, from Hoban as you said. Never met him myself. Looks like he's an 'E'."

"What's an 'E'?" Sam asked.

"An Ephysian, it's a sect within the Hospitalers. Lots of secret stuff and special projects. Too stuffy for me. I like being a free-wheeling Knickerbaum."

"Ennez, how concerned should I be about this chemical? I have no idea when Kay and the others shall return. Might they be in danger?"

"Maybe. Until I know for certain, I'd like to err on the side of caution and treat them with the antidote as soon as possible, just to make sure. I'm certain they're fine, but I want to examine them all just in case."

Sam was worried. She stood and paced the room, hand on her chin.

"And you've no way to contact them?" Ennez asked.

"No, I don't know where they are. The *Goshawk* is gone. Castle Bloodstein, you mentioned? I could try to Com the castle and see if they answer." Sam went to the Com. "Andorra," she said.

A few moments later, Andorra answered. "Yes, my Countess."

"Will you please attempt to raise the *Goshawk*?"

"Aye, my Countess. I will have my colleague in the Com center begin the query immediately."

"Thank you. Inform me right away when the *Goshawk* is reached. If you are unable to reach the *Goshawk*, then try to raise Castle Bloodstein and enquire if they are there."

"Yes, ma'am."

They sat in the gilded room for a while. Several plates of refreshments were brought in. Lady Tellerran seemed to have a big appetite, eating cookies and cakes with abandon.

After a time of waiting, with Sam a nervous wreck, Andorra Commed. "My Countess, the *Goshawk* cannot be reached."

Sam huffed. "Thank you. What about Castle Bloodstein?"

"They do not answer our Coms, my lady."

"Thank you." She had a thought. "Ennez, can you take me to Castle Bloodstein?"

"Why?"

"Because you said they might be there, and I was told that I might find answers there as well—Sarah said so. If Kay's health is at risk, I want him treated as soon as possible, and at the moment, Castle Bloodstein is my best option for locating him promptly. Apparently, I can't simply have the staff fly me out—something about protocol and scheduling."

He laughed. "That sounds about right. Well, I can't fly. If you'd like to ask my lady here, she might be happy to fly us out. She flies me around all over the place. Lord Davage himself taught her."

Lady Tellerran smiled and put her endecar back into her pocket.

Sam dreaded the prospect of having to ask a Fphenook for something, for anything, and she addressed her in a sour, unladylike voice: "Lady Tellerran, may I entreat you to take me to Castle Bloodstein? I shall be happy to pay for your time and fuel."

Tellerran shrugged her shoulders. *"I canna' reconcile your meaning,"* she said in Conox.

Sam replied in Anuie. *"Yes, you can! For the love of Creation, I'm desperately trying to not become frustrated with you, Lady Tellerran, therefore, would you please be good enough to take me to Castle Bloodstein? I would greatly appreciate it."*

"Oh, Anuie is such a purty language, init? Hmmmm. You Astralons think you so high and mighty, don'ya? You think we jus' clean yer castle. I demand we wrassle Lake Style, jus' you an' me, Fphenook vs Astralon. No kickin', no scratchin', but punchin' an' har pullin' is allowed. Them's my price fer takin you to Castle Bloodstein, how 'bout that?"

" *'Har'?"* Sam asked. *"What in the Name of Creation is 'har'?"*

"Har, har! All that long, black, purty har you got! I'm gonna'

pull it out!"

"I have no time to waste rolling around with the likes of you."

"Then you not goin' to Castle Bloodstein ... is ya?" Tellerran crossed her arms and would not budge.

Sam threw her hands up. *"Fine, fine—if you wish me to thoroughly thrash you and put you back in your proper place, then I shall do so—but not until my husband has been located and made safe."*

Tellerran was defiant. *"No! We're wrasslin' now! Understand? Or you go nowhere. An' I want Ennez to watch. I like him ta' sees me 'n action."*

"My husband expects me to behave like a Vith lady, and this is foolish Monama behavior."

Tellerran slapped her sides. *"Ya? Ya .... you looks like ah Monama to me, girly. Ya seem ta wants ta be a Vith, but you ain't no Vith, is ya? Yer a Monama, jus' like me, an' this is wha' Monamas do. Square up with it!"*

"I'm warning you, little Conox peasant, if you wish to fight me, you're going to get hurt ... bad."

"Mayhap and mayhap not. We's agreed? It's you an' me in th' water, right now!"

"I refuse to fight you in the water and have my expensive clothing that my husband bought me ruined."

"Then nude ..."

"I will not place my bare skin against yours."

"Then behind the castle somewhere right now!"

Sam reverted to League Common. "Fine!"

"What?" Ennez asked. "What's going on?"

"Nothing. I was negotiating with the good Lady Tellerran. Such a fragile delicate thing she is."

Ennez was shocked and pushed his silver helmet back. "Fragile and delicate? Tellerran?"

Tellerran pulled her endecar back out. "So, what are we waiting for?"

They exited the Firth House, Sam leading them through the landscaped passes, through the Castle and out into the Grove.

"Where are we going?" Ennez asked.

"To a spot in the Grove I know. It's just up here."

"What for?"

Sam turned to Ennez, her eyes flashing. "To fight. Your tiny little lady wants a match, otherwise she'll not take me to Castle Bloodstein."

Ennez was beside himself. "Oh, for Creation's sake! Tells, you promised you wouldn't start anything today. She does this all the time, Sam. Everywhere we go she's got to challenge somebody to something."

Tellerran blew Ennez a kiss. "You know you love it," she said through the endecar. "You know it gives you a thrill."

They entered a small Vith ruin near the lake. Tellerran led Ennez to a convenient spot off to the side and seated him. She gave him a kiss and then removed her flight jacket, folding and handing it to him.

Sam removed her collection of rings and bracelets, most given to her by Kay, and set them aside safely behind the wall. She rolled up her sleeves and stepped out of her sandals. "I hope your lady knows what she's getting into, Ennez. I'm in really no mood for this and am in fear for Kay and my cousins. I'm going to ..."

In a blur, Tellerran sprang and tagged Sam across the cheek, knocking her down. It was a ferocious punch, squarely landed; something Sam didn't think a Conox would have in her. Sam felt one of her teeth come loose in a warm flow of blood.

Tellerran dropped on top of her and they came to grips, Tellerran staying close, trying to prevent Sam from using her superior strength. She fought dirty, biting Sam's cheek, drawing blood. She grabbed a handful of Sam's hair and wrapped it around her neck, trying to choke her out.

"Tells, play nice," Ennez said from his seat.

Through the curtain of her hair, Sam felt the sole of Tellerran's boot come up and get her hard on the chin.

"*No kicking!*" Sam cried.

"*Who's kickin'?*" Tellerran growled as she followed up with another kick to Sam's ribs. She then plunged her claws into Sam's chest, just below the ribs. It was a common tactic in Monama fighting, meant to cause debilitating pain.

Sam's chest was blasted in agony. She heard another voice. "Come on, Sam! You can take this little shrimp! Get mad!"

Sounded like Sarah.

Sam flailed about with her hands. She latched onto cloth and ripped down, tearing Tellerran's white shirt and taking some skin along with it. She clamped on and got two good fistfuls of Tellerran's black hair. She pulled hard and wrenched the fistfuls out of her opponent's scalp. Tellerran gave a ragged scream as Sam rolled on top of her. She reared back and kneed Tellerran twice in the gut. Sam got to her feet, lined her up and socked Tellerran hard across the cheek with a sickening slap, returning the favor.

Tellerran slumped and went down, breathing heavily.

Sam wanted to keep going, to teach Tellerran a lesson with hand and claw not soon forgotten, but she relented and stepped away, holding her chest, leaving Tellerran panting in a heap. "Ennez, you might wish to tend to your lady," she wheezed as she began to feel real pain from her wound.

Ennez helped Tellerran up. Sam seated herself and watched as Ennez looked Tellerran over. She had to admit, pulling Tellerran's hair out had felt good, helped wash away some of the lonely disquiet of the morning. When Kay got home, she would be able to say in good faith she had upheld her Monama honor and that of the House of Blanchefort without resorting to cheating. She was certain Kay would understand and be proud of her conduct.

"*Now then,*" Sam said in Anuie, "*once you get yourself together, darling, let's get headed out to Castle Bloodstein, or shall we have round two?*"

Tellerran raised her hand. "*Wait ... ah'm not done fightin' yet. Gimme a moment and we'll go again ...*"

Sam smiled and cracked her knuckles, savoring the prospect of beating on Tellerran some more. "*Sure, anything you want, darling ... Anything you want.*"

As Sam waited, the familiar figure of Andorra appeared at the mouth of the ruin. She was frantic. "Ne-Countess! Ne-Countess! Oh, thank Creation I located you here! We are receiving word from the locals in the village that a pirate ship is heading into Blanchefort Bay and is ignoring control efforts to steer it."

"A pirate ship? A bloody pirate ship?"

"Yes, come quick!"

Ennez was still tending to Tellerran. "You better go. I'll take care of Tells. She's got a broken jaw. She was asking for it."

Sam put her sandals back on and, favoring her wounded chest, left with Andorra.

3—Observing a Wedding

Rrrrrrrrriiiiiiinnnnnggggggg ...

"*Ki?*"

Magistrate Kilos walked down the windy beach fully dressed in her old Marine uniform: red tailed coat, white pants and tall Brussard boots. She loved her old Marine boots, up to the knees in stout leather with a sole hard enough to kick a man's teeth out; the most comfortable things she had ever worn.

The beach she walked on was mostly pristine with sugary white sand marred by the occasional patch of driftwood or seaweed. She had to stop herself from picking up the driftwood and taking it with her; as an impoverished child near the city of Tusck, she used to collect wood with her brothers and sisters to sell in the city streets; they did anything they could to earn enough for their next meal. It took practice and a fair amount of skill to walk fully shod on the sand and not get bogged down. She grew up with beaches and the sea; walking on it was like nothing to her.

By the way, where was she? The beach was a long, perfect curve. The water roaring in at a steady rate was an awesome shade of aquamarine tipped in orderly lines of white foam and a haircut of squawking of sea birds looking for an easy meal. Only the Big Blue on her home world of Onaris, the deepest and clearest ocean in the

League, was that shade of blue; she would know it anywhere. But she wasn't on Onaris, the place where she grew up. She was on Kana—Kana was her home now, along with her husband and her son and a few of her sisters. And she wasn't a Marine anymore, not in decades.

She must be dreaming. Ki had always been good at detecting a dream as it was happening. She was fully capable of analyzing the dream, to appreciate it if it was a good one and to wake herself if the dream wasn't to her liking. She usually dreamed of her toddler son, Sebastian, and her husband, and her faithful Silver tech tweeter bird who was never far from her side. Her goal was to one day "give" Tweeter to her son, but that was way down the line once Sebastian was grown. Despite being alone on the beach, she felt this was a nice dream so she would just let it play out. Maybe her son and her husband and her bird would be waiting for her somewhere.

Up ahead was a small church; just an unpainted plank cabin on weedy pylons beyond the wave-line, scoured smooth by sand and wind. The church was decorated in fronds and strings of nice white flowers caught in the wind. Two people came out to greet her; suntanned, waving, all smiles.

Ki recognized them. It was Phillip of Blanchefort, wearing loose white clothing made for the wind and the beach. Look at Phillip, all grown up, so handsome; just like his cousin, Kay, though Phillip had a more conservative, more rugged look to him. He was great-looking, but not so much that he was unapproachable. Kay was almost too good-looking, Kay was like a Vith god; Phillip though, more earthy, more normal-looking, was just right. Ki had known Phillip since he was a boy, the second son of Lady Poe of Blanchefort. He was quiet, soft-spoken, a brainy, reliable type, sort of like Ki's husband. He was the kind of fellow Ki favored and was attracted to. He was totally unlike his knickers-in-a-twist blue-haired twin sister, Sarah, who was a total loud-mouth and impulsive hothead.

At Phillip's side was Thomasina the 19th, an imperious woman from the Xaphan city of Waam who had fallen for Phillip some years back. Ki had never figured mild-mannered Phillip as someone who favored wild, strong, opinionated women, and Thomasina was all that in spades. Tall, tautly muscled, long-legged, Thomasina looked like a half-civilized warrior princess; Ki knew she was greatly respected as a Portator and prohibitionist in Waam. They stood together by the church. Thomasina was wearing a wrap-around beach thong and no shoes. Her hair, which was normally dyed a leafy shade of green, was back to its natural brown, though the wind and sea had stained it to a healthy blondish shade. Her born name was Rose, but only Phillip got to call her that.

"Hey Ki, glad you could join us," Phillip said, warmly shaking her hand. "We're getting married, me and Rose. We didn't want a big Vith ceremony so we decided to do it here, by the sea. We've fallen in love with this place. We didn't have time to invite anybody, but since you're here, why don't you join us? Help us celebrate our marriage?"

"Sure, and congratulations!"

Phillip and Thomasina went inside the church. Ki trudged through the sand and followed them in. A sign by the door read:

Wedding of Mr. and Mrs. Illibuck

"Mr. and Mrs. Illibuck?" Ki asked.

"That's us. We're using an alias in case anybody came looking. Would you like to get comfortable, Ki?" Thomasina asked. "I've got some extra beachwear here somewhere."

"Nah, I'm good. Thanks."

Inside, the uneven wooden floor was dusted with sand; her boots scraped in a gritty fashion across the planks. They had a metal washbasin full of ice. Bottles of good Onaris ale peeked out through the ice in an inviting fashion. Ki took two out by the necks and grabbed a seat on a creaky pew.

As she got comfortable, she heard a great deal of noise coming from the back of the church, lots of banging and sounds of wooden planks being lifted and then dropped in a workmanlike fashion. Ki got annoyed—this was Phillip and Thomasina's moment, and some fool was ripping the place up while they were trying to do it. Ki got up, still holding her ales, and went to the back, determined to take control of the situation and put a stop to the racket.

Near the back wall, a girl with fuzzy blonde hair and wearing a light beach robe was flopped on her hands and knees doing something with the floor, pulling up planks and setting them aside. She had opened a hole in the floor several planks wide, and Ki could see the shack's previously hidden footers pounded into the sand littered with accumulated beach trash.

"What are you doing there?" Ki asked. "My friends here are trying to get married."

"I'm hiding something," the girl said. She had something long and skinny hidden under a sheet.

Ki set her drinks aside. "Here, let me help you. You're making too much noise."

The girl pulled the sheet aside, revealing an odd metal device. It was a round dial about two feet in diameter composed of polished brass and striking midnight blue metal; very impressive construction. The dial was mounted atop a long pole, also midnight blue, and it reminded Ki of a street lamp.

"What's that?" Ki asked.

"Control column," the girl replied.

"Control column to what?"

"The Bower Chest. It's very precious, and I'm hiding it from Her. She wants to destroy it."

"Yeah, ok, whatever."

The girl wrestled the whole thing through the hole in the floor, wedging it in the footers. They replaced the planks and returned to the pews. The girl didn't seem to be in a festive mood and sat slumped in her pew, hugging herself as if she were either cold or just painfully shy, and stared at the floor. The girl was killing Ki's mood.

"What's the matter? This is a wedding," Ki said. "Supposed to be happy."

The girl's light robe revealed pale arms and legs. She didn't answer.

"Do you know Phillip and Thomasina?"

Again, she didn't answer.

"Come on, this is a nice dream I'm having. You're messing it up. Want an ale? It's good stuff. I got two." Ki held out one of the sweating bottles.

The girl rustled a little and looked at the bottle. "For me?" she asked shyly.

"Sure. They've got a whole tub-full. You better grab it before I change my mind and drink it myself."

Tentatively, the girl reached out and took the bottle. She reacted to its cold wet surface and the smooth glass with wonder. She touched it with the pads of her fingers. She rolled the glass across her cheek, savoring the feel.

"It actually tastes better than it feels," Ki said, taking a drink. "Ahh!"

"So amazing," the girl said in awe. "It's been such a long time since I felt such things. To see the color of the bottle, to feel the water droplets on my fingers ..." She took a drink, savoring the taste of the ale. She giggled and came out of her shell a bit.

"I am Chrysania," she said.

The name was familiar to Ki. "Chrysania? As in Lady Chrysania of Bloodstein?"

"Yes."

"The one who was sick? The one with no face I heard about?"

"I was sick, yes. I couldn't see or hear. I had no tongue to taste with and no mouth to give my tongue a home. I had no hands or feet. I was entombed within my own body."

Ki was horrified. "That sounds terrible." Chrysania certainly appeared to be healthy; pretty, nice complexion, soft hands and feet. In this dream Ki was having, she seemed to radiate good health.

"Your friends helped restore me, Lord Blanchefort and his party. I am grateful to them." She took another drink. "Such kindness they showed me. I love them all."

The ceremony began, the preacher reading from a holy book, Phillip and Thomasina standing before him holding hands.

Chrysania seemed enraptured. "Oh, I've been married many times," she said.

"What happened?" Ki asked.

"They … they died. I lived and they died. My children too. Over and over."

Ki polished off her beer. It was good. "So, that thing back there you hid—who you hiding it from?"

"From Her …"

"Who?"

A shadow fell across the window facing the sea. Chrysania covered her mouth in fear. "She's here for me," she said.

"Who is?" Ki asked.

A dark figure stood at the window gazing into the church, glaring directly at Lady Chrysania. A woman stood there, bone-white features framed with a carpet of impossibly thick black hair. Her hands were placed on the sill, her claws digging into the wood. She had a menacing presence and gave Ki a start until she recognized the face. She composed herself and laughed.

"Oh! It's just Sam," she said to Lady Chrysania. "She's a Monama; the pale skin, the black hair—it's all Monama stuff. She's a sweetheart. Sam, you gave me a fright! Come on in. Phillip and Thomasina are getting married."

Sam marched into the church and approached, bringing darkness with her. As she neared, Ki noticed something not quite right with Sam. Sam was always such a happy person, married to Kay, deeply in love with him, eating Vith food like a horse, always arguing with Sarah.

This Sam was different. There was no trace of her happy, so in-love expression. No warmth, no smiles, no feeling; instead, she bore the demeanor of a cold, cruel, conniving woman bent on doing no good. Those cold black eyes, missing Sam's usual light, gave Ki chills. She came up to Chrysania and wrenched her from the pew. Sam's fingernails were much longer than normal, like a series of black daggers. Chrysania squealed and dropped her bottle of ale.

"No, please! Leave me alone!" she cried.

"Think you could get away from me?" Sam said, dragging Chrysania out of the church by her arm. "Where would you be without me? Lost! Imprisoned! Come along, it's time for you to go back where you belong."

Ki didn't like this one bit. "Hey! Sam, what are you doing?"

Sam threw a hateful glance at Ki. "Stay out of this!"

Ki set her drink down and followed them out.

Outside, dusk had fallen in a cyan line across the surf and the stars were out. Sam was way off in the distance, dragging the struggling Chrysania inland through the sand. Ki ran after them.

Moving steadily inland, Ki saw an odd structure looming up in the darkness. Built in an architectural style not found on Onaris, Ki didn't recognize it at all. It was a partially ruined walled enclosure guarded by two crumbling spires. An archway was built into the far wall. It went down into the ground at a steep angle. Sam headed right for the archway, dragging Chrysania through it. Ki could hear Chrysania's screams and pleas for mercy echoing as they passed through.

Ki, following, entered several minutes later. Through the archway was a tunnel heading down. The walls of the tunnel were lined with glass display cases, like one would see at a museum. The cases were full of gorgeous swag all laid out and lit up with carefully concealed lighting. The items in the cases must have been worth a fortune.

Ki didn't have time to admire the displays, for ahead, she heard sounds of a struggle. She saw a figure supine on the ground. "Chrysania, is that you?" she asked. As Ki approached, she got a good look at the figure and was horrified.

The figure had no face; no eyes, nose, mouth, hands or feet. It was a pitiful blank creature, like a mannequin. With its stumps, it clutched at its throat, trying to breathe but having no nose or mouth to breathe with.

Ki picked her up and held her, desperate, not knowing what to do or how to help her.

A voice spoke from the darkness. "And now, Magistrate, time for you to join her …"

Ki saw a figure approaching, hands raised in a threatening fashion. Ki could feel a haze of malice, of pure evil, coming from the figure. She reached for her SK pistol, but it wasn't there.

She'd had just about enough of this dream. It had gone from warm and homey to brutal and terror-filled. She closed her eyes.

Wake up! Wake up!!!

* * * * *

Must still be dreaming …

She plunged into horrifying delirium. She could see nothing, she could hear nothing. She could feel the vibration of her heart beating and also feel the galling sting of cold metal piercing her body. She was seated in something hard and cold, like a rough-hewn stone chair, and she felt coarse, loose fabric draped around her body.

Humid, it was very humid where she was, and terribly cold.

She struggled for breath, feeling herself smothering with each failed attempt. Of all things, she wanted to take a refreshing cleansing breath; forget not being able to see or hear, to not be able to breathe was the worst, most terrible sensation of all, like being perpetually on the verge of suffocating, yet not dying, lingering forever at that horrible moment. The machines plunged into her kept her alive, kept her existence going, but they provided nothing else.

Chrysania had no face …

She would go mad soon if she couldn't take a breath. If she could have screamed, she would have. She didn't seem to have a mouth to scream with. She put her hands to her face, but she had no hands, just stumps.

I have no face either!!!!

I can't wake up!!

Something came and fluttered before the smooth roundness of her face. She felt the churning of beating wings and the occasional ticklish brush of something delicate and warm.

It was Tweeter, her dutiful little bird. He had come to her at last. She felt him land on her shoulder and sit. She knew he was there, though she could not see or hear him.

Ki felt crushing sorrow. No eyes to see her son, no mouth to kiss him, and Tweeter sitting by her doomed side.

No, Tweets, go to my son. Don't stay here with me. My son needs you. For the love of Creation, go to my son!! Please, abandon me!!

But, Tweeter would go nowhere. He was forever connected to her life force.

He would sit there with her in the dark forever, come what may.

4—Visit from Sarah

Ki was troubled all the way to her office in the heart of Blanchefort Village.

Bad dreams. Terrifying dreams, actually.

Usually, Ki's dreams didn't faze her much; they were always cloudy and farcical and mostly forgotten before breakfast. She often dreamed of beating up her sister, Maia. She and Maia were similar in age, similar in size, and similar in temperament, so when they came to blows, which was often growing up on Onaris, it was a toss-up who would win. One fight in particular that she lost to Maia, Ki sometimes revisited in her dreams; *if I'd moved this way, or if I'd thrown Mother's prize vase or kicked some dirt in her face, I'd have won.*

She loved Maia. Those were good dreams worth having. Lately though, her dreams were ghastly and unsettling. She woke up sputtering and coughing, desperate for a clear breath. The dire images stayed with her all day long. They were full of smothering and helplessness. That was the worst part; being helpless, watching her friends die and not knowing where her son was.

Ki took the tunnels to her office. There was a nice easy tunnel in the Grove that went all the way down to Cyan-Towne, popping out in a garden Fox Shrine a short walk from her office, and she didn't even have to crawl or get dirty. That way, she could be alone with her troubled thoughts.

As always, Tweeter sat on her shoulder, providing light and energy.

When she got into her office, a person was waiting to have a word with her on her Com. She disliked first-thing-in-the-morning communications. She liked to settle in, read her Posts, toss back a nip and decide what issues to tackle that day. People waiting for her right off the bat made her feel rushed, and nobody was going to rush Ki.

She removed her coat and made herself a drink with deliberate slowness, hoping to punish the early morning caller with a lengthy delay. She seated herself and leaned back. Tweeter flapped over to his bell stand and went to work on the bells as was his habit, pecking out a pleasing tune.

The Com relentlessly blinked, demanding to be answered.

At last, Ki sighed and answered the Com.

"Magistrate Kilos," she said in a dry fashion.

On the screen appeared a businesslike man she had never seen before. He was clearly a Hospitaler, wearing his black and silver uniform with starched, particular care. He had short sandy hair parted in a conservative fashion. He gazed at her, mirthless and serious.

"Good morning," he finally said. "My name is Raal, Lord of Niles. I am a Hospitaler."

Ki nodded. "Yep, I can see that. What can I do for you?"

"The question is, Madam, what can *I* do for *you*?"

Ki wasn't in the mood for games. "What?" she said with a sour note.

Raal checked his screens. "You have resisted our standard efforts to keep you in calm sedation."

"What?" Ki repeated, becoming perturbed.

More checking of his screens. "We've had numerous events, four today, three yesterday and five the day prior. All calamitous given the RDP running and all very consuming of my assistants' time. Frankly, I'm not quite sure what to do with you."

Ki set her drink down. "Listen, buddy, I'd have figured a Hospitaler would have more important things to do with his morning than Com me up and play a dumb joke. Did Krummie at the Drunken Eel put you up to this?"

"I'm afraid I do not know a person named 'Krummie'."

"Maybe you're not a Hospitaler. Maybe you're some sick freak who likes wasting my time. Slot off, ok, and be glad we're not face to face, otherwise I'd be slugging you in the mush!"

"Please, Magistrate, I am speaking of matters of the utmost gravity. I'm afraid we might have to terminate this venture."

"Terminate?" Ki cried. "Sounds good to me! Let's terminate!"

She cut the link before Raal of Niles could say another word.

Ki sat there and stewed.

What a sick freak.

She finished up her work and then headed out to her bar several blocks to the north near the cathedral. Ki loved her bar and business was good. She went in, rubbed elbows with the regulars for a bit and then exited to the private area in the back. She stumped up the stairs and went into the dark and leathery environs of her private lounge.

Somebody was waiting for her.

It was Sarah.

"Oh, here's trouble," Ki said, walking up to the bar and pouring herself a drink. "What's up, Sarah, and no—I don't have anything for you to look at right now if that's what you're wanting."

Sarah stood by the picture window overlooking the bay. She seemed unusually straight up and serious, very unlike the wide-eyed, hyperventilating, head on a swivel way she usually was. She offered a small smile. Ki expected the usual crowd of people with her: her brother Phillip, Thomasina if she was around, Kay and Sam. The Gang, the Crew. Though Ki was a loner and rather salty, she also liked being part of a *select* group of close friends whom she knew well and trusted. Ki, despite her complaints, liked being part of 'The Gang', but, today, it was just Sarah.

"Morning, Ki, how are you?" she asked in an unusually quiet voice.

Ki tossed back her drink. "I'm fine." She looked around. "Where's everybody? You don't roll alone if you can help it."

"Just me today." She gazed at Ki with a concerned, almost care-worn expression. To be burdened by the troubles of the world, that was not Sarah of Blanchefort, always fresh, always new and full of life, ready for the next adventure; annoying certainly, but steady, consistent and also comforting in an odd way.

Sarah didn't waste time. "I'm worried about you, Ki."

"Worried about me? What for?" Ki felt a headache coming on. "You want a drink?"

Sarah shook her head. She came forward, taking Ki by the hand. She had a pained, mournful look on her face. "I'm worried, Ki. I'm worried we're going to lose you. You're like family to us." Her voice cracked with growing emotion. "You've been there my entire life. Part of who I am, and Phillip and Kay too, is thanks to your example."

Ki was confused. "You're welcome." She tried to take her hand back, but Sarah wasn't letting go. She clung to it, almost desperate.

"Where am I going, Sarah? You're not going to lose me, this is my home now. This is my place. You and the gang, you're going to be mentors for my son." Ki felt herself growing short of breath.

For once in her life, Sarah didn't seem to know what to say. She opened her mouth and considered each word carefully. "I …"

"Spit it out."

"I need to level with you about a few things." She seemed on the verge of tears.

"Oh yeah? What things?"

Ki had seen Sarah like this once before; weeping over Kay as he lay in his deathbed. Sarah, unabashed, grieving for him full force, thinking he was going to die.

"Hey, hey, what's wrong? Sarah, you can tell me."

Sarah put her arms around Ki's neck and wept into her shoulder. After a few minutes, Sarah pulled back, her eyes puffy like she had gone face-first into a briar patch. "I'm trying to save you, Ki. I don't want you to die."

Ki tried to reassure her. "I'm not going to die, Sarah. I'm fine."

Sarah shook her head. "No ... no, Ki, you're not fine, and you know it. You're at the end of the line here."

Normally, Ki should be annoyed by all this, should be boxing Sarah's ears and throwing her out of the lounge on her butt. But having known her since she was an infant, Ki knew how to read Sarah, could determine when she was on a freaked-out bender with her head in the clouds or when she was serious; and right now, she was deadly serious. Ki fetched Sarah a cup of coffee. Sarah took the cup and held it in her hands. "You've had a terrible dream lately, haven't you? About smothering, about being buried alive in your own body. The worst dream you could ever have. Tell me I'm right."

Horrid memories flashed across Ki's thoughts.

breathe ...

can't breathe ...

going mad ...

Tweeter, abandon me! Go to my son!!

Ki nodded. "Yeah, yeah, that's right."

Sarah struggled for words. "And ... and you know, deep down, that it wasn't a dream. This is the dream. Right here, right now. The reality is that horrid place where you can't hear or breathe or see."

Ki stared at Sarah in horror, trying to be impassive, trying to maintain her cool.

Sarah went on. "You are in a dream, Ki, and you're fighting it. So damn stubborn, you won't just lay back and dream. You know you're in trouble and you won't let them help you."

Ki took another drink of her coffee, having difficulty swallowing.

"The Hospitalers have had it with you. They're ready to pull the plug. As a last ditch effort, I decided to come to you and be as square as I can." Sarah choked up a moment. "You know I love you,

Ki. You're like family, like a big sister. I looked up to you, standing by my uncle's side all those years. I wanted to be you."

Ki blushed a little. "You should pick your role models a little better, kid."

"No, no way! It was from you that I learned to be bold and tenacious, to be loyal, and that to love someone means you're not afraid to bust them in the mouth when they need it. I couldn't have had a better role model, Phillip and Kay too. All of us have been enriched by your presence and I'm not letting you go. And now here I am, trying to save your life. I would never stop missing you if you were gone."

Sarah stood and leaned over Ki's bar. "So, this is me busting you in the mouth."

Ki gazed at Sarah and saw much of herself in this blue-haired Vith kid. "All right, Sarah, I'm listening. What do I need to do? I certainly don't want to die, I want to watch my son grow and become a young man, I want to have more children with my husband, I want to sit on the terrace and go to Brandtball matches and eat at the table with you and everybody else. I guess I'd miss you too. So tell me— what do I need to do?"

Sarah brightened and wiped her face. "That's what I wanted to hear. So, get ready. I'm going to Game you up. You're going to have the weirdest dreams of your life; just ride them out, let them play. I know you're going to get through this. Ready?"

"Sure …but wait. What happened? How did this happen to us?"

Sarah shrugged. "Castle was infiltrated and they got every one of us. We're all sitting in that room with you, blanks … like Lady Chrysania. We've been betrayed."

Betrayed?

A blinding light came from under the door. The light surged with energy.

"Who betrayed us?" Ki asked. "How can I help?"

"Don't know yet. But they got us. Castle Blanchefort has fallen. Go through the door, Ki. That's how you can help."

Ki took a last look at Sarah and went to the door. She opened it and was engulfed in blinding light.

Part Two

The Immortal

1—Laika

A lithe silver bird flashed across his dreams and spoke.

"... speak the words ..."

Kay slowly awoke.

He had been troubled by strange dreams ever since their encounter with the Dead Man. It was probably the noxious gasses from the Dead Man's tanks he had breathed in, for they had been horrid and his dreams dangled in multicolor before him in a nightmare collage. He dreamed of a strange place of wet stone and broken glass trussed up by lengths of rusty barbed wire. He wandered the place, his Sight unable to cut through the preternatural darkness. He was convinced something inhabited the dark with him, something frustrated and anxious. As he awoke, he heard an angry disembodied voice cry out:

"SPEAK THE BLOODY WORDS ..."

Coupled with his odd dreams, he was also worried about Sam, resting in their bed after nearly being killed by the Wunderlucks' Hemolizer murder device. He loved Sam so; seeing her injured and weakened was troubling. Sam was so powerful and strong, he had never felt the husbandly need to protect his wife until now.

The steady chiming of a bell roused him to alertness.

He opened his eyes. Kay was lying fully dressed on a small bed that he imagined a villager of meager means might sleep on; it was coarse and lumpy and badly sagging on one side. Instead of the familiar airiness of his ornate bedroom in Zorn Tower, he was in a completely different place. The room around him was small and modest, the walls and the ceiling knotty with varnished wooden boards instead of the smoky mortared stone of Castle Blanchefort.

He sat up. His body was surrounded by a colorful selection of aromatic wildflowers that appeared to have been freshly picked and carefully placed around him.

Flowers? He had a vague memory of flowers all around him.

He rose and looked about, hoping to gather his wits and make sense of this situation. His weapons were gone. His CARG was nowhere to be found. Patting his vest pockets, his Poltava was also missing.

Sitting nearby at a small table was a smiling woman wearing a jeweled gown of rare beauty. The gown appeared to be old Vith in style; well made and fabulous, encrusted with blue, red and green gems—no doubt the gown was priceless. She had long, honey-blonde hair stacked up in a heady royal style with sparkling jeweled brooches peeking out of the curls. Her hair twisted down to a long single braid at her back. Her hair was something that might have taken a team of skilled setters hours to accomplish. Seated in the nest of her hair was a golden crown. She had sparkling green eyes, very haunting in their beauty, rather like his mother's eyes.

"Good morning, Lord Blanchefort," she said in a pleasant voice. The simple wooden surroundings seemed out-of-touch with the fabulous gowned, green-eyed woman who belonged in a grand manor of ages past.

Kay looked around, assessing his situation. A quick Sighting revealed no hidden assassins, no aimed weapons or monitoring equipment. He appeared to be alone and unobserved with the woman.

He took in her features and recognized her. "Roethaba of George?" he asked. He had seen her before in Waam, and in his own Grove as he battled the Dead Man from Mare. Roethaba of George, the adversary of his charge, Lady Chrysania of Bloodstein.

She smiled and gave a modest bow. "Indeed. I told you we might meet again. I'm certain you have many questions. I can assure you that, at the moment, you are safe." She reached out to touch him and he backed away, his hand searching for his CARG that wasn't present. She pulled her hand back. "I don't bite," she offered.

"And I am your prisoner, is that correct?" Kay asked.

Roethaba put her hand to her mouth in a modest way and

giggled. "Of course not. How could I imprison such a strong young man? You are our guest, and we are honored to have you. I hope the room is cool enough for your liking. I know the Vith like things cold, I certainly do. There is a door just there to the outside, try it. You'll find it unlocked."

There was a wooden door to Kay's left. He slid off the bed and tried it. The door opened easily into a gulf of cheerful sunshine. He stepped outside. "See," Roethaba called to him. "Unlocked." She did not follow him out.

He was in a large walled courtyard landscaped with many varieties of hedges and flowering plants blended with well-tended ponds filled with slow masses of lazy colorful fish. Behind him, the cottage he had slept in was painted in a cheery color, two-story with a steep thatched roof and bright shutters adorning simple windows.

"Isn't it a lovely day?" Roethaba asked from within, the sound of her voice strong and clear. "I hope you're hungry. We'll be serving breakfast soon."

Kay quickly noticed the sky: a rich brownish color like the waters of the Withelwell River, clear save for a few cursive-writing lines of high altitude clouds and a single pearly moon hanging on the southern horizon. He noticed blinking lights clustered about on the moon's surface, indicating an advanced settlement was present there. There was only one place he could think of in the League with such a sky and with an inhabited moon: Hoban, and its moon, Lauralea. He was on Hoban, far away from his home-world of Kana. Why was he on Hoban? Kay composed himself, determined that he was in no immediate danger, and decided to gather information. He had to have it.

"And why, may I ask, am I on Hoban, kind hostess?"

The woman inside the cottage considered her response. "We brought you here to protect you. It's a simple answer, and it happens to be the truth."

"And you are Roethaba of George, the rival and adversary of my charge, Lady Chrysania of Bloodstein."

"Oh, I have had many names in my long life. A name, I have found, is fleeting and short-lived. A name is only good for so long, then it must be discarded. And, yes, I am a rival of sorts of Lady Chrysania of Bloodstein. She too has had many names, did you know that? If I may offer an opinion, you were assisting the wrong side in our on-going contests."

"Was I? By serving Lady Chrysania? Are you saying that the stories she told me, my cousins, and my Ne-Countess were lies?"

"Not lies so much. Incorrect information would be a better way to put it. We shall make all plain for you in short order. We are at your service."

"I see."

Kay filed the exchange away for later reference. He scanned his surroundings. The courtyard was surrounded by an ivy-covered brick wall that he estimated to be twenty feet high. Beyond the wall were hints of treetops and countless leaves alive and chattering in the afternoon breeze. He Sighted through the wall and saw a dense forest going for miles in all directions. His knowledge of Hoban was poor at best. He had no idea where on Hoban he might be.

"Fine then, Madam Roethaba, if you are at my service, then when may I expect to be taken home?" he asked.

"When? Whenever you wish. Now, if you like. Unfortunately, I don't think you'll be very happy when you arrive."

"And why is that?"

Out in the courtyard, an eastward-facing door swung in. Someone wearing a simple butternut robe with a hood pulled over their face shambled through. The figure carried a straw basket full of fresh grocery items.

"Because you'll not find many of those you love there, especially your Ne-Countess," Roethaba answered.

"What have you done with my wife?" Kay demanded.

"I have done nothing. Nevertheless, terrible things have been performed upon her."

Kay had had enough. "I see. Thank you for that sinister revelation. On that note, I bid you a fair afternoon. I go to assist my wife. Goodbye."

He strode out into the courtyard to take his leave. The robed person who had entered blocked his path. "Your pardon," Kay said. He made to step around the robed figure and was met by a soft but impossibly strong hand holding him where he was.

The figure in the robe rose up and up, uncoiling like an inflating balloon until it stood over ten feet tall.

It set the basket down and cast its robe aside, revealing a slender, curvy, giant-sized female wearing a pair of tarnished banded-mail pants, rugged well-worn leather boots with frayed laces and a dinged-up banded-mail breast plate. She was wearing a great belt from which hung two large swords and several holstered pistols. Her face was pretty but expressionless, and her hair was a fawn color, wrapped up and twisted around with an iron chain.

She also had six bare arms ending in gauntlets at her wrists, and six breasts of descending size fitted into hammered protrusions on her breastplate.

"A Haitathe warrior!" Kay cried, backing up. He remem-

bered seeing this Haitathe in Waam in the chaotic Temple of Wilhella Cormand-Grande, her head emerging from the stump of the old one as the Wunderlucks tried to assassinate her.

And she had been in his Grove, watching him battle the Dead Man; the Cam-X sensors had revealed her presence. The old Vith in him recoiled. The Haitathe were the ancient enemies of the Vith and thought to be long extinct, but here was a live one towering in the flesh.

"Lord Blanchefort, may I please introduce you to Laika? She was out getting you breakfast," Roethaba said. "Laika, you've been wanting to say hello to Lord Blanchefort, now's your chance. Don't be shy."

Kay knew from his lessons that Haitathe were alien creatures, partially male and partially female. He couldn't detect anything male about this one; it was slender, hippy and very female in appearance, though her extra arms, her extra breasts and her giant size set her apart as an alien species.

The Haitathe said nothing. She reached out with one of her giant-sized hands and he responded with a maneuver Ki had taught him. He seized her by the wrist and, in a sudden move, pulled her great mass over him and down into the flowery surface of the court-yard, spread-eagled with a cottage-shaking, weapons-clanking crash. That was his lone unarmed fighting move, after that he had nothing. The Haitathe's expressionless visage blossomed into an open-mouthed smile, her eyes wide with delight. She stood after a moment and unclipped her belt, tossing it aside, apparently content to fight him unarmed.

"Wrestle?" she said with taut excitement.

Kay knew when to stand and fight and when not to; without weapons, he didn't have much of a chance against a gigantic Haitathe Warrior. He made to Waft away, leaving this cottage far behind.

With incredible speed, she reached out, her arm stretching like rubber, and seized him. She lifted him effortlessly into the air, pulling him to her face, regarding him close up.

Kay struggled to free himself. He Cloaked himself into invisibility. The Haitathe gripped him tight and squinted, trying to see him. The pressure of her grip was incredible.

Roethaba, still inside the cottage, went on as if nothing were happening. "You have much to thank Laika for, Lord Blanchefort. She knows you saved her life in Waam from those horrible, horrible Wunderlucks. I've told her the story many times how you chopped the Hemolizer from her neck; she enjoys hearing it. She, in turn, saved your life the other day in the Telmus Grove as your Castle fell to the enemy, otherwise you would be dead. She has also watched over and protected you ever since."

Kay tried to speak but couldn't get any wind with which to talk. Laika had him gripped tight.

"Wrestle?" she said again through her teeth, squeezing the life out of him.

Roethaba chuckled. "Laika was hoping you would wish to wrestle with her, Lord Blanchefort, it's her favorite thing. She hasn't stopped talking about it. She often wrestles with the bears in the woods, but they've gone into hibernation for the season. Laika, put him down, please. He doesn't understand how excited you've been to make his acquaintance."

To Kay's surprise, the giant Haitathe put him down and released him. Laika swiveled her head around looking for him, unable to see through his Cloak. "Jarlcon?" she said in a soft, accented voice.

"It would be nice if you dropped your Cloak so Laika can see you," Roethaba said. "I assure you, you've nothing to fear from her."

Kay mulled over his options and decided to drop his Cloak and allow events to unfold. He could always put it back up again should he need it. He appeared before the Haitathe.

"Jarlcon!" she said again with joy. She seized him behind the neck and, before he knew what was happening, threw him into the carpet of flowers. She launched herself atop him, placing him into a tight headlock. Her giant-sized body was surprisingly light.

"Release me!" he cried from underneath, his voice muffled as she wrenched the headlock tight.

"Laika, I don't think Lord Blanchefort wants to wrestle right now. I'm certain later, after breakfast, if you ask nicely, he will consent to have a match with you. Let him go, please, it's time to eat."

Laika relented and stood. "Jarlcon will wrestle Laika later?" she asked tentatively

Kay stood, indignant. "I will not!" he barked. To his surprise, she seemed saddened, as if he had just greatly disappointed a small child. Frowning, she picked up the basket and remained quiet.

"I've seen you before, in Waam, haven't I?" he said. "In Wilhella's Temple, and again in my Grove as you spied on us?"

Roethaba answered. "Well, to be frank, that was 'monitoring,' not 'spying,' and technically, that was Hruntha you saw in Waam, not Laika."

"What?"

"Hruntha in Waam," Laika said. "This armor, these weapons, all Hruntha's."

Roethaba answered for her. "Haitathe live several distinct lives with a corresponding head inside their body, rather like a seed ready to germinate. Each head they possess is distinctly different from the next. It's like several people living in one body, each wait-ing for their turn to take over—imagine that. I sent my trusted servant Hruntha to Waam to help guard you in the horrid temple of Wilhella Cormand-Grande, and she died there, lost her head to your Ne-Count-ess, as did another whose name I do not know. Those Wunderluck people tried to kill her."

"Hruntha tried to kill Sam," Kay responded.

"She wanted to test her strength, sure enough," Roethaba agreed. "Always so competitive and short-tempered Hruntha was, and she lost her head in Waam. The last is Laika, thanks to you. Were she to lose her head now, that would be the end. There are no heads left inside of her. She is shy and unsure of herself, but she managed to get out of Wilhella's Temple alive and return home to Hoban. She is so very different from Hruntha and I love her as my own daughter."

Kay could not imagine a giant, flesh-starved Haitathe shy and insecure like a little girl.

"You said the Haitathe saved me. Saved me from what?"

Laika raised her hand. "Not here," she said in a thick accent. "Enemy might be listening. We go inside. Talk there."

"What enemy?"

Laika shook her head. "Talk inside."

She picked up her belt and motioned for Kay to enter the cot-tage. He went in through the small door and seated himself at the tiny table. Roethaba seated herself across from him. Still outside, Laika got on her hands and knees and peered in through the open door, too large to possibly enter; her shoulders were wider than the door frame. Setting her weapon belt aside, she pushed her basket through and then she somehow compressed herself down, rubberlike, easily squirming into the room. "Now, it is safe," she announced. Squashed and twisted about on her side, she reminded Kay of his sister Ki playing in her old doll house which was too small for her growing frame. Holding the basket, she slithered into the kitchen.

"Are you comfortable in here like this?" Kay asked.

Laika seemed confused as she emptied the basket, setting fruits and wrapped bits of meat and eggs on the countertop. She tilted her head, struggling with Kay's question. "Comfortable?" she asked.

"This house is obviously far too small for someone of Lai-ka's size, but she never says a word of complaint," Roethaba said. "Hruntha complained about it all the time, but not Laika. She is very stalwart."

Laika's network of arms worked in complex unison: turning

on the simple stove, grabbing bowls and utensils from cupboards, cracking eggs and beating them, seasoning meats and greasing pans all at once.

Kay watched her work and admired the artistry. "So then, I would appreciate an honest discourse, if possible. Again, why am I here?"

Roethaba clasped her hands together and placed them in her lap. "To begin, you correctly identified the coffee-brown skies of Hoban. To be precise, you are on the Croatoan continent, Hemsdale Forest, near the Gold Coast. The locals believe this is the finest place in the League to be. The best of everything is available here."

Kay internally disagreed, as clearly the Vithlands of Kana were the finest in the League. "I see. And where is the nearest land, sea and space port?"

"In the city of Croatoa, about seventy miles to the south along the coast."

"Yes, thank you." Even having been told where he was, Kay still couldn't gauge his position. The only area of Hoban Kay was familiar with was Zama and its towering buildings shaped vaguely like people. He would have to study up when he returned home—his father and Sam would be most disappointed with his lack of non-Kanan geographical knowledge.

Roethaba continued. "There is an extensive and unused network on Hoban, though scattered about all over, that I can make use of, and so Laika was good enough to bring you here and watch over you. She has hardly left your side in several days. I'm certain she is very disappointed you don't wish to wrestle with her. She has spoken of it frequently."

"What network?" Kay asked.

"Krant," Laika answered from the kitchen amid the sounds of eggs frying and meat sizzling. "Come. Laika show you. Heat has been lowered to 37 degrees Celsius to simmer. Breakfast will not be ready for another five minutes, thirty-seven seconds. Come ..." She crawled away, her bare shoulder blades rubbing up against the ceiling, and pulled open the door to the broom closet. She slithered in on her hands and knees. "Come," came her voice from within as the bottoms of her boots disappeared through the doorway.

Kay was dubious. "How is it you have obtained the loyal services of a Haitathe warrior?" he asked.

Roethaba laughed. "I've had Laika and her various 'sisters' with me since she was a child. We discovered her hiding in the very tunnels you are about to enter. The Haitathe are not all gone, they still roam about the League. Many can be found here on Hoban, hidden in the wild places. Sometimes they walk among us in disguise. Unlike what is said, Haitathe can be tamed, Haitathe can be loyal. I think of Laika as my daughter and I love her very much."

"Is it a 'she'? Haitathe, as I understand, are both male and female."

"The male in her was killed years ago during an attack. His head was lost, his brawny arms dried up and fell off, along with his various other workings. He's buried out in the garden in a tended plot. She is as female as she can possibly get, though she's not an Elder."

"Jarlcon?" came Laika's voice from the broom closet.

"What is 'Jarlcon'?" Kay asked.

"It's a Haitathe word," Roethaba answered. "It implies strength and trust. It means she respects you. She is grateful for what you did for her in Waam. She was impressed by your fighting skills in the Grove as she watched you battle the Wunderlucks and the horrid Dead Man of Mare. The respect of a Haitathe is not something to be taken lightly."

Kay took the compliment, got up and went to the broom closet. A secret doorway in the back was open, revealing a tunnel heading down. The tunnel was small, requiring full-on hands and knees crawling to enter. His mother, Sygillis, had taught him to love crawling through tunnels and exploring. He savored the thought of going into the tunnel. "Are you coming, Great Lady?" he asked, not expecting the regal Roethaba in a priceless gown to get down on her hands and knees and crawl.

As expected, Roethaba remained seated at the table and shook her head. "No, no. Go on, Laika is waiting for you. Hurry, you don't want your breakfast to burn."

Beyond the closet was a steep, rather low-hanging tunnel. He couldn't imagine how the gigantic Laika managed to squirm through this snug passage, it was a little tight even for him. At the end of the tunnel was a circular room filled to near capacity with droning computerized equipment wired together in a complicated spider web of braces and thick cabling. Heat poured from the machines; a giant vent nearby pushed in cooling air with a roar. The machines were all tall and rectangular, like a city of dark tombstones linked together with sagging runs of thick wire. Laika crouched off to the side nearby, her armored knees pulled up into her chest. Her fawn hair moved in the breeze of the vent. She sat quietly, arms placed on her legs, careful not to damage anything.

Roethaba spoke again, her voice clear and ever-present despite the roar of cooling air. Kay was shocked; as she spoke, lights in the towerlike machines came on, blinking in time with her voice. "This is my Mentralysis Deck," she said, her voice strong and vast. "I have many such decks prepared all over Hoban, Kana, and elsewhere. My friends maintain them for me. Here in this humble cottage we live-test the latest models. It is with these systems that I am able to communicate with you now. Obviously, I'm not actually here on the Gold Coast with you. In truth, I'm very far away."

"What are you?" Kay asked.

"I'm a friend," came her voice from the pulsing machines, jewels of light matching her voice. "A friend."

He Sighted back through the walls of the tunnel to the table where she had been seated.

Roethaba was gone.

"You see, Lord Blanchefort, this is the life I live," her voice said through the machines.

The lights blinked again. "Is it possible, might I call you 'Kay'?"

Kay studied the systems, though he had little knowledge of such things. They were noisy, generated heat in uncomfortable waves, and appeared rugged and complicated.

"Did you set these machines up?" he asked Laika.

She shook her head.

"Then who did?"

Roethaba answered. "Laika will show you. My time, for now, is short, and I must go. Laika, after breakfast will you please take Lord Blanchefort to see Raal?"

"Yes, Mother."

"Thank you. I shall let him know to expect you."

"Where are you going?" Kay asked.

"To sleep." Her voice faded away. "I shall return." The lights on the machines modulated once or twice, and then scattered into speckled, blinking randomness draped with static.

"Hello?" Kay asked.

No response.

Laika stirred. "Mother sleeps." She sat there, folded up, boots placed side-by-side on the floor, and appeared sad. A tear leaked down her cheek.

Kay saw it. "Laika? May I call you Laika?"

She nodded.

"Why are you crying?" he asked.

She shrugged and put her face into her knees. "Jarlcon promised to wrestle Laika."

Kay was perplexed. "When you say the word 'Jarlcon', you are referring to me, yes?"

She nodded.

"And so, I promised to wrestle with you?"

She nodded again.

"When did I do this?"

"While Jarlcon slept."

Kay had no idea what to make of that, but: "I pride myself on never knowingly breaking a promise. If I promised to wrestle with you, then I shall do so." Off-handedly, he wondered how he would fare unarmed in such a mis-match of size and strength.

Laika's normally impassive face transformed into a wide, toothy smile. "When?" she wanted to know.

"Later, when things have been sorted out."

Laika, with new enthusiasm, crawled past Kay and went back up the tunnel on her hands and knees, her great body filling it up. "Come, breakfast ready in one minute, twelve seconds, then we go."

"Where are we going?"

"To see Hospitalers. Mother has requested it. Must be careful and swift, Enemy might be about."

"The enemy?"

"In woods. Very dangerous. Go fast. Must not be seen."

"What enemy?"

"Spies. Very dangerous. Come ..."

Kay followed her back up the tunnel. Laika exited, crawled into the kitchen, and served breakfast, Kay eating at the table and Laika on her side stuffed into several rooms at once.

"Can this place be comfortable for you?" Kay asked.

"Home," Laika replied.

As they ate, Kay felt himself relaxing. Laika didn't seem to be a danger. She ate her breakfast with manners and grace. Whatever story she had to tell, he was eager to hear it.

Roethaba, or Lady Chrysania? Which was to be believed? Which was the enemy, which was a friend, and what had happened at Castle Blanchefort?

Where was Sam?

After breakfast, they gathered their things and went outside into the sunshine. Laika stood to her impressive full height and buckled on her belt. "We walk several miles. That way!" She pointed to the west. "We go fast. Laika carry if distance too far."

"I'm certain I can manage. Thank you, though."

She checked her pistols to ensure they were fully loaded; four LLAG automatics with extended magazines. Good workmanlike guns. Hers were battered and dirty.

"Will weapons be required on our trip?" Kay asked.

"Enemy might be in woods. Laika protect you."

"I can fend for myself. I certainly wish I had my CARG and Poltava."

Laika drew one of her swords and offered it to Kay. It was far too big and heavy for him to wield.

"Thank you, no, it's a bit too big."

Laika once again seemed puzzled. She took the sword back. With that, they exited the colorful courtyard and trudged into the woods. Kay looked back—the walled enclosure was cleverly Cloaked, the whole thing appearing as nothing more than a prickly tangle of briars. Laika led him deep into the Hoban woods on a narrow, barely passable trail. Striding on her giant-sized legs, she could have easily left him in her wake, however, she slowed her gait, looking back often to make sure he was there.

"I must admit that, to me, Haitathe are creatures of fable and legend. A rampant Haitathe adorns my House coat-of-arms," Kay said, a touch out of breath from the effort of keeping up.

"What this word: 'rampant'?" she asked.

"Rampant? It think it means to rear back, to elevate your arms approximately level with your shoulders. I've never really thought about it much."

Laika arched her back and raised her six arms, holding them out in front of her. "Like this?" she asked.

"Yes, after a fashion. If I may ask, where do you come from? Are there anymore of you here?"

"Just Laika," she said. Kay hoped she would offer more, but she was mum. She came to a small fork in the trail and veered to the left. "Come, no time. This way." She quickened her pace into a run, moving at amazing speed, covering vast stretches at a stride. Kay couldn't possibly keep up. He Wafted ahead, appearing in the trees with a blast. As Laika passed he Wafted again, on and on, covering miles until she came to a stop.

She was impressed. "Jarlcon moves with many winds! Laika

looks forward to wrestling Jarlcon."

"Is wrestling important in Haitathe culture?"

"Wrestling Laika's favorite thing." Laika took a good look around and listened intently, apparently searching for eavesdroppers. "Come. No enemy. We go."

Into the woods they traveled, moving steadily west, Laika stopping every few miles, checking for 'the enemy'. They encountered no one.

Kay wondered what she was looking for. He Sighted about, casting a wide net. The forest was alive with various woodland wildlife native to Hoban: wooly hoofed beasts, strange birds, and various mammalian predators giving them plenty of space. Far to the west were the beginnings of a great brown mountain range shimmering in the haze, similar to the rugged Vithland mountain rage of home, only they weren't as snow-covered here. It was a very pretty, pristine woodland, free of people. A great river flowed far away to the north.

Wait! He cycled his Sight back a day and saw pockets of people milling about, searching the surroundings, shining lasers and other scanning beams. They were armed: snipers were set up in the trees, scouts placed in the brush. Winged ships took flight and orbited about. They appeared to be gone at present.

"I see people, Laika, to the north. They were there yesterday, but are gone today. Lots of airborne scanning technology. They were armed."

"Enemy," she said.

2—The Cult of Roethaba

They continued on, moving through several more miles of dense brush until they reached a clearing. A simple house sat innocently in the clearing, landscaped with pebbled walks and scrolled stone benches. A quick glance with his Sight revealed the place to be much, much more than a quaint residence. The simple house was revealed to be a metal and glass tower hidden behind a complex Cloak. It was approximately fifty feet high and quite sophisticated. The flat roof of the tower was studded with communications equipment. He also saw people in black uniforms roaming about the grounds. Black uniforms and silver helmets with articulated wings: they looked to be Hospitalers.

"The Hospitalers here," Laika said.

"I see them," Kay replied.

They stepped out into the clearing. Two Hospitalers, a male and a female, came out to meet them. They dropped out of the Cloak and didn't appear to be happy.

"You know not to approach from the forest, you might be followed as before," the male said in a stern voice. He wore his uniform with spit-polish perfection. His winged silver helmet was impossibly shiny. He removed it, revealing neat, sandy-blonde hair and a thoughtful face.

Laika shook her head. "No, no, not followed. Mother wished Jarlcon brought here with all speed. East, fastest way. Not followed."

The female was skeptical. "You're positive?" The female was wearing a lovely black dress of a style Kay found unfamiliar, with long sleeves and a conservative collar. Her dress was inlaid with silver sequins. A complicated silver medallion was pinned to her breast. She wore dark gray hosiery and black shoes with a modest heel. She wore no helmet, though she carried herself like a Hospitaler. Her dark brown hair was pulled back behind her ears with two long tendrils of hair near her temples coming down to rest on her shoulders; Kay recognized the style. That was how unmarried ladies from Bazz wore their hair.

"Yes, yes," Laika said.

They turned to Kay. "Lord Blanchefort, welcome to the Gold Coast of Hoban," the male said. "I am Raal, Lord of Niles, Samaritan,

Mentralysist, and member of the Ephysian order. We were informed you would be arriving."

The female bowed. "Lord Blanchefort, I am Jana del Lavi, Samaritan, Mentralysist-in-Training and member of The Jones."

"The Jones?" Kay asked. "You're from Bazz then? The Jones are the local Hospitaler sect on Bazz, is that correct?"

"Correct. Named after one of our local heroes of the past, Darius Jones."

Raal motioned for Kay to follow them into the complex. "We have been expecting you. Please, this way."

Kay turned, but Laika stood where she was, not moving. "Are you coming, Laika?" he asked.

She shook her head. "No, no ..."

"The Haitathe is not allowed to enter our sanctum. It knows that full well," Jana said. "It might well destroy half our equipment if allowed in. Please, this way."

Kay reluctantly followed them. He glanced back once and saw Laika sitting motionless on a stone bench, her swords splayed out on either side. "Will she be all right out there?" he asked.

"Who, the Haitathe? It is a menace and we tolerate the creature only because our leader insists that we do so," Raal said. "It has its uses. It guards our test cottage in the woods."

"Will she be served food and beverage while she waits? We have journeyed a long way."

"If you require refreshment, Lord Blanchefort, we shall get it for you. Enough of the Haitathe," Raal said. "We have much to discuss."

They entered the complex. It was neat and orderly in the Hospitaler fashion, decorated in their usual blacks and silvers, polished stones and inlaid bronze. Like most Hospitaler places, the entrance looked more like the lobby of a fine hotel and ballroom than a place of learning, research and healing. The centerpiece of the ground floor was two towering, twelve foot high portraits, both lit up with reverent directional lighting and centered with potted plants and padded benches. One portrait depicted a hauntingly beautiful woman wearing a jeweled gown of a style a Xaphan Marist might wear. She resembled Roethaba from the cottage, though her dress and hair were styled in a different manner. A complicated golden locket hung over her heart and she seemed to be wearing some sort of elaborate tiara or headset with a pair of antennas sprouting out over her ears. Kay puzzled over it for a moment. Opposite the portrait was an equally large paint-

ing of a thin, somewhat frail man standing before a host of towering machines. Kay didn't know who the man was and couldn't place his attire; he did, however, recognize the tall, heavily cabled machines in the background: Mentralysis Decks from the cottage.

"This way," Jana said, hurrying him along. They entered a windowed corridor that dead-ended in a set of doors. A complicated security panel was mounted next to the doors. Through the windows, Kay could see Laika sitting outside on the bench. It had begun to rain and she was getting soaked. She stoically sat, allowing the rain to drip off her head.

"The weather has taken a turn for the worse. We need to invite Laika inside," Kay said.

"Don't concern yourself with the Haitathe," Raal replied as he entered the security code. The doors opened, revealing a lift. They invited Kay to step in.

Kay stood where he was. "I'm sorry. I don't know how things are done on Hoban, but on Kana we show courtesy to those who have been kind to us. I was told Laika has watched over me and rescued me from some sort of danger."

"Is that what it told you?" Jana asked.

"That's what Roethaba of George told me."

Raal and Jana exchanged glances.

Kay was not going to step into the lift until this matter was settled. "I find your dismissive treatment of Laika distressing. I would like her brought inside immediately and made comfortable. I would also like refreshments to be made available to her while she waits."

"Comfort and refreshment? You are assigning needs and wants to the Haitathe that it does not possess," Jana said.

"Regardless, I want her brought in and refreshed."

The two Hospitalers sighed. "There's that Vith stubbornness manifesting again, Jana, do you see it?" Raal said.

"Indeed."

Raal pulled a small communicator from his breast pocket and spoke into it. Several moments later, Kay watched two Hospitaler Chancellors trot out of the sanctum into the rain and fetch Laika. She appeared surprised that she was being let in. She slowly stood and followed, towering over the Chancellors.

"Now then," Raal said, "shall we?"

Kay stepped into the lift and they went down a surprising number of levels until the doors opened, revealing a bustling, factory-like complex deep beneath the ground. Hospitaler Chancellors moved about in organized stages, hand-constructing sturdy computerized equipment at vast workbenches. The air was filled with the smells of hot metal and burning solder.

"Doubtless you have many questions," Raal said over the bustle of the factory. "This facility is one of several we maintain here on Hoban and elsewhere. We have chapters in Hybernia and Walla as well, but here is where we design, build and test the latest of our Mentralysis Decks. It is an ongoing process and each incarnation is superior to the last, if I might dote on our own product."

Kay saw the devices they were building: tall and boxy, crammed with circuitry and studded with jewel-like lights and thick plugs.

"I saw these machines in operation under the cottage," Kay said.

"That cottage is one of our live test facilities where we install our latest designs and put them to trial. We have several layers of protection over it; the simple country cottage appearance to fool any passersby, the Cloak, and the Haitathe watchdog should an attack occur."

"An attack?" Kay asked.

Jana del Lavi spoke up. "We have a presence all over the League and in Xaphan space as well, however, we are most prolific on Hoban. The Krant system here, used during the old EX days, provides us with a vast pre-wired network readily available for our use and is ideal for our needs."

"Laika mentioned something about that."

"Did it?"

They led Kay to a small, well-furnished office away from the noise and smoke of the main factory floor. They seated themselves. On the far wall hung two portraits, the same lady and man Kay had seen earlier on the main sanctum floor, only these portraits were much smaller. Nearby, a Mentralysis receiver built into a fine wooden cabinet flashed with random lights and grunted clouds of hypnotic white noise. Jana turned it down so they could talk without shouting.

Raal appeared to be a fastidious man. He set his helmet aside and wasted little time. "We have much to go over and I'll thank you to give us your full attention. So, let's get right to it, as I'm certain you have questions. First, let me assure you that your wife and your kin are safe."

Kay had many questions, but Raal moved on to the next topic without pause.

"Next, what is Mentralysis? Mentralysis is a method of communicating with sleeping or otherwise comatose or stasis-locked individuals. With the decks in proper tune, one can hear their sleeping voice as plain as can be. Wondrous technology. We did not invent Mentralysis, but have perfected the art here and make new discoveries every day. Mentralysis is a burgeoning science, it is a precise science, and we long for the day when we can present it to the League as a proper and safe form of therapy and treatment for any number of ailments."

"Comatose individuals? I was speaking to Roethaba of George in the forest cottage via these devices," Kay said.

"You are correct. Roethaba of George is our leader."

"Your leader? And what was I speaking to? A construct? An automaton?"

"You were speaking to the Sleeping Self, or 'SS', of Roethaba of George," Jana replied.

"I was speaking to a sleeping woman?"

"Correct," Raal said.

"Are you certain of this?"

"Yes."

Both Raal and Jana had a dry, clinical way about them, very unlike the bubbly, engaging Ennez Kay knew so well. He felt like a random patient being spoken down to by a pair of haughty clinicians who inhabited labs for most of their waking hours and had limited social skills. He desperately wished to be elsewhere, with Sam; however, he was certain these two were going to fill his ear for quite a while to come. "So, a sleeping Xaphan socialite and reputed harlot is your leader? What is to be gained by speaking to her while she's sleeping? Why not simply wait until she awakens and speak to her then?" he asked.

"Ahh, why indeed," Raal said. "A bit of patience and all shall be revealed. You were speaking to Roethaba of George, and yes, she was asleep while you were communicating with her via the Mentralysis Decks."

Jana pointed at the receiver. "She faded into silence, which means she woke up and the connection was broken. When she goes back to sleep, the decks that we have placed near her proximity will lock on, and her SS voice will return."

Kay was confused. "I'll ask again, why do such a thing? Why go to such lengths to speak to a sleeping person? What is gained? I don't see the need for it. Speak to her at your leisure while she is awake."

"The need is clear," Jana del Lavi answered. "Have you ever wondered about yourself, Lord Blanchefort, about what lurks within? Ever had a dream that you were convinced came from someone else? Ever been frightened or ashamed of your dreams, of what you do in them? You wake up unsettled and say to yourself as the memory fades: 'Could that be me? Could I have done such a thing?'"

Kay thought about it and dismissed the notion. "I don't recall much of my dreams and what I do remember is nonsensical. I pay them no mind."

Raal disagreed. "That is a clear sign of low transient Beta. If you had a detailed scripting of your dreams as they play out each night, you might find that your wants and needs as an unconscious person differ greatly from those when you are awake. It is a fact that the waking mind and the unconscious mind are two entirely different entities; sometimes only marginally so, yet at other times they are diametrically opposed. In such cases of extreme opposition, the Sleeping Self and the Waking Self are actively at odds with each other, clashing in the cerebral ocean of one's own mind."

Jana pointed to the portrait of the lady. "As we mentioned before, that is the portrait of our exalted leader, Roethaba of George. She is a genius, a visionary and a saint. You saw her in the cottage, correct?"

"I did. She is certainly very beautiful—I had heard as much; though I am still unconvinced that she is a saint of some sort. I am in the service of her rival, Lady Chrysania of Bloodstein."

Jana responded. "Yes, we know, and you erred in that decision. Let us turn the clock back a bit, shall we? 'Roethaba of George' is merely one of many names our leader has had going back through the centuries, and some of them are rather notorious. Recall your history, Lord Blanchefort. Have you heard tell of the Xaphan Queen Ghome of Trimble?"

"Queen Ghome? The tyrant and murderer?"

"The very one."

Kay thought back. "If I'm recalling my history lessons correctly, Queen Ghome of Trimble lived around three thousand years ago."

"That is correct," Jana del Lavi said. "Let us spare you further mystifications. Our leader, Roethaba of George, and the murderer, Queen Ghome of Trimble, and the Lady Chrysania of Bloodstein, are one and the same person. She was, and is, immortal. She has lived, by our calculations and her somewhat incomplete recollections, nearly six thousand years so far, as measured on Kana."

Kay sat there, not quite certain what to do with this information. "I have it on good authority that Lady Chrysania is a Rundlepharge as the learned folk call them. An oddity."

"That is correct."

"And you're saying Lady Chrysania and Roethaba of George are the same person? Not sisters, as I've been told?" Kay asked.

"We are, because it's a fact," Raal said.

"And she is immortal as well?"

"Correct."

"Rubbish," Kay said.

"It is our belief in the Ephysians that we are all, to a greater or lesser extent, immortal," Raal said. "We do die, of course; however, that seems to be something artificially imposed upon us. We are still investigating the matter and our findings at this point are confidential, but what we are certain of is that there are some, like our leader, who walk among us immortal, never dying. As you mentioned, the Hertogs often refer to them by the code word 'Rundlepharge.' Very quaint. They attempt to track these Rundlepharges back into time. We have hidden Roethaba from them. We do not wish her tracked. The Sisters, should they become aware, do not tolerate such people."

Kay was perplexed. "If I'm remembering my history, Queen Ghome was responsible for the death of millions and was the instigator of a number of capricious, self-serving armed conflicts with the League and other Xaphan Households. Assuming what you're telling me is true, why would you choose such a person as your leader?" He thought back to his brief encounter with Roethaba; she seemed a regal lady of proper bearing with a definite commanding air about her. Though he hadn't had the occasion in the cottage, he fancied he would have had difficulties saying no her, such was the force of her presence. He detected no hint of mania or tyranicism about her. A sociopath like Queen Ghome would certainly carry an off-putting buzzing cloud of despotism. And, what about Lady Chrysania?

"Yes and no," Raal said. "We follow Roethaba of George, the *Sleeping Self* of Queen Ghome, mind you. Not the waking woman of lore, the sleeping one. Queen Ghome is the WS, the Walking Self; Lady Chrysania is merely one of her many guises. The sleeping woman and the waking one could not be more different."

Jana continued. "In our Mentralysis lexicon, she is known as a DO Archetype, or 'Diametric Opposite' from her wakened self, the most extreme case we've yet encountered and documented. Though she is one person, Ghome/Chrysania is evil, while Roethaba is a saint."

"You're saying Lady Chrysania, into whose service I pledged my CARG, is an evil immortal?"

"Yes. You were deceived. You wouldn't be here otherwise."

Kay sat there listening to the random tapping and popping coming from the Mentralysis Deck. It was astounding to consider that at the other end of all that noise was the blank, frail woman he gladly helped. Lady Chrysania, an immortal Xaphan criminal.

"She's a person with multiple personalities, then?" he stated.

"No," Raal replied. "Absolutely not. Multiple Personality Disorder is a brain malady, a symptom of a weak, recessive personality. Everyone has an SS, a sleeping self; it is part of the natural brain function. Only very few people have multiple Waking Selves sharing their mind. It is rare to the point of being a statistical impossibility."

"A little history," Jana del Lavi said. "You must understand; the Queen Ghome portion of her life was but a fleeting moment for her. She was actually born in the early days of the League, and her name was Chrysania of Bloodstein. Imagine, six thousand years ago, the strange glances and pointed fingers as all those people around her, her family, her friends, died, yet she continued to live. For her own preservation, she eventually moved on, discarding the name 'Chrysania' and rolling from one life to the next; a slow moving vagabond, basically. She eventually amassed a fortune in coins, weapons and artifacts gathered bit by bit over the years. We don't know if she was born evil, or if the slow roll and indifference of unending time made her that way; in any event, she eventually found the confines of the League and the watching eyes of the Sisters too uncomfortable for her liking and she moved into Xaphan space, becoming wealthier and wealthier, assuming a number of notorious guises along the way, that of Queen Ghome being merely the most noted in history. The history of Mentralysis begins squarely during her reign as Queen Ghome."

Kay got up and rubbed his temples. He felt tired and overwhelmed with the information and couldn't fathom its relevance. He stood in front of the Mentralysis receiver—the sputtering waves of static it put out was sedating.

"All right, tell me," he said.

"It was the time of the Two Queens of Trimble. Queen Ghome, a widow of the recently dead Queen Xo of the House of Sevarr and alone on the throne of Trimble, was a prolific suitor, always with a new man at her arm, and quite a few of them didn't survive her attentions. She robbed some and killed others; those seeking her hand were certainly facing death in doing so. Eventually, two men came to the forefront of her attentions: Wilmer of Sorrander, a warlord and thrill-seeker, and a more unlikely fellow, Vehelm of Waam, a designer of technological wonders and a jeweler of legendary skill."

Kay pointed at the portrait of the gentleman hanging on the wall. "And I assume this portrait is a depiction of one of them, correct?"

"Yes, that is a portrait of Vehelm of Waam, the father of Mentralysis," Raal said with reverence. "Queen Ghome always enjoyed receiving gifts from her suitors. She demanded of Wilmer a gift of a million corpses. He rode off with his battle fleet and made war all over Xaphan space, leaving Vehelm alone to occupy her time—Wilmer assumed the meek and studious Vehelm would not survive Ghome long in his absence. Vehelm's task was to create for her the most beautiful jewelry ever seen by man or woman, and he worked long, crafting glittering treasures of gold and silver in the Gardens of Zama. Vehelm was charming and Ghome was suitably impressed with the resplendent jeweled creations he made for her. He became favored in Wilmer's absence, eventually sharing Ghome's bed."

Jana del Lavi jumped in. "Vehelm of Waam soon discovered that Queen Ghome wept in her sleep and mumbled without end. She spoke, though he could not understand what she said. He was, however, certain as he observed her that she seemed remorseful of the evil she did, that it weighed upon her and she was pained by it. Night after night it was the same thing—the weeping, the talking and recriminations in the dark. He hit upon the idea that, if he could successfully communicate with her sleeping mind, she might have remarkable things to say."

"At great risk to himself, he slipped her a Malik, intending to keep her asleep indefinitely so that he could study her," Raal said.

"How did he explain away her absence?" Kay asked.

"He told anyone looking for her that she was off holding vigil at the tomb of Queen Xo. Really, the only person interested in seeing her was Wilmer, everybody else in the Court of Trimble was glad she was gone—it was like an extended sabbatical, tirade and death free. So, with a free hand, Vehelm began designing the first Mentralysis Deck. It was exhaustive work designing systems tuned specifically to pick up her theta and delta waves. Once he had a working prototype, he then was faced with the task of deciphering and decoding the unconscious human mind; a daunting assignment of sorting out the various cesspools of dead memories, nightmare images, vortices of ego and mania and the pitfalls of unbound emotion and wants. Hidden under all that was a rational consciousness with which he could converse.

"He found it was similar to speaking to a computer, it was very literal and direct and difficult to conduct a meaningful conversation with. He also had trouble locating the 'I' of the unconscious mind; sense of self appears to be a waking attribute. He developed an extensive language that we call SD-2 with which to communicate with the unconscious mind and make it understandable. With the basics in place and a proper language to help decipher her mind, he tuned his prototype Mentralysis Deck and heard her sleeping voice clearly for the first time. It was magical. The sleeping woman whose voice Vehelm heard through the Deck was everything Ghome was not during the day: she was intelligent and kind, she cared for the people of Trimble and wanted to undo the harm her waking counterpart had done. She began a long oratory, which Vehelm took down; in time these oratories became known as the 'Edicts of Ghome' and would change Trimble for the better. Vehelm was enchanted with the sleeping woman; he called her 'Roethaba' after a type of flower that the blooms at nightfall and can be appreciated by only the most diligent. As he read the Edicts to the people, her subjects thought that this woman could not possibly be the same brutish Queen Ghome they had suffered through previously, and referred to her as Ghome II.

"Eventually, they clamored to see Ghome II, to shout her name in praise as their liberator and savior. 'Bring her to us! Bring her to us so that we may worship the ground she walks upon!' they said. Vehelm found himself with two significant problems; one, he had to produce Queen Ghome II so the people could see her, and two, he found he was falling in love with Roethaba and was no longer satisfied with only her voice over the Deck. He devised a method to 'animate' Roethaba, to give her control over her body. Assisted by a friend of his, Vehelm developed a wondrous golden necklace which would keep her in a sedated state and allow Roethaba to control her body, and a headset allowing her to remain in contact with the Mentralysis network. You can see them on her portrait—see there, the peculiar headset and the necklace. Those are the artifacts he created," Raal said.

"And, wearing them, there was Ghome II before her people, a carpet of flowers laid before her feet. Vehelm and Roethaba made love in the Gardens of Zama, and she gave her heart to him. It was a golden time on Trimble."

"What does all this have to do with me and Sam?" Kay asked.

Raal and Jana stood. "Walk with us, and we shall show you."

They stood and left the room, walking across the bustling factory area manned by dozens of Chancellors. They entered a small hallway at the far end.

Raal spoke. "Fate was not kind to Vehelm of Waam. Wilmer of Sorrander returned to Trimble with his million corpses gift and found Queen Ghome radically changed, her hand extended to Vehelm. Wilmer was no fool: how could this have happened? What had come over Ghome to foster such a transformation in her formerly brutish demeanor? He reasoned that Vehelm must have done something. He saw the necklace and headset and suspected some sort of treachery. She took him into the gardens to explain to him in person that she had fallen in love with Vehelm and selected him as her consort. She never should have done such a thing. Wilmer was enraged. He removed the headset and necklace by force and Roethaba fell back into her Ma-liked state. Wilmer introduced a countering Malik and Queen Ghome awoke, quite unaware of what had happened and how long she had been asleep. Listening to Wilmer, she assumed Vehelm had tried to Malik her and usurp the throne. She tore down the Edicts Roethaba had introduced and put the people of Trimble to the lash. Wilmer then hunted Vehelm down as a fugitive and executed him before her throne as she watched. So fell Vehelm of Waam and so began the reign of Queen Ghome III, the most ruthless of the lot. Trimble fell into the darkest night of all."

Raal produced a key and opened a small door. "This way, please." Inside was darkened room. At two opposing sides of the room were two circular raised platforms.

Two unmoving female figures stood on either platform. On the platform nearest to Kay was a woman in a jeweled gown, bathed in the pool of light. Kay recognized her as Roethaba of George, the woman he encountered in the cottage. The other figure stood obscured in the shadows.

Jana del Lavi continued. "But that was not the end of Ve-helm's work. He anticipated things might take a turn for the worse and spirited away the designs and research he'd accumulated for the Mentralysis Decks to several couriers. They escaped Trimble with the data. And here we have been ever since, the Cult of Roethaba grown from those fleeing couriers, the hidden light of Roethaba almost but not quite extinguished. Our goal is to bring about the second coming of our leader and return her to glory. We hear her voice and are in-spired anew every day. We follow her commands. We have perfected and expanded upon Vehelm's original designs and language, we have installed an extensive secret network. We have even created a sophis-ticated Cyberling for her to inhabit: Roethaba of George."

"And how deeply has your order invaded the Hospitalers?" Kay asked.

"We have Hospitalers of all sects counted as our trusted members; the Hopkins, the Knickerbaums, the Boblytes and Ephysians, and the Jones as well," Jana said. "We also count members of the Science Ministry, of academia, of the world of business and trade, some of the Fleet and of the Stellar Marines. We even count select Xaphans in our membership. All of us are dedicated to this task."

Raal pointed at the unmoving woman standing on the illuminated platform. Kay Sighted her; she wasn't real. She was a complex hologram, complete with a holographic skeleton, hair, skin, internal organs, blood and a web of intricate finducers allowing her 'touch' to feel absolutely real. Without his Sight he never would have known, she was the most convincing hologram he had ever seen.

"A hologram," Kay said.

"Actually, the proper technical term is: Fintron, because of all the finducers woven into her holographic framework," Jana said. "Much more complex than a mere hologram. Her database and the units housing it take up three floors of this facility."

Raul gazed at the hologram with reverence. "Roethaba of George does not exist, yet she has a birth date, has bank accounts, she has IDs, and receipts marking her passage. She has friends all across Xaphan space. She has attended balls and taken lovers. She is listed in the Sisters' Book of Xaphan. She is an unreal Cyberling guise that our mistress inhabits. Our goal is to cast aside the Cyberling, the programmed Fintron, and bring about the real, flesh and blood woman, freed at last from her evil waking self. We therefore seek the artifacts Vehelm created on Trimble: the necklace and the headset. With them, she may be freed."

"So, what's stopping you? You have all this funding, technology and organization—recreate them."

"We cannot," Jana said. "The necklace and headset were prototypes, no technical drawings or plans of them exist that we know of. Additionally, we believe Vehelm had help creating the artifacts from a peer of his, Lord Revis of Want, another man of legend known for his skill in creating arcane devices. The necklace and headset are treasures we cannot reproduce. We cannot, at this point, grant the Sleeping Self access to the body as Vehelm had accomplished. If we had the artifacts, we could study them, unlock their secrets and reproduce them."

Kay became impatient. "Then quest for them if they still exist after three thousand years. Again, what does that have to do with me and Sam?"

"It has everything to do with you and your Ne-Countess."

The lights came up on the other platform. The figure standing there was a woman of similar proportions to Roethaba, though she was only sparsely dressed in a light, revealing white linen. She gripped in her hand a rather cruel-looking scepter of black iron studded with spikes. Her downcast face was obscured by a long curtain of black hair—hair rather like Sam's.

For a fleeting moment, his heart jumped. He thought it might be Sam standing on the platform, but the figure's general shape and height were not like Sam's at all—Sam was much more wiry and up-and-down. He Sighted the figure: hologram, complex, well-made, like Roethaba's.

"What you are seeing on the far platform is a technical marvel, the end result of a great deal of effort via both technology and our vast and tireless spy network. This is an up-to-date analog of Queen Ghome, as she currently appears," Raal said. "We receive frequent updates regarding her dress and appearance from our spies, and we modify the analog accordingly."

As Kay watched, the hologram of Queen Ghome changed. He saw tiny lines and swirls of decorative color in various shades come and go from her arms and legs, erasing, redrawing themselves in subtle, but noticeable, waves.

"The need for this analog is clear. Queen Ghome was, and still is, known for frequently changing her appearance. Many in her court on Trimble wrote that she rarely appeared before them looking the same way twice. They called her the Woman of a Thousand faces," Jana said. "Behold."

The image of Queen Ghome transformed before his eyes. Gone was the linen she was wearing and the iron scepter, and the black hair. She now stood before him in a simple Bloodstein gown, her hair a curly light brown shade. Her face was simple and pretty with a fresh smile.

"We can, with great accuracy, follow the evolution of Queen Ghome back into antiquity. What you see now is how she appeared six thousand years ago in Bloodstein; just a pretty young lady with her whole life ahead of her," Raal said. "But watch as we move ahead in accelerated time ..."

Kay watched the hologram change. The beautiful young woman's fresh, lively smile transformed to a sinister straight line, an uncaring expression indicative of a cold woman, weary of the world, gone to indifference, and then to evil. Her face also seemed grotesque somehow, out of place, as if her eyes, ears and mouth no longer fit or belonged on her face. Kay watched her features vanish into a blank, nightmare face devoid of features, not even a mouth, draped with a coarse hood.

"I saw this—this blank face! It was Lady Chrysania, not more than a few days ago. I saw this with my very eyes."

"Continue on, see it all," Raal said.

As Kay watched, he saw the hologram transform radically in appearance a bewildering number of times in a halo of rapid clothing changes; each transformation preceded by a brief glimpse of the monstrous blank self.

The dizzying gallery of changes passed by at a rapid rate. Kay caught glimpses of horns growing from her head, scales, sharp teeth, wings coming and going, and piercing red eyes. Kay wondered when they would come to an end.

Jana del Lavi spoke up. "Observe the radical changes in appearance she has undergone over the years, and not simply topical changes in hair color and dress. These faces are completely different, down to eye color, dentition, sinus depth, facial distal, and nasal size. She's also taken to decorating herself, attaching animal parts to her head; a variety of horns, reptilian skin, shark's teeth and unsettling red eyes."

"The reason for all these myriad changes is because not all of her body is immortal," Raal said.

"How do you mean?"

"Her immortality is incomplete. Her skeleton is mostly immortal, as is her brain and her trunk with its vital organs. However, her eyes, ears, nose, tongue, hands, feet, mammaries and genitals are not immortal. They eventually wear out, die and rot. Yes, most terrible, isn't it, to be buried alive within one's own body with nothing but endless life to look forward to. Perhaps that is what soured her, turned her bad. Imagine her distress, centuries ago, as her eyesight began to fail through rotten corneas, her hearing and sense of smell dulled to nothing and her tongue bloated and rotted in her mouth. Imagine her terror as she sat there trapped deep within the smothering darkness of her own immortal body, struggling to remember light, color and sound. She began the practice of murdering girls, waifs and vagabonds who wouldn't be missed, and stealing their body parts like a ghoul, like a grave robber, adding them onto herself via surgical methods, restoring, at least in a small way, her sight and sense of hearing. She employed Xaphan Cabalists to perform the work for her and the results were shoddy at best, horrific and botched at worst.

Cabalists have never reached the level of the Hospitalers, and surgical techniques for transplanting delicate organs like eyes and ears six thousand years ago weren't overly advanced. She needed a better way, and, in time, she found it."

Raal pointed at the hologram. "Notice these odd blank sequences that come later on. About a thousand years into her immortal life, she appears to have hit upon a system of refreshing her lost face and other parts that is much better than mere surgery, and much more bizarre as well. She seems to be employing a method by which her entire face is lifted seamlessly away, leaving her with a smooth, blank face, as you saw in Bloodstein. She then has a complete replacement face placed back on as if she were merely swapping out bad parts on a machine with new ones. The replacement is seamless and perfect in every way, fully restoring her lost senses and giving her a brand new appearance."

Jana added: "On Trimble, they speak of parties Queen Ghome once threw. She invited only the most beautiful people and when they were assembled in the ballroom, she would lock the doors and gas the attendees with a sedative. At her leisure, she walked among her guests, picking and choosing the parts she wanted, trying them on even until she hit upon the look that satisfied her. All the rest would be murdered."

"Yes, Jana," Raal said. "That is a colorful story. We are not fully certain how she is managing the theft of these parts. The process she uses is unknown; we have sought the answer to no avail. We hear stories, such as the one Jana just mentioned, and we pick up bits of information here and there. Even Roethaba herself doesn't know. She has described something to do with a pool of clear water and a touching of hands, but that is all. Nevertheless, the results speak for themselves. Whatever process she uses, it is flawless."

The rapid transformations ceased. The hologram stood there as before, iron scepter in hand, long black hair covering her face.

Kay had had enough. "Friends, this is all fascinating, and certainly tales to frighten children with, but again, I want nothing further to do with this matter. I simply wish to return to my wife and my home. You seem to have an abundance of ready money; use it to purchase a capable mercenary. I recommend someone local. Hoban has its share of heroes, certainly."

Jana del Lavi pointed at the hologram. "Lord Blanchefort, look."

The hologram of Queen Ghome lifted its head, the black hair

parting. Kay was horrified. It was Sam's face, pale as a bone, high cheekbones, proud nose and a veil of bumpy coal-black hair—only he didn't recognize her expression. Sam was always so full of light, full of smiles, and her beautiful pale face radiated joy.

There was no joy in the face staring back at him, in fact, quite the opposite. It was the face of a cold, vindictive woman whose cupboards were bare of things like love, mercy and tenderness. There was murder and mirthless ruin in her eyes—wait! Her eyes! They weren't Monama black; instead they were icy blue. Vith blue.

They were Sarah's eyes, Kay would know them anywhere. And her hands; slim, tapered fingers ending in long, iron-hard nails. Sam had begun wearing her nails short so as not to frighten the people or the castle staff. Here, her nails gripped the scepter, long and sharp, ready to kill.

"Queen Ghome, Lady Chrysania, whatever you wish to call her, has stolen your wife's parts for herself," Jana said.

Kay choked back his welling emotions and forced himself to speak calmly. "You said my wife was safe and my cousins were safe ..."

Jana del Lavi dropped her Hospitaler mask of cool indifference and placed her hand on Kay's shoulder—very Bazzlike. People from Bazz were very 'touchy'. "No! No, Lord Blanchefort, have courage. Your Ne-Countess is safe, but she is not fine. We did not say she was fine. She and your cousins are blanks kept alive in stasis. We know that the parts Ghome has stolen cannot live if the original host is dead. We don't know how the process works or how the disembodied parts continue to be linked to the original donor, but we do know one cannot survive without the other. Ghome and her followers go to great lengths to keep the host alive. Your wife and your cousins are alive."

The hologram of Queen Ghome with Sam's face was chilling. Kay was livid. "You are telling me my beloved wife and my cousins are currently imprisoned somewhere bereft of their senses, kept alive by tubes and machines like Lady Chrysania at Bloodstein?"

"Yes."

He reached for his CARG that wasn't there, a habit he had acquired over time when he was angry. "Then where are they, and why have you allowed this practice to carry on when innocent people are made to suffer such atrocities? Where is your Hospitaler oath? Why have the Fleet or the Sisters not been brought into this?"

Raal raised his hands. "You must understand; our hands are

tied in a number of different ways. Roethaba has her cult of followers, us; and so too does Ghome, and the very nature of her followers makes it problematic for us to act."

"Why?"

Jana spoke. She sounded sad. "Many of her followers are not evil people; they are merely misguided, duped and a bit desperate. Most of her current followers are not Xaphans; rather they are citizens of the League. They are men and women of The Jones, my very order. We of The Jones seek a being known as Bellathauser, a creature we believe to be the pinnacle of human perfection and our knowledge in the medical arts shall increase a thousandfold with its study. And some of us are so desperate to discover Bellathauser at last that they will listen to anyone or anything that seems promising. Ghome has poisoned some of the good men and women of The Jones, turning them against us."

"We cannot go against our own, Lord Blanchefort, that is an oath both we and they have kept," Raal said. "We do not shed each other's blood. We do not go into each other's sacred places and we cannot engage the Sisters and the Fleet. Wars have started that way and we are committed to be against such things, thus we have kept this to ourselves. Victory or defeat in this matter is wholly dependent on the acquisition of Vehelm's artifacts, and they must be acquired by one not of our Order."

"So then, while my wife and my cousins suffer, you sit placated on high ground with unbroken oaths. Perhaps I shall go to the Sisters then if you will not! They will hear me in Valenhelm. They will listen."

Jana again violated Kay's space. "If you do such a thing, the life of your Countess and your cousin shall be lost."

Kay was incensed. "And how so?" He made to exit the chamber, but Raal and Jana blocked his passage.

"Because we have your Ne-Countess and your cousins. If you bring in the Sisters, they shall storm into this facility, confiscate our research and our equipment and leave your Ne-Countess and cousins for dead as casualties of war. They are known to do such things. We are trying to protect their lives."

Kay was incredulous. "You have my Ne-Countess?"

"We have secured their return to us in barter. They are in our care."

"And why did you not tell me this from the outset?"

"We wished to ensure you were properly armed with knowledge first. It is much to take in and understand, and we wanted to provide you with a proper baseline of information. We didn't intend to withhold this from you," Jana said.

"And they are here at this facility?"

"Yes."

"Take me to them."

"It is not something you should see."

"Take me to them at once!" Kay again reached for his CARG, which wasn't there.

Raal and Jana del Lavi exchanged glances and then silently agreed. "This way," Raal said.

3—The Infirmary

They exited and crossed the room, where the hologram of Roethaba of George was absent from the platform. The hologram of Queen Ghome was now nude, her eyes closed—apparently asleep. They reached another lift, entered and went down several more levels.

The lift opened to a somber infirmary, sterile and cold. They entered a large white room. A thick, sanguine smell floated in the air.

"This is our infirmary where we tend to these poor souls," Jana del Lavi said. "The enemy knows we are adept at caring for these victims, and it benefits them that they are kept alive for as long as pos-

sible. As the body lives, so too do the stolen parts."

At the far end of the room were several white, vaguely man-shaped capsules lined up in a long row. They hissed ominously, venting humid gasses. Terminals situated around each capsule printed data in steady, workmanlike streams. Chancellors moved among the capsules, checking screens, clearing hoses and making fine adjustments. One capsule in particular seemed to be giving them trouble and occupying much of their time. Alarm lights and warnings went off regularly, sending them into hurried activity.

Kay cautiously approached a capsule, doing his best to stay out of the Chancellors' way as they worked. There was a square window built into the top of the capsule, situated approximately where a person's head should be. The window was rimed over with ice, obscuring the occupant. Full of dread, Kay Sighted through the metal case.

Inside was the blank sleeping form of a person, nude, covered with a light sheet. The face was blank: mouth, eyes and ears gone, hands and feet gone, the breasts were removed, even the hair was missing. Who was this unrecognizable person? The only recognizable aspect of its body was its complexion, general size and shape. The truth hit Kay.

"Sarah?" he piped.

Jana del Lavi checked the terminal screens. "Yes. This subject is Lady Sarah of Blanchefort."

Kay was speechless. Machines hung under her throat and pulsating tubes plunged into her skin supplied her with oxygen and nutrition. She lay there on her back unmoving, so unlike the rolling, kicking, blanket-stealing Sarah he knew from their frequent sleepovers as children.

Seeing her like this, Kay was overcome. "Oh, Gods, Sarah ..." he whispered, his voice trembling. "What did you do? What did you get into?" Here was his cousin, his friend and life-long companion, a helpless bag of nearly unidentifiable meat in a capsule.

They continued on. Looking back once, Kay saw the screen attached to Sarah's capsule go blank; all the scrawl of data littering the screen cleared by itself, leaving a single tiny phrase in the center of the screen.

Kay zoomed in. It read:

"feelin' fine"

As Kay puzzled over that, several capsules away alarms sounded. The Chancellors rushed about.

"What is wrong with that capsule?" Kay asked, concerned for the well-being of the occupant.

"She's being stubborn," one of the flustered Chancellors said, adjusting the capsule's controls.

Kay went to the capsule. "Who is in here?" he asked with dread, not wanting to Sight.

"Magistrate Kilos of Tusck," Jana said.

Ki too?

"Why the alarms? What's her status?"

"She's fighting stasis, trying to wake up," Raal said.

"Is she in danger?"

"For the moment, no."

Despite it all, Kay chuckled. Stubborn and a handful; that was the Ki he loved.

Dear Ki, always causing trouble.

He felt a pair of hands touch him on the shoulders. Kay turned and there was the tall, sympathetic hologram of Roethaba of George standing over him, proud and regal, a splash of glittering color in the otherwise plain white room.

"Now you see. I've no words for this, Kay," she said. "I've seen this same scene unfold countless times, so many victims." She stood there, hands on his shoulders, the finducers programmed into her holographic makeup making her touch feel absolutely real via nerve induction.

Kay wanted to be angry, to be enraged, yet, even as a hologram, Roethaba carried with her a simple grace and commanding presence. He couldn't be angry with her.

"Up at last, Great Lady?" Kay said.

"I am returned," she said. "If I might allay your fears, your cousin and your friend dream right now. The Magistrate's dreams are intense, fouling the machinery. Each occupant requires extensive custom tuning. My Hospitaler friends will get it right. They are dedicated and tireless. It's a small consolation, but she has no idea what has happened to her."

"Where is Sam?"

Roethaba pointed several capsules down. "There," she said. "There is your Ne-Countess."

At the end of the row, a quiet capsule breathed in regular gasps. Slow data printed in timed spasms.

"And she dreams as well?"

"She does."

"And you are currently seeing through her eyes, hearing through her ears?"

Roethaba winced a bit. "*She* does, yes."

"I wish to speak to my Countess. You have these magnificent machines that serve as a conduit to the sleeping mind. Prepare them. I want to speak to her immediately."

Roethaba disagreed. "The well-spring of the mind is a complicated and unpredictable thing, Lord Blanchefort. Her Sleeping Self might not be who you expect. She might be totally different. She could be a DO, as I am. I would hate for you to have to experience that. I will ask the Chancellors to perform analysis upon her."

"Analysis is not required. Awake or asleep, she is my Sam."

Roethaba nodded. She turned to Raal and Jana and, without her having to say a word, they bowed to her wishes and exited. While he waited for them to return, Kay inspected the rest of the capsules.

Two people Kay thought might possibly be Blanchefort Castle staff members occupied the next capsules.

A little body rested in a capsule farther down the line, large enough to be a toddler at best. Could that be Sebastian? Ki's son? His heart broke again.

Ki's little boy ...

No Phillip, no Thomasina. That was something. They appeared to have escaped whatever happened at Castle Blanchefort.

Dear Creation ...

And then Sam, her lonely capsule at the end of the row. He couldn't bear to Sight into her forlorn capsule. He didn't want to see what rested within; he didn't have the courage. Roethaba patiently stood by and allowed him to take it all in. He could smell her holographic perfume.

"How did this happen?" Kay croaked.

"Several members of The Jones came to your castle. They were welcomed warmly; your staff had no reason to suspect the Hospitalers of treachery. The Jones are masters of hypnosis. It was a bloodless attack. No one even put up a struggle. They passed into The Jones' spell and meekly surrendered. They were then harvested for their parts. I don't know how the process works, but the results speak for themselves."

"What about Phillip and Thomasina?"

Roethaba shook her head. "I don't know. We have only what's before us."

"How did I escape?"

"You didn't, Lord Blanchefort. You fell into their spell along with the rest."

"Why am I not in one of these capsules then?"

"You were to be killed—*She* commanded it, for with your passing she shall have further access to the Blanchefort fortune as your widow. She craves your money; she requires it. They marched you out into a quiet area of the Telmus Grove. A quick sword thrust or bullet to the head and that would have been all. You would have fallen and been found in the next day or so. As I said before, Laika saved your life."

"Why was Laika there?"

"Because I asked her to be there, and she crouched in the cold for days; no food, no water. Though she is huge, Laika is quite stealthy; a trait Hruntha did not possess."

Raal and Jana, followed by several Chancellors, re-entered the room. They came forward and swarmed around Sam's capsule, hooking up cables, setting up portable terminals and other devices Kay couldn't identify. They worked with crack precision.

The speakers came up: static issued from them; the Chancellors adjusting their equipment, causing the machines to sputter and pop.

Raal seated himself at a terminal and keyed in information. "I don't have boost!" he said angrily, causing the Chancellors to bustle about and check their work. They adjusted several cables and turned dials. Raal seemed satisfied with the corrections. He called up a screen. "There! There's the theta wave, nice and strong. Very skewed, very irregular—possibly due to her alien physiology." He snapped his fingers. "Take notes!" and the Chancellors obeyed.

He adjusted several dials and cleared his throat. "About?" he said into a microphone. "About?" he repeated. More fine adjustments. "Give me more beta!" he demanded. The Chancellors took action.

"About ..." Raal said again into the microphone.

"About what?" Kay asked Jana as he watched the process unfold.

"It's a key word meant to elicit a response," Jana whispered. "We are tuning the connection, seeking the inner voice. It is exacting work, sometimes more art than science. Please, give us a moment. Raal is a master Mentralysist and he is very skilled at establishing a connection."

Raal said the word several more times. "About ... About ... About ..." More fine tuning.

"About ..."

Then, like a ghost's voice, there was a machinelike reply through the speakers. "ABOUT ..."

The Chancellors stopped what they were doing and watched, as if this was the moment they had been expecting.

Raal flipped a few switches. "Continue."

No answer. More adjustments. "Continue," he said again.

"CONTINUE," came a response.

"Aftermath."

"AFTERMATH."

"Melancholy."

"MELANCHOLY."

Raal seemed satisfied and stepped away from the terminal. "The Mentralysis connection is ready. Go to the machine and speak into the left microphone. Remember, we have a standard RDP running and your Ne-Countess does not know what has happened to her. You would be wise not to say too much; the reality she inhabits at the moment is quite fragile. And, most importantly, keep in mind we have no analysis on Ne-Countess Sammidoran at the moment, therefore we have no idea what she'll be like as her Sleeping Self. She could be an MC Archetype, which is most common; in Elders, that is. MC means 'Moderate Change,' in which case you won't notice too much difference in her demeanor. She could, however, be an NC, SC or DO, and be radically different than when she is awake. You must be prepared for that possibility, Lord Blanchefort. She is a Monama and we have virtually no baseline analysis to fall back on, no textbooks to consult. We are, at this very moment, gathering the data; we are at this moment writing the textbooks for our posterity, and therefore every word you say shall be critical. What we learn here will help us better serve Monamas in the future."

Kay approached the portable deck and the Chancellor technician moved aside. "This one?" Kay asked, pointing at the left-hand microphone.

Raal nodded.

"Sam?" Kay said into the microphone. "Sam, can you hear me?"

No response.

"Sam?"

There was a clicking sound, and then, "Kay?" came an excited voice over the speakers. "Kay, is that you?"

"It's me, Sam."

The screens around Sam's capsule flashed with fresh data. Her heartbeat monitor increased significantly, her skin temperature rose, and her respiration quickened in a cone of steam.

"I have been so worried! I woke up this morning and everybody was gone. It was like a bad dream. I should be very angry, but I cannot be cross with you, Kay, I love you so. Where are you?"

"I ... was called away. I'm sorry, I had immediate business to attend to. Such things happen."

Sam sounded hurt. "And you didn't get me? I would have liked to come with you."

"I know, darling, and I'm sorry. It was late in the night and ... you needed your rest after all that had happened. I didn't want to disturb you. How is your neck?"

"It hurts a little, and I'm having a little trouble with my nose."

"Your nose?"

"I can't smell anything."

Raal flipped a switch and paused the connection. "Her RDP is based on Elder patterns—the sense of smell is the least concern in such cases, and her inability to smell is to be expected. It is not normally noticed."

"Sam's sense of smell is very keen and a vital part of how she perceives the world around her; of course she'd notice it."

"We have taken note of that and will correct the problem for the future when dealing with Monamas. We don't have a Monama RDP at the moment and this session shall assist us in creating one. Please continue. You are doing well." He flipped the switch again.

"When are you coming home?" Sam asked.

"Soon. This very day. I'm nearly finished. Would you like me to bring you a present?"

"You're all I want."

Kay glanced at the sterile surface of the capsule and placed his hands on it. A tear fell from his eye. He longed for Sam.

"Where are you right now, Sam?"

"I'm in our favorite reading room snuggled up on the couch, catching up on some reading. I'll not leave until you return. You know, I see many flaws on this pillow I embroidered. I need to make another one and do it better."

Kay controlled himself, and forced his voice into a steady state. "It ... was your first attempt. Mistakes are to be expected. I cherish it ... because you made it."

He heard the voice give a short laugh, then: "Are you coming home soon, Kay? By dinner perhaps? May I expect you? I saw Sarah. She's here."

"I'll try, darling, I'll try ..."

"And, may we head south to the lake this weekend? I'd like to continue working on our jar. I cannot wait to be pregnant with our children, feeling them grow in my belly. I long for it."

Kay put his hand to his face and wiped away tears. He couldn't respond. He was overcome. The Chancellors made a few adjustments to the terminal.

"Kay? Are you still there?"

The terminals flashed alarms and printed warning data.

"I ..."

Raal came up and flipped a switch. "Steady yourself, Lord Blanchefort," he said, struggling with the terminal. "Her well-being depends upon not suspecting her circumstances or questioning her RDP. Do not cause her further distress. Now proceed." He flipped the switch again.

Kay composed himself. "Yes, yes, I'm sorry. I must away,

darling, and conclude my business. There is much to do and I wish to be home as soon as possible to share dinner with you."

Over the speaker, Sam's voice reverted to Anuie: "*I love you, Kay.*"

"*And I love you too.*"

Raal ended the connection. Static returned. The lights on Sam's capsule reverted to random blinking. Vapor hissed from its tubes.

Roethaba's hologram stood there, silent. She touched his shoulder. "Was she different, Lord Blanchefort? Did you detect a change?"

Kay knelt down and hugged the surface of Sam's capsule, gripping it as hard as he could, pressing his cheek into the window glass. "N-no," he wept. "She was exactly the same."

The Chancellors and Roethaba watched for several long minutes as Kay, a proud Vith lord, openly wept by the side of Sam's capsule, his body wracking in spasms. He fell to his knees.

Everybody stood there, watching the spectacle in silence.

"H-how many?" he sputtered. "How many have endured this fate?"

"Too many," Roethaba replied.

"One too many. One life too many …"

Kay stood and composed himself. He wiped his face. "There is a Machine I know, one that has the power to undo this, all of this. I shall use it now and save Sam and my cousins and friends. That will be the end of it."

Roethaba shook her head. "I believe I know the Machine to which you refer; a wondrous creation of Lord Revis of Want, if I'm not mistaken. I'd know his work anywhere. I'm afraid your cousin, Sarah, told The Jones about it under hypnosis and they used her to show it to them, to demonstrate it. 'She' was very keen to learn more about it, to use it perhaps in her various schemes. They have your Machine."

"What?"

"She and The Jones stole it and other items as spoils of conquest."

"You're lying."

The Chancellors milling about reacted with a bit of shock.

Roethaba smiled. "I never lie, Kay, I am not 'Her', and I never hide the truth either, no matter how much it hurts. I beg you to not forget your emotions, but to properly use them, to make this a good end. Will you help us?"

"I will not. I will take my Countess and my friends and my staff members home and watch them in my care, and I shall determine a way to make this right."

"Your home is compromised and overrun with The Jones. I'm sorry things have come to this. I'm sorry, I tried to warn you, remember? I warned you of the curse. And now here we are."

Kay stormed out of the infirmary.

"Where are you going?"Raal asked.

"To the Sisters, to the League Ex-Commons, to any who will stand with me and rally against this indignity! Our House shall go to war over this!"

Kay went down the hallway. Roethaba's hologram appeared before him, hands clasped to her heart. "Your Countess and the others will be lost."

"They will not, for I will extract their bond." He moved past her into the lift. She was waiting for him within.

"Not giving up, are you?" he said as the lift began to move.

"I'm thinking of your Countess … and of others as well. The Sisters will set us back decades, our research impounded, our devices and materials seized, and your Countess and your mentor and staff will be lost in the process."

"My loved ones will not be lost. If you and your people will not take decisive action in this matter, then I shall do it for you. One life too many slumbers in those capsules."

Roethaba was silent for a moment, then she seemed overcome with emotion. "One life too many?" she said in a pained voice. "Shall I tell you about one life, Lord Blanchefort?" She placed her hand on the lift control panel and it ground to a halt between floors.

Her hologram stood there in the lift, weeping. "My 'One Life' came and went centuries ago. My Vehelm, how I loved him, the man above all others who heard my voice and risked his life to bring me into being. Just one life in centuries, I will love no other. And I watched him die, by my hand. What is it the Vith say about death, Kay; that our loved ones wait for us in the Gallery of the Dead? Does Vehelm wait for me there, knowing that I will never walk down that path, immortal in my loneliness, immortal in my guilt? And now, here you are, a Vith lord, kin of mine, weeping over his wife. I have lived long and known many Vith lords. I have seen them cry over fallen battlefields, over destroyed castles and squandered fortune, over lost ships and dead colleagues. But I cannot recall ever seeing one weep simply for the love of his wife as you have just now. We all have our 'One Life', Lord Blanchefort, do we not?"

Despite himself, Kay could not shield his heart. "What do you want?" he asked.

"I want to make right what 'She' has done. I want to be free to atone. You have been to Wilhella's Temple and lived to tell the tale—Laika too. We have never had such an opportunity. We have never been so close. You are not driven by a need for conquest and fame, you simply want your wife and kin back, and with such love fueling you we couldn't possibly fail. What do I want? I want you to help us."

Kay stood there in silence. Roethaba adjusted her gown and restored motion to the lift. It began moving with a jerk.

The lift brought Kay and Roethaba back up many levels to the surface. The doors opened and there was Laika sitting at a table, holding a glass of wine in one of her hands. Several plates of food had been brought to her; she had eaten the meats and breads, but ignored the fruits. When she saw Kay and Roethaba, she stood up. "Jarlcon," she said.

"What is your decision, Kay?" Roethaba asked.

He made up his mind. "If by helping you I save Sam and the others, then so be it. You have my CARG."

Roethaba lit up. "Laika, Lord Blanchefort has agreed to help us."

Laika lifted the glass she was carrying and tossed its contents back. "Hail, Jarlcon! We go!"

4—Sleep?

They flashed across the head of the great constellation Serpens toward Kana, flying an old Vith *Venera* ship. Laika was sitting in the giant-sized control seat, her six arms moving in fluid coordination. The ship was one of many Roethaba and her evil counterpart Ghome had collected over the years; she had them sequestered on most League and Xaphan planets in case a quick getaway was needed. The *Venera* consisted of a single open bay that went back one hundred feet all the way to the engines. It was spacious and commodious compared to the rather small ships Kay was used to flying in. It was also high enough inside that Laika didn't have to stoop.

Kay sat on a plush padded couch nearby, anxious to begin this strangest of quests.

His thoughts spun.

Sam faceless in a capsule; Sarah and Ki too.

He felt lifeless and drained, as if he were in a capsule as well, dreaming a pre-programmed dream.

"Where are we going, Laika?" he asked. He honestly had no idea.

"Tereth Norr," Laika replied. "Kana."

Kay hardly processed the information. "Tereth Norr? Where's that?"

"Kana," Laika repeated.

"Where on Kana?"

"Hospitaler sanctum three point eight-four miles south of the Withelwell River. Get re-supplied there and briefed on where to go."

Sam was fond of telling Kay the story of how she dreamed of him before he was born and how she longed for him, to come into the world with her. That is how Kay felt at the moment, that Sam was slumbering inside a great automated uterus, and she would not emerge until he made it possible for her to do so.

Sam, Sarah and Ki's life or death depended on him, and he had no idea what to do. Kay had been so caught up with Sam and Sarah and with his own pervasive feeling of loneliness that he hadn't realized he was starting this quest for Queen Ghome and the elusive artifacts she may or may not have with no starting point, no plan of attack, no nothing. Sarah was the planner. She would have been all over this. He certainly wasn't.

He was just flying through space with Laika.

"So, the Hospitalers at Tereth Norr will brief us on Queen Ghome's current location, re-arm us and lay out some sort of plan of attack? I currently have no weapons."

"Jarlcon's weapons at castle," Laika said.

"I would like to go home and get my CARG and my Poltava. I feel naked without them."

"Home not safe," she said. "Hospitalers at Tereth Norr will have weapons for Jarlcon."

Kay stood in the open bay. "All right, that sounds fine. We'll figure out our bearing once we get there."

A Mentralysis Deck and holo-emitter was mounted to the ceiling of the ship. The deck flashed with random lights. "Is that another Mentralysis Deck, Laika?"

"Yes."

"Does Roethaba speak and appear through this deck?" he asked.

"Yes, but not now. Mother sleeps," she said.

Roethaba sleeps. If the Hospitalers were correct, then that meant somewhere out there Queen Ghome was awake, seeing through Sarah's eyes and hearing through Sam's ears, surrounded by her Jones servants. It was all too much to ponder. Kay felt numb and immensely tired. He seated himself on the long cushioned bench. "How long until we arrive at Tereth Norr, Laika?"

"Twelve hours, sixteen minutes, forty-five sec-"

"That's good enough, Laika. Thank you."

Kay unbuttoned his vest and untucked his shirt. "I think I'll turn in for some sleep myself; I'm feeling pretty worthless right now. You should set the auto or whatever automated functions are available and get some sleep as well. We need to be fresh when we arrive on Kana."

"Sleep?" she asked.

"Of course. Don't you need to sleep?"

"Laika protects Jarlcon."

Kay looked around at the empty *Venera* ship. Despite everything, he felt a growing fondness for Laika; she had an honest, innocent quality he found inviting. A Vith friends with a Haitathe? Who would have ever thought such a thing was possible? If she weren't there with him, he felt certain he would go mad with melancholy.

"I think we're safe at the moment. Come and sleep."

Kay lay back and stared at the ceiling of the ship. The engines, centuries old but tried and true, throbbed in a soothing fashion. At the control seat, Laika adjusted several knobs and pushed the chair back. "Laika may sleep?"

"Of course you may. You needn't ask. Um, I'm sorry, do Haitathe need to sleep? I assumed as much, but I ..."

"Laika likes to sleep."

"Then get comfortable and rest."

The word 'comfortable' seemed to give her difficulty, as if the concept was something she wasn't familiar with. She pondered it for a moment.

"How does Laika become 'comfortable'?" she asked.

Kay stretched. He closed his eyes and dozed. "How? It's amazing how complicated it can be to explain a topic that is normally taken for granted. Well, I suppose you might let your hair down, you might loosen or remove any articles of clothing that pinch or bind. Your boots, perhaps, and I'm certain that armor isn't very pleasant to wear."

"Laika needs boots and armor to fight. Must protect Jarlcon."

"There is no one to fight here. We are perfectly safe."

She again pondered the thought and seated herself on the opposite bench. She gazed down at her boots and then began unlacing them, the old leather creaking as she did so.

"Where did you learn to fly?" Kay asked as he rapidly descended into the first stages of sleep. "My father is an amazing pilot, my sister as well. I, however, seem to have inherited my mother's flying skills, which are negligible at best."

Laika removed her boots and set them aside, uncovering her pale skin and surprisingly delicate feet. "Hospitalers taught Hruntha. Hruntha flew mother's ships. Now, Hruntha gone. Laika must fly." She removed her gauntlets, revealing her giant-sized yet dainty wrists, and then set to work uncoiling her long fawn hair, her six arms working in complex unison.

Kay drifted to that pleasant estuary between wakefulness and sleep. He heard metal rattle as Laika unclipped her banded mail pants and removed the plates.

"You fly very well, Laika," Kay said, groggily. "You should give yourself more credit."

"Hruntha flies, not Laika."

"Hruntha died in Waam, her head was mounted on a post in the Wunderlucks' compound and put on display. I don't see Hruntha around here anywhere, just you."

There was a heavy clunk of metal—what was that, Kay wondered? He was too sleepy and content to open his eyes and look or use his Sight. Sleep nearly had him.

He expected Laika to stretch out on the adjacent couch, though she was much too large for it. Instead, he felt her crawl up next to him and situate herself on the padded couch. She was nude. He felt the heat and smoothness of her taut bare skin, smelled the faint aromas of her naked body. He felt three slim arms drape over him like a warm, inviting cage.

"What are you doing?"

She spoke, her mouth right next to his ear. "Sleep. Jarlcon said Laika could sleep. Comfortable. Laika comfortable next to Jarlcon."

Was he awake or asleep? He wasn't certain. Memories bubbled up, while he was asleep in the cottage on Hoban: Laika watching him sleep, lying next to him, placing flowers around his body.

Laika's arms around him ... The heat of her body ...

Laika groaning in pleasure. Kay groaning in pleasure, engulfed in her.

Where were his sensibilities? Where were his principles and his loyalty to Sam? He should be recoiling right now, demurely shying away from her. But, he might be asleep, and someone else appeared to be in control.

The Sleeping Self, the Hospitalers said: a different person.
Different person...

His right arm came up all on its own and probed behind him, coming into contact with Laika. He felt his hand traversing the alien and inviting giant-sized mountain range of Laika's six breasts, the towering primary ones, followed by the lesser rows, like foothills progressively dwarfed by the larger peaks. He felt the rise and fall of her firm, rubbery skin, very different in texture from Sam's silky skin. Her six hands moved up and down every bit of him.

He could feel Laika gently trying to turn him around to face her while another hand fumbled with his pants. His Sleeping Self argued for him to give in and turn around, for certainly Laika was offering herself to him. He could make love to an alien Haitathe warrior; how many Vith, short of Homma of Telmus Falls, could say that?

His more rational Waking Self, the one that was committed to Sam, resisted, and the matter passed, the argument won. He put his arm down at his side and moved her wandering hand away from his pants. Laika relented and snuggled in tighter, holding him like a teddy bear, and soon was asleep.

✷ ✷ ✷ ✷ ✷

"Speak the words," drifted through his head. Something in the dark nearby. Something angry.

SPEAK THE WORDS!! I CANNOT HELP YOU!!!

Kay awoke to the sounds of the Com near the control chair going off.

The interior of the ship was dark. Laika was all over him, lightly snoring.

"Laika, we're being Commed. Can you let me up, please?"

She rustled a bit but didn't wake. Kay Wafted out of her grasp. She searched around for him and then curled up, and continued sleeping.

Kay seated himself at the Com and accepted the message.

"Lord Blanchefort?" came Raal's voice. "Is that you?"

"It is."

"What is your ETA to Kana? Your *Venera* ship doesn't appear on our scopes."

Out the front glass, Kay saw the gallery of open space charged with color. The stars were so bright he couldn't make out familiar constellations. "I'm not certain."

"Where is the Haitathe? Why is it not flying the ship? Are you qualified to pilot a *Venera* V4 vessel?"

"Laika is asleep, and, no, I am not. The ship is on auto, I believe."

Raal was shocked. "Asleep? Haitathe have no need for sleep. It ought to be manning the controls at all times."

"I have allowed her to get some rest; perhaps we'll need it once we arrive. I think I see Codis in the far distance, that bluish star that stands out from the rest. We are in no danger."

"Can you enable your Ponder and we shall get a fix on your position."

Kay surveyed the vast panels full of buttons and switches and had no idea what he was looking for.

"It will be in the left-hand quarter-panel, labeled 2-N," Raal added, predicting Kay's lack of knowledge of the *Venera*'s instruments.

Kay searched for it and found the switch Raal described. He enabled it. "There, now, what can I do for you?"

Raal hesitated. "I wanted to inform you that we are having significant issues with one of your kin. She is resisting stasis."

Kay thought back and recalled Ki's blinking capsule in the infirmary giving the Chancellors fits. "Ki? Are you referring to Magistrate Kilos? Is she is danger?"

"No, though she is also giving us trouble. I'm referring to your cousin, Sarah. She established a holistic link out of her capsule and was wandering our Krant system for a short time, even accessing files. She hid from us in a database located in Hibernia and rewrote Lady Sammidoran's RDP. We had to isolate her capsule and stand it on its own to prevent her further escape. Does she have any technical skills regarding networking, holographics, cerebonics or holistrophy?"

Kay scratched his head. "Not that I am aware of. I have no idea what any of those topics are, and I'm certain she doesn't either. Why?"

"Has she attended the University of Arden or participated in any of the Sisters' technical seminars at Twilight 4?"

"Absolutely not. That, I'm certain of."

"Hmmmm …" Raal's tone sounded interested. The master Mentralysist and Hospitaler in him came through. "Hmmmm," he said again, "it is very possible that your cousin Sarah is an Ultra then."

"What is that?" Kay asked.

"It's a Mentralysis Archetype. We have discovered there are seven basic types of people, or Archetypes, depending on how much deviation exists between the Sleeping Self and the Waking Self. The Ultra is a special class of Archetype. The Ultra is unique in that the Sleeping Self displays skills and talents the Waking Self does not possess—it's normally the inverse. The Ultra, for example, might be a master painter or a great writer, even if the Waking Self has had no training or exhibits no particular talent in those areas. It's very rare, but we have documented cases of Ultras displaying incredible skills. The Ultra can also exhibit traits of any of the other six Archetypes; only with analysis will we know which one your cousin is. We will hope at this point that she follows the standard statistics and is an MC, in which case the difference will be negligible."

"What are you planning to do with my cousin?"

"I believe we are going to do something unprecedented. I am going to authorize the removal of some of the restrictions on her capsule and give her low-level access to the Krant network and some of our other ancillary systems. I want to observe what she is capable of. I assure you, she is in no immediate danger. The opportunity to observe an Ultra should never be missed."

"What about Ki?"

"We shall continue to monitor her."

"Keep me advised, please."

"I will do so. Your Ponder data is in. You are on course for a median polar orbit of Kana, ETA two hours with a descent to our banking facility at Tereth Norr."

"A banking facility? Tereth Norr is a bank, did I hear you correctly?"

"It is. Tereth Norr is an outlet of the Standard Bank of the League. It's rather like a self-contained community and commune for bankers, so I'm told."

A commune for bankers? Kay winced. "That sounds … lovely."

"I'm sorry, but that is our largest facility on Kana at present. Once there, we will determine a plan of attack. In the meantime, I recommend you wake the Haitathe and do not allow it to sleep again. I repeat, Haitathe have no physiological need for sleep. Be advised, allowing them to sleep can foster a psychological need in them to do so, akin to encouraging them to become drunk or indulge in recreational drugs, and it might behave erratically. It might even attempt to have sexual intercourse with you—Haitathe are known to behave most erotically when in a sleep-ready state. Sexual intercourse with the Haitathe is counterproductive to our mission and I advise against it, unless you fancy such things, in which case that is your business. I will be here at our Gold Coast sanctum bells deep and will be available if you need me."

"How is Sam, Raal?"

"Stable. Raal out."

Kay closed the Com and approached Laika. She was a nude tangle of arms and breasts supine on the couch, her calves and feet dangling over the edge. He shook her. "Laika, it's time to wake up. Laika."

She smacked her lips and stretched. Two of her hands found his shoulders. "Come … sleep with Laika," she purred, her eyes still closed.

"It's time to get up. We're nearing Kana."

With gentle strength, she pulled Kay down onto the warm couch. "Still have time …" she mumbled. "Still have two hours, four minutes, thirty-six seconds until interface. Laika comfortable. Lie with Laika."

Kay had heard the Haitathe had eidetic, computerlike brains able to keep track of complex and minute detail, never forgetting a thing even when addled with sleep. Seeing it in action was impressive. Kay sighed, and allowed himself to fall back to sleep in a warm, six-armed embrace.

He thought better of it, but her body felt so good and nothing was happening, so why not?

Why not? came a voice in his head.

5—The Ultra

Kay awoke a while later, still wrapped up with the sleeping Laika all over him.

Someone stood in the darkened bay looking down at him. "Well, this is cool. Don't worry, I won't tell Sam or nothing."

Kay stirred. "Lady Roethaba, is that you?" he asked.

"Nope! Guess again."

Kay rose to full wakefulness. Standing over him was Sarah of Blanchefort, blue-haired, pony-tailed and smiling, wearing her usual black duster, pants and boots. He did a double-take. "What in the name of Creation?"

"Hi, Kay!"

He Wafted out of Laika's arms and stood there before her for a moment, elated. He threw his arms around her. "Creation, it's good to see you, Sarah!" He squeezed her tight and she squeezed back.

"Good to see you too, Kay!"

Something occurred to him. "Wait—how did you get here?"

"Oh, I'm not here. I'm back on Hoban, butt naked in that funky capsule they've got me in with no face. I'm a mess right now, aren't I?"

She beamed with her usual energetic smile.

Kay took a step back and Sighted her. "You're a …"

"Hologram? Yeah, isn't it cool?" She slapped him once on the cheek with surprising force. "Feel real too, don't I? Actually, I'm not a stupid hologram. Technically, I'm a Fintron. Got more finducers programmed on me than you can shake a stick at. Ha! Even now I could kick your butt!"

"Did the Hospitalers program this hologram for you?"

"Whaaaaat? Heck no, screw them. I did it myself. It seems that when I'm asleep, I'm a real whiz at these sorts of things. I just up and got into the Hospitalers' network and helped myself to a bit of database room. I programmed this Fintron from scratch, done deal. It was easy."

"They called you an Ultra."

"I know! I love it!" She glanced up and her eyes got that dreamy, distant look typical of Sarah when she was about to go on a self-indulgent rampage. "Sarah of Blanchefort—Ultra. Doesn't that sound cool? How about Sarah of Ultra, or just Ultra Sarah? Yeah, yeah, I like that. Wait until I tell Phillip!"

"Can you hear right now, can you see?"

"Well, yeah! Not being able to hear or see would suck hard!" She whirled around and pointed at Laika. "I can see a naked Haitathe lying over there on the couch. I can hear her snoring too. Did you have sex with this Haitathe, Kay? My Fintronic nose tells me she's emitting."

"Of course not. I'm committed to Sam, you know that." He thought about what she had just said. "Emitting what?"

"Pheromones, Kay, a lot of them. Listen, when you're awake you're committed to Sam, but what about when you're asleep? Huh? Ever thought of that? The Hospitalers did some analysis on you when you were asleep in their test cottage on the Gold Coast and, you know what? They've got you penciled in as an SC; that means 'Significant Change'. That means you're way different asleep than when you're awake, though you're not a cool Ultra like me. You could be a real horn-dog when you're sacked out, you know?"

"Impossible."

"Nope, not impossible. This Mentralysis stuff is actually pretty cool."

Kay was shocked. To think that in the deep bowers of his mind he might be somebody else; someone not fully committed to Sam. The thought made him feel ashamed and disloyal. Sarah detected it.

"Hey—hey, I didn't mean to put you off. Of course you love Sam, you adore her, you're loyal to her, there's no question of that; it's just how the mind works. How you are when you're sleeping may not be at all how you are when you're awake. There's nothing you can do about it and it's not your fault. Don't worry about it. I'm sorry I even mentioned the subject."

Sarah moved on from the awkward moment. She raised her arms and whirled around. "So, what do you think?"

"You're the Pride of Castle Blanchefort as always."

"And to think I've been wasting all this talent putting on pajamas and going to bed every night—we're going to have to install one of these machines at home." She whirled about in a frenzy, the tails of her duster fluttering. "Hey, Kay, let's wrestle! Come on!" She got him in a headlock. The fabric of her duster and the bend of her holographic arm felt completely real. Kay could even smell the threads of her duster.

Laika reacted like an angry beast. She rose off the couch, jumped across the room and drew her swords, poised and ready to attack.

"No, no, Laika," Kay said, freeing himself from Sarah's grasp. "This is my cousin, Sarah. She's a friend. She's a friend, it's all right. Please lower your weapons."

"It will be Laika who wrestles Jarlcon!" Laika growled at Sarah in a surprisingly vicious voice. "Not Sarah!"

"No, no, no, Haitathe, he's my cousin. I've been wrestling him since he could crawl. Buzz off, ok? You don't get to play!"

Without another word, Laika surged forward and slashed Sarah through the midsection with blinding speed.

Eyes bulging, Sarah clutched her stomach and slumped to the floor. "Sarah!" Kay cried. He turned to Laika. She stood there with her swords raised, defiant.

Sarah rolled over and beat her fists and boot heels against the floor. She laughed hysterically and sat up. "Oh ... oh this is too much! Sorry, Toots, I'm a Fintron! A sword to the belly isn't going to do much good, is it? You got nothing! Right? Nothing! Hahaha!"

Laika fumed.

Sarah sauntered up to her and tapped her on the thigh. The lighting inside the ship fluctuated as blue bolts of energy surged through Sarah's hand into Laika. The Haitathe leapt back in surprise. Sarah howled with laughter. Her fingers sparked. "Yeah, I added that. Isn't it cool? I'm tapped into the ship's thermoplant. Take that, you damn Hospitalers. I'm wired to kick ass!"

Laika frowned and showed her teeth, enraged. "Perhaps someday, little girl, we shall meet in person, and what will Sarah do then?" she grumbled.

"Oh, I'm scared! Go fly the ship or something! Piss off!"

Laika scowled and turned away, throwing her swords aside. She seated herself in the control chair, sulking.

"I think this Haitathe likes you, Kay, did you see how fast she tried to bisect me?"

"Do not listen to the construct, Jarlcon. Sarah is a fool," Laika said from the control seat.

"Yeah? At least I programmed myself with some clothes on. You might want to get dressed sometime soon, babe."

Laika blushed and got out of the seat. She padded across the bay and gathered her clothes, beginning the long process of donning her armor.

"Feeling a little happy with yourself, Sarah?" Kay asked as Laika dressed.

"I sure am. Watch this …" Sarah waved her hand and a shimmering line of monitors and diagnostic screens appeared in midair. "See? I've got this holographics stuff knocked. This is the security camera system back home at Castle Blanchefort … in real time, too."

Kay could see all the various places in the castle he was familiar with: his tower, the great ball rooms, the kitchens and so on. "How did you …"

"I hacked into it. It was easy. You know, now that I know I'm so bad ass asleep, there's going to be no living with me. We're getting one of these rigs for the castle and that's all there is to it!"

Laika picked up her giant-sized breast plate and maneuvered it into position. "Laika pities Jarlcon then, to be forced to listen to Sarah all the time."

"Here, let me help you with that," Sarah said. She touched the bluish metal with her finger and sent a jolt through it. Laika took the shock with gritted teeth and stepped away.

"Will you leave her alone, Sarah? Gods, you're as bad as the Hospitalers!" Kay said.

"I'm just having some fun, Kay. She's a big, tough Haitathe so she can take care of herself. Ok, where were we? I've been reviewing the camera logs. So here's what happened. The day after the battle with the Dead Man in the Grove, The Jones came in and brain-bagged the lot of us, and they did it really fast. Remember that fellow Mother was so keen on me seeing in the Firth House the other day? His name is Tal de Roga and he's the ringleader. He brain-bagged me but good in the Firth House."

"Brain-bagged you, Sarah?" Kay asked.

"Hypnosis, Kay. The Jones are really good at it." She blushed a bit. "So, this de Roga guy hypnotized me that afternoon and I guess I spilled the damn beans. I told him about the Perlamum pieces and Lady Chrysania, and about King and the Machine too. He grilled me hard about the Machine." She kicked at the metal floorboards. "I guess I blew it, didn't I? To think I almost let the guy kiss me and everything."

"You couldn't help it, Sarah."

"I know, but you'd think I'd be a little tougher than that. Anyway, after the fight with the Dead Man, The Jones infiltrated Castle Blanchefort and took us all down. They also infiltrated the staff, so home isn't too safe right now."

Kay thought a moment. "What about the Professor? What happened to him?"

"He's at a seminar on Brindval. He's not due back until next week. Never around when the sky falls, is he?"

"Doesn't seem like it. Still, his wife and his son are next to you on ice right now in the Hospitalers' complex. Whether he's at the castle right now or not, he's involved. What about Phillip and Thomasina?"

"I don't know," she said, puzzled. "They took off in the *Goshawk* a little while before the attack. I haven't been able to raise them yet. I think they went off into Xaphan space. I hope so. I heard Phillip mumbling something about marrying Thomasina on the down low. She doesn't like big Vith weddings, so they probably snuck off to elope. They'll turn up—I've got my ears pressed to the network. They make a peep, and I'll be all over them."

"What about King? What happened to him?" Kay asked.

"I don't know. I don't see him on any of the cameras. He might have run his course and is dispelled."

"Dispelled?"

"Yeah, Mother put a 'Self Destruct' in all Kings she created after the little mess I made in Bern last year—remember that? Mother doesn't like having active Kings sitting around, so once their mission is completed, they are compelled to return to the Servant's Graveyard in the Grove and enter, causing them to disencorporate."

"That's a shame. I rather liked King."

"I did too, and we could sure use him right about now. Once they get the suicide bug in them, I think you can stop them by re-reciting the summoning litany if you catch them in time. Looks like we missed him." Sarah's eyes lit up with that familiar mischievous light. "Kay, can I zap you once with my fingers? I'm just asking."

Laika finished buttoning her pants and reached for her boots. "Do not shock Jarlcon!"

"He's my cousin; I'll shock him if I want to!"

"Laika is tired of the sound of Sarah's voice," she said. "Don't need Sarah!"

"Oh yeah? Am I getting on your nerves? La, la, la, la .... You know, Toots, Kay's married to a woman who could beat the living tar out of you, so shaddap and fly the ship. You might also want to do a better job of monitoring engine five—it's running a little hot."

"Laika flies ship!"

"Fly it better."

She shot Sarah an utterly deadly gaze.

"Gods, Sarah, awake or asleep you love to antagonize people, don't you?" Kay said. "And, remember, Haitathe never forget anything, so you might have to settle up with her later over this."

"Well then, you two get me put back together and out of that stupid coffin on Hoban, and I'll step out with her and we'll go at it. I'm not afraid to fight this chick."

Kay was relishing this. He needed no analysis as Raal had mentioned: this was Sarah, Ultra or not, and her presence was just what he needed to pull him out of his funk. She gave him strength.

Sarah pointed at the monitors and went on. "Let's turn our attention back to the castle. So, Tal de Roga comes and puts the hurt on me in the Firth House, and I guess I sang like a bird. A couple of days later, they return, get the staff to let them in, and they bag us one by one and frog march us out. It only took them the time it takes to make the grand tour of the castle. Kind of a low point in the history of Castle Blanchefort, if you ask me."

She turned to Laika. "After centuries of attacks, no damn Haitathe ever got that far."

Laika swatted at her in a dismissive fashion.

"Now, I hate to show you this, Kay, but I think you need to see what we're up against. Watch."

Sarah expanded one of the camera screens. Kay recognized the scene. It was his bedroom. Kay saw himself being led in by several dour people dressed in long operatic black cloaks. He watched as he then disrobed and got into bed.

"Those guys in the cloaks are The Jones," Sarah said.

The Jones parted, as if someone of great reverence was passing by, though Kay saw nothing on the monitor.

"That's her, Kay," Sarah said. "That's who we're up against. That's Chrysania of Bloodstein, or Queen Ghome, or whatever—call her what you want. Somehow, she doesn't show up on the security logs. It's not a Cloak, I don't know what she's using. I'll look into it further."

As The Jones watched, Kay seemed to engage in heated sadistic sex with someone unseen. Kay stared in horror. When it was over, he watched one of The Jones offer a black robe to an unseen person. The robe vanished as the invisible person put it on, and another member of The Jones handed the unseen person a cigarette.

Kay was then roughly dressed and taken from the room.

Sarah became uncharacteristically meek and a little emotional. "They … um, are taking you out to be killed, Kay. Sorry, I—guess I get a little teary seeing that. You're my cousin and best friend and I love you, you know. At this point the rest of us are, basically, what you see now—blanks, our parts stolen, our bodies being kept alive by machinery and being bartered off to the Hospitalers."

"I Sighted you in the Hospitaler Sanctum, and it was just like what we saw with Lady Chrysania at Bloodstein," Kay said. "Your head was a solid piece of meat, no sinus, no nasal cavity; no orbits for your eyeballs, and your esophagus went nowhere; like it had no function at all. How did that happen? What procedure was used?"

"No clue, and the Hospitalers don't have one either," Sarah said. "They have odd theories, but none of them are promising. That's something we're going to have to figure out. So, let's get organized."

"We're en route to Tereth Norr on Kana," Kay said.

"Yeah, I know," Sarah replied. "See, Raal and his flunkies over there on Hoban might be great Mentralysists and all, but they really don't have any idea what they're doing other than that. They think they're going to track down Queen Ghome via financials. They figure she and her Jones dogs robbed Castle Blanchefort dry and they'll be able to track her movements that way, as if she was going to step in an SBL somewhere and deposit all our stuff into a traceable account. They have no idea where Queen Ghome is, and heading to Tereth Norr is going to be a big waste of our time."

"Then where should we go?" Kay asked. "Do you have a better thought?"

"Castle Blanchefort."

"Why?"

"I've a hunch. Hey, before I go too far, let's make sure we understand what we're doing and what our objective is, and then I think you'll see why going home is the correct move. Here are our tasks. First, our primary task is the capture of Queen Ghome."

"You mean Lady Chrysania," Kay said.

"Let's get our terminology down. Lady Chrysania of Bloodstein, in my opinion, is dead, long dead. I like to believe that the woman we helped, the one we felt sorry for in the dark at Bloodstein, was a just woman, a righteous one, and that she is now in her grave. Our adversary is Queen Ghome; let's refer to her as such from now on."

"Fine," Kay said.

"So then, our first task is to locate and capture Queen Ghome. Raal and his Hospitalers want her so they can resurrect Roethaba of George. We, on the other hand, want her because she's wearing Sam's face and my eyes, and we both want our stuff back. That is our second objective, to determine how Queen Ghome is able to steal and swap body parts like it's no big deal. Her exact whereabouts are unknown. Her Jones henchmen, though, are still present in our castle, so that's one of the reasons I think we should begin our investigation there."

Kay gazed at the monitors. "One thing I'm quite concerned about is the staff. My parents are out of the League questing with my brother and sister to Eng with a full science armada; your parents are still at their winter home in Esther with the Duke and Aunt Torrijayne. My sister Kilos is in Zenon at an endurocon hosted by the House of Zenon, so the castle is undefended at this time. We have to get the staff out for their own safety."

"The Hospitalers think The Jones have messed with their minds. More hypnosis," Sarah said.

"That could very well be, but that's irrelevant. They are our people to keep safe. I think if we can get them out of the castle, they'll be fine."

"Leave the staff to me, I'll figure out something," Sarah said.

Sarah flipped the screens around. "Now, while I'm taking care of the staff, you and Toots over there need to do the hard part and get the Artifacts of Vehelm: the necklace and the headset. That's objective number three. It won't do Raal and his men on Hoban any good if they have to keep Queen Ghome Maliked forever because she's not a nice lady when she's awake. With the artifacts, Roethaba can live, stand up, walk and talk like anybody else."

"And where are these items supposed to be?" Kay asked. "If she's been alive for six thousand years as the Hospitalers maintain, she's had plenty of time to hide them, both here in the League and in Xaphan space. That's a lot of ground to cover."

Sarah's eyes got wide with excitement. "Well, here's the thing, the Hospitalers think she keeps them in her Bower Chest."

Kay was stunned. "What?"

"Yep—a freakin' Bower Chest. Right out of the pages of Vith mythology. Isn't that cool?"

"Bower Chests do not exist except in old books and children's stories."

Sarah disagreed. "Well, maybe and maybe not. I've been doing a lot of reading since I've been in the coffin, going through the Hospitalers' archives like a boss. It seems, back in the early EX days of Kana, about six or seven thousand years ago, Vith Households like ours and the Bloodsteins were pretty darn powerful, maybe even more so than the Sisters. The old books call that time the 'Splendor of the Vith'. I love that! We could control the weather, we could animate the inanimate, we could influence people's minds; it was awesome."

"How were we able to do these things?" Kay asked.

"Gellar magic. By collecting powerful arcane items, by hoarding them in places like Castle Blanchefort and Castle Bloodstein, we became powerful ourselves. The more stuff you've got, the tougher you get—that's Gellar magic. And from what I've read, our ancestors stockpiled their most fabulous of treasures in giant-sized animated treasure vaults crafted to look like animals and beasts of lore: the Bower Chests. In the old days, the Bower Chests, loaded with treasure, shook the ground and darkened the skies over Vithland; the Zenons, the Remnaths and all the rest, including the Sisters, had nothing like them. They must have been magnificent, those great silverbacks lurking in the woods, those jeweled birds with wings of gold and obsidian beasts winging through the clouds; those glittering ophidians full of treasure, so huge their serpents' tongues flicked the heavens. Forget the stupid Gifts of the Mind, we were godlike during the Splendor." Sarah paused a moment. "You want to know why we are no longer Gellars like we were? You want to know why there are no more Bower Chests roaming Kana? The Sisters, that's why. They didn't like us so powerful, and they managed to sly the power out of our ancestors over time, all the Bower Chests fading to dust. The only Gellars left on Kana are the Sisters themselves. They don't like anybody being more powerful than they are."

Sarah stewed for a moment. "It kind of pisses me off; they took all the magic out of us, all the giant things that made us great. How could our ancestors have allowed the Sisters to steal most of what they had built without so much as a whimper? I would have loved to have lived during the Splendor—that's where I belong. Anyway, I think our lady, Queen Ghome, has managed to keep hold of the Bloodsteins' old Bower Chest, kept it hidden and out of the Sisters' reach and has all her best stuff stashed in it. That's where she's keeping the Artifacts of Vehelm, I reckon. The bad news is, if that's the case, you're going to be in for a rough time of it, Kay. Bower Chests were said to be tough, almost invincible. They walked and they flew; the more items they carried, the tougher they got. They were intelligent and could defend themselves against intruders. And, if you happened to manage to steal something from them, no matter how small, they'd come after you hard until they got it back. That's what you're going to be up against, boyo; as if Queen Ghome herself and her

Jones servants aren't tough enough."

"Jarlcon and Laika not afraid!" Laika said from the control seat.

Kay sighed. "So then, where is this fearsome Bower Chest that's waiting to kill us?"

"That's what we're going to have to figure out. The old reading says some of our ancestors hid their Bower Chests from the Sisters' view in a secret, well-defended place where no Sister has ever set foot. That secret place never fell to the Sister, our nutty ancestors simply forgot about it and the wonders hidden there over time. That's where we need to go."

"And did your reading happen to mention where this hidden place might be?" Kay asked.

Sarah examined the screens of Castle Blanchefort. "No, but I think I know where to get started." A screen popped up displaying the familiar and orderly environs of the Mystery Library, a place where Kay and Sarah had spent much of their childhood. Kay squinted, taking in the detail.

"The Mystery Library? What about it?"

"Hold on, give me a sec," Sarah said. The camera panned further into the familiar rows of shelves and cabinets. Though Sarah had designed the place as a kid, she had done an amazing job. It looked like a real, functioning library. "I saw this and I think it's important."

The camera centered on a statue standing amid the rows of books. It was a full length terracotta statue of a tall, rather skinny female in a gown. She was wearing a pair of protruding goggles that covered her eyes. She cradled a thick vellum book to her chest. "Where'd that statue come from, huh? I don't recall a statue like that in my Mystery Library," Sarah asked.

Kay stared at the statue. "I think I remember a statue like that. Remember, Sarah, in Gods Temple on Xandarr? There was a statue of a goddess wearing a pair of goggles that seemed to be following us around the temple as we looked for Carahil. She had Wilhella's Perlamum piece. What's she doing in the Mystery Library?"

"You tell me, Kay. If this goddess was following us around Gods Temple and now she's squatting inside my library, then she must be trying to help us. Maybe she's looking for worshippers or wants a favor or something? I think the book she's holding is going to be important for us. It might have valuable information. It might tell us where the Bower Chest is, or what process Ghome is using to steal body parts. I guess this goddess wants to help us out."

"What's in it for her?"

"I guess we're going to see."

"Yes, Sarah," Laika hissed, "let Jarlcon discover how to put you back together so Laika can take you apart again."

"Ha! Whatever!" Sarah responded. "Kay, just remember, Queen Ghome is probably one of the most evil calamities who's ever lived, and she's wearing Sam's face and she doesn't show up on security cameras. From what I can gather, she's a full-blown Gellar, so she's going to be a handful. You better not go all weak-in-the-knees on me when you see her."

"I will simply have to control my emotions, won't I?"

Laika returned to the control chair. "Kana comes. Time to prepare for landing."

"Laika, change of plans. Recalibrate our entry. Forget Tereth Norr. We're going to Castle Blanchefort instead," Kay said. Laika adjusted the course.

Sarah stood. "I have to go, Kay. My Fintron is using up a lot of the ship's power and I don't want to foul up the landing sequence. I'll keep snooping around from my end, and don't worry about the staff. I'll take care of them." She turned to Laika. "Haitathe!"

"Sarah, her name is Laika; please show her a bit of courtesy. I'd appreciate it."

"Ok, sorry. Laika, when you two get to the castle, go into the lower levels in the southern wing and find the core of the old Bobby system we used to use when we were kids. Remember, Kay, those old boxes containing the handset and receivers we used to play with? They were from the days of our great grandfather Maserfeld and have fallen into disuse. Turn it on and then find a handset, any will do. Make a Com to AAANB47Z8999AA and we'll be able to talk. I have a connection there."

"How am I going to remember that? Let me get something and write it down," Kay said.

"No need. Laika will remember it. Now, one last thing you need to know, and pay attention because this is important. Everybody back here on Hoban is doing fine so far except for Ki. It's like she's stuck in a nightmare and it's getting worse and worse. The Hospitalers have noticed her readings and are trying to keep her calm, but her nightmares are getting pretty bad. We've got to get her out of this and soon. I'm afraid for her sanity."

"Understood. Thanks, Sarah—and, before you go, I'm glad you're here with me."

She winked at him, shimmered, and was gone.

Kay sat down in the seat next to Laika. In the glass, the blue and green ball of Kana along with its two moons grew large.

"Did you hear the number Sarah gave us?"

She scowled. "Laika remembers. Laika does not like Sarah."

"Sarah is family."

"Don't need Sarah. Laika comfortable before Sarah come."

"You'll become accustomed to her. Sarah always likes to ruffle feathers a bit."

"Laika would like to kill Sarah."

Kay was taken aback. Laika's fairly innocent demeanor and affection for him masked the fact that she was still an alien Haitathe warrior with very stark and brutal sensibilities, and until Sarah managed to win her respect, Laika wouldn't think twice about killing her if she could. Good thing Sarah was just a hologram at the moment and beyond Laika's reach.

"You can't kill Sarah, Laika. All right? You can beat her within an inch of her life in a fair unarmed contest if you are able, but you can't kill her. Are we agreed?"

Laika flushed up and remained quiet as she brought the *Venera* ship down into orbit. Kay Cloaked the ship and they came down fast, apparently unobserved.

6—Castle Blanchefort

They flew north on the rim of the Gaston Way and then veered east past Castle Blanchefort to the outer reaches of the Telmus Grove. Kay watched the sprawling red castle go by, a place he intended to spend his years with Sam and raise their children. It was a proud place, unconquered in centuries; until now.

Invaded ... by a sect of Hospitalers. A very unexpected enemy.

"Laika, let's put down past the eastern wall of the Grove, there's plenty of cover and good places to park the ship. From there, we'll Cloak it ourselves and scout back through to the castle. Our first task is to get my weapons and then get to the Mystery Library."

Laika steered to the east. At the eastern frontier of the Telmus Grove was a towering one thousand foot wall going down into the cloudy valley below. Beyond were the Great Vithland Mountains; a corniced, brutal range of jagged peaks capped by towering Mt.Vith, the tallest mountain on Kana. It was a hulking shadow only a few miles farther to the east.

"That mountain was once a Haitathe bastion, cloud-wreathed and full of dread," Kay said. Laika gave the great black cone of the mountain an impassive glance and brought the ship down near a small frozen lake. Kay helped Laika strap on her belt dangling with weapons. He took stock of her arsenal. She had two giant-sized long swords, both sporting a five-and-a-half foot blade length and each weighing over a hundred pounds. "Hruntha's swords," she said. She also had four LLAG automatic pistols that were so dirty and well-used it looked like she had run them through the mud once or twice.

"Hruntha's pistols," she said. The pistols were regular-sized. Though Laika was a giant, her hands were rather small and delicate for her stature; not much larger than Kay's own.

With her load-out of two swords and four pistols, she should be well able to unleash chaos.

"I think first we should go to the site where I was nearly killed. Perhaps my weapons are there, since I was under hypnosis and was no threat to The Jones. I would like to have my things back; I feel naked without them. Then, we'll hit the castle and head into the Mystery Library."

Laika wound her hair back up in short order and opened the hatch, allowing a blast of frigid northern air to howl in. Laika was bare-armed and bare-shouldered, wearing only a metal breast plate, armored pants and leather boots; none of which was insulated to any degree. Kay was immune to the cold, but what about her?

"Will the cold be an issue for you, Laika?" he asked.

"Why does Jarlcon keep asking such things?" she asked as she stepped out of the hatch into the howling wind.

Kay followed. "Because I'm concerned for your well-being. I'm immune to the cold, are you?"

Outside, it was a gray day in the mountains. Laika shut the hatch and Kay Cloaked it back into invisibility. She stared at the empty space where the ship once was and probed about with her hands.

"It's still there, just invisible," Kay said.

She stood tall and breathed in. "Laika not comfortable," she announced impassively as clouds of condensed vapor issued from her mouth like smoke from a chimney.

"You're not?"

"Cold."

"You're cold? Will you be all right? Do you have a coat or blanket?"

She didn't answer. Her arms and shoulders were livid with gooseflesh. Unmindful and uncomplaining, she leaned back and had a good look at the wall. The wall was towering, rising up into the clouds. The wall also wasn't straight up and down. Instead, it bowed out like the rim of a bathtub.

"Why this wall here?" she asked.

Kay struggled with how he should respond. He decided to be honest. "To keep out the Haitathe. Long ago, they roamed here in vast numbers and made war with us."

He wondered how she would take the news. Wearing her usual frown, she seemed indifferent; the tribulations of the past, the conflict, the blood that had been shed, meant nothing to her. Sentimentality was not something Haitathe had in excess.

"This wall no barrier," she announced. She picked Kay up and set him on her bare shoulder. Laika quickly scaled the wall, her arms moving in spiderlike unison, weapons clanking together as she climbed. Her arms also stretched like rubber when handholds were not within easy reach. About halfway up, she reached the most convex section of the wall and was climbing well past 45 degrees, her weapons dangling down past her hips like a set of kitchen knives. She couldn't place her feet, five of her arms were fastened to the stone. She tired with the labor, her breath coming out of her mouth in steamy puffs.

"Let me help you," Kay said.

"Laika fine," she said.

"No, no, you're exhausting yourself. I'm very impressed how far you've gotten so far. Let me help you."

He looked up and gauged the distance to the top of the wall: about four hundred feet. He put his arms around Laika's neck.

"I'm going to Waft us up. Ready?"

She reacted to his touch. "Jarlcon warm," she said.

Kay Wafted to the top of the wall with a crash. The difference in temperature on the rim was marked. It was still cold but much of the bitter edge was removed by underground hot springs that ran beneath the Grove.

"Warm here," Laika remarked.

"Yes, it's much warmer. Is this temperature more comfortable for you?"

"Laika comfortable." She nodded and gave Kay two quick slaps on the back, blows meant to be affectionate but which nearly put him on his knees. "Laika comfortable," she repeated as her gooseflesh flattened out. She peered over the edge of the wall at the long drop. "Again, Jarlcon moves with the wind," she said admiringly.

Kay recovered from the blows. "All right. We're Cloaked. We can see each other and we may speak normally, but to anybody else we are invisible and silent."

Laika nodded again, gazed at her hands and marveled. "Come, we go where Laika rescued Jarlcon."

"Is it far?"

"Not far."

Kay stopped her. "Before we set off, I want to have a look around first." He lit his Dark Sight and focused ahead through the distance and dense trees, seeing everything. "I can see the castle; it's about three miles to the west. I see a few staff members rolling about, but not many. We normally have about a hundred staff in the castle at any given time. Sarah must have gotten them out somehow—that was good work."

"Sarah is fool," Laika replied.

"I don't see any Jones roaming about. Good."

Laika stood there and nodded. Whenever she nodded, it seemed to be an outward indication she was very impressed. It was important to show her what he could do and not be shy about his Gifts; she had to respect him, otherwise she might turn, though she had shown him nothing but loyalty so far. He was certain she was trustworthy.

"The rest of the Grove is pretty empty right now."

He turned his Sight to the clearing where the Machine was located. Roethaba had told him the Machine had been stolen by the Jones. Sure enough, there was a great ragged hole in the ground where the Machine had once stood. He rolled his Sight back. Two days prior, the Jones had thundered in with a giant earthmover. They couldn't see the Machine as it was Cloaked in Whispers Veil; however, they appeared to have a very good idea where it was located, as Sarah had told them where it was under hypnosis. Working blind, they simply scooped it up, Silver tech disguise and all, and hauled it away. Yet another thing stolen from Kay's family.

"Let's go ahead and see the area where I was meant to be killed," he said.

Laika waded off into the trees and Kay followed, dwarfed at her side. Rather ironic, he thought. The history of Castle Blanchefort was rife with wars and battles, sometimes with other Vith House-holds, once or twice with the Zenons, and many times with the old Haitathe hordes hungry for Vith flesh; now gone in the tamed, more civilized modern League. How many Haitathe just like Laika had fallen here, pierced by Vith weapons? How many had trudged off with Blanchefort prisoners and dead to throw onto their bonfires? How many dead Haitathe was Laika walking over at that very mo-ment with every stride?

Now, he walked the Grove side by side with Laika, a Hai-tathe, and one he was becoming fonder of by the day. One he had nearly made love to while half-asleep.

"You're pretty different when you're asleep ..." Sarah had said. *"A Horn-Dog."*

They passed an old marking stone covered with fallen leaves. Kay stopped and brushed it off, seeing the carvings on the face. "Lai-ka, a moment, please. I want to show you this."

She stopped and stared down at the stone. The Blanchefort Coat of Arms was carved into the face in weathered relief. On the left-hand side of the shield was the profile of a six-armed Haitathe. "See that, Laika?" Kay asked, pointing. "That is a Haitathe adorning our shield."

Her expression was inscrutable. "That is 'rampant'?"

"It is, yes. When I was a boy, I didn't think Haitathe really existed. I thought they were simply monsters from Vith mythology. Then my Sight began working, and now I see past images of them all the time."

"Laika exists," she said.

"Yes, you do. This is probably the first time … ever that a Vith and a Haitathe have walked these passes as friends. You're the first."

She stared at the marker and then shook her head. "Jarlcon not friends with Laika."

"Why do you say that?"

"Jarlcon did not mate with Laika on ship."

Back to that again.

"No, I didn't. I'm married. I love my Ne-Countess and am devoted to her. Wouldn't you think less of me if I proved untrustworthy, if I betrayed my Ne-Countess when she needed me most? But that doesn't mean I can't be fond of you as well. I have become very fond of you."

She turned to him. "Laika does not understand. What is 'fond'?"

"It means I like you. It means I enjoy your company and value your opinion. It means I am concerned for your well-being. Two people can be fond of each other, can care deeply about each other, without being intimate."

Laika thought about it and nodded. "Come, this way."

"Are you square with that?"

She didn't answer. "Come."

They left the stone behind and moved farther into the trees and soon reached a clearing.

"Here, here is where Laika rescued Jarlcon."

"Here?" Kay looked around. They were in a fairly remote part of the Grove. "Where did you come from?"

"From the north. Laika parked ship there. Many miles. Moved with caution, shadowing Jones. Laika picked Jarlcon up and ran back to ship."

"Ran? Who was out here with me?"

"Two Jones."

"What happened to them?"

"Laika killed Jones, rescued Jarlcon and ran to ship."

"I want my CARG, Laika. Did I have it on me when they brought me out here?"

"What is 'CARG'?"

"It's a weapon, like a sword. It's silver and it glows."

Laika laughed. "Ah, toy weapon. Yes, is here." Laika led Kay away a few paces and dug through the grass.

There was Kay's CARG, covered up by leaves. She picked it up and looked it over. She wasn't impressed. "This too small. This CARG is toy." Laika once again offered him one of her massive long swords.

"Thanks, but those are too big. This CARG does just fine. I've slain many with it, though that's not something I'm proud of."

"The battles Jarlcon has won do not please him?"

"I'm proud of my home and my family and my commitment to my Countess. I'm proud of my friends and of my kinship to them. I'm nostalgic about the battles I've fought and the faces of those I've killed, and perhaps someday those experiences will help me better prepare my children for the world and what might face them. When I raise my CARG, it is because I have to, not because I wish it."

He took his CARG back from her and savored its feel. He checked around in the leaves for his saddle and his Poltava.

"Laika remembers all Hruntha has killed and is proud. Laika likes to fight. Laika would like to fight Jarlcon, sword against CARG. It would make Laika 'proud'."

He wondered: did she mean play fight, sparring, that sort of thing? He didn't think Laika would be very good at pulling her punches or her sword cuts, and there was still this wrestling match she wanted to have. "Later," he said.

Kay found his saddle in the grass and put it on, slinging his CARG at his waist. Laika still eyed it with distrust. "Where did the Jones fall?"

Laika stepped a few paces to the north. "Here, and here. Laika killed Jones with LLAGs."

Kay inspected the ground. No bodies. He ran his Dark Sight back and there they were in their white shirts and black cloaks, shot dead to the chest, hauled away by The Jones later on. He Sighted around looking for his Poltava, but didn't see it. He wished he could re-claim it. His Poltava had been a gift from his father.

"Let's head over to the castle and determine the situation there. We'll then follow Sarah's suggestion and enable the Bobby system."

Laika stood. "Laika does not like Sarah."

"Yeah? But we're going to need her." He Sighted ahead. "I

don't see anybody, the way is clear. Let's go."

They stuck to the northern passes, avoiding the courtyards and cobbled paths, following the cold waters of Blanchefort Run as it veered south to the castle proper. An elaborate stone bridge came into view.

"That's the Dragontooth Bridge," Kay told Laika. "We're here."

As they watched, a staff member from the kitchens wearing a light shawl came out and walked across the bridge. Laika instinctively made to hide, but Kay stopped her. "It's all right, she can't see or hear us. With my Gifts, we've nothing to fear."

The girl walked right past them and continued down the path. Kay Sighted her as she walked.

"She's packing a knife in her sash, just there!" Kay pointed. "And the knife appears to be smeared with a thick purplish resin."

Laika lifted her chin and sniffed the air. "Malik," she said. "Laika knows the smell. Hospitalers showed Laika."

"All right then, now we know what we're up against. The Jones no doubt have the staff hypnotized to attack us with Maliked knives. Laika, I don't want any of our staff hurt; they are good, hard-working people and they are innocent in this matter."

"And if staff attack Jarlcon and Laika?" she asked.

"Then we subdue, we restrain, or put them safely out of commission. I repeat, these people are not to be hurt in any way. If we are inconvenienced in the process of subduing them, so be it. I am their lord, and it is my responsibility to protect them."

They entered the castle and moved through the familiar lofty passages. Laika admired the stonework. Kay had to fight the urge to offer her a guided tour—that could come later.

"We're going to go down into the lower levels. I think I remember the equipment Sarah mentioned; it's in the southern wing, two levels down, but it's a little tight to get to it. Can you manage?"

"Laika comfortable in small places."

Kay came to a pillar with a hidden doorway concealed in the stone. Using his Sight, he located the cleverly hidden lever and pulled the door open, revealing a tight spiral staircase leading down. "My mother, who is a first-class castle explorer, showed me this passage once. It'll take us down two sub-levels near the Bobby equipment."

He considered the passage: tight, barely wide enough for him to take at an angle because his shoulders were too broad to fit.

He considered Laika hovering over him, at least twice as

wide in the shoulders as he was. She had gotten along with ease in the tiny cottage on Hoban, but this was a good tight squeeze, possibly a rating of three or four stones out of five on his mother's scale for determining the difficulty of squeezes in the castle. He didn't think there was any way Laika could fit. Kay squeezed in and went down the gritty stairs. Before he knew it, there was Laika, squeezing in after him like a rubber doll with only her armor occasionally catching on the stone walls. In fact, she seemed even more fluid and at ease going down the cramped stairwell than he was.

Kay got to the bottom; it was a small maintenance level about three feet high. Crawling on his hands and knees, he moved south, Laika slithering behind him. He got to a dead end that was barely large enough for him to ball up into the fetal position and change direction; just like his mother taught him when in a confined space. Patience was needed. He saw a side passage—that's where he needed to go. He inched his way into position, slow and steady.

And then Laika plowed in, filling the space solid with her massiveness. Unable to breathe, Kay Wafted out into the passage, scolded her for being too eager, and continued on.

Ahead was a junction filled with old, dusty equipment. A series of black boxes were bolted to the wall; they sprouted thick cabling in several directions ending in a confusion of metal pins blossoming with even more untidy wires.

"I think this is the old Bobby system. It's a primitive sort of Com. You have a handset and a receiver and you can hear a person talk on the other end. My great grandfather Maserfeld put it in. It hasn't been used in years, except when we used to play with it as kids.

Kay looked the equipment over. Seemed dead and inert. "Laika, help me look for a way to power this up."

Laika rolled over onto her back and probed the boxes with her hands. "Here. Is here. Switch behind unit."

Kay saw it. "That's right, I remember now. I think Sarah had a stick around here somewhere that we used to turn the system on. It's too tight back there to reach with our hands."

"No need stick." Laika removed the gauntlet from one of her arms and reached in the tiny space behind the boxes, her bare arm flattening out. She found the switch, flipped it, and the ancient Bobby system thrummed to primitive but reliable life. "What now?" she asked, placing the gauntlet back around her wrist.

"Now, we find a Bobby box." Kay searched around and found one nearby. It was just a plain metal box with a spring-loaded door.

Inside was a small metal receiver painted olive green and a dial pad. A rusty can of red gasol, a relic of their childhood adventures and a favorite of Sarah's, lay crushed up inside the box. Kay removed the can and picked up the receiver, untangling wires. "Laika, what was the code Sarah gave us?"

"AAANB47Z8999AA," she repeated back without a hitch.

Kay marveled at Laika's infallible memory as he punched in the code. He heard tones sound through the receiver.

"What we wait for?" Laika asked on her knees.

"I'm not certain," Kay replied.

He heard tones for a few seconds more and then he put the receiver back in its box. "Well, I think ..."

Riiiiiiinnnnngggg ...

Kay opened the box and pulled the receiver back out.

"Hi, Kay!" came Sarah's scratchy, distant-sounding voice. "It's me. Great job getting the Bobby going—now I'm tapped in. Ha! I told you I'm bad ass now!"

"Great job with the staff, Sarah, the castle's near empty. How did you manage it?"

"How? I'll tell you how. I sent a note to the head of staff thanking everyone for their hard work and offered them a complimentary trip to Bern on the Hospitalers' dime. You should have seen it—they went for it like pigeons to bread. I even booked a transport to take them to Bern, all on the Hospitalers' expense. How's that for a laugh? I watched them stream out of the castle in droves, carrying suitcases and sun tan lotion. Most of them are gone."

"Good, good. How's Sam?" Kay asked.

"The same. She's fine for now, wandering around in a facsimile of the castle, getting ready to have a fight."

"A fight?"

"Yeah, I punched up a little RDP sub-routine, something to keep her busy and entertained. Remember that weird little Monama girl Ennez married?"

"Lady Tellerran? The friend of my parents, the one with the flight jacket?"

"Yep, that's her. She challenged me to a fight, and I remember hearing that she wanted to challenge Sam as well. With the Dead Man and all, we never got to fight; maybe next time. So, right now, I've got Sam and Ennez' wife getting ready to duke it out behind the castle. You know what? Initially I had cooked up this grand setting where Sam and #6 were going to settle their differences once and for all. It was going to be an awesome brawl, but I thought that might be a little too intense, so I switched it. Our good friend Raal had Sam up in your reading room sewing a pillow. How boring is that?"

"Raal told me about your status as an Ultra and that he was going to allow you low-level access to their systems in order to observe you."

"Oh, *'allowed me'* did he? I tell you, me and this Raal guy are going to have words when this is all said and done."

"I'd leave him alone if I were you, and, by the by, I think I'd feel better knowing Sam was safe and sound working on her pillow rather than going off fighting with either #6 or with Lady Tellerran. You know Sam doesn't like #6."

"Oh Gods, Kay, really? You'd rather Sam spent all her time sewing rather than having a satisfying knock-down drag-out with a woman she absolutely hates? Would you rather have a warrior at your side, or a *seamstress?* Oh Creation—don't answer that. I don't want to know. Anyway, the Tellerran_Fight_In_Back_Of_The_Castle RDP program is running and I'm not going to change it—neither you nor Raal can do anything about it at this point. Once Sam's beaten the poop out of Tellerran to my liking, I've got her going up against a pirate ship that I dreamed up. Isn't that cool? She's not going to want to wake up from that!"

"Sure. Thank you, Sarah. What about Phillip and Thomasina?"

"Still haven't located the *Goshawk*. Don't worry about them, it's damn Ki that's the problem."

"How is she?"

"Not good. It's starting to dawn on her that she's trapped in a nightmare and she's fighting against it. I'm trying to keep her busy with cool stuff, but you know Ki, always a pain in the butt. The Hospitalers wanted to shut her down. They think her theta wave has gone into an Insanity Curve and they say they can't fix that. They say she's going to wake up a blabbering idiot."

"Do not let them terminate Ki's treatment!" Kay said, alarmed.

"Don't worry, I won't. I've taken extreme measures. If they work, Ki will be ok."

"Then we've no time to lose. It appears The Jones have hypnotized the remaining staff in the castle. We're under Cloak and haven't been detected yet."

"Ok, ok. Hey!" Sarah said. "Before you cut the line, you

haven't seen King flying around, have you?"

Kay thought a moment. "No, I haven't. You were probably correct. He seems to be gone."

"That really sucks! We need him."

"That's a shame, it really is. I liked King. He had a wise soul."

"You could use King's firepower right now, that's for sure. I'll Com-up Mother and see if she's got any more Kings stashed somewhere. In the meantime, get on up to the Mystery Library as quick as you can. Oh—I need to tell you that Ghome, the lady wearing Sam's face, is trying to withdraw a fortune in Blanchefort money. We're making it hard on her; 'we', listen to me talk. There are several members of the SBL in Roethaba's cult at Tereth Norr, and they're busy moving the money around so she can't get to it. The problem is, she's got a whole bunch of accountants and bankers from the Jones on her side working for her, so it's sort of a toss-up at the moment. They're really going at it right now, from their desks in front of their terminals, anyhow."

"Thanks, Sarah. Do what you can for Ki. We're on our way to investigate the Mystery Library. We'll be in touch."

Laika pulled the receiver from his hand and spoke into it. "Hello, Sarah," she said in a purring sort of voice. "Laika is looking forward to seeing Sarah in person. Laika wishes to have nice chat. Jarlcon and Laika shall put Sarah back together only to have Laika take Sarah apart again."

Kay heard the tinny stirrings of Sarah's voice piping over the receiver: "Yeah, oh yeah? Bring it on, you cow, you …"

Laika replaced the receiver in the box.

"I'd really appreciate it if you didn't fight with Sarah," he said.

"Sarah annoys Laika. Laika will prove to Jarlcon that Laika can fight by beating Sarah into pulp."

"You don't have anything to prove to me."

Laika didn't respond. They made their way out of the tight confines of the sub-level and went to Sarah's Xyotle tower in the central section of the castle. The Mystery Library was on the 50th floor. The ground level door was open. To Kay's surprise, there was somebody sitting in the foyer drinking a cup of tea. It was a young man wearing a loose white shirt with a large unbuttoned collar, and a pair of black pants. A large black cloak was folded neatly on a nearby couch. He had out several books from the Blanchefort library, all pertaining to demonology.

"Jones," Laika said, her hands going to her weapons.

So, Kay thought, here was his first up-close look at a member of The Jones—Hospitalers from Bazz, healers; people in the service of the enemy. The fellow seemed decent enough. He looked like he was ready for an evening out on the town, though he sat quietly reading.

A girl wearing the usual pinstriped blue uniform of the House staff came in, bearing a tray of cookies. An apron was tied over top of her uniform. "Henk, I saw the demon again," she said.

Demon, Kay wondered. What demon?

"Where?" Henk replied.

"In the North corridor. I could see his eyes. They scared me."

"Thank you, don't be scared. Keep me updated."

"We've made you some cookies," she said in a cheerful voice. "Would you like some?"

Henk turned from his books and smiled. "Thank you, yes, I would. Christine, is that your name?"

She blushed. "Yes."

Henk took one and ate it. "They're very good."

Christine fidgeted. She appeared troubled.

"Is there something on your mind?" Henk asked.

"I ... picked a good knife from the butcher's block. Do I really have to cut Lord Blanchefort with it? He's such a nice young man. I've always found him so handsome."

Henk spoke in a soothing voice. "It's for his own safety. We'll take good care of him, you'll see."

Christine listened to his hypnotic voice and seemed convinced. "All right then. I'll make sure, if I see him, I'll get him in the arm."

"That's very good. I'm certain he'll appreciate that." He returned to his books and Christine walked out. Laika snarled as she passed.

"Shall Laika kill Jones?" she asked.

"No," Kay said. "Watch this ..." He lit his Dark Sight and zoomed in on Christine as she walked away. There was the knife sticking lazily out of her sash; a trained assassin she certainly was not. As Laika watched, he reached out and the knife from her sash appeared in his hand. Not blinking, not taking his gaze off it, he held it up.

"I can use my Gift of Sight to interact with objects near or far, past, present or future. The only catch is that I have to concentrate on the object. If I blink or look away, even for a moment, the object falls back to where it came from. I've perfected the process to a maximum of two minutes. I want to test the efficacy of this Malik."

Sure enough, the blade of the small kitchen knife Christine had selected was smeared with a purplish resin covered in lint from her cotton sash. Without wasting another second, Kay stepped toward Henk and gave him a swipe across the shoulder, drawing a bit of blood. Henk reacted, stood up and then quickly fainted, dropping to the floor face-first in a tangle. Kay wiped the blood and resin off the blade using Henk's shirt as a cloth and then blinked his eyes. The knife vanished back into the unaware Christine's sash, where it had come from.

Laika rolled Henk over and tested his pulse. "Heartbeat slow, steady. Good Malik."

"Yep, that's a fast-acter. We need something to bind his hands, as we have no idea how long this Malik is set for."

Laika found a table-top iron lamp and effortlessly bent it around his hands.

"Make sure it's snug but not so tight as to cut off his circulation."

She molded the metal with her powerful hands. "Jarlcon is very concerned for enemies."

"Aren't I, though? All right, excellent work. I'm going to take him up to a place I know he'll have difficulty escaping from." Kay approached Henk and put his arms around him. "I'll be right back, just stay here a moment." With that, Kay Wafted away, down into the darkened interior of the Chapel of Countess Fercandia, the place he had first met Sam years ago. It was dark in there and impossible to get out of without crawling through very tight passes. As Henk was a Jones and probably from Bazz, he shouldn't have the gift of Waft, so he would be stuck in there. He laid him out on a pew and Wafted back to Laika. "That takes care of our boy Henk, now let's get on up to the fiftieth floor."

7—The Mystery Library

As nobody was around they took a lift up through the levels, passing the ones Sarah frequented until the doors opened on the fiftieth floor. Awaiting them was a small, clean vestibule and then a set of double doors leading into the Mystery Library, Sarah's beloved bastion in the castle. The ceiling was a bit low and Laika had to stoop, which she did without complaint.

Kay pointed at the doors to the library. "In here, Sarah says she saw a statue holding a book. The statue came from Gods Temple on Xandarr, so we're keen to see the book it is holding and what's in it. The goddess might have favored us. The book might contain a clue on how we should proceed. This is a room we used to hang out in as kids—we still use it as a convenient gathering place. This might lead to nothing, but we'll check it out anyway."

Kay passed through the doors into the fresh natural light of the library. Laika hesitated and remained in the stony vestibule.

"Come on, Laika," he said.

She shook her head. "Enchanted."

"What's enchanted?"

"Library enchanted."

"No, it isn't. Come on."

Laika refused. She backed away toward the lift.

"Oh, come on, you big baby, there's nothing here to—"

Laika reacted like she had been punched. Her face turned a flushed shade of red and she huddled up and began weeping.

"What's wrong?" Kay asked, emerging through the doorway.

She spoke through her hands. "Laika … Laika disgrace. Laika coward."

"No, you're not. Did I hurt your feelings just now calling you a 'big baby'?"

She continued to sob. Kay wasn't quite sure what to do; a sobbing Haitathe with hurt feelings? He had not imagined such a thing was possible.

"Hey, I'm sorry, I didn't mean it. Come on, you're a ten foot tall giant. You can fly a *Venera* ship, you're a lot stronger than I am, and you remember everything you see or hear. I can't do any of that."

Laika continued to cry. He tried to appeal to things she might like. "After we investigate the library, we'll go out into the Grove, find some muddy ground, drop our weapons and have a good old fashioned mud match; just me and you."

She looked up. "Jarlcon wishes to wrestle with Laika?"

"Sure do, and I'm going to kick your butt!"

She seemed to cheer a little. "Laika promises to wrestle well."

"I'm sure you will. So look, I need you here with me, and—"

That seemed to get her full attention. "Jarlcon needs Laika?" she asked, eyes puffy but hopeful.

"Of course I do. Now, please, stop crying." She seemed to be in need of a hug and Kay gave her one. He felt her six arms coming around him, pulling him in close to her, suffocating him a little.

"Are you feeling better?"

She nodded.

"Ok, now tell me, why do you think the Mystery Library is enchanted?"

Laika let him go and pointed at the doorway. "Laika feels energy. Enchantments. Very strong."

Kay studied the library. Through the doorway he could see the usual open space; the crush green carpeting and the assortment of stuffed chairs and mismatched couches arranged along the walls, interspersed with broad windows admitting cheery daylight. Seemed like it always did, going back to when he was a child; the only things missing were the old colorful posters Sarah used to have hanging on the walls but had taken down as her tastes matured.

He recalled something that Carahil once told him, that the library was one of his 'little temples' and that Sarah was one of his 'high priestesses'. Carahil had said he kept things in the library, things he wanted to be safe. Kay didn't take any note of it—thought it was simply exaggeration or hyperbole. Maybe Carahil wasn't exaggerating. Maybe the Mystery Library was a temple of some sort and Laika had detected its hidden power.

Next to the doorway was Sarah's beloved slate indicating who was welcome to enter and who was not. According to Sarah, anybody not listed or on the "FORBIDDEN" side was not allowed to enter. She was very particular about it. Laika's name was not there on either side.

Kay decided to appeal to Laika's sense of logic. "Laika, I think maybe you're correct—perhaps this library is enchanted. This slate here determines who is allowed to enter the library and who is not. This is Sarah's library, so if we can get Sarah to add your name to the list, you should be able to enter without fear. Does that sound reasonable?"

She nodded and gazed at the doorway.

He headed into the library. "There's a Bobby receiver in here. I'll ask Sarah to grant me permission to add your name. Wait right here. We're going to take care of this."

Laika seated herself and tucked her knees up into her chest. Kay moved into the room; he always marveled how neat and organized it was. The eastern end of the library contained the tables and chairs, a holo-terminal, and a few coolers Sarah kept full of snacks— it saved them having to run down to the kitchens far below. In the center of the room was a great Nadine wood table that his father, Lord Davage, had given to Sarah. It was a relic of old Castle Durst and he liked seeing it still in use, so he gave it to Sarah to keep in trust. Sarah took meticulous care of the table, dusting it often and tending the wood with various oils. A set of old wooden coasters adorned with Sarah's Blanchefort coat of arms sat in their box and were required to be used when beverages were introduced. He recalled the innumerable times he had sat at the table with Sarah and Phillip, her eyes dreamy, discussing their next adventure.

Beyond the Durst table was a small maze of bookshelves and cabinets full of books, papers, documents and artifacts Sarah had collected over the years; and the collection was impressively enormous. Sarah had a precise knowledge of every item stored in the library, down to the smallest crinkled paper and hand-scrawled note. Though Sarah fancied herself an adventurer, fighter and swordsman supreme, 'librarian' was clearly her true calling and this amazing, well-organized and maintained space was proof of it. He wandered into the shelving, taking the twists and turns, smelling the old pages and leather-bound covers lingering in the air. Sarah's layout of the shelving made maximum use of the limited space.

The tangle of shelving went on and on. Kay had forgotten, or didn't realize, how many books Sarah had. There had to be ten thousand books shelved here, and Sarah had probably read each and every one front to back at least once if not more times. He reached a long corridor that went on for quite a ways. He had no memory of that corridor. The corridor seemed too open and far too long to fit in the space of circular Xyotel Tower. Down the corridor about three hundred yards was a tan, unpainted statue of a tall female in a gown, a pair of over-large goggles on her face; it was the statue from Gods Temple on Xandarr Sarah had shown him previously in the security cameras. The statue was oddly placed. It wasn't situated in an alcove or some other out-of-the-way spot where a statue might logically go; it was plunked square in the center of the corridor. It was as if a passing lady walking down the corridor had simply turned to stone were she stood.

In her thin arms she carried a rather thick book. That was their objective, to get the book; and Kay decided to simply go and grab it. He Cloaked himself, just in case who-knows-what might be waiting for him, and Wafted down the corridor, amazed by its size and length. He arrived at the statue. The statue was situated in the center of a drafty crossroads; a parallel corridor cut across left and right with either end going off a long way. Too long. None of this would fit in Xyotel Tower; therefore, this corridor had to be some sort of arcane portal going to who knows where. Laika and Carahil were correct; the arcane was at work in the Mystery Library. To the left, the corridor extended into a dark, yawning sort of space. A chill wave of humidity issued from it. He thought he saw bits of stone and tangled wire—and something else.

Something was down there, hiding in the dark, watching him. Something angry.

The demon, Christine had said. There was a demon is the castle.

Was a demon hiding in the dark? Kay could feel it. Something small but intense and foreboding waited for him down that passage. He wanted to avoid the dark space if he could.

The statue before him was familiar. He had seen it before on Xandarr in Gods Temple. They had gone there to gather one of Wilhella Cormand-Grande's Perlamum pieces and, if possible, to curry a favor of the gods. They had hoped to commune with Carahil, a god they knew well, but were unsuccessful in reaching him. This particular statue of a girl wearing a gown and a pair of goggles, presumably a goddess, seemed to have taken notice of them, and it followed them about the Temple, blocking their passage and following them as they exited. And here she was again in an arcane node of the Mystery Library, holding a book that might have information that could assist them.

He tried to take the book and head back out to get Laika. The book wouldn't budge from her hand. It was impossibly heavy. Kay's strength-level certainly was nothing like his father's. He would need Laika to lift it.

He headed back into the more familiar area of the Mystery

Library. He was glad to be gone from the dark room to the left and the demon that might be hiding in it. He dropped his Cloak. There was a Bobby box, mounted on the floor covered up with a Carahil plush toy. He moved the toy aside and pulled the receiver out.

A scratchy voice filled his ear. "Joe's Pizza!"

"Pardon? Who is this, please?" Kay asked, tentatively holding the receiver.

He heard laughing. "Oh, Creation, Kay—it's me! Who else?" came Sarah's voice. "Don't be so wet!"

"We're here at the Mystery Library. Laika refuses to enter. She says it's enchanted."

"Enchanted?"

"I stumbled into an arcane corridor in the back of the library, so maybe she's correct. In order to humor her, I would like you to grant me permission to add her name to the WELCOME side of the slate."

"A bloody Haitathe in my library? No way! She can wait outside in the vestibule."

"Sarah, we don't have time to bat this around, ok? I need her help, so lighten up. I'll make sure she doesn't get into anything or break your stuff. She's not a dog, you know, she hasn't broken anything yet."

"You promise?"

"Yes, yes, I promise."

"Ok, but it's going to be me and you doing a couple of rounds in the Grove if I find anything messed up once I get back."

"You might have to get past my new Haitathe bodyguard for that."

"I think me and the Haitathe are going to be doing some rounds regardless, so after we settle up, I'll be coming for you. Just make sure she doesn't break stuff or remove anything from its proper place, ok?"

"I promise."

"So, here we go: I, Sarah of Blanchefort, daughter of Lady Poe and Lord Peter of Ruthven, grant unto Kabyl, Lord of Blanchefort, son of Lord Davage and Countess Sygillis of Blanchefort, the *temporary* right to annotate the official welcoming slate of the Fabulous Mystery Library in any manner he sees fit, good until I set foot in the library proper once more, at which time the privilege shall be revoked. There, that ought to do it."

"Thanks. I saw the statue. The book is there."

"Did you take it?"

"No."

"Why didn't you take the book if you saw it?"

"It's too heavy for me to lift. I need Laika."

"Oh, Creation, you're a wimp, Kay. Well, hurry it up. I want to know what's in it!"

"All right. Let's hope this bears fruit."

Kay hung up the receiver and went to the entrance of the library. He could see Laika huddled up by the doorway solemnly peeking in. He found a marker and went back into the vestibule.

"I just spoke to Sarah, and she granted me permission to make changes to the slate." He showed her the marker. "See this? I'm going to add your name to the WELCOME side and then you will be able to enter without fear. Will that be sufficient?"

She nodded.

"I saw the book while I was in there. I'll need you to lift it. It's way heavy."

Kay wrote her name onto the WELCOME side of the slate. "There, all set. Come on in."

Laika licked her lips and stepped in. Nothing happened. She stood just inside the doorway and waited for him to follow.

As Kay put the slate back on the wall, he noticed there were several new entries on the WELCOME side that hadn't been there previously: 'The Jones' was one, and 'Tal de Roga' was another, all in Sarah's distinctive hand. Sarah must have added them there while under hypnosis. If that was the case, then The Jones had already been in the library and the notion that they were waiting inside to spring a trap seemed a distinct possibility. Had he not been Cloaked, they might have attacked. He struggled with the idea: enemies in the Mystery Library, their childhood play area—the safest place in the world.

Just for good measure, Kay scratched their names off the list and added them to the FORBIDDEN side. He then placed the slate back on the wall.

There was an explosion of noise within the library.

"Jarlcon!" came Laika's voice in a scream. Kay rushed inside. A strange tempest had appeared inside the library, throwing the place into a chaos of smoke and cloud. Fierce winds whipped through Laika's hair. Through the torrent, Kay saw several people come tumbling out of the maze of shelves like man-shaped pieces of paper caught in a fierce wind: white shirts, fancy cloaks fluttering dramatically. Mixed into the tempest were a number of long, tubular objects, shattering, spinning in chaos.

Jones, and they had been armed with sniper rifles. As he suspected: an ambush!

Kay counted twelve people and their weapons and various kit go spinning by, tumbling head over heel past the Durst table and out the doors where they clattered into the vestibule like toppled bowling pins.

The torrent ceased. Kay led Laika by the hand into the shelves, where they took cover. "The Cloak's back up. They can't see us," he said as she drew her LLAG pistols and cocked them.

"We fight!" she cried.

"We wait! Just wait."

Through the door, Kay saw The Jones picking themselves up, milling about in confusion; some injured, some holding their heads in pain. One tried to reenter the library and was violently rebuffed, sent flying back toward the lift.

The enchantment on the library was potent and proved real.

After a moment, one Jones, a thin young man with short blonde hair, approached the doorway, leaned down and examined the slate. He took his time, carefully reading the names printed there. He smiled and said a few things to his fellows. They retreated to the back of the vestibule.

"Hello?" he said, standing in the doorway. "Lord Blanchefort, is that you?"

Laika took aim.

"Laika, no!" Kay cried, but too late. The LLAG discharged in a gritty cloud of burnt powder and gun smoke. In Kay's Dark Sight, he could see the twisting condensation trail of the bullet as it sizzled through the air toward the man's head with a fast twist.

In a nonchalant manner, the young man standing at the doorway reached up and plucked the high caliber bullet out of the air like it was no big deal, and let it fall to the floor in a harmless roll.

The young man spoke again. "I say, that certainly wasn't very sporting, was it?"

A moment of silence passed as he awaited an answer. Kay partially let his Cloak drop and spoke.

"And what you did to me and my kin without provocation, was that sporting? Was waiting for me in ambush in this tower sporting?"

The young man gave a short laugh. "I suppose not. Well then, we'll call it even for the time being, shall we? I must say, I've visited quite a number of fancy Kanan Households of late, and I'm certain I like this one most of all—most impressive. Allow me to introduce myself. My name is Tal de Roga, I'm certain you've heard my name before."

Kay bristled. "Indeed I have."

"And how is Raal these days?" Tal asked. "Zenons, especially ones from Hoban, are so stodgy, aren't they?"

"I'm not interested in engaging in a session of false civility with you, sir," Kay shot back.

"Ah. How Vith you are."

"Perhaps you'd like to discuss with me how it is your leader is currently wearing my wife's face, holding her tea cup with my wife's hands, walking to the bank to steal our money on my wife's feet, and so on. I am most keen to discover how that process works."

Tal de Roga laughed and shook his head. "Yes, I'm certain. Just business is all. Your pardon—I'm not accustomed to dealing with someone whose position is so at odds with my own. I'm accustomed to a bit of tacit civility."

"You are in the service of a tyrant and a thief and a liar, and you may count me as your mortal enemy. Let's be clear on that point," Kay said with fury.

"Acknowledged, and that is a great shame as I am not a bad person, and I am certain you are not one either. Fate, it seems, has pitted us against each other."

"Fate had nothing to do with it, sir. When your master chose to come at my wife, assault her, steal her goods, discard her for dead and invade my home ... that is when we became enemies!"

Tal de Roga raised his hands and let them fall. "I understand how you feel, truly I do. What can I say? Guilty as charged. My mistress fancied your wife's face and that was all there was to it. You should take that as a compliment. I must say I find the candor of this situation unique and uncomfortable."

"I suppose a more stealthy theft and murder, free from that awkward moment when you have to face those you have wronged is more to your liking."

"You must understand; I am not a cruel or evil man. I do not sit in my home, or in our sacred places, and dream of doing evil things. None of us do—we are not Xaphans."

"Fine words. Xaphans, at least, do not attempt to rationalize away their misconduct. I have never been so wronged by a Xaphan."

Tal's voice took on a hard edge. "Truly? Wounded and suitably enraged, are you? From my perspective, you, sir, are standing in the way of progress, of making a better day for the League. We are pledged to serve humanity, understand?" He gestured, his hand cutting through the air, driving home his points. "In order to do that, we must increase our knowledge. Bellathauser is within our grasp at long last. With Bellathauser, our knowledge of the human analog will be complete. Nothing will be left to chance; there will be no questions for which we will not have an instant answer. Imagine it! It will be a new Age of Man, a revolution of thought and of cure, with lowly Bazz at its center."

"Meanwhile, you bow in fealty to a creature wearing my beloved wife's face!"

"A creature who will lead us to Bellathauser!!" Tal de Roga shouted. "What is a life or two in the service of Man?"

"One life and millions more!"

"Yes, and millions after that! All nameless dead in the service of total knowledge! An acceptable loss and we are willing to pay it!"

Kay fully dropped his Cloak and stepped out into plain sight. "Of all those nameless dead, one of them indeed has a name, for it is Lady Sammidoran of Blanchefort and it is also Vengeance!" He brandished his CARG.

Tal waved his hand and snapped his fingers. Kay fell into an immediate trance and stood erect like a statue.

Tal de Roga laughed. "Ah, the Vith," he said in a suddenly calm voice. "So dramatic and easily stirred." He turned to his fellow Jones. "He's ready." He turned back to Kay. "Come here, Lord Blanchefort, you've some documents to sign, some funds to transfer, and we're certain there are more coffers in this castle to empty. You shall lead us to them. Living an immortal life is expensive, I'm certain you understand. You wanted to see our leader, and we shall take you to her, make no mistake. All this House has, including your blood and the hearts that pump it, belongs to my mistress. And then you are going to die, all in the name of progress. Come on, come to me." He gestured for Kay to come to him.

Entranced, Kay moved toward the door.

BLAM! BLAM! BLAM! BLAM!

Laika came thundering out from behind the shelves, blasting away with her LLAGs, shooting over Kay's head. De Roga caught one bullet and dove aside as more shots whistled in, kicking up cones of pulverized stone as they hit the wall. "Haitathe!" de Roga cried. The Jones moved about in the vestibule in confusion as she maintained her fire. With two free hands, she picked Kay up and ran back into the shelving, taking cover. She set him down and shook him.

"Jarlcon?" she asked, probing him with her hands. "Jarlcon bewitched!"

Kay, eyes glazed, roused from his trance a little. "Slap me …" he whispered.

"What?" she asked. She brought her ear down to his mouth to listen. "Speak again!"

"Slap me, Laika!" Kay repeated, and, without hesitation or pause, Laika slapped him in the face nearly hard enough to sever his head from his neck.

Kay jostled on the verge of unconsciousness for a moment. Laika raised her hand to slap him again. "No … no, I'm all right," he stammered; another slap might kill him. He lolled about, trying to gather his wits. Laika hovered over him, her eyes wide.

"I'm fine, give me a moment."

From the doorway came Tal de Roga's voice again. "We're prepared to negotiate, we are not unreasonable. You cannot have your wife's accessories back, nor any of the others we've taken, for those have already been promised, and neither shall you yourself be spared; I'm sorry, but there it is. However, think of your staff and the rest of your family and the continuation of your House. Think of all those things—they are on the negotiating table as of this moment. Perhaps we won't have to make your staff have illegal sex with each other, or fight, or kill, or devour one another. Perhaps they can be safe and unharmed, weeping before your empty grave, remembering you as a fine lord and kind benefactor. Perhaps we shall not need to lie in wait for your parents and siblings to return to the League and welcome them with force of arms. Perhaps we need not pay a visit to your aunt in Esther. Such is in my power to argue their case before my master. Think of that."

Kay felt his wits returning by the moment as he listened to Tal de Roga.

Hearing nothing, de Roga continued. "Very well, you've forced me to take … 'grotesque' … measures."

Activity at the doorway caught Kay's attention. The Jones bustled about in the vestibule. From the lift, they hauled in a large cryochest on floats. The Jones were setting up a temporary command post in the vestibule—very organized, very Hospitalerlike in their methods. They were also girding themselves for battle; trucking in an arsenal from the lift, donning war gloves armed with Man-to-Man rockets, huge D4 Tremblay gas guns and gangly Battle Armor suits; all weapons and systems meant to take down very large, very powerful quarry. In this case, it was clear they were kitting out to hunt and kill Laika as if they were on safari.

Where was all this gear coming from, Kay wondered? The castle had been empty, save for a few sentinels, only a short time ago. He focused on them and ran his Sight back. There they were, docked in the village in four *Mercaba*–class transport ships, each loaded for war and teeming with Jones. Clearly, they had been waiting, hoping he would return to the castle. And now, here they were, powered up and arrayed for battle. Kay was thankful that Sarah had managed to get most of the staff out of the castle—that was one less thing to worry about.

They presented the floating cryochest to Tal de Roga. He opened it; bloated, heavy cryo-mist came out and trailed down to the floor, lingering there like swamp fog. He reached into the smoking interior and pulled out what looked like a delicate human hand and wrist, rounded off and smooth at the nub like a hand gently removed from a marble statue.

Kay quickly ran his Sight back through time, seeing the hand bathed in water, sprinkled with dust and then attached to a female arm.

Sarah's hand! That was Sarah's disembodied hand de Roga was holding!

Tal de Roga selected a small device from the chest. The device was squared-off and functional, sporting a flexible cable studded with a thick gauge needle. He stretched the cable out and inserted the needle into the base of the hand's wrist. The fingers came to life, moving with a spidery, machinelike beat. De Roga fine-tuned the device and the fingers came under full control. He presented the hand with a marker and placed it into its grasp, the fingers positioning it to write. He was going to use Sarah's disembodied hand to write on the slate and grant himself admittance. As it would be Sarah's hand doing the writing, the enchantment conditions protecting the library would most likely be met and disarmed. The Jones would then surge in, hunt and subdue him, hunt and then kill Laika.

Kay Sighted the chest. Inside was a menagerie of disembodied parts: hands, feet, breasts, male and female genitalia and a series of faces: Sarah's, Ki's, those of several staff members, and there was a little boy's tiny face there too: Sebastian, Ki's son. Inside this chest was a frozen treasure-trove of their stolen parts, all stored and collected for safe-keeping.

How arrogant! The Jones, believing themselves to be in complete command of this situation, had brought this wondrous cache of stolen booty into his presence, unmindful of the possibility of a counter-attack. That was a grave miscalculation; that chest contained the prizes his loved ones so desperately needed and he was going to have it back at all costs.

He had recently told Laika that he preferred to fight only when he had to, that Vith modesty and decorum dictated his usual routine. If ever a moment called for violent action and a display of power, it was this one. The chest was going to be his and The Jones were going to suffer in its taking.

Kay Cloaked himself and Wafted out into the vestibule where The Jones were readying themselves for battle with Laika. A nearby Jones in a black battle suit had nearly finished powering up his Unit as super-cooled fuel was pumped in. The suit was a gangly, servo-driven metal framework that fit around his body and mimicked his movements with cold fusion power. A good Battle Unit rig would allow him to punch through a stone wall and mangle steel. Kay wasted no time and showed no mercy. He took the operator's head off with a swing of his CARG.

"He's here!" someone shouted. "Tal, he's here!" A moment later, another Jones was dead, headless.

Tal de Roga was incensed at seeing his people fall. "Mist him already! And remember, we need him alive!" He held Sarah's hand in a shaking fist.

One of the Jones tossed an egg-shaped device to the floor. It cracked open and red, grainy mist filled the vestibule. Laser light from the Battle Units panned about and Kay's Cloaked body lit up plain as day in a red silhouette.

"He's there!" a Jones cried. Kay Wafted to the other side of the vestibule. Tal de Roga had already proved he could hypnotize him into a trance in mere seconds; Kay had to keep moving, avoid eye contact and keep The Jones guessing. He Wafted in front of a Jones wearing a pair of Man-to-Man rocket gloves. He took off the Jones' left leg at the kneecap; the person fell and screamed, gushing blood, creating chaos and confusion and wounded to be tended. Kay chopped through their terminals and screens. He severed their exposed fuel lines: fire, sparks and dense mist from the spewing super-cold fuel turned the vestibule into a no-man's land of dead and dying.

"Lock him up!" they cried.

"He won't hold still!"

They attempted to move into a semblance of a battlefront; however, they were encumbered with heavy weaponry designed to slay large quarry, far too slow to properly engage a fast Wafter. One after another went down, cloven through the arms, legs; gut-pierced and hamstrung. Moans and screams for help from the distressed Jones mingled in a horrid chorus.

Kay fought his way to Tal de Roga.

BOOM! Kay Wafted behind him, but de Roga, unarmed, punching light and fast with incredible skill, was all over him. He even hit Kay with Sarah's balled-up hand. Kay tried to use his CARG, but de Roga crowded him in, stilling his arm. Kay had no room to use his weapon.

"Look at me, Blanchefort!" de Roga demanded, slavering. "Look at me!"

More punches, fast and savage. Sarah's hand went to his throat. Fighting unarmed was not Kay's strong suit and he was badly out-classed. He felt himself being beaten unconscious. He tried to Waft away but he couldn't concentrate. De Roga's fellows were closing in.

Kay tried one last ploy. He bull-rushed de Roga and forced him through the doorway of the library. Almost instantly, de Roga was spat back out with mystical fury. He flew through the doorway like a cannonball, plowing into The Jones, Sarah's hand lying next to him like a spider, fingers twitching. Kay, staggering, collected the cryochest and pulled it through into the safety of the library.

"Blanchefort! Get back out here, you cowardly Shinepole!" he heard de Roga roar from the vestibule. Kay twisted and turned into the maze of shelves, taking his prize with him; though Sarah's hand remained with the Jones.

8—H-Grenadiers

Kay moved into the shelves. Everything was spinning. He was not whole after his encounter with de Roga.

"Laika?" he cried. "Laika, where are you?"

"Jarlcon!" came her voice from a good way off. "Laika comes!"

Troom! Troom! Troom!

Kay located a Bobby box and opened it. He slumped to the floor as he took the receiver.

"Talk to me, Kay!" came Sarah's worried voice.

"I got your stuff back," he mumbled through stinging lips.

"What stuff?"

"What stuff? Your face, your breasts, the whole assortment except for your eyes and one of your hands."

Sarah was elated. "Are you all right?"

"Not really, no ... Tal de Roga gave me a pretty decent beating."

"He is a Hospitaler, you know? Hospitalers can fight. See, I've always told you and Phillip—you can't always fight with a weapon; sometimes you've got to duke it out. Where did the Jones get all that gear from?"

"Transports parked in the village. I ..."

"Kay?"

Kay passed out, dropping the Bobby receiver.

Laika came around the bend. "Jarlcon took many Jones lives," she said proudly. She picked him up, and she picked up the cryochest as well and carried them deeper into the library.

Riiiiiiiinngggggggg ...

The sound brought Kay back and cleared the cobwebs a little. Laika located a Bobby box and set Kay down. Groggy, he opened the box and pulled out the handset.

"Sarah, what is it? I need to pass out somewhere."

"Kay, shut up and listen!" came Sarah's frantic voice through the receiver. "The Jones! The Jones got through the library just now. They're coming, Kay! They must have used my hand. I saw dozens of them through the cameras, and they are trucked out for war, you—"

From behind one of the shelving units, a female Jones wearing Battle Armor fired a Man-to-Man rocket at Laika. She drew one of her swords and met the incoming rocket with the blade. The tiny but lethal warhead went off and the explosion, though blunted, was still fierce, knocking Laika down. She dropped the cryochest. The Jones lumbered into view to get the chest while two more moved into position among the shelving.

Kay dropped the Bobby receiver and flash-Sighted the area to get a feel for what they were up against. Sighting through his swollen eyes, he saw ten Jones Battle Units coming forward, arranged in a tight formation. From his days playing chit war games with Sarah and Phillip, Kay knew how The Jones loaded out for battle, as Phillip always selected them for his side. Kay's head ached, his eyes were swollen shut. All he wanted to do was crawl into a hole somewhere and rest.

Leading the attack were five Jones strapped into augmented Battle Units, granting them immense strength and protective armor-plating against counter-attack. The control seats at the heart of the Battle Units were rather small and their operators were almost always tiny females or suitably small men who could fit in the tight space without much fuss. Their armor was studded with ten Man-to-Man rockets; quick, accurate and deadly.

Behind the front line of armored Jones were two GW units. As the Jones were from Bazz and had no Gifts themselves, they employed mobile 'Gift Warfare' units designed to neutralize or eliminate the Gifts of the Mind altogether. They droned with a haunting noise meant to drown out the Dirge. They lobbed No-Cloak dust pellets and trawled the area with scanning laser light, illuminating any Cloaked person who might be about. They panned about with bright spotlights meant to blind an enemy using the Stare, and they broadcast frequencies meant to jam a Wafter into Waft-lock.

With the GWs operational, Kay could not Waft and he could not Cloak.

Farther back, he saw three Jones males armed with high-powered Tremblay gas guns moving into position atop the shelving to provide sniper fire covering the GWs and the forward units.

And, farthest back and theoretically safe from the fighting, were the dreaded H-Grenadiers; the Jones' audible hypnosis units. They looked similar to The Jones' Battle Units, just with a lot more gear attached to them. The droning H-Grenadiers broadcast a hypnosis wave and, given enough time, could lock-on and get into one's head from afar. Covering one's ears did no good as the frequencies they produced created bone-inducted sounds. Phillip once drove Sarah to flipping the gaming table over with rage by using his H-Grenadier units with frustrating effectiveness. They needed to be eliminated as quickly as possible.

Man-to-Man rocket Battle Units, GWs, gas gun snipers and H-Grenadiers; that's what Tal de Roga and his infernal master arrayed against two people: a half-conscious Kay and Laika with two swords and four LLAG pistols.

Wearily unsaddling his CARG, Kay took aim and let loose a blast of Silver tech. It stretched out in a deadly killing streak, obliterating two Battle Units and, farther back, his intended victims, the H-Grenadiers. They vanished in a storm of silver, eliminated from the fight.

Chattering over their Coms, the Battle Units turned from Laika to attend to Kay. They had been unprepared for his Silver tech attack.

Kay waded into the fray. He had to conserve his CARG's Silver tech, for it was only good for a few blasts before needing to recharge. The Jones had taken away his Waft and his Cloak, but what they could never take was his third Gift—his Dark Sight—and with it, he could turn the tide of this battle in a number of ways. With it, he could see into the near future, anticipate their actions and take countermeasures at his leisure; his father Captain Davage had survived countless battles using that same tactic for decades. Though his eyes were swollen shut, his near-Future Sight was the equalizer.

He could see that the tiny, black-suited operators strapped to the Battle Units were armed with Drogbas, short-range pistols manufactured on Bazz holstered near their left armpit for dealing with any random enemy who happened to get in close with them. With a gun,

Kay could once again use his Dark Sight to take command of this situation. Normally, he would have his trusty Poltava with him; however, since he was without it, the Jones' Drogbas would do nicely. Kay had to get one from them and then he could unleash hell.

That was his first task: get a gun.

A forward Jones Battle Unit moved in and picked up the cryochest using the powerful hydraulic arms like a forklift to lift it over her head. The operator traded fire with Laika, who blasted away with her multiple LLAG pistols from behind a shelf. Flanked by two other Battle Units, The Jones turned to march away to Tal de Roga with her prize.

Kay shot out, running to engage the unit. The Jones operator spotted him, Commed in for support and backed away. A flanking Battle Unit moved in to cut him off.

Man-to-Man rockets from loaded wargloves locked on. Apparently, taking him alive was now off the table. Dead would do just fine. Just another moment or two and rockets would rain down on him.

He zoomed in on the nearest Battle Unit with his Dark Sight and found the Emergency Fuel Dump Switch located on her finger pad. He hit the switch. Super-cold fuel vented from the tanks, spewing thick mist. His ability to interact with objects via his Dark Sight was completely unknown to The Jones. The operator, wreathed in clouds of condensation, cursed in surprise and fumbled with her controls, trying to see through the dense mist. She wailed in distress over her Com.

Sight: Sniper fire coming in to cover the downed unit. Kay threw himself behind a shelf just in time to avoid several sniper rounds from the Tremblays above. Laika, to his left, returned fire with her pounding LLAG pistols, brutally pinning the snipers down.

Kay advanced and closed in on the Battle Unit, easily able to Sight through the mist. Proximity alarms went off. The operator saw him coming at the last moment, unstrapped her left leg and foot from the suit and lashed out with a savage frontal kick. He knew from his Sight she was going to trying kicking him, but he hadn't counted on the speed of the attack. She connected with Kay's jaw, stopping him in his tracks. She followed it up with a sweeping kick to the left, knocking Kay down. She unstrapped her right arm and reached for her Drogba.

Too late. Kay zoomed in with his Sight and took the gun from its holster before she could get at it. He then aimed it at her forehead and fired. The headless operator went limp in death. Kay blinked, cancelling his Sight. The Drogba returned to its holster. He was there a moment later and pulled the gun from her holster just as a wall of sniper fire cascaded down.

BOOM! BOOM! BLAM! BLAM! Both sides traded deafening gunfire as Laika fired her LLAGs and reloaded at the same time.

Two more Jones Battle Units moved in to attack, readying their rockets, as the one bearing the prized cryochest continued to retreat.

Kay could not let de Roga recover the chest, and now that he had the Drogba in his hand:

Sight. Zoom in on the operator's forehead. BLAM!

Dead.

It was that simple. The Battle Unit with the now-dead operator veered off track and plowed into a shelf, dropping the cryochest.

Kay tried to recover the chest and then retreat, but so much was going on around him.

Sight: a sniper was lining Laika up for a kill shot. Kay used the same deadly technique on the sniper as he had on the Battle Unit operator; a moment later the sniper was dead, shot through the forehead and tumbling head over heels from the top of the shelving in a dramatic cartwheel, The Jones around him astonished and terrified.

Laika came out from her cover and cleaved a Battle Unit down the middle with a massive sword cut. Ports opened. Kay saw what was about to happen.

"Laika—rockets!"

She sprang over the top of the shelving as four rockets darted out of their launchers and blew a great hole of splintered wood and shredded paper. Kay Sight-attacked again, and another Jones was dead. It was ridiculously easy, and this wasn't lost on The Jones as the battle unfolded. Though they couldn't be sure what was happening, they knew full well that Kay, a Vith lord with obscure ways and mighty powers, was no doubt behind it all. They chattered in panic over their Coms, telling Tal de Roga somewhere in the rear that Kay could, as if by magic, kill any he so chose in mere moments. Kay, all by himself and with only a handgun, had cleared out the entire front line of Jones, sending the rest retreating in confusion.

They backed away, trying to regroup and reassess. Laika came in and attacked a GW unit, smashing its laser emitters and prying its operator from within. The operator screamed, blood flew, and an armless, legless body came out in Laika's hands. The second GW began a quick retreat.

"Laika! Get the chest!" Kay cried.

She tossed the dead Jones aside and moved toward the chest still gripped by the fallen Battle Unit. In Kay's Sight, sniper fire glittered off her body.

Kay killed two more snipers in quick succession. Mag empty. He would need to reload his Drogba or secure another one.

His eyes were stinging, his head tumbling in a slow roll. He needed to rest.

Phoom! Phoom!

The snipers lobbed some sort of grenade forward. The grenades burst open, emitting thick smoke laced with a cloying, perfumy sort of stench. It quickly got into his nose and stank there.

Wait! His Sight was going blind; with each passing moment the open book into the future was closing. It must be these grenades, doing something to his Sight.

Without his Sight, he momentarily panicked, not certain what to do. That's when he began hearing the pensive voice in his head, quickly growing loud.

"... kay ... kay ... Kay? Kay? KAY!!! KAY!! KKKKAAAAAAAAAAYYYYY!!"

H-Grenadiers? The Jones had hauled in three more, standing well to the rear of the fight doing their dreaded work. They were dialed into his brain, quickly incapacitating him. Blast, he should have taken a moment to check the rear for reinforcements.

Laika, take Laika and flee.

"... KAYKAYKAYKAYKAYKAYKAYKAYKAYKAYKAY KAYKAYKAY!!!!!!!!!"

Too much! Too much. He was too weary to fight. He fell to the ground, near senseless.

"Jarlcon, Laika comes!"

"No! L-Laika! Run! Take the chest and get away! Go!"

Laika wrenched the chest free and came to his side as the Jones, emboldened by Kay's fall, came in fast, the Battle Units met by Laika's swords, metal ringing.

The snipers, shooting. Laika hit, over and over.

Rockets, smoke from their tail fires, hitting Laika in the chest. She recoiled, reached out with six arms and mangled the operator. So much blood.

More Battle Units. Laika's pistols spent. She took a rocket square to the face.

Blood and smoking flesh.

Surrounded.

Kay managed to raise his CARG and loosed another Silver tech blast. Three more Battle Units and the remaining GW were swept away.

Bleeding, badly wounded, Laika picked Kay up and tried to retreat from the area. More explosions. Rockets coming in, taking a terrible toll on her. Her blood dripped down on Kay.

Laika fell, the Jones coming in for the kill ...

CARG spent, no Silver tech left.

No Gifts. Couldn't see.

Kay lay there in a daze, contemplating his life, his failure.

Failed Sam, dreaming in her capsule.

Failed Sarah. Failed Ki.

Failed Laika, who had trusted him.

He thought about dying, far away from Sam, never having given her any of the children she so wanted. His thoughts flashed to the servants' graveyard deep in the Grove. Sarah uncovering the little bulge of silver, her eyes full of excitement and wonder.

The birth of King.

What had happened to King?

Sarah thought he was gone ... disincorporated. His tasks done.

Images flashed across Kay's mind. A silver bird floating in his dreams.

King, seeing The Jones land. "ALERT!!" he had cried as he swooped away.

Words growled in his dreams: ... *speak the words* ...

The thing in the darkness.

SPEAKTHEWORDS!!!!

King was on his way to disincorporate.

Sarah's voice over the Bobby: "He won't come back until we say the litany ..."

One last memory, in the Grove summoning King, his mouth murmuring the words:

> *'King, King, guide my steps,*
> *King, King, guard my path.*
> *King, King, light the way,*
> *King, King, your flock awaits.'*

There was a flash!

Something whistled on the air.

9—1000 Carahil Park

"Lord Blanchefort?"

Kay tried to open his eyes but they were still swollen shut. He felt like a battered, swollen mess. He Sighted through. He was lying prone in a sea of pleasant smells. He was in some sort of brightly lit marketplace with shelves and orderly aisles trailing off a surprising distance in all directions. He heard soft music playing somewhere in the background.

He wondered for a moment if he was dead and this was the Vith Gallery of the Dead, where all his ancestors waited. If so, it was certainly much cheerier and sweeter-smelling than he would have guessed; serenaded by pleasing music to pass eternity with.

Perched overhead on a lacy iron beam was a silver bird with

shiny feathers.

Looked like King. Actually, there were several Kings perched across the beam in an orderly procession. He must be dreaming, yet, after a moment, he determined most of the Kings looking impassively down at him were some sort of stuffed toy designed in King's image, with the real one sitting quietly in their midst.

"King?" Kay asked. "Is that you? You're back! Where have you been?"

From behind, King spoke. "My mission was at an end. I was

headed to my disincorporation in the servants' graveyard, as I am tasked to do by my Creator. I witnessed the Jones land and commence their attack. Per my Creator's wishes, once I commence my journey to the graveyard to disincorporate, I am considered deactivated. As such, I can no longer take action until the summoning litany is re-uttered. I also could not return to your side until the litany was re-uttered. I waited in the library node. You summoned me and I was returned at last. There was no need for me to re-imprint; that aspect remained."

"We'll have to talk to Lady Poe about that disincorporation thing. It's good to see you, King."

"I am pleased I did not complete my journey to the grave-yard."

Kay took in his situation. He was in a large, well-stocked marketplace of cheery pastel colors. Directly overhead was a rotunda made of wrought iron and glass, admitting an abundance of daylight. A purple sky shone through the glass which looked to Kay like Xan-darr's distinctive sky. Kay was sitting atop a round decorative island made of shale and sand rising up in a gentle miniature mountain. A ring of clean water surrounded the island, enclosed by a lacy iron fence. A harem of live seals milled about at the base of the shale mountain. Their whiskered faces all looked up at Kay, distressed that their home had been invaded.

"Where are we, King?"

"A node deep within the library."

"A what?"

Nearby, Laika was prostrate on her side and not moving. Kay feared the worst. He stood and went to her. King flew up and perched on the iron fence, silently watching.

Laika was badly wounded in the chest, shoulders, arms and neck; she was lying in a pool of her own thick Haitathe blood, paint-ing the shale red. He was certain she was dead. A wave of dread and grief passed through him. "King, what happened to The Jones?" he asked as he attempted to tend to Laika. She was such a wreck, he didn't know where to begin.

"I destroyed many of them and they retreated in confusion. I did not pursue, I tended to you instead. I was able to drag you to safety here. I assumed, given your past actions and tendency toward sentimentality, that you wished the Haitathe saved as well."

"You assumed correctly."

Laika was alive, but barely. Her heart still beat and what was left of her blood still flowed. From below, at the base of the island, the seals barked up at them in dismay.

She was a quivering bullet-riddled, rocket-scarred disaster. Her girl-like face was mutilated and barely recognizable.

The Jones shot Laika in the face with a rocket.

It wouldn't be long.

It was a bit much for Kay. His beloved wife Sam was in a stasis capsule on Hoban, and now here was Laika, whom he liked very much, about to die.

Laika groaned and Kay knelt over her. He propped her bloody head up. A Jones rocket blast had removed a healthy portion of her cheek, exposing broken teeth and the hollow of her mouth. "Laika? Laika?" he said.

"The Haitathe cannot hear you. She is soon to die from her wounds. Shall I put her out of her misery?" King asked. "I can make it quick."

"Her name is Laika, and I'd appreciate you using it."

Kay came down and away from the island, scattering the seals. He hopped the fence and searched for something, anything to help Laika. He found a number of linen shirts folded neatly on a shelf. A stamped patch on the right breast read 1000 CARAHIL PARK, XANDARR. He quickly returned and dabbed her bloody face with the shirts.

"King, are we on Xandarr?"

"Possibly."

"How can that be?"

"This is a node hidden in the library, clearly arcane in nature."

Laika's body was half destroyed. She had taken multiple rocket hits to her side, her back, and her face. One of her arms was nearly severed, many of her fingers were broken, and some were missing entirely. Kay tried to Sight, but it was slow and unresponsive, a lingering effect of The Jones' grenades. He concentrated and pushed their effects from his head and the Sight opened before him.

What he saw was truly horrifying. Laika had more bullets lodged in her body than he could easily count. She was ruined and shrapnel-riddled. She was partially disemboweled. How she remained alive in such a state was beyond him.

Laika painfully stirred. "Jarlcuuuu…n," she lisped.

Kay moved in close. "I'm here, Laika."

She wheezed. "Hrrrrr, not cuuuumfortable … Hrrrrrrr, not …"

"Don't speak. Don't speak. Save your strength. Let me help make you comfortable." He unclipped her belt and struggled to move it aside. King fluttered up and took it, able to carry vast weights well beyond his tiny kingfisher size. Kay unlaced her boots and, with great effort, pulled them off and set them aside. He unclipped and unbuckled her breastplate. Blood lay everywhere underneath. King lifted it away.

One of her uninjured hands came up and took his, squeezing ever so slightly.

"You were very brave, Laika. You fought well, took many lives."

She closed her eyes. "Sssstay … withhhh Laikkkahh ..."

"I'm not going anywhere."

King impassively observed. "She suffers, Lord Blanchefort, and there is no hope of healing her. I can give her instant peace."

She fell into a fitful sort of sleep. Kay stood and looked at the abundance of things all around. A market this large should have a proprietor or two. Perhaps they could summon help.

"Hello!" he called out into the hollow air. "Can someone help us?"

He received no reply. "Watch Laika, please," he said to King and Wafted down to the floor past the iron fence. He saw a sales counter in the distance and hurried there. He didn't have time to appreciate any of the wonders placed on the shelving as he passed. He saw a case full of confectionery, all in inviting colors. He smelled the aroma of pie and frosted cakes, hard candies, chocolates, assorted fruit and baked goods and a long chilled case of ice cream in endless pastel colors. It smelled so good. It cleared the remnants of The Jones' grenade from his nose.

As he neared the counter, he passed a number of statues, some in the shape of giant-sized cats of various species and some in the shape of seal-like aquatic mammals: a walrus, a furry seal pup and a sea lion. Standing tall over the statues was a slender human female sculpture in an alluring gown carved in the act of sighing: head back, mouth slightly open, and a demure hand pressed to her cheek. Her face was partially hidden by a large pair of protruding goggles, rather like Sam's goggles from Hoban, only these were much larger and more protruding.

This statue …

He stopped dead in his tracks. He had seen it before, in Gods Temple, and in the Mystery Library where she had carried the large book. Now, here she was right in front of him. This time, she carried no book in her slender arms.

He reached the counter. Nobody was present. There was a stack of business cards in a clamshell that caught Kay's attention. The cards read:

1000 CARAHIL PARK GIFT SHOP
XANDARR
Where fun and mystery are where you find them.

He held the card and took heart. He had heard that Carahil maintained a wondrous shop of sorts where he allowed those who pleased him to roam about and have whatever they wanted. The store was full of Carahil's charm and light: Oh, to be a child here.

If any could save Laika, it was Carahil.

"Carahil!" he called out. "It is I, Kay! Carahil, I have urgent need of you!"

His voice echoed in the giant space. Kay stood there holding the card. "Carahil!"

An alluring voice from behind him spoke. He felt breath on his ear. "Something you like?"

Kay whirled around. Standing there was a thin female, on the tallish side, wearing a fine teal gown of extraordinary quality. She reminded Kay of his aunt, Lady Poe: her figure and turn of the cheek was similar, along with her complexion, her lean upright body and her head of boy-short platinum blonde hair. Her shoulders and line of the neck were the same, only she was more cut, more provocative than Lady Poe. She wore an elaborate pair of telescoping silver goggles that obscured her eyes and much of her face above her nose. The lenses glowed with ethereal purple light.

Here stood the statue, given life at last.

She leaned in and encroached on his personal space, giving him no room. Kay tried to gauge her age, but it was impossible; sometimes she seemed like a little girl fresh with life, other times she gave the impression of great age and wisdom. She carried with her a fierce presence, an invasive, aggressive sort of quality that Kay found off-putting. Though she looked rather like Lady Poe, she acted nothing like her.

"Who are you, please?" he asked.

She adjusted her goggles and spoke, carefully articulating her words. "My name is Atha."

Kay searched his memory for the name, certain it had great significance, but couldn't recall it. "I'm sorry, I don't know the name. We saw you in Gods Temple, did we not, and again in the library?"

Atha laughed. "Of course you did." She came in close and lifted her arms as if she wished to embrace and possibly kiss him. Kay sidestepped to his right and created some space.

"Are you the proprietor of this store, Lady Atha?"

"My father is," she replied.

"And who is that?"

She laughed. "Why, Carahil, silly."

Kay was thunderstruck. "Carahil is your father?"

"Yes, of course."

Kay looked her over. Carahil was a newly minted 'god'; therefore his children would also be gods and goddesses. Atha had a vast presence about her, she could possibly be a goddess, but he assumed Carahil's daughter, if ever he had one, would be different somehow; more like Carahil himself, perhaps. Tattooed at the end of her left collarbone was the tiny glittering image of a resplendent seal—Carahil himself.

As if reading his thoughts, she answered. "Were you expecting a daughter of Carahil to be a little animal of some sort? We can be whatever we want. I could be an animal if I wanted."

"Then why aren't you?"

"Because I like being a human ... so few expectations come with this form. Come, I'll prove it you." She held out her hand.

"My friend is dying. If you are Carahil's daughter, can you help her?"

Atha smiled and adjusted her goggles again. "The Haitathe, you mean? I find it odd that a Vith should care so much for his ancient enemy."

"Laika is not my enemy."

"That remains to be seen. Come, I've things to show you. I promise she'll not die for the time being." She held out her hand, impatient for Kay to take it. He glanced at the island and Laika's still form at the top, along with the audience of seals gazing up at her from below. King's shiny bird eyes blinked back at him from the rail. Tentatively, he took Atha's hand and she led him away through the rows. The selection of odd neatly-shelved items was bewildering. "Where is Carahil?" Kay asked.

Atha led him to an aisle lined with toys in colorful boxes. Her grip was soft, but strong at the same time. "He's far away. In Gods

Temple, you asked for help and I heard you. Here I am. I stayed near just for you."

"Phillip and Sarah asked for Carahil."

"Sorry. You got me instead."

"And you are Carahil's daughter?" Kay asked again.

Atha ignored his question. She released Kay's hand and browsed the vast collection of items on the shelves. She leaned down and pointed at a box. "Ah, here! Come see."

She pointed at a child's doll in a duraplas box. It was a foot-high effigy of Atha as a young girl, wearing a complicated gown and a crooked little smile. The doll's platinum blonde hair style was the same; the eye-obscuring goggles were there as well. Bold labeling on the box read:

THE CHILDREN OF CARAHIL SERIES:
ATHA OF THE QUEST, YOUNGEST DAUGHTER OF CARAHIL
AND MABSORNATH
GODDESS OF OCCASIONAL CHAOS

Kay stood there looking at the labeling and was somewhat stunned. Atha laughed and covered the last line with her hand. "Don't worry about that last part," she said. "I'm harmless."

Kay looked over the myriad other boxes on the shelf and was amazed by what he saw. There was a doll of his mother, Countess Sygillis, complete with gown, red hair and Shadowmark, and also one of his father, Captain Davage, in his Fleet uniform. There was Sarah and Phillip, Thomasina in her green and brown armor, Magistrate Kilos in her black suit and ...

He pulled a box off the shelf. There was a doll of himself, purple-haired and green-eyed, and another box, this time with Sam, bone white and jet black holding her orange Anuian Jar. And another with Laika, uninjured, standing tall wearing a miniature belt dangling with duraplas weapons.

Laika, nearby. Dying.

Atha once again read his thoughts.

"The wonders available here are not to be taken lightly. Nothing is beyond reach or out-of-the question here. If there's any place your Haitathe friend can be saved, you've found it." Atha took his hand and pulled him down the aisle. They reached an area profuse with toy doll houses of various sizes, some quite large and complex. Situated amid the doll houses was a large and rather complicated doll in a clear duraplas package. It read, in splashy lettering:

QUEEN GHOME—WOMAN OF A THOUSAND FACES
DELUXE SET

Kay picked it up. It was big, nearly covering his full arm-length. In the center of the package was a doll in roughly female proportions. The doll had no face, just a smooth blank spot where a face should be. It had no hands, feet, hair or breasts. Surrounding the doll were dozens and dozens of masklike faces with different colors and styles of hair. There were also hands in various alien configurations, feet, scaly wings, tails and other odd accessories.

"This is the enemy, the one who has stolen my Ne-Countess' face. The process she uses to achieve this is not understood," Kay said.

"It's understood by me. It's all there on the package, if you look carefully," Atha answered.

Kay tore the packaging open and pulled the faceless doll out. He took one of the faces included in the package and tried to put it on the doll's blank face, but it would not stay.

Atha barged in. "You're not doing it right. You'll never get anywhere that way. Let me show you."

At the bottom of the package was a small tube. Atha took the tube and removed the cap. She squeezed it and a puff of golden glitter came out, coating the doll's blank face. She then took the face Kay was holding and attached it. It held fast and wouldn't come off. The previously faceless doll now had a perfect, seamless face, like it had always been there.

He noticed a splash on the package's surface:

INCLUDED: ETHYLBERRY (NOBERRY), QUEEN GHOME'S
MAGIC DUST.

"Ethylberry?" he asked.

Atha smiled. "Ahh, yes indeed. Well, a facsimile. Let me show you the real thing. Come." Atha led him away to a distant part of the store, so distant that he could no longer see Laika on top of the island without Sighting.

They arrived at another, slightly smaller rotunda flush with purplish daylight. Basking under the rotunda was a lacy iron fountain gurgling with clean, fresh-smelling water. Surrounding the fountain

was a bed of apparently hard-packed, ill-kept earth covered with a dull patch of thorny weeds. The weeds were a dirty olive color hiding an occasional speckling of drab yellow flowers. The weed-bed seemed most out-of-place surrounded by the clean aisles and sweet-smelling environs of the store. It looked like something that would be growing wild in the cracks in an alley.

"Here we are!" Atha chirped. "This is a wonder seldom seen."

Kay looked around, not certain what he should be seeing. "I'm sorry, I …" The water smelled clean and inviting.

Atha seated herself on a bench near the fountain. "Would you mind loosening my gown?" She showed him her back; it was slim and curvy, her spine well-defined. Kay undid the laces and Atha sat with her bare back to the stone bench. "So, you want to save your wife and assist your Haitathe lover, is that correct?"

"Laika is not my lover."

"Really, Kay, there is no need to lie to me. I won't tell. So, do you want Ghome's secret, yes or no?"

Kay noted a definite change in Atha's bearing. From the tone of her voice and her deliberately aloof demeanor, he knew she wanted something, was attempting to 'prep' him for some sort of pending shock. "Yes, I want it," he replied.

"And what would you do to secure this help, Kay?"

"Pardon?"

"It's a simple question. I am not my father, I don't do things for free. I can help you; the question is, what are you willing to pay for my help? What are your wife and your Haitathe lover worth to you?"

"Their worth is invaluable. I would pay anything."

Atha smiled. "How nice." She produced two unglazed clay flower pots and a silver flask. "Here, Kay. Fill the flask with water, and put one plant in each of these pots." She handed them to Kay.

"I've no time for gardening," he said.

"Of course you do, if you want to save your wife and your lover. Go on."

Kay unstoppered the flask and filled it to the brim with clear water.

Atha removed one of her shoes and dipped her foot in the water. She sighed with pleasure. "This water comes from the Spring of Salonmae. This water is the beginning of dreams and is served at the table of the gods, cold and clear. Now, fill those pots. Mind the thorns, they're rather sharp."

Kay knelt down and began the process of filling the pots. The going was rough; the ground around the fountain was hard and unyielding.

"May I have some tools?" he asked.

"No, sorry. Cultivating these plants by hand is a tradition. Please proceed."

Kay dug his hands in. The weedy plants were studded with savage thorns that quickly shredded his fingers. They caught on his clothes and tore his sleeves like tissue. As Atha watched, he continued on, though his hands were soon bleeding. He wrenched two plants from the hard earth, placing them in the pots.

"Those thorny little weeds you're struggling with are Ethylberry, Kay, the mythical Dust of the Gods. Don't look like much, do they? Ethylberry is, sometimes, the very first plant to grow on a new world. It's prickly and ugly, but its dust seethes with life and possibilities. The old goddess Anabrax often planted it on new worlds and once life took hold, she would harvest them and move on. Now that Anabrax, thanks to the Horned God you know so well, is gone, Ethylberry's pretty hard to find these days. Fortunately, she taught me how to plant and tend to it. I'm the only one who ever listened to her. Good thing you got me at Gods Temple, Kay, otherwise your little wife might be spending the rest of her life in that capsule back on Hoban."

"In the corridor, you were carrying a large book. That's why I went into the Mystery Library, to fetch it. What was in the book?"

Atha blushed and swished her foot through the water. "Oh, nothing. It was just a prop to entice you to come to me. Worked, didn't it? It looks like you're done with the pots. Please give them to me."

Kay presented her with the pots containing their unassuming cargo. His blood coated the pots. She took Kay by the hands.

"Just look at you. I know your hands are hurting, and the Ethylberry thorns are covered in poison. I'd say you've only a short time to live."

Kay looked at his bloody hands. His blood was bubbling, turning a putrid shade of brown. He felt the poison in the first stages of killing him. "Gods," he stammered.

Atha put the pots down. "Come here, Kay." She took a decanter and drew some water from the fountain. "Hold out your hands," she said kindly and washed his torn flesh with the water.

As she worked, Kay fell into a prismatic dream full of flowers and scents. Images flashed into his head as Atha tended to his hands.

The modest cabin on the Gold Coast of Hoban.

Asleep but moving.

Nude.

Many arms around him.

A giant body all over him.

Moving together. Grunting in ecstasy.

Making love to Laika, fast asleep.

Somebody else inside him.

He awoke with a start. Atha was still cleansing his hands. She laughed. "The dreams this water inspires …. Ohhhh. And you needn't worry about the poison, the water has nixed it. Just one of the many things this water can do. I wasn't going to let you die, silly. I wonder what my father would have said about that? Now, for a sight rarely seen."

She put her decanter down and carefully plucked a single flower from one of the pots Kay had filled. She tapped the flower and a cloud of vivid golden dust drifted out, coating his hands. The feel of it settling against his skin was indescribable.

"That dust is Ethylberry, pure and rare. The power of life, the unbound energy, the healing itch. Do you feel it?"

"The Dust of the Gods comes from a lowly weed?" Kay asked, only half-conscious.

"Tsk, tsk, great things often have meager trappings. Watch what it can do. See what can be done." She worked Kay's hands like a sculptor, molding his flesh like wet clay, and his wounds closed. With her thumb and forefinger, she plucked one of his fingers clean off; no blood, no hole, just a clean rounded stump as if his finger had never been attached to his hand in the first place. Just as quickly, she popped the finger back on.

"And this is the process Queen Ghome is using?" he asked, his excitement growing. He was discovering something monumental.

"It is."

Kay marveled at his flawlessly repaired hands. Queen Ghome's secret was now revealed and proved under the bright lights and serene music of Carahil's store. Possibilities flashed through his head. "With this I can save Laika!"

And Sam ...

Atha held out the pot. "If you like. Here ... take it. Go save your Haitathe lover; I know you're dying to. I'll be here when you're done." Atha leaned back, watching him, her eyes hidden under her goggles.

Kay took the pot and the silver flask and went back across the store to the top of the shale island with its chorus of unhappy seals. Laika had crawled a few feet from where she had been, leaving a trail of blood. She lay on her hands and knees, trying to raise one of her swords. She was weeping.

"Jarlcohhhhn," she gasped. "Not ... not chhhhomfortable. Chhhhannot chhhhontinue. Khhhill ... Khhhill Laikhhha. Phhlease ..." She moaned in agony, no longer able to hide the fact.

Kay came to her side. "Laika, I've something that will help you, I promise. Have courage for a bit longer."

"No lehhhhhve. No lehhhhhve!" she pleaded.

"I'm not going anywhere, Laika, I promise." He turned her over. "Now just lay flat." She painfully stretched out on the shale and Kay surveyed her ruined body. The most obvious wound was an open rocket blast that had burrowed into her chest cavity and rented her ribs, exposing her innards. "King, get up here!" he demanded. King fluttered to the top of the island.

"What have you there?" King asked.

"A remarkable substance and the key to the mystery regarding Queen Ghome."

"What is it?"

"Ethylberry."

King ruffled his feathers. "Ethylberry is the stuff of children's stories."

"Nevertheless."

"And you are going to assist Laika with it?"

"I am."

Laika painfully breathed in and out. Kay reviewed in his mind how Atha had used the water and the Ethylberry. He had to be careful; he could not afford to waste any of it.

"King, I need some clean damp cloths, please."

King flew down the island past the barking seals and turned into one of the aisles. A moment later he returned with a pair of colorful towels grasped in his silver feet. The towels were thick and soft, like something one might take to the beach. He hovered a moment and let them soak in the water at the base of the island as the disgruntled chorus of seals noisily watched, then he flew up.

Kay took one of the towels and cleaned the wound as best he could. "I hope that doesn't hurt too much, Laika," he said. "I wish I had something to deaden the pain."

She moved a little in response.

First, the water; he opened the flask and allowed a few drops to moisten the interior of the gaping wound. Now, the dust. Setting the flask aside, he selected a flower from the thorny mass inside the pot. He tapped out a few grains from the flower, hoping to conserve as much as he could, and carefully dabbed the ragged wound. He could see the fine, glittery dust coating the interior. A little seemed to go a long way.

Now what? He had partially expected the wound to spring to life and seal itself up, but it didn't do anything. "Should we be seeing something?" King asked as he watched.

Kay wracked his brains. He recalled Atha treating his hands, how she had laid her hands on his and worked his fingers like wet clay.

It was worth a try. He reached in and touched the jagged remains of Laika's ribs. To his amazement, the ribs became pliable under his fingers; they flexed and molded. It was like smoothing out the wrinkles of his bed sheets. It was hard going. He added more water and it became much easier. With gentle, fluid movements, Laika's ribs were made whole again under his touch. The interior began to dry and he applied more water from the flask. Soon, he had the wound cleaned out and rebuilt. He draped in the layers of muscle and fat, dabbed her skin into place and sealed the wound shut, clean as could be like it had never even been there.

"Laika, does that hurt?" he asked as he moved on to another wound.

She spoke in delirium. "Laikhhha very fffohhnd of Jarlchhhhn," she rasped. Two of her hands came up and touched him as he worked.

With growing excitement and skill, Kay moved on. He was out of water and gave King directions to refill the flask. King fluttered off and quickly returned. Kay attended to the grotesque wound on her face, splashing water, dabbing and smoothing her gums and teeth back into service and closing the large hole in her cheek. She had a chunk taken out of her tongue as well, which he also fixed. Completely repaired, her face showed no sign it had been wounded at all. She looked like Laika again.

He spent hours repairing her. King fetched a large bucket and made numerous trips to the fountain as Kay went through bucketful after bucketful, anointing Laika, healing her. Eventually, he removed over seventy Tremblay bullets from her body, and over twenty pounds of metal and composite fragments from Man-to-Man rocket hits, mostly in her back from where she had tried to protect him. He found he could Sight the bullets, plunge his fingers into her flesh and pull the bullet out, leaving no hole. He repaired fifteen lacerations, two feet of destroyed small bowel, three mangled breasts, a shattered spinal disk, a broken thigh bone and a lacerated stomach. Her calves, ankles and feet, as far as he could tell, were mercifully undamaged. Soon, Laika was no longer writhing in pain. He took her down off the island to a nearby bench where she could sit up as he worked.

"King, will you please try to find something for Laika to wear; her armor needs to be cleaned first." King sped off. Kay wasn't certain what sort of clothing King might find for her to wear, but anything was better than that destroyed, gore-soaked breastplate.

"Jarlcon has healing hands," she said with wonder.

"It's not the man, it's the stuff. This dust is amazing. We'll have you and everybody else put back together in no time. This is a moment to celebrate, for we have the knowledge at last! If only Raal and his buddies knew how easy this is." He continued working. He had gotten used to looking square at her bare, six-breasted chest. It wasn't a big deal anymore.

"Laika belongs to Jarlcon," she announced.

"What? No, no ..."

"Laika belongs to Jarlcon!" she shouted.

He moved on from her torso and legs to her arms. Aside from being a bit grabby with her many arms, Laika was a good patient, eyes closed, enjoying the healing attention. "Hungry. Laika hungry," she said.

"We'll see what we can find once I get you squared away."

Her arms were a mess. The third arm on her left side was mostly severed. A generous splash of water and several dabs of Ethylberry and he had it back on, muscle repaired, bones mended, tendons reattached, skin stretched and smoothed over. He also repaired over twenty broken or, in some cases, mangled or missing fingers. He even found a few patches of diseased flesh, not a result of the battle, merely something she had been living with. Laika was not Elder and she suffered maladies of the flesh that Elders did not. He smoothed the disease away as well, leaving pristine skin.

Soon, he could find nothing more to fix. All the Tremblay bullets that showed up in his Sight as glittering stars were gone, piled up in a bucket; all the lacerations repaired, all the holes plugged. "Laika, how do you feel?"

She checked herself over, and gave Kay a grand, crushing, bare-chested embrace, lifting him into the air, spinning him around. She laughed strong and clear, bursting with energy. She threw him down into the water near the island, scattering the seals, flopping on top of him, wanting to wrestle. They rolled around in the water and laughed. After they had rough-housed a bit, King returned. He had brought a garment of light white cloth folded into a square. Kay took the garment and unfurled it; certain it would be much too small for her. To his surprise, the garment was huge and billowy, stamped with Carahil's smiling face. What's more, it had three arm holes on each side—it was almost as if the garment had been custom-made for Laika.

"Where did you find this?"

"On a display of shelving units not far from here. There were a number to choose from in various gaudy shades and paintings. I naturally chose a conservative color."

Kay checked the tag. It read: Gx3. He was perplexed. "Gx3, what's that? The 'G' must be for 'Giant' and the 'x3' for three sets of armholes," he mused.

King appeared neither amused nor impressed.

Laika took it and pulled it on. It fit perfectly, though he thought she looked a bit odd wearing it.

"Very comfortable. Laika like," she said happily.

They moved out into the aisles looking for food. Kay could smell the pastel aromas of sweet confections floating about. There was an abundance of candy here in the store; Carahil was a big fan of sweets. He hoped they might find something more substantial to help Laika regain her strength. Laika quickly found a terraced dining area lined with inviting shelves and display cases full of a treasure trove of candy, chocolates, frosted cakes, ice creams in gorgeous pastels, hard candies in bags, spun sugar, taffy and other treats. Before he could stop her, Laika was pulling bags of candy off the shelves six at a time.

"Hey, I just got done fixing your teeth and now you're going to mess them up again with candy?"

Laika brought an impressive armload of bagged candy and tore into it, popping in loaded handfuls. "Good!" she announced.

"Such confections are not furnishing your system with useful calories," King said, fluttering near her head. She swished him away.

"Away, bird. Laika not care!"

Kay watched all this and was elated. They had stumbled into Carahil's wondrous store and happened upon the key to saving Laika, Sam and the rest. The secret the Hospitalers had long sought to recover was in his grasp and had proven effective in saving Laika from certain death. As Laika and King bickered over sweets, Kay went to find the fountain and gather more Ethylberry. He would need gloves as he didn't want to tear his hands up again, and a larger vessel for the water, as he had found a lot of water from the pool made the procedure easier.

When he arrived at the fountain, a metal cage of lacy black iron, like a birdcage, had been dropped down over it. A sign reading: DISPLAY CLOSED hung over the locked gate. He tried it and couldn't get it open. He tried Wafting through and it resisted. He stood in frustration. "Atha!" he called out.

"Yes, Kay?" came a voice from behind him.

There was Atha, sitting comfortably on the stone bench. "Your friend is all better, I see? Up and around hoarding candy, is she? I'll be certain my father sends you a bill for all that, by the by."

"Why is the fountain locked?" he asked.

"Why? Because Ethylberry is precious, that's why, and it's not exactly plentiful anymore, is it? When Anabrax died chained to the Horned God's stone, most Ethylberry lore died with her, except that which she taught me. You'll find it nowhere in the wild, except for right here around this fountain."

"I need it."

"Sorry." Atha produced the second pot Kay had picked, the weedy leaves and thorns glistening with his blood. "You picked this one, you bled for it, so you can have it. It's enough to correct one person and one person only. The water is fairly common—you're resourceful, you shouldn't have trouble acquiring more."

"There are many to save," Kay pleaded.

"I'm sorry," she said. "This is all the Ethylberry I can spare. I have to tend to an entire Universe, after all."

Kay wasn't going to give up. "I'll pay for it."

"Pardon?"

"I'll pay, whatever you want. Name your price."

Atha smiled and adjusted her goggles. "My price? Goodness, what would a goddess need or want? Hmmmm …"

Atha stood and walked around him in a playful manner, nudging his back and arms with momentary wisps of goddess touch.

"Would you sing to me? Would you pledge me your CARG? Would you quest on my whim?" Her voice took on a dark note: "Would you offer me your flesh? Would you engage in perversions and travesties? Would you slit a thousand throats? Would you lie in my bed, your arms around me?"

Though Kay couldn't see her eyes behind her goggles, he felt them burning.

"Would Carahil's daughter ask such a thing?" he asked.

She didn't answer.

Kay lost patience. "I have no time to waste. I shall consult with Carahil in person, inform him that his daughter might require additional training in the art of civility, and not be satisfied until he has given proper ear to my plight."

"Going to tell on me? Good luck with that," Atha said.

Kay took the pot and walked away. He had taken several steps when Atha called out to him. "You shouldn't give up so easily."

Kay stopped.

Atha held out her arms. "I thought you'd put up a bigger fuss before promising to run off and tell my father how bad I am. You need to learn to be a better negotiator, like your father. Come here, Kay."

"I don't have time for continued games."

"Come and sit, please."

Kay returned to the bench near the fountain and seated himself. Atha stood over him. "There is something I want, Kay. Everybody wants something, even the gods."

"What do you want?"

"Come on, Kay, think about it. What would a goddess want and why would she need to come to *you* for it? I have something you want—Ethylberry—and you have something *I* want, otherwise we wouldn't be having this discussion. I will offer you my help if you promise to help me in turn."

"I'll ask again, what do you want?"

Atha refused to be pinned down to specifics. "Do we have a deal, yes or no? Whatever it is I want, certainly it doesn't compare to your current needs; your Ne-Countess' needs, does it? Tell me truthfully and I will help you."

Kay answered without thinking. "Fine then. Help me now and we'll sort out the ramifications of this later with your father."

"Do we have a deal, yes or no?"

"Yes, we have a deal."

"When may I collect my payment?"

Kay thought about it. "When my Countess' jar is completed."

Atha laughed. "Done! Wonderful, I'm certain my father will give me a nice earful over this at another time." She produced a large vessel full of water. "Here's some water, more than you'll need to tend to one person unless you waste it."

Kay took it.

"Now, as I said before, I can't let you have any more dust from here, but I'll tell you where more can be found, more than enough to tend to your people. Anabrax once had a wondrous urn full of a seemingly magical golden dust that she used to experiment with various flora and fauna, and to grant favors when she was so inclined. I know what you're thinking, but the urn did not, I repeat, *did not* contain Ethylberry; instead it overflowed with a sort of lesser Ethylberry. 'Noberry' I call it. It can't do many of the things the real stuff can, and it cannot breathe life into the dead, but for simple temporary parlor tricks, for extracting sickness and for altering the flesh, it works just fine. None of the things accomplished with Noberry last forever—maybe only for a couple hundred years. Your immortal, Queen Ghome, learned of this urn full of Noberry long ago. She knew of rumors and children's stories that caught her attention; she had much time to contemplate being blind, deaf and mute, wearing rotten stitched-on parts that worked only so well. She pursued the legend into Xaphan space, taking a lifetime or two, spending several fortunes and stepping over the corpses of her various lovers until finally discovering the secret. Ghome discovered the location of Anabrax's Temple, raised an army and captured the urn centuries ago, using the dust and the water to give herself new, fresh parts whenever she wished, or whenever the effects of the Noberry dust wore out. Imagine, to be freed at last from the tomb of her immortal body. She became drunk with the possibilities. She learned her art well and changed her appearance often—sometimes she would even become a man or an exotic beast; she does have an amazing imagination. She had a great Wailing Room on Trimble where she kept the victims of her caprices alive; for if they died, the Noberry could not sustain the stolen parts, yet another of its limitations."

"And where is this fabled urn?" Kay asked. He felt he already knew the answer.

"It's one of her most cherished possessions. She keeps it, most often, in her Bower Chest behind lock and key—you didn't need me to tell you that, did you?"

"Bower Chests, per antiquity, are said to be invincible."

Atha shrugged her shoulders. "That is true. Look for a way to deactivate it. That's up to you to discover. You're a capable fellow, I'm certain you'll be successful."

"Where is it? Where is Queen Ghome's Bower Chest?" Kay asked.

"Ask your Magistrate."

"What?"

"Oh, so many questions, Kay. I have already given you invaluable information, so use it and save your Ne-Countess. I repeat, if you have questions, ask your Magistrate. And remember, when your Ne-Countess' jar is complete, I shall be calling on you for my payment. And don't try to trick me, Kay, your jar will be completed."

"I require more beyond mere hints and promises of toil to come," he said.

Atha shrugged. "What more do you want?"

Kay held out the pot. "I want you to deliver this pot and the water to the Hospitalers on the Gold Coast of Hoban at once."

"I am not a delivery service, Kay."

"And I am not in the habit of giving out favors. I care not who your father is; our jar will be finished when I desire it to be finished. Either deliver these goods to the Hospitalers on Hoban or our deal is off. Sam will never work on her jar again, I shall make certain of it. We shall remain childless if need be."

Atha thought a moment and then laughed. "You're a bit more devious than I thought. Very well, I shall deliver these goods as asked, but expect no more of me."

"The pot with the Ethylberry and the tankard of proper water."

"Yes, of course."

"And you will take them in working order to the Hospitalers precisely as…"

"Yes, yes, Kay. I know where to take them, and never fear, I'm not out to trick you and twist your words or get out of a promise. When I say I'm going to do something, I do it. Your instructions are vaguely worded and leave much to chance, but my father's teachings were not lost on me. I know what you want and where you want them go. I will deliver them as is and they shall work flawlessly. But do not ask one iota more. This is all I can give you. Remember, what would my father say? Oh yes, Balance, I can't upset Balance. Very dangerous. Now, I must leave."

She walked away and spoke over her shoulder. "Farewell, Lord Blanchefort, but not goodbye …"

She faded and was gone, leaving the fountain and its weedy treasures secure behind their iron cage. Alone, Kay tried the cage one more time.

Locked. Not budging. Before Kay's eyes, the fountain, the weeds and the cage vanished, leaving only a sign on an iron stand:

ETHYLBERRY DISPLAY TEMPORARILY REMOVED FOR
MAINTENANCE

Somewhat dejected, Kay returned to Laika and King.

Laika was grabbing everything she could find. She had collected a massive assortment of bagged candy, a pile of colorful shirts like the one she was wearing, and numerous toys. Even with six arms she was having trouble carrying it all.

"Jarlcon!" she cried, holding aloft a bag of candy. "For celebration!" she said, tearing it open. She popped in a handful of jawbreakers and merrily crunched on them. She had a giant cloth bag which she stuffed everything into. In went the candy, half a dozen shirts, Carahil mementos that had caught her eye, and a number of posable dolls in boxes. Kay stopped and had a look at one. The dolls were likenesses of his parents, Captain Davage and Countess Sygillis, dressed in miniature clothing packaged with accessories; CARGs, pre-shaped Shadow tech, the works. There were also dolls of Sarah and Phillip with SAPP accessories, one of Thomasina in her green and brown armor complete with a MT CALM club, and several of himself wearing different outfits. Conspicuously missing from the lot was a doll of Sam. Kay found himself wanting one. He returned to the aisle Atha had shown him and had a look. Laika had rifled through the boxes, making a grand mess in the process. In sorting through some of the boxes, Kay found a doll of King, a sinister one of Tal de Roga with balled-up fists, and a number of Sam—none of which Laika had chosen to take with her. In some, Sam was wearing her old black Monama gown, in others she was wearing colorful Vith clothing, a bathing suit and even a nightgown. He found one of her holding her earthen jar. Seeing her beautiful pale face so full of love resting on a nest of black hair nearly brought tears to his eyes. He stared at her for many minutes.

"Lord Blanchefort," King called, ending his musing.

He took several Sam dolls with him and headed back. "Come. It's time to return to the castle. First things first—we strike at the Jones. Our objective is the recovery of the damn cryochest, and this time it shall be we dictating the terms of battle, not Tal de Roga. Castle Blanchefort is ours and its secrets are our own."

King blinked in agreement. Though he said nothing, he was clearly eager to have at the Jones.

"Laika, it's time to move out. You need to suit-up."

Laika frowned. She seemed quite happy roaming the store bootless in her giant-cotton shirt. Kay went to the island and, with difficulty, dragged her mangled breastplate down to the water and cleaned it off as best he could. The armor was destroyed by the Jones' Man-to-Man rockets and seemed unwearable. Laika saw the damage. "Laika just wear shirt," she announced, "and no boots."

"You'll need protection and you need your boots."

"Jarlcon heal Laika again."

He brought her down her boots and, reluctantly, she pulled them on and laced them up. King returned carrying a large black garment. "I located something she can wear in place of the armor." It was a corsetlike composite garment, giant-sized and sporting multiple armholes with small round disks of metal sewn onto the material. Laika took it from King and eyed it skeptically.

"Seems to be a lightweight composite material. Seems very durable," King said.

She pulled off her cotton shirt and wiggled into the composite. Oddly, it seemed to fit quite well on her alien Haitathe form and had numerous pockets. Kay pulled the straps tight for her.

"You good?" Kay asked.

She nodded and strapped on her weapons belt, her swords freshly cleaned in the cool shale island water.

They headed out of Carahil's wondrous store and out into the node between places.

10—Hyper Staff

As they moved through the long node toward the Mystery Library, King gave Kay a full report. "The Jones have largely quit Castle Blanchefort, and Kana for that matter, and are on their way back to Bazz. They have helped themselves to some of the more exotic artifacts lying about Castle Blanchefort, including the Machine and Mallus Mirror, and they have Queen Ghome herself with them under their protection. The Jones brought in a Gilead Heavy Earth Mover and scooped up the Machine out of the Grove, Silver tech defenses and all. They still cannot get past the Silver tech defenses around it and, should they succeed, they will find the Machine inert, as I have the powering stone hidden. That should foil them for some time to come."

"Well, that's something, at least. All right, so, here are our objectives: Recover the cryochest containing the stolen parts; capture Queen Ghome and recover all items stolen from Castle Blanchefort including the Machine, or ensure its disuse."

"And then revenge on Jones!" Laika added.

"If we succeed in our plans, then the natural outcome will be the downfall of The Jones. The Jones have proved themselves entirely complicit with Queen Ghome, the enemy, to the point of committing mayhem and murder within the walls of a sovereign Great House."

"Laika hates Jones," she said with a slight growl as she popped more candy in.

"Our final objective is the enemy herself. We must secure Queen Ghome and return her to the Gold Coast of Hoban, where she may give up the parts she stole from Sam and Sarah and be fitted with the Mentralysis artifacts. How are you doing for ammunition, Laika?" Kay asked.

"LLAGs near empty. Thirty-seven rounds remaining."

"We'll see what we've got in the castle armory. We should be able to get you re-armed, provided The Jones haven't sacked it."

Following King, they plunged deep into the node, and it was a surprisingly long walk. They came to the intersection. Atha's statue was still there. The book she had been carrying was gone; in its place was a large earthen jar of a distinctly orange color. The jar was unmistakable; it was a facsimile of Sam's Anuian jar, whose completion would require Kay to 'pay up' to Atha.

King perched on the jar. "This intersection links all of Carahil's temples. We just came from his 1000 Carahil Park store; ahead is the Mystery Library in Castle Blanchefort. To our left is a passage leading to an odd plane. It's very small; only a few miles in length before it ends. It seems to be fully enclosed. This is the only entrance or exit."

Kay gazed down the corridor and Sighted. He saw the corridor end, opening up in what looked like a bluff overlooking a lovely beach. As King said, it only went on for a few miles before it doubled back on itself, ending up where it started.

"It is Carahil's Porch, a place where one can be alone with one's thoughts. To the right is the final place," King said.

Kay looked. To the right of the intersection was the dank and gloomy patch of darkness lurking with wet stone and rusty metal nestled in layers of darkness that he had seen and recoiled from before. It had a forlorn and lonely feel to it. Laika gazed down the corridor and stepped back. "Bad enchantment," she said.

"What is that?" he asked. "Something about that area gives me pause."

"Cathedral of Bone and Wire," King replied. "You saw me there. It is one of Carahil's temples, certain enough, and it is not a pleasant place. All angry things are welcome there. I waited in the darkness for you to summon me."

Kay contemplated that for a moment. He couldn't picture darkness and Carahil in the same thought. "How is this dark gulf a place Carahil would reside? I can imagine a nice beach being someplace Carahil would like, but this?"

"There is darkness in us all," King replied.

"Come," Laika said, tugging on Kay's sleeve. "Jones await."

They continued on, leaving the passages to the secluded beach of Carahil's Porch and to the Cathedral of Bone and Wire behind. Soon, Kay spied a point of light in the far distance, which eventually grew into the now familiar passes of the Mystery Library. The room was heavily damaged by the Jones as they traipsed back and forth with their Battle Units: shelving was knocked over, books lay everywhere, and the venerable Durst table was on its side. Kay struggled to set it back up on its legs; Laika assisted and it came over easy.

"Sarah's not going to be happy," Kay said. "She loves this place. I do too."

He checked the Bobby box, hoping to contact Sarah, but the

Jones had crushed it under foot, destroying the receiver within. For now, the three of them were on their own in the castle.

They went back out into the main area of the library, seeing it in ruins. Kay immediately noticed the same odd perfumy scent hanging in the air that he had smelled previously during the battle. The smell crawled far up his nose and festered in his sinuses like a wet rag.

"Lord Blanchefort, cover your nose," King said.

"Why?"

"That scent is pollen from the Horvath Creeper. It will foul your use of Gifts."

Kay covered his nose and mouth. Laika reached into the bag and gave him a Carahil shirt to breathe into.

"Laika and bird get rid of Creeper," she said.

Laika and King went ahead. Kay hung back and waited a few minutes. He Sighted ahead to see what they were doing.

There were numerous potted vines scattered about the library, left by the Jones as they departed. Many had toppled over, spilling black, loamy dirt onto the carpet—yet another fightable offense in Sarah's book. Each bore a large single white flower with a meaty pollen stalk. Laika and King worked together, picking up

the plants and throwing them out the window. As Kay Sighted, the heavy floral perfume laced with pollen got into his nose despite the shirt he was breathing into to filter it out. It was a good smell at first whiff, but grew heavy and unpleasant very quickly. It was a smell one would never wish to experience twice. Very quickly, Kay's Sight clouded and went down to nothing. His Gifts were diminishing fast. He couldn't Cloak any longer and his Waft was unusable as well. He went into the main library area.

"Oh, these stink," Kay commented, holding his nose. "My Gifts are done."

Laika grabbed the rest of the vines and sent them whizzing out. "Horvath Creeper," she said. "Plant fouls Gifts. Laika heard Hospitalers speak of them. Jones use plant often."

"Pollen from the Horvath Creeper is a prime ingredient in The Jones' anti-Gift grenades," King stated.

"Well, the bloody plants are gone now; let's see what the damn Jones are up to." Kay tried to release his Dark Sight and look in on the distant reaches of the castle, but his Sight wouldn't open. Try as he might, nothing happened, just like before during the battle. Kay's heart sank. "No, I can't Sight."

"Plant no good for Gifts," Laika said.

He tried to Waft; nothing happened. He tried his Cloak.

Failed.

"Gods!" he spat. "I've got nothing. All my Gifts are useless. I didn't think the pollen would have a lingering effect." He clutched his head, hoping to will his Gifts back into service. His brain felt numb and dormant; he could still smell the cloying perfume of the Creeper charging through his nose and knocking about in his head.

"Jarlcon no need Gifts. Jarlcon strong!" Laika said, offering encouragement.

"Glad you think so. We have no idea what's in front of us, could be a whole legion of Jones. King, can you scout ahead please, and give us a report?"

King complied and fluttered out the door. As they waited, Laika began cleaning up a little. She pushed the Durst table back into place and put fallen books back on the shelves, though she did so without the care and grace Sarah would have used.

Soon, King returned, fluttering through the windows. He was carrying something in his tiny silver feet.

"King, what's our status?" Kay asked.

King replied in his dry voice. "I'm afraid I have grim tidings. The Jones have left a great quantity of Horvath Creeper all over the castle interior. Very fresh, very potent. You may expect to have no use of your Gifts anytime in the near future. The Jones have largely quit the castle; however, the castle is not empty. Several staff members are drifting about the corridors."

"How many?"

"Ten. All are armed with knives and under The Jones' influence, ready to kill. Given what I've seen, The Jones have induced a Hyper-State onto the staff members."

"What's that?" Kay asked.

"A Hyper-State hypnosis. It super-charges the subject, imparts upon them heightened physical attributes and skills they would not ordinarily have. They will also feel no pain. Some that I saw have mutilated themselves, and you must be prepared for what you are going to see in the castle proper below. The Hyper will invariably kill the subject if they are not freed from it in short order."

Kay listened and ran his hand through his purple hair, worried for his staff. Laika adjusted her new black composite armor and appeared unfazed. He unsaddled his CARG. "Then we can't just sit here and let our staff be killed. Our staff is, as are the Cyans of Blanchefort Village, under our protection. They and their ancestors before them have served this castle for ages, and we have a sacred trust to keep them safe. There are usually over a hundred staff members in the castle at any given time. Sarah, thankfully, got most of them out. Now it falls on us to protect the rest."

"Laika ready!"

King spoke. "I located your PtVa pistol, Lord Blanchefort, in the Grove near the creek." He set it down on the table. Sitting there was Kay's Poltava; an enameled purple work of art. He picked it up—fully loaded, he could tell by its weight. It felt comforting to have it back.

"Good eye, King, thank you." He cocked the gun and slid it

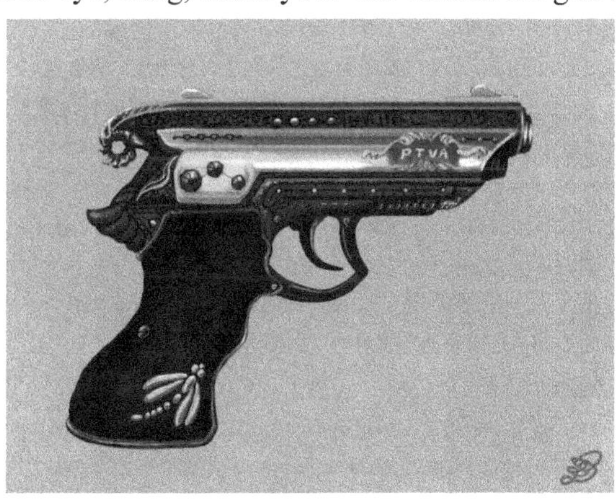

into his vest pocket.

They went out into the vestibule. Detritus from the Jones lay strewn about everywhere: shell casings, cables, discarded medical assortments from the triage they performed on their wounded fellows, pools of dried blood, and so on. "Our first task shall be freeing the staff from their Hyper-State and we must accomplish it with all speed. We will fight to incapacitate. We will then secure them as best we can and take the tunnels to the castle armory just in case The Jones left any surprises for us in the Grove. There we can kit out with heavier weaponry and contact Sarah. Here's what is going to happen: Raal is going to send in a team of Hospitalers to tend to our staff whether he likes it or not."

They headed down the stairs, moving fast past fifty floors. The atrium to the tower was just below. "Remember, the staff is not to be harmed. Defend yourself as best you can, but we fight to assist the staff. King, what can you do to help out?"

"I am designed to kill, Lord Blanchefort, not to engage in non-lethal interdiction."

"Then adjust. Figure it out. I've got faith in you. No killing."

"No matter. Laika and Jarlcon fight!" Laika cried, ready to go.

"You too, Laika. No killing," Kay demanded.

Laika offered an uncharacteristic growl in response. They reached the atrium at the base of the tower. It was frustrating for Kay to not be able to Sight, to not know what was around every bend ahead of time—the Horvath Creeper was a horrid plant indeed. King fluttered ahead, checking for any surprises.

"Clear," he said. "The staff was concentrated near the kitchen area; that's where we should encounter most of them."

"The kitchens are too small," Kay said. "We need room to incapacitate them. The Grand Ballroom is nearby. Laika, you wait there. I will attempt to draw the staff into the open space of the Ball-room where we can properly subdue them."

They headed north down the main corridor. So far, they had met nobody. Here and there were potted Horvath Creeper plants; pretty and festive with their huge white flowers, filling the air with their horrid perfume.

"There's the Ballroom. Laika, await me in there." Through the doorway was a colossal room decorated in Vith finery large enough to berth a medium-sized starship. Laika walked in, her weapons clanking. Her ten-foot frame was dwarfed by the sheer size of the room.

"Don't make a mess in there, ok?"

She didn't answer.

Kay and King resumed walking down the corridor toward the

kitchens. He held his CARG at the ready.

"Alert!" King cried.

A girl wandered out of the side corridor from the kitchens wearing the cheery light blue apron and ruffled shirt of a staff member. She saw Kay and smiled. "Lord Blanchefort! We've been so worried about you!"

She drew a curved knife from her sash. "May I prepare you some breakfast?" She attacked at a breathless run, moving straight for Kay, knife poised to kill. King hovered up and lit his Sight, throwing out two silvery beams in the girl's direction. She evaded the beams and came in, knife flashing. She thrust and Kay countered with his CARG. He pushed her knife aside and gave her a thump on the side of the head, hoping to render her unconscious. She took the blow and attacked again. Kay parried, landing a blow on her wrists, knocking her knife away.

Her breast was wide open, he could kill her easily, but he allowed the moment to pass. She reached behind her apron and pulled out another knife. "May I make you some pancakes?" she asked, raising it up. She smiled the whole time, unaware of what she was doing. Kay fled down the hallway toward the Ballroom, the staff girl in hot pursuit. Exhibiting incredible speed, she caught Kay from behind, tackling him, ready to stab him with her knife.

She winced, dropped her knife and slumped to the floor. There was King, hovering behind her, holding her first knife in his arrowlike beak. He let it fall. "The knife she dropped is Maliked. I nicked her with it below the right shoulder."

Kay stood and picked up the knife. "Well, that at least gives us an easy method to safely incapacitate the rest of the staff." He picked her up and moved her into the Ballroom under Laika's watchful eye. Readying himself, he and King went into the kitchen.

Nine staff members stood within. "Lord Blanchefort!" came their voices in a joyous chorus.

He stood there for a moment, shocked.

The kitchen was a place he loved, had fond memories of. Sneaking there as a child to get a snack, the smells of baking delights and boiling syrup, the roasting meats and simmering sauces. The smiling faces of the staff, the giggles.

The kitchen was a slaughterhouse dripping with blood. The staff milled about, performing the ghost of the work they normally did, going through the motions, stirring nothing, baking nothing. One had her own hand on a chopping block and was slicing it like a head of lettuce. Another was capering about with the kitchen cutlery plunged into her arms and legs like a grim butcher's block. Another had partially cooked herself in one of the stoves.

They had the Jones' cryochest full of parts and were in the process of preparing the parts within for cooking. Faces, hands, feet and other assorted parts were laid out on a cutting board ready to be sliced into bits.

What had The Jones done? What sort of game was this? Heartbreak and rage filled Kay. The staff that were able to do so brandished knives and came at Kay. Many were too weak to stand and simply crawled.

Kay cut one with his Maliked knife and she fell. The rest pressed in, smiling, bleeding, offering to prepare food for Kay even as they attempted to slash him. Kay and King fell back into the hallway and went into the Ballroom, pursued closely by the staff, all in various stages of disfigurement.

Laika was waiting. She perched high on the near wall, like a giant spider. She reached out with an unbreakable grip, arms stretching, and lifted the staff high into the air. King hovered up and Maliked them in turn, and they went limp. Quick as that, the battle with the staff was over. Kay returned to the kitchens and mopped up the rest. With tears in his eyes, he tended to the staff's wounds as best he could, whispering into their ears that he was their Lord and he would protect them. They then returned the staff to their beds in high up Harper Tower. Most of the beds were empty, the bulk of the staff diverted away by Sarah.

"Come, they should be safe here for now until Hospitalers arrive to tend to them," Laika said.

Kay didn't want to leave them.

"Come," Laika said again.

Returning to the kitchen, Kay and Laika collected all the parts and returned them to the super-cooled interior of the cryochest. Fearing the worst, Kay inspected each one, wondering what damage had been done. A hand and a face were on a cutting board, partially diced into cubes. Kay dreaded to learn who they belonged to. Performing a quick inventory, he found Sarah's face, her hands (including the missing one de Roga had taken), Ki's parts and her son's as well. He collected everything and placed them back into the cryochest, shutting the lid with a hiss.

As he puzzled over why The Jones had left the chest in the kitchens, Laika and King entered. "The Jones must have left the chest here hoping I'd react and kill the staff. Every bit of this is an unforgivable outrage!"

As they exited the kitchen, Kay enabled the automated high-pressure steam cleaners which were run once a week to sanitize the area. He closed the door and heard the jets come to life, scouring everything with heat and steam, washing clean the gore.

Pulling the chest with them, they came to the darkened Hall of Portraits. Hundreds of life-sized portraits hung in the hall from the floor to the lofty ceiling. "What these paintings?" Laika asked.

"My ancestors, going back through the antiquity of the House. Mine and Sam's portrait hang here as well. Come. There's a secret passage just there we can take to the armory."

Laika stared at the portraits of the Old Blancheforts, some from the beginning of the League. She pointed at one hanging high above. "Haitathe," she said. "This Haitathe, like Laika."

Kay looked up. She was pointing at an old painting of a fierce Blanchefort countess from long ago. Her painting was difficult to see in the dark. Kay had forgotten how dark the Hall of Portraits was without his Sight. King shone his light on the painting.

"That's Countess Mirzathorn, I think. A great matriarch in the old EX days," he said.

"Mirzadan," King corrected.

"Yes, that's right. Thank you. She goes back several thousand years."

"Mirzadan, Haitathe," Laika announced. "Eyes. Haitathe eyes."

One of his ancestors might have been a Haitathe in disguise? Kay didn't have time to ponder that odd notion. He examined the stone wall near the portrait of Lord Sadric, his grandfather. "Somewhere here is the hidden door to the passes below which will give us access to the Grove tunnels." He couldn't find it. Not having use of his Dark Sight was maddening. "King, I need your light, please."

King flew in and illuminated the wall. They probed the wall, testing the stone with their hands. "We're looking for a hidden lever." Good thing Sarah wasn't here to see this, she would certainly laugh. With a good deal of searching, Kay found the lever and the door swung open.

The passes below were terribly dark. King went ahead and lit the way with his Sight. Kay crawled behind him and Laika brought up the rear, her mass filling the tunnel, dragging the cryochest behind her.

"Many passages," she said, taking note of everything, filing it away into her eidetic brain. They moved northeast, safely under the Grove, toward the armory. They pressed on, the tunnel becoming damp as they neared the lake. Soon, they went up through a hidden passage and into the Castle Armory, which was disguised as a Vith ruin from the outside. Weapons of many kinds were slung up on the walls and boxes of standard ammunitions were neatly shelved. It was a wonderland of weaponry. Laika wandered out into the room, taking it all in.

"Look around and take what you want," Kay said. "I'm getting Sarah on the line."

Kay found a Bobby box. "Sarah!" he yelled.

A scratchy voice replied. "It's me, Kay. What happened?"

"The Jones came at us hard: Battle Units, GWs, H-Grenadiers, the works."

Sarah cursed. "I didn't see anything. The Jones must have rigged our security cameras. Are you all right? How'd you get out of that?"

"King. He swooped in and got us out."

"King's still functional?" she asked.

"He is, and a good thing too."

Sarah laughed with joy. "A-ha! Atta' boy, King!"

"Sarah, is this line secure? The Jones could be listening."

"I don't know, probably. There's no way to know for certain. This is a pretty low-tech connection, so it's hard to tell." There was a pause. "Hold on. Let's drop the line, I'll be right there."

"Sarah?"

No reply, the line appeared to be dead.

"Alert!" King cried, hovering high into the air and lighting his Sight.

A figure appeared out of the dim lighting at the far end of the room. Laika dropped what she was carrying and drew her gigantic swords, ready to fight.

"Hey, hey," Sarah said, showing her hands, "it's just me!"

Kay saw her and was elated. "Sarah! Where in Creation did you come from?"

"Well, I ..."

Laika's hand shot out, stretched, and got Sarah by the neck, cutting her off in mid-sentence, lifting her into the air. Sarah gagged and kicked.

"Hello, Sarah, did you think Laika would forget?" she said,

savoring the moment, bringing Sarah in close to her face. "Answer Laika!"

Sarah reached out and put a jolt into Laika's ear. Laika yelped and dropped her.

"So sorry, Toots," Sarah said, standing up. "Fintron again. You'll have to wait another day to beat me to a pulp, if you can."

Laika scowled. "Jarlcon said Laika could beat Sarah into pulp and Laika intends to do just that."

Sarah laughed. "Did you tell her that, Kay?"

"I sure did."

Sarah turned to King. "And where were you, just now? Were you going to let her wring my neck or what?"

"I can see you are a heavily finducered hologram, Sarah," King replied. "You are currently in no danger."

Kay and King came down. Kay gave her a grand hug. "It's so good to see you again, Sarah. The staff, did you see what happened? What The Jones did to our staff is unforgivable."

"I saw them up in their tower, Kay. Obviously some of them didn't make it out of the castle and were overwhelmed by The Jones. I wish I could have been there with you. You did the right thing by them."

"Get Raal right now and tell him I want a team of Hospitalers sent en route at once to tend to our people and clear the castle of The Jones' influence."

"I know what he's going to say."

"I don't care what he's going to say. Get rough with him if you have to. How's Sam?"

"Sam's good. Got her fighting pirates right now in her RDP. You know, she's a pretty sadistic little bunny rabbit when she gets pissed. She's doing things to those pirates I'd not thought she would have. Everybody's good except for Ki, who's in bad shape. I'll fill you in later."

Kay suddenly realized something. "How are you here, in holographic form?"

"Yes," Laika growled. "How is Sarah here? Laika wants real Sarah, not holographic Sarah."

Sarah grinned. "How? Get kitted out and come outside when you're ready. You'll see. I'll be waiting." She waved-off Laika and vanished.

They continued loading out. Seeing Sarah energized Kay. He was certain the staff would soon receive the medical help they needed for their condition. Now, he could press on, though he was worried about Ki. "You've got four LLAGs, right Laika?" he asked.

She nodded.

"LLAGs are ok, but you'll probably want something with a bit more punch. Let's see ..."

He wandered around, seeing many types of weapons. The famous Blanchefort PtVa was not present, as Lord Sadric had disposed of the bulk of them. Also, the Grenville 40 series was not present, as the Blancheforts would not carry weapons produced by their one-time rivals. "What do you suggest, King?" Kay asked, genuinely perplexed.

"I suggest a weapons system with more explosive power. I suggest the Dare D3D4 combat rifle. It fires a potent hardened dart, completely armor piercing and frangible, which should play havoc with the Jones' equipment."

Kay pulled a 'DeeDee' rifle off the wall and presented it to Laika. "Here, Laika, what do you think?"

She looked at the weapon with wonder. "Is Jarlcon offering this weapon to Laika?"

"I am. It's a little heavy, but I'm certain you can manage."

"Laika has no weapons—all belong to Hruntha."

"Not this one. This DeeDee belongs to Laika, if you want it."

She stood there for a moment staring at the rifle.

"Go on, take it," Kay said.

She took it from him. "What do you think?" he asked.

"Well-made, not heavy. Laika very happy."

"Not heavy, huh? We'll see about that once we get it loaded." Kay searched around and found a bulbous two-hundred dart drum.

"I suggest a load-out of brindacyte darts, as they will create the most damage," King said as Kay worked.

"Two hundred brindacyte darts will be extremely heavy."

"I am certain Laika will be able to manage."

Kay loaded the drum and lugged it around, having issues with its weight. "Laika, this weighs over forty pounds, that's why DeeDees fell out of favor, because they're so heavy. Loaded out with a drum like this, it's supposed to be mounted. What do you think?"

She took the drum like it was nothing and loaded it onto the rifle. She waved it around with one hand. "Not heavy," she said. She leveled it to her eye and gazed through the sights. "Good feel. Laika will kill many Jones with rifle."

Kay found a bandolier holster and fitted it across Laika's

shoulder. She holstered the DeeDee with approval.

Kay took a few boxes of ammunition for his Poltava. "Laika, do you want to replace any of your LLAGs? Help yourself."

Laika rummaged around the armory but was apparently happy with her unglamorous and battered but reliable LLAGs. She reloaded them and filled the pockets of her composite armor with extra magazines.

Kitted out, they exited the armory into the sunshine of the Grove. Sarah was sitting on a stump nearby. "Took you guys long enough," she said.

"We're fully stocked up," Kay replied. "So, Sarah, how are we seeing you here?"

"It's coming now. Look!"

Flying low over the treetops making a horrendous racket came a gangly, singularly ugly fixed undercarriage transport ship studded with four elephantine industrial power plants in vectored shrouds. It was painted a dinged-up bright yellow.

"That's how I'm doing it," Sarah announced happily. "This baby's a surplus Tubruk 444 hauler that I got for cheap, way cheap. I used some of the funds Ghome tried to pull out of the Blanchefort coffers. I Commed the yard up and bought her done deal. It's perfect; with those four big Grenville mass drivers generating sixteen megawatts each, it oozes power."

The ship came down in a clearing with a clank of gangly linkages, and the hatch slowly opened. "First thing after I bought it, I had it delivered to a chop shop on Brindval and had a butt-load of holo-emitters installed. With these four engines online, I've got a 1400-mile range circular all day long. When they got the holo-emitters online and I appeared out of nowhere, those boys dropped their lunches. You should have seen it! Ha! It was great!"

Laika scoffed. "Sarah buys ugly ship," she said. "Sarah's ugly face scares mechanics."

"Yeah, Toots? She doesn't look like much, but she's got it where it counts. I call her *The Ultra*; cool, huh? I also loaded her out with a full spread of Monties."

"Monties?" Kay asked. "You mean missiles? You loaded this hauler out with missiles? That's illegal."

"So? I won't tell if you won't. I slipped the guys at the chop shop a little extra and they installed 'em no problem. You need something illegal installed on your ship, they can make it happen for you on Brindval. I've even got surface mounts in case we want to go Surface-to-Air. Come on, let's get aboard. I've got the factories in the Village emitting a sensor lock over the Grove right now, just in case The Jones are trying to monitor us. It won't last forever, so let's get a move on."

Laika shook her head. "No need Sarah's ugly ship. Have *Venera* ship waiting. Much faster."

"Yeah, and The Jones will spot you coming the moment you blast off. Remember, we're not dealing with a bunch of pirates or Xaphans here; The Jones are plugged into the sky and have their eyes on everything. This innocuous vessel is the way to go."

They piled in. The interior was functional and clean, though it smelled faintly of grease and old oil. There were several crew cabins in the rear along with a good functional cargo hold. Laika set the cryochest down. The hatch closed and Sarah flopped into the pilot's chair. A few moments later, the big Grenvilles growled and the ship lifted off, lumbering nice and smooth over the castle and south into the Gaston Way. Laika stood next to the pilot's chair, crowding Sarah's space.

"Give me some room, right? We're on our way to Bazz. Should take about seventeen hours to get there. I've even got a fake manifest and bogus flight plan filed so we look totally legit if The Jones snoop us over. They'll never know it's us."

Kay took a peek at the cargo bay. It was fully stocked with hermetic containers and had a good-sized industrial winch. "Does the winch work, Sarah?"

"'Course it works. Everything works on this ship. We'll be needing it to get our stuff back once we take The Jones down."

Kay selected a cabin. Laika stood by the pilot's chair, observing the process, memorizing the layout of the gauges and dials. King settled onto the co-pilot's chair and quietly watched. Kay took Laika's sacks of things from Carahil's store and placed them on the bed in a nearby cabin.

"Give me a few minutes and I'll get Raal on the line," Sarah said.

The Ultra broke orbit a short time later and eased into the shipping lanes toward Bazz, moving at a leisurely rate of speed. Several other haulers came and formed up with them; a standard practice, for haul ships always traveled in numbers in case any found themselves needing assistance. Sarah locked the helm and got up out of the chair. Laika readied to flop down into the seat.

"Ah-ah, keep your big butt out of there, sister," Sarah said.

Laika grumbled some sort of curse and came away.

There was a table mounted near the hold complete with monitors and chairs. Sarah sat down cross-legged as usual and Kay joined her. Laika stood next to Kay, her hands on her swords, guarding him. "So, then," Sarah said. "Let me get Raal out of bed here; it's only two bells on Hoban right now, so it's good and dark." Sarah waved her hand and a monitor came to life. The image of a fine bedroom appeared. Someone peacefully slept, arms encircled under a thick pillow. "Watch this," Sarah announced.

Several jolts of bluish light danced across the room and the sleeping person sprang from the bed with a cry. "Out of bed, Raal!" Sarah yelled. "We've got some action items for you to take care of! Can't wait! Come on! Chop, chop!"

Raal, pajama-clad, sat by his bed and rubbed his eyes. He stood and walked out of the holo- screen's eye. "Hey, where're you going?" Sarah demanded.

"Let's give him a moment of privacy, Sarah, please," Kay said. Laika excused herself and went into her cabin. A few minutes later she emerged, bootless, her weapons belt and composite armor removed, wearing a light blue shirt from Carahil's store. His smiling face was stamped on the breast. She held several bags of candy.

"You look ridiculous in that," Sarah remarked.

"Quiet, Sarah. Laika not care. Laika comfortable," she said, seating herself next to Kay.

"Where'd you get all that stuff?" Sarah asked.

"Carahil's store on Xandarr," Kay answered.

"Carahil's what?"

"It's a long story, Sarah. I'll tell you later."

She gazed at the bags. "Is that candy?"

"It is, Sarah. While we wait for Raal, what is everyone's current status?" Kay asked.

"Everybody's fine, except for Ki, and she's not good."

"Did the Hospitalers receive the items I sent over?"

Sarah paused. "One sec, let me check. They received an earthen pot with a crappy weed in it that they were going to pitch, and a tankard of heavy water that they're analyzing. Is that what you're talking about?"

Kay was alarmed. "Yes! Do not let them throw that plant away! That plant is the key to Ghome's flesh-stealing technique. Sarah, you tell Raal to be careful with that 'crappy weed'. They also need to quit analyzing and testing and start doing for a change."

"Ok, ok, I'll tell him. You know, he's not a bad fellow, really, Raal."

"I thought you two were going to have words."

"We did have words. I barged right into his terminal and we came to a nice understanding. I sort of like him now. He knows what he's doing with this Mentralysis stuff, that's for sure. He needs to loosen up a little, but other than that ..."

Laika tore open a bag of candy and popped a handful into her mouth. She offered some to Kay. "No, thank you," he said.

"Must eat," she insisted.

"It's just candy, Laika. It's not really food."

"Are those jawbreakers?" Sarah asked.

"Probably."

Sarah appeared a little dejected. "You know, one thing I didn't program into this Fintron was finducers for taste, so I can't taste anything right now. What flavor are those jawbreakers?"

"Mixed fruit, I believe," Kay said.

Laika took a colorful handful and showed them to Sarah. "Awww, poor Sarah cannot taste. Such a pity." She popped them into her mouth and crunched away. "Good!"

"You want me to shock you again, don't you? When you guys get me out of the ice box, you're going to have to show me this cool Carahil store. I want to see it for myself."

As they waited for Raal, Kay noticed Sarah's blue pony-tail seemed to be slightly flowing and twisting about, as if in an ethereal wind; a rather otherworldly enhancement to her otherwise perfectly convincing hologram that she probably couldn't resist adding.

"Raal's ready. Let me get him. Oh, one thing, if he starts getting uppity, let me do the talking, ok? I know how to deal with this guy." She opened the monitor and Raal appeared, fully dressed in his Hospitaler uniform, conservative and quiet-mannered as before. King found himself a good spot and silently observed.

"Hi, Raal, we're all here," Sarah said.

"Hello, Sarah," he replied.

"Hey! It's *Ultra Sarah*, Raal, we discussed this, remember? You said you'd call me Ultra Sarah!"

Raal sighed. "Yes, yes, of course ... And, might I add, '*Ultra Sarah*', that if you ever shock me out of bed again, I'll personally go down to the infirmary, pull your blank naked body out of the ready capsule and slap it silly. Understand?"

"Now you're talking!" Sarah cried. "Get rough with me.

Don't take my crap!"

Raal turned his attention to Kay. "Lord Blanchefort, we received the items you sent to our facility here on Hoban. How did you manage that?"

"Not relevant at this time. Take great care of those items— they are of critical importance, especially the plant. We managed to recover a cryochest with all the stolen pieces except for Sam's parts and Sarah's eyes. Some of the parts have been damaged." He turned to Laika. "Laika, do you mind?"

She put down her bag of candy and retrieved the cryochest from the hold. Kay opened the lid and a bluish cloud of condensed mist drifted out. Sarah leaned over and looked in.

There were the stolen parts; a ghoulish display of faces, hands, feet, breasts and other workings. Sarah reached in and pulled her own face out. It hung there in her hands like a latex mask draped in blue hair. Sarah's holographic expression was, at once, horrified and morbidly enthralled. Sarah loved such things and holding her own face in her holographic hands only added to her wonderment. "So this is my face, huh? Wow! Wow … *I'm gorgeous* ..." She looked it over with a critical eye. "Do you think my hair's bluer in the back than in the front? Hey, I didn't know I had a mole there."

She presented her face to the monitor. "What do you think, Raal? Aren't I cute?"

He shuffled in his seat. "You have a fine profile, Ultra Sarah."

"Ohh," Sarah laughed. "Now you're flirting with me."

"Did you recover these parts from The Jones?" Raal asked.

"No, from our staff. The Jones vacated the castle and left the chest behind."

Raal seemed perplexed for a moment. "Odd that they would leave it there. Well, in any event we shall want them back on Hoban as quickly as possible for proper inventorying and preservation. We can send a ship to fetch them."

"Not a good idea," Sarah said, still admiring her limp face, shaking it a little. "The Jones will finger us. We need to remain hidden."

Kay had a thought. "Sarah, I saw hermetic containers in the hold. Are they functional?"

"Sure they are."

"Good. King, how quickly can you make the trip to Hoban from our current position?"

"Eighteen point five hours, Kanan," he replied.

"That will do. I'm thinking we box up the chest in one of the containers and have King fly it to Hoban. He's small and fast—The Jones won't notice, and, if he's set upon, he can defend himself."

"That's a good idea," Sarah agreed. "Raal, we're sending the stuff to you and be careful with my face, ok?"

Laika went to the hold and returned carrying a heavy hermetic container, specifically designed to withstand the rigors of space. She set it down and Sarah opened the lid with an air-tight hiss. They returned all the parts to the cryochest, Sarah lovingly placing her face within. "Try to resist the urge to kiss me, Raal, at least until I can kiss back, ok?"

Raal didn't respond.

"Some of the parts have been greatly damaged," Kay added.

"Leave that to us. As long as we have most of the material and it is still viable, we can repair them," Raal assured.

They sealed the chest and Laika hauled it into the hermetic container. Sarah closed the container and pressurized it.

"Ready, King?" Kay asked.

He fluttered up from his perch and followed Laika to the airlock. "Safe journey, King. You are authorized to use whatever force necessary to complete your mission. Speed well," Kay said. Moments later, the doors closed and King and the container were released into space. Kay marveled as the tiny King, dwarfed by the container, gripped it with his Silver tech feet and was gone in a streak.

They returned to the Holocone. Kay seated himself and spoke. "The cryochest is on its way. It should be there tomorrow afternoon. Let us turn our attention to Magistrate Kilos. Sarah has informed me of her precarious situation. I would like her restored to full health as soon as possible."

Raal raised his eyebrows. "Pardon, sir? How are we to do that? I would not advise surgery to re-attach her parts; the significant internal restructuring of her body would make that impossible without disfiguring and possibly killing her."

"Surgery? No, no, just use the items I sent."

"The items you sent?" Raal repeated. "We received a potted

fibrous plant of a highly toxic nature and a tankard of slightly heavy water. What import are they?"

"What import? They are how Ghome is stealing parts; using the water and the dust from the plant. I've seen the process in action sure enough."

"Elaborate, please."

"The plant, though it looks like a mere weed, is pure Ethylberry. The water is from some place called Salonmae."

Raal made a few notes. "Ethylberry? I see. And the water is from Salonmae, you say? Salonmae is a spring located on Trimble in Xaphan space. The water is said to possess remarkable qualities."

"It does have remarkable qualities. I have been made privy to Ghome's secret. The water, in conjunction with pollen from the plant, is the secret to Ghome's technique."

"We know, of course, of the various legends from League and Xaphan worlds surrounding a magical substance called Ethylberry. We know the fanciful stories and so forth. We have quested for such a substance in the past; the Knickerbaums performed an investigation into it, I believe. However, we have never been successful in securing any specimens. We therefore believe Ethylberry to be a substance of myth and nothing more. Where did you acquire this sample from, please? I'm assuming you are not a botanist by trade."

"You assume correct. It was given to me by a notable source, and I have witnessed it in operation. Laika was brought from the brink of death with it."

"And who performed this healing?"

"I did. With the Ethylberry and the water I was able to restore her to full health, and I am no Hospitaler."

"Haitathe, is this true?" Raal asked.

Laika crunched away on her jawbreakers and didn't answer.

"Ultra Sarah, would you please scan the Haitathe?" Raal asked. Sarah stood and put her hands on Laika's shoulders. Laika reacted and pushed her away.

"Hold still, Toots, will you?" Sarah said.

"Do not touch Laika's shirt! Laika hates Sarah!"

"Stop it. Just pretend I'm Kay, all right? I need to scan you. Quit fidgeting!"

Laika pulled away and Sarah followed, the two rolling around on the floor with Sarah all over her. Laika shrieked and made a fuss, trying to seize Sarah's holographic form and throttle it. Finally, Sarah jumped off, leaving Laika scowling.

"Damn, that was harder than it needed to be," Sarah said.

"Laika not forget, not forget," she spat, sitting up.

Raal checked his screens. "The finducer data are coming in. Here we are. I am not scanning any trace of injury on the Haitathe. Were the Haitathe grievously wounded I should see traces of it, and I see none. Therefore, she has not been injured recently."

"She had more Jones bullets in her than I could count, along with a hole in her chest large enough for me to put my arm in. The Ethylberry works marvels. Flawless healing."

"Wait!" Sarah cried. "You got it from Carahil, right? In his store?"

"Who is Carahil?" Raal asked.

"He's a source we can trust," Sarah said.

"But, what are his ..."

"Tsk, tsk, Raal. Trust me, ok?"

Though Raal tried to hide it, he was clearly astounded. "Then, we shall perform analysis at once."

"No, no, the time for analysis is over—the time to act is now," Kay said, feeling impatient. "Sarah has told me that Magistrate Kilos cannot hold out much longer, that her sanity and possibly her life are at stake. Use the water and the dust and save her the moment King arrives with the cryochest. Unfortunately, there is only enough dust for one person at this time, so use it on Ki."

Raal made some notes. "Magistrate Kilos is in a Level 3 Insanity Curve. She will awaken a mindless vegetable."

"So? How's that any different than normal? Just do it, Raal," Sarah said.

"Can we acquire more materials, from this Carahil person, perhaps?" Raal asked. "We must test and prove this. We do not perform procedures on patients without knowing precisely what we're doing. We are not Xaphan Cabalists."

"No, though I have been informed where a quantity of lesser dust is available. Ki doesn't have time; she needs to be out of that capsule immediately. You keep mentioning the need to add to your knowledge, so now's a fine time for it."

Raal made notes. "I dislike sounding grim; however, I would not advise using the materials on Magistrate Kilos," Raal said.

"Why not?"

"As I said, because her sanity is probably already lost. Her beta and theta waves show signs of massive degradation. She should already be dead, per our calculations, but Ultra Sarah pushed us to run a Gaming Session on her."

"That session saved her," Sarah said. "She was heading to Deadsville and I wasn't going to allow that to happen!"

"What is a Gaming Session?" Kay asked.

Raal answered. "It is a caustic introduction of sentotarcin, a highly acidic, hyper-tropic alkaloid developed from a type of fungus that plays Mary-Kale with one's brain functions. Injecting it into the cerebellum is known as 'Gaming Up' a subject, and the duration of its influence is known as a Gaming Session."

"Why? It sounds horrible."

"It's a radical step," Sarah agreed, "but Ki was in desperate straits. Raal's not joking about the Insanity Curve she was falling into. The Gaming Session forced her to concentrate on the dreams she's having and not the horrible reality she is currently in. Ki is a tough bird, and I know she'll be fine."

"Sarah, I was told that should I have questions, I should consult with Ki," Kay said.

"Who told you that?" Sarah demanded.

"My contact in Carahil's store. She said Ki would have answers."

Sarah rubbed her chin. "Hmmmm. A Gamed-Up patient's dreams are often hyper-psychic."

"That is not fully proved," Raal said.

"Check your database, it is proved," Sarah replied. "She might have much to tell us when she wakes up."

"If she wakes up," Raal corrected.

Kay worried for Ki. "Magistrate Kilos is a fighter, and she has much to live for. Raal, please use the materials I sent to you and revive her as soon as possible. Simply wash her in the water and then dust on a fine layer of Ethylberry, just a little goes a long way, and re-attach her parts. You'll see instant results. If I can do it, you can do it."

Raal made notes. "We will do what we can. And your Ne-Countess? She is to remain in her capsule?"

Kay felt his heart tug a little. "Sam is in no danger?"

"Not at present, though I disapprove of the psychedelic and rather violent RDP Ultra Sarah has running for her. The Ne-Countess is killing people in her RDP, even as we speak."

"Yeah, Raal, like the bore-me-to-tears RDP you subjected her to wasn't punishment enough," Sarah retorted. "Sam's having fun in the little wonderland I created for her. She's storming St. Vith Cathedral right now, kicking pirate butt! She thinks they've got you captured in the cathedral, Kay, and she's tearing them apart to get to you. She just loves you to death, doesn't she? She's going to be thanking me when she wakes up."

Kay jumped back in. "Then she must remain where she is for now. Ki's need is greater and we do not yet have Sam's stolen parts in any case."

"As you wish, Lord Blanchefort. We will do our best, but I promise nothing, you understand that, correct?"

"I do. Thank you," Kay said. "Now, onto our next pressing topic. The Jones have proved themselves to be a pack of unprincipled barbarians. They came at us in our home in full battle array: Battle Units, GWs, snipers, H-Grenadiers, the works. They also committed atrocities upon our staff, and that is unforgivable by any measure."

"The effects of their hypnosis will not last more than a day or two."

"Oh? They did more than just that—they Hypered them," Kay said. "The staff are innocent people in our care who have been violated! Mutilated! And I demand they be tended to at once!"

"We have covered this ground before, Lord Blanchefort."

"Aye, and we shall cover it again! You're fortunate that I'm not going to the Sisters with this outrage—since when does a Hospitaler sect kit out in full array against a League Great House and its servants?"

Raal stirred. "You know the reasoning. They are under Ghome's influence. Introducing the Sisters into this situation will result in the certain deaths of your Countess and your friends."

Sarah winked at him. "You don't want to see me dead; right, Raal?"

He offered a small laugh. "No, Ultra Sarah, actually I don't. I look forward to the time when I may properly introduce myself to you in the flesh." He turned back to Kay. "I warned you to be careful and to expect nothing less than their best effort, did I not? The Jones are under *Her* sway, and will treat you, and your people, with no mercy; and, as you have seen, they are quite deadly. I hadn't thought it needed repeating."

"Attacking me and Laika is one thing, but extending the conflict to include our House staff is completely unacceptable. I demand the Hospitalers immediately tend to the medical needs of our staff and cleanse the castle of their wretched Horvath Creeper plants while it's still relatively empty. I'd like Ennez of Innari or Bethrael of Moane to supervise the process. They both may be reached via the Knickerbaum Sanctum in Minz."

Raal appeared conflicted. "There are complications ..."

Kay was ready to explode. Sarah waved him into silence and jumped in. "Well, listen, Raal, my uncle, Captain Davage, and my aunt, Countess Sygillis, have gotten wind of the goings on at the castle in their absence, and they are on their way back to Kana with a small armada in tow. If they arrive and then head on to Bazz to blast The Jones to smithereens, the Sisters are certainly going to get involved."

Raal rubbed his forehead.

"Oh, come on, Raal," Sarah said. "We talked about this earlier. We're out here putting our butts on the line. Help us out a little bit. Throw us something, will ya? Help our people."

Laika protested. "Laika does not recall Sarah there when Jones attacked. It was Jarlcon and Laika who faced Jones, not Sarah."

"Yeah, but I was all worried and everything. I was there in spirit."

Raal relented. "All right, Lord Blanchefort, I agree that your request is not unreasonable. I'll make the arrangements at once. You needn't worry about your home or your staff. Tell Lord and Countess Blanchefort not to intercede at this time. I am thinking in the best interests of your Ne-Countess."

Raal checked his screens and appeared troubled. "Lord Blanchefort, have you been exposed to a Horvath Creeper?"

"Yes, The Jones left them all over our castle and they robbed me of my Gifts. Why?"

"Because I'm reading from Ultra Sarah's finducer information that you are infected with it."

"I'm what?"

"The Horvath Creeper is, among other things, parasitic to those with Gifts of the Mind. Gifted brains, such as yours, are the perfect ground to germinate a Creeper. Its spores embed themselves in your head by way of the maxillary sinus and go dormant until you encounter a sizable pool of fresh water. Thus infected, you will not be of your own sound mind. In the presence of calm water, the spores will activate and compel you to go into the water and drown yourself. Several weeks later, after feasting on your brain matter, the Creeper will burst out of the water straight from your head."

Kay sat there a moment, horrified. He felt sick to his stomach. "That ... sounds terrible."

"Never fear, we have remedies to treat it. However, until you receive such treatment, you will want to avoid close proximity with shallow pools of fresh water."

"I'll make it a priority. You can count on it."

"You have Ultra Sarah and the Haitathe with you, insure they monitor your activities at all times. The immediate effects of exposure to Creeper spores will last about a day, and then your Gifts will return. Also, be advised, your Gifts will behave erratically until the spores are extracted. Use them with caution."

"Excellent, thank you for the advice," Kay said. "Please let us know what Magistrate Kilos' status is once she has been made whole. Be bold and aggressive in her treatment, Raal. Do not relent until she is restored and do not waste the materials I have provided you. We are to Bazz to pursue Queen Ghome and take her into custody."

"Understood. Raal out."

Later, Sarah and Laika were having a heated argument.

"Let go of the controls, you six-breasted bitch!" Sarah screamed.

Laika was perched in the pilot's chair and was not budging. "Laika hates Sarah!" she roared. "Laika ready to fly!"

"This is my ship and I'll be doing the flying, so get your big butt out of my chair or I'll shock the hell out of it!"

Laika clung to the chair for dear life.

"I'm going to light you up!" Sarah roared. "You've got ten seconds!"

Kay laughed to himself. "What is going on?"

"Your buddy is a pain in my rear!" Sarah said. "Kay, tell her to get out of my chair right now before I decide to get really nasty."

Laika grit her teeth. "Laika is going to enjoy wringing Sarah's neck! There will be no peace between Laika and Sarah until one is dead!"

"Now you ..."

"Sarah, Sarah, one moment, please," Kay said. He took Laika's hand and helped her out of the pilot's chair. Laika quivered with rage and appeared to be ready to fight Sarah to the death, her hair fluffed up and frazzled. "Laika, Sarah has been nice enough to let us fly in her ship. This is her vessel, let her pilot it in peace, please."

Laika turned a bright shade of red and hugged herself around the waist.

"Laika wanted to show Jarlcon Laika could fly ship."

"I'm certain Sarah will be nice enough to let you pilot the

ship later on, right Sarah?"

"She's had no training!"

"She never forgets anything she sees, Sarah. By now, she should be fully briefed on piloting this type of vessel, so you're going to let her pilot it later, right?"

Sarah thought about it and kicked at the floor with her holographic boot. "Well, all right. You can fly later after we're done at Bazz, and don't bug me about it and don't piss me off until then."

"Great, did you hear that, Laika? You can pilot the ship later on. Thanks, Sarah. See, it's not that hard to get along, is it? So, Sarah, what's our ETA to Bazz?"

"About ten and a half hours."

"Ten hours, six minutes, twenty-three seconds, Sarah," Laika corrected. "Jarlcon requires precise information."

"Whatever," Sarah replied. "I've already got a nice quiet berth booked for the ship, which will give me plenty of range with the holo-emitters and the Monties should we need them."

"Good thinking." Kay stretched. "I'm going to lie down for a bit. Wake me up when we begin the landing sequence."

He went into his cabin and sat down on the bed. He felt very tired and far away from Sam, slumbering in her capsule on Hoban. It had been a while since he'd had a proper sleep. He stretched out on the bed and quickly faded into dreams.

The door to his cabin opened and Laika padded in, bootless, but still wearing her Carahil shirt. She pulled the shirt off, revealing her taut, six-breasted chest, and began the process for removing her armored pants.

"Laika," Kay said. "I have to be firm—these encounters must end. I am very fond of you, you know that, but I am here questing for my Countess, whom I love above all else."

The pants fell to the floor. Laika stepped out of them and stood there nude. She climbed on top of him, allowing him to savor the heat of her body, her giant size swallowing him. Six eager hands quickly undid his clothing and peeled it aside.

"Laika, please," he said.

She brought her head down close to his. "Love Laika ..." she whispered. Her tongue wandered into his ear. "Love Laika ..."

"I cannot."

She moved into him, reaching for his private places, trying to stimulate him into action. She kissed his cheek.

"Laika, stop!" Kay pushed her away. "I said stop, and I mean it! Now go!"

She gazed at him for a few moments, then climbed off and stood there nude, six-armed, six-breasted. He hadn't wanted to yell at her, and he didn't want to disappoint her either, but he could not violate his sacred trust to Sam. He thought he knew Laika well enough at that point that she would be bashful and hurt, quietly taking her things and sulking away to her cabin.

But she didn't do that. Instead, she leaned down and whispered in a seductive voice: "Laika will just wait, then, for Jarlcon is always most eager for Laika when he sleeps. Jarlcon will come to Laika when he is ready for love, and Laika will be waiting."

She gave him a sweltering look and exited.

Kay lay there on the borderlands, unsure if he was awake or asleep. He thought he heard Sarah's voice. *"... I'm going to lock the door for you, Kay ... "*

11—Visitor in the Dark

Sometime later, Kay awoke. It was dark in his cabin. He had no idea what time it was.

His Gifts were still down. He had a miserable notion; wondering if they would ever come back.

He felt there was someone else in the room with him. He thought perhaps someone was standing over him, or possibly sitting in the corner. He saw a flash of gems. He felt someone in bed with him, warm arms around him and the heat of an intimate embrace.

Was he dreaming?

"Kay?" came a voice both near and far, whispering into his ear and dancing on his breath.

"Who's there? Laika?" he replied, his voice groggy.

"It is I, Roethaba."

"Roethaba?"

"I wanted to speak to you, in private. I hope I am welcome to do so."

"Always."

"First, and with all my heart, thank you for being a friend to my Laika, Kay. Raal is wise and skilled, but he has much to learn about certain things. Haitathe feel everything we do, perhaps some things even more so; they simply hide it better. Thank you for your friendship and for saving my daughter's life."

He struggled to respond. "Laika is ..."

"I know, I know. I should have put a stop to it, but she was so happy and it did my heart good seeing her that way. You love your Ne-Countess, you are devoted to her, yet your Sleeping Self is not so loyal. Asleep, you sought out Laika and took her repeatedly. I should have stopped it. Be firm with her, tell her how things must be, and she will respect that."

Roethaba's voice paused. Kay thought he felt her lips touch his. *"I have a number of fears. I haven't shared them with Raal or my other Hospitaler friends; it's just a feeling I have. Sometimes my friends are guilty of thinking too much, of relying on charts and data, and not seeing what's unquantifiable yet plain. And so, I am afraid. With you, I can be candid."*

"Afraid of what?"

"That this is the end, one way or another. Something is not right. My Waking Self, Queen Ghome, knows of me, just as I know of her. We do not, however, know each other's thoughts. She hates the fact that I exist, has pondered it, puzzled over it, wondering how the great Queen Ghome can bear something so mundane and ordinary as a conscience and a heart. And she has tried to stamp me out of existence for centuries. She has cast spells and taken potions; she has mutilated her brain; yet still I exist. Her one true method of defeating me is to take her rest in protected places where the Mentralysis Deck's broadwave cannot reach. She is adept at it. There have been long stretches of time when I have not been seen at all. I think she sleeps in the deep belly of her Bower Chest monster, near to all the things she has stolen. There she is safe. However, about a year ago, she stopped taking whatever safeguards she had been using in the past, and I began appearing every night to my Hospitaler friends on faraway Hoban. Raal attributes it to our people's tireless efforts to broaden the Mentralysis network throughout the League, and in Xaphan space as well. He believes we have achieved a much greater coverage, and that could indeed be the case, but I don't know. I have my doubts. I have a notion that She wants me out amid my people, that She's using me for some sinister purpose. I've been puzzling over it. Many of the things She has done do not make sense."

"What things?"

"Lady Chrysania told me. Please understand; in all this, poor Lady Chrysania is trapped in between us. There are two Waking Selves and one Sleeping Self inhabiting our body. I have told Raal this many times. In the arena of the mind, Raal has strong opinions and believes I am mistaken; he cites any number of medical treatments and statistical improbabilities explaining away my beliefs. I am, however, not mistaken. Lady Chrysania was the original; she the Waking Self and I the Sleeping Self born thousands of years ago in Bloodstein. We were in harmony together; she living the simple life she so desperately wanted, and me hoping to inspire her in dreams. She did not understand her situation; her immortality. She was lost, terrified, grieving over her dead loves as our mutual immortality manifested itself. She sought the help of the Sisters and went to them in Valenhelm, desperate for assistance.

"The Sisters do not tolerate the bizarre. They did not help her; instead, they imprisoned her there, for how long I don't know, but I believe it was a long time, long enough for her to fall into utter despair. In her loneliness and suffering under the Sisters' heel, Ghome

came for the first time, riding the turbid seas of our inner-psyche, whispering in the gentle, easily-swayed Chrysania's ear, promising to free her. All she had to do was relinquish control over our body to Ghome, just for a short time, and she would be free. Chrysania relented and Ghome took over. True to her word, through ruthless exploits, Ghome got us out of Valenhelm; however, her persona was so powerful she never relinquished control, banishing Lady Chrysania into the nether regions of our own mind, keeping her there like a bedraggled servant.

"Ghome uses her from time to time, letting her have control in those select moments when she needs to feign innocence before discriminating Staring eyes and when she is blank and without senses—a terrible cruelty. The quiet, despairing woman you spoke with in Castle Bloodstein was Lady Chrysania, not Ghome. If you had Stared her, you would have scanned Lady Chrysania's placid, love-starved mind, not Ghome's evil, raging one. I'm certain that what she told you at Bloodstein she believed to be true—after all this time she still listens to Ghome's lies, desperate for them to be true. Chrysania still has some insight to the outside world and Ghome's activities. Sometimes she tells me things, and what she recently told me, I must share with you."

A knock came at his cabin door. "Kay, we're on approach."

Kay blinked and Roethaba's voice continued. He could feel her holographic body next to his.

"Chrysania didn't understand why Queen Ghome would attack your Ne-Countess and steal her face. Of course, your Lady Sammidoran is very beautiful. She is a Monama, very exotic certainly, but there are many beautiful, many exotic women out there across the worlds, and beautiful men as well, and Ghome has been many of them. Chrysania told me Ghome once took a fancy to the Bers of Trimble; a gypsy people roaming the countryside, very pale like your Sam. And there were the Dames of Carina, whose dim world makes them very pale. She has worn their faces as well. And, She has been Monama too, long ago before She left Kana. She thought she would have free rein, as the Monamas are so isolated and secretive, and She took their faces and attached them to her via surgical methods. The surgery didn't take; the Monamas' flesh is so alien, it..."

Kay felt her body shudder. *"It was a disaster and She developed an aversion to Monama flesh ever after. Chrysania said She swore to never wear them again, a vow She has kept for centuries, until now. So, I ask, why is Ghome suddenly wearing your Ne-Countess'*

Monama face? She has some sort of alternative purpose, I'm certain of it. What it is, I don't know."

Another knock at his cabin door. "Kay. Re-entry. Get up!"

Kay sat up and got himself together. The horrible perfume of the Horvath Creeper that had plugged up his head seemed to be diminishing. He tried Sighting and, to his delight, he saw through the wall and out into the main area of the ship. He saw Sarah's hologram standing outside his door. He recalled what Raal had said, about the Creeper's spores embedded in his head waiting to snare him and sprout. He was eager to be treated and be rid of them.

He felt a pair of arms come around him. He could see their holographic patterns of force.

"This is the end, Kay, one way or the other. I haven't said anything to Raal and the others; they certainly would not take it well. They would insist we pull back and wait, let things die down. Though he hides it well, Raal is a very passionate person, all my friends are. I cannot allow this to continue. Either I will be made whole, or this is the last I will ever be seen. Ghome or Roethaba, only one of us will survive this episode at long last. I'm sorry Lady Chrysania is caught up in all of this; should we be successful, I swear to share our body. My Hospitalers will work night and day to give her time in the sun. You are our champion, sir, mine and Lady Chrysania's. I place my faith in you, to keep your wits about you, to save your Ne-Countess and to do what needs to be done, whatever needs to be done. I cannot depend on Raal or anyone else to do the right thing, they are too close to the matter."

"Are you asking me to kill you?"

"If need be."

"Can you be killed?"

"Anything can be killed, even She and I. We shall meet again, sir, either in this world or the next. I hope there is a place for me there with my Vehelm."

That comment touched him. He turned to see her. He had to see her, and there she was, glittering in her jewel-encrusted holographic gown.

Kay embraced her, taking comfort in her finducer-generated touch.

"How could there not be?" he said.

12—Helios-Mason

Kay buttoned his vest, pocketed his Poltava, saddled his CARG and went out. Ahead, through the front glass, the misty aqua-blue sphere of Bazz hung large like a celestial robin's egg. Laika was standing next to the unoccupied pilot's chair, closely watching the landing sequence process. She had on her boots, but still hadn't finished donning her composite armor.

Kay smiled and tried to put the seduction incident behind them. "Did you get some rest, Laika?"

She turned and held up her composite armor. "Would Jarlcon help Laika with armor?"

Laika turned around and Kay fastened the various clips and straps holding the heavy piece in place as she slid her six arms into the sleeves. "This thing looks very uncomfortable."

"Armor comfortable," she said. "Much better than Hruntha's armor."

"We'll need to replace your banded mail pants and your boots are looking a little old too."

"She's not a dress-up doll, Kay!" Sarah snapped, appearing in the pilot's chair.

"Keep flying, Sarah. As soon as we get this matter settled, we're going to get Laika proper fitted clothes."

Sarah sighed. "Whatever. About ten minutes and we'll be on the ground. There's no need to Cloak us or anything. We're just standard haul traffic."

The Ultra plunged into the formless haze of Bazz's thick atmosphere. The size and weight of the ship made the normally bumpy ride through the rough air fairly smooth, though Laika wasn't impressed. "Fly ship better, Sarah!" she demanded. "Too much V.4."

"Shaadaap!"

Below, the tumbled and meteor-pocked landmass of Bazz appeared through the murk, fully terraformed and filled in with warm water. The prominent Endax Sea to the west was clearly a flooded ancient crater. Eventually, the newly created wind and weather cycles would smooth out the land and the jagged scars of Bazz's primordial past would erode away, but for now, Bazz enjoyed a uniquely wild and pugnacious topography.

The water, greenish-blue, danced with churned up minerals and fresh sediments. It looked oddly inviting to Kay; nice and cool to wade in and have a nice splash, it …

Wait, the Creeper! Water! The Creeper wanted him in the water so it could emerge. He forced the thoughts from his head.

The Ultra came down nice and slow, quietly merging into the well-traveled lanes with other ships from all over the League. Kay thought the lines of traffic looked like strands of hair floating in a bowl of soapy water.

"Here, Laika, take over and follow the heading I've preset. I'm getting tired of flying," Sarah said, stepping out.

Laika hopped into the seat, took the controls and flew like she had been doing it for years. She gripped the control sticks with her middle set of arms, which seemed to be her preferred set. With the lowest set she adjusted dials and flipped switches. Her topmost pair did nothing. "Great work," Kay said, patting her on the shoulder. "Wish I could do that." She beamed with the compliment.

"How are your Gifts doing, Kay?" Sarah asked, scanning him.

"They're back. I tell you, if I see that stupid plant again, I'm going to freak out. That was horrible, and the fact that its residue is in my head and ready to parasitize my brain is enough to send me screaming."

"You'll be fine. Raal and his cronies will have it out of you in a jiffy. But, and I hate to break it to you, The Jones love using that plant against Gifted enemies. Don't think you've seen the last of it, because you're going to be seeing it a lot more."

"If I see anybody coming near me with one, they're getting shot, and I'm not joking."

"Speaking of The Jones," Sarah said. "I was able to briefly hack one of their less well-defended portals. Looks like, after kicking your butt, they came in and had a ceremony featuring a visiting dignitary of high regard at their main sanctum in Helios-Mason the other day."

"I suppose we can guess who that is," Kay said.

"Yep. Then, the dignitary and a contingent of Jones headed out to their research facility in Gallia, which is just west of the city. I'll bet all of our stolen stuff's there too. Gallia Palace. That's where she is right now; ripe for the taking."

"Once we're down, we'll need to formulate a plan against The Jones. This time, we'll be operating on their home arena."

"You didn't have 'Ultra Sarah' with you last time, did you? Trust me. We'll do it from the ground and be absolutely secure. Laika—bring us in!"

"Jarlcon does not need Sarah," Laika said.

"Why don't you just call him 'Kay'?" Sarah asked. "You're going to give him a big head or something, and I don't need that. I've got to live with this guy."

"Because Jarlcon has earned Laika's respect and devotion."

"Oh, that? You do know as soon as Sam's back on her feet, you're history, right?"

"Sarah, please stop antagonizing her," Kay said.

"Just keeping things real."

Laika flushed up.

The southern continent of Bazz grew large in the glass. Laika followed the fairly heavy traffic moving over Helios-Mason, one of the larger cities on Bazz. The messy sprawl of low, iron-wrought buildings came into hazy view. To the west near the coast of the Endax Sea was a great collection of smooth black spheres pushed high into the sky, dappled with red lights and golden struts, dominating the surrounding skyline with obsidianlike glassiness.

"That's The Jones' Sanctum over there," Sarah said. "Too bad we can't just haul off and put a full spread into 'em just for dragging us to Bazz."

A transponder signal came in. "Laika, follow that signal; that's our ship park. We're not landing in Helios-Mason; we're heading west to a little place called Willom-Lester. We're supposed to be picking up a load of Zemuda in a day or so. I faked everything, even an illegal load out. If you want to look legit, be illegit."

"If you're faking everything, then why not fake us something legal?" Kay asked.

"Oh please ... What fun is that?"

Laika veered away from the streams of traffic over the city, following a route west over the dry Bazz countryside to a small city huddled up against an impressively high wall of black stone that ran north and south.

"That's the Gallian Wall," Sarah said. "It runs all the way from the Endax Sea to the ocean, about five hundred miles." Sarah regarded Kay intently. "How you doing? Is the water freaking you out or anything?"

"No, Sarah, I'm fine, thank you. What's the wall for?" Kay asked.

"It's to protect the Gallian Torr, an endangered beast that roams the Gallian Plain. It's sacred here on Bazz. The wall is to keep people out."

The beam Laika was riding led them to the outskirts of the city, to an isolated yet secure ship park just outside of the city proper. A mixture of high and low rent shipping, some needing a paint job and some body work, was scattered about on their platforms. Laika skillfully brought *The Ultra* down and landed it with hardly a bump.

Sarah called up a holoscreen. "Ok, I'm going to set the ship's engines to idle at 5000 Mags, so my holo-emitters will have maximum range without attracting any unwanted attention." She rapidly adjusted settings on the screen. "The Monties are online and ready to go should we need them for Surface-to-Surface action. Great, let's move out!"

Laika checked her LLAG pistols and slung her new DeeDee rifle over her shoulder into its holster. She tied her bag from Carahil's store to her belt. Kay Cloaked Laika into invisibility and altered his appearance. Sarah shut off her hologram visualizations and faded into invisibility, though Kay could Sight her holographic lines of force. They piled out of the ship, Kay instantly withering in the humid Bazz summer warmth. Heat, humidity, it was like a wet glove all over him; a flexible unpleasant membrane from which there was no escape. Sarah shut the hatch and locked it behind them.

"Gods, it's hot," Kay said.

"Quit complaining, will you?" Sarah replied. "You should feel what it's like to be in the damn coffin I'm in back on Hoban. It's so cold in that capsule, if I had boobs right now they'd be standing on end, saluting. And, I'm getting fed hot mush through a straw. Now that sucks!"

"Laika, are you ok in this heat?" he asked. She nodded and took her place at Kay's side.

"Let's find a good inn somewhere in the center of the city that'll be ideal for our needs. We'll need one with a dense D-band into the Bazznet," Sarah said. "I saw a few adverts for a place called the Inn of the Hidden Surprise. They had a pretty decent Holo-Temple. I think that will do nicely."

"We don't have time for an inn, Sarah."

"No, no—an inn will be perfect! Perfect! We can patch into the Bazznet network and send an untraceable message off to Raal and his Hospitalers on Hoban to see if they have any intel for us. The Jones won't be able to trace nothing. Hard-wired into the Bazznet, I'll fix it so they'll never find us."

They wound their way through the twisting streets wrought with brick and iron and filled with sweaty locals wearing gaudy clothing and pungent with the strong smells of the red spicy food characteristic of Bazz. A noisy people never shy about public dramatics, the Bazzers filled their ears with shouts and casual cursing. Bazzers pushed and shoved each other yelled from balconies, yelled from street-level, turning minor disagreements into a full-blown spectacle right out in front of everybody.

"Very warlike people," Laika remarked, seeing all this happening around her.

"Yep, you'd love it here," Sarah said.

Ladies with the usual sicklelike Bazz sideburns presented themselves to Kay as he passed, twirling them around their fingers and winking at him. They lingered in doorways and at the top of stairs; some smoking pipes filled with muddy-scented tobacco blew impressive smoke rings at him.

"You know what the sideburns mean, the Mollocks, right?" Sarah asked.

"It means they're unmarried. A Bazz tradition."

"More than that, it means they're looking," Sarah said.

One of them, holding a tray of steaming baked goods, tried to give Kay a friendly kick in the shins. He had to restrain Laika from drawing her swords in reprisal.

"They're making it plain they're interested in you, Kay," Sarah said. "Shin-kicking is a Bazz thing. I kind of like it. Kana's too bland and proper sometimes. You like somebody, go ahead and kick 'em one in the shins. Let them know all about it. I gave Raal a nice boot to the shins the other day. You should have seen him."

"Why?" Kay asked.

"'Cause I like him. He's smart. He's really good at what he does. I think he's handsome too. What do you think? You see me and Raal as a couple?"

"No!" Laika answered. "Sarah will not be very pretty when Laika is finished."

Kay laughed. "Sarah, I think we're finally seeing a little deviation between yourself and how you are when you're awake. Raal is not your type at all—you don't fancy intelligent men, you go for meatheads. You always have. Remember, you had that big crush on that idiot Lord Merc from the House of Park? The man was a disgrace."

Sarah winkled her nose. "Ewww ... I don't want to court a dumbass. I want to have a conversation, I want to find out things. I'll bet the walking-around me goes for knuckle-draggers to get an edge or something—that sounds like something I'd do. Well, I like Raal just fine. I guess you're going to have to get my head on straight or something. I don't want an idiot. I want a man who looks good and thinks fast. I want Raal—maybe tonight, when he's in bed, I might just have to show him how well these finducers on me work, *all* of them. It's pretty cool I can be here on Bazz saving your butt and there on Hoban getting all snug with Raal at the same time. Hey, Kay, promise me you're going to have a talk with me, ok?"

"Yeah, sure." Kay wrinkled his nose. "The smell of the food alone is making my nose hurt."

"Smells good to me," Sarah said. "Too bad. I wish we had time to grab a bite. I love Bazz food, it's got heat."

"Sarah cannot taste," Laika said.

"I fixed that problem, small fry. Gimme one of those jaw-breakers. Come on!"

Laika refused.

They entered a square in the heart of Willom-Lester lined with iron-wrought shops and cafes pungent with spicy aromas laced with hints of wild animal smell and a dash of body odor. Seated in the center of the square was a jostling crowd of Bazzers, each one invading the personal space of the others. Foreigners from across the League were scattered about, some seeming rather nervous while others took in the controlled chaos all around them with glee. Some had Atmospherics hired to create them a personal bubble of cool air to squelch the pounding Bazz heat. Kay rather envied them. He hated the heat.

Members of The Jones were seated here and there in the square having lunch. Some were getting nickel-and-dimed by the locals hoping for free medical advice. Laika and Sarah were Cloaked and Kay had altered his appearance, so they passed without issue.

"The Jones sitting out there are giving me the creeps," Sarah said, gazing at them with caution.

"Not all Jones are in the service of Queen Ghome," Kay replied.

"Yeah, but which is which?"

At the far end of the square was a landscaped inn curly with iron terraces and painted brick walkways lined with exotic Bazz plants bursting with tropical color. It was a place clearly too expensive for the locals to afford, and they eyed it with scorn.

"Here's the place, I think," Sarah said.

"This one?" Kay asked. He read the sign. "The Inn of the Hidden Surprise. Seems like a decent establishment."

"Yep," Sarah replied. "It features a dense D-band connection to the Bazznet network. It's also air-conditioned, Kay, which I assume you can't live without."

"Thanks, Sarah," he said. "Good thinking."

"It's perfect!" Sarah chirped, eager to get inside. "I wonder what the 'surprise' is?" Even as a hologram, Sarah loved hanging around inns and ordering room service. She reached into her holographic duster and pulled out a Credstick. "Here, use this." She handed it to Kay.

"What's this?" he asked.

"It's a holographic Credstick. I programmed it up myself. It works just like the real thing and, what's better, it's got a fake Meta trail, so that if The Jones happen to scan it, they'll think we're from Tantan. How's that for thinking?"

"So, this will still be an honest transaction; the innkeeper won't be cheated?"

Laika beamed. "Jarlcon is honorable."

"Of course he won't," Sarah replied. "This Credstick's hooked into the Hospitalers' account on Hoban via back-channels. This one's on Raal and he'll be lucky if we don't order a big lunch or something on his tithe," Sarah said. "The Jones aren't playing around. They've got an army of networking engineers snooping for us high and low rent, and if they catch wind of our trail here on Bazz in their backyard, it's on."

Dubious and with the Cloaked Laika flanking him, Kay approached the innkeeper and rented a suite with the holographic Credstick. The transaction went through without issue and they moved through the complicated courtyards of the inn dotted with benches and swimming pools; had they not been on a specific mission, it would have been an interesting place to explore. All the hidden alcoves and little turns, and …

Swimming pools! Kay stared at them. They seemed so cool and inviting, so calm and clear; to plunge in, to allow the water to wash away the layer of Bazz heat and filth …

"Hey!"

Kay found himself lifted into the air by Laika, dangling from her hand by his vest. He was dripping wet. He thrashed about and

Laika set him down, keeping a firm hand on his shoulder. "What happened?" he asked, coughing up water.

"You jumped in the freakin' pool and sank to the bottom, that's what happened," Sarah said. "Toots here had to fish you out. Remember, this Creeper business is serious stuff and until you get rid of it, you cannot be expected to control yourself." She glanced up at Laika. "Got it, babe? If he jumps in the damn water, you pull him out. Slap him up if you have to."

"Laika watches over Jarlcon," she said. "Laika protects Jarlcon."

"Well, at least you're earning your keep," Sarah said. "Come on." They pressed on until they found their room deep within the lacy labyrinth of the inn, Laika hovering close to Kay. He unlatched the door. Inside was a spacious, cooled room complete with two bedrooms and a private terrace that looked out onto yet another swimming pool.

"Jarlcon, Laika wishes to become comfortable," Laika said, removing her weapons belt and tossing it onto the couch with a clank.

"Go ahead."

She laid her DeeDee on a chair and wandered into one of the rooms. Kay soon heard the shower come on, while Sarah immediately began fooling with the room's networking equipment, pulling out wires and boards and conjuring holo-screens and displays in mid-air.

Kay, drenched, watched with awe; it was like witnessing the Professor at work. "You really know what you're doing?" he asked as he wrung out his hair.

"Yep," she replied as screens whizzed around her head. "I'll have us all setup here in just a sec and we'll be untraceable. I'm going to increase the power a little from *The Ultra*, and then we hunt Queen Ghome." She flicked her hand across the air; a holo-screen appeared and she rapidly worked the controls.

"Is there any risk in doing that with the power?"

"Sure. The Jones could detect us if they are monitoring the Bazznet; and if they're actively looking for us—which is a distinct possibility—they might more easily discover our location. But I think we need to risk it. We can't let Queen Ghome get away from Bazz. We'll never find again her if she escapes back into Xaphan space."

He shut the thick drapes and locked the doors. Sarah fiddled with her displays. "Look at that … the Bazznet's in the mud. Oh, The Jones are looking for us, all right. They're slowing the whole network down with all the sub-processes and traces they're running. They've got their hooks into everything. If we had Credsticked a lunch or sent an open Com to Kana, they would have made us instantly. But thanks to me and my mad skills, they think we're still on Kana."

"You did all that just now?" Kay asked.

"Ok, ok, my boyfriend Raal and his cronies on the Gold Coast and Tereth Norr helped out a little. Just a little, mind you. I'm going to be a while here sorting this out; why don't you scope out The Jones and see if you can get a visual. Tal de Roga and What's-Her-Name should be west of here in their testing grounds at Gallia Palace. Don't go outside unless you need to and are Cloaked. The Jones are probably Sat-Scanning for us as well; they can make us from orbit just by scanning the top of your head." She took note of his drenched clothes. "You should get changed, and mind the bath tub. Honestly, we're probably going to have to have Toots monitor you at all times when you're near any sort of water or water-bearing vessel."

"Change into what? I didn't bring a change of clothing. It's not like we had time to properly pack for this trip."

"They probably have a robe or something in your room. Go on, I'll be a little bit."

Kay wandered into his room and searched the closet, finding a thick robe made of some sort of plush Bazz fabric. He changed into it and laid his clothes out to dry. The room was fairly nice and clean, with cool air clanking steadily through a vent. A glass door opened onto a sunlit patio. He closed the drapes and checked the door; could be Jones out there, he mused.

Through the bathroom door, he heard Laika bumping around having her shower. He imagined her, giant-sized, leaning over, water dripping off and covered with soap. He found the bag from Carahil's store and fished around through the contents. He pulled out the Sam action figure he had tossed in. He took in her pale, delicate features and coal-black hair. So beautiful, holding her jar that would one day carry their children. He placed the box by the head of the bed and felt comforted by its presence. He wondered where King was with the container and how he was getting along. He should be arriving on Hoban right about now.

He relaxed and let his Sight go. It felt so good to have it back after having it squelched by the Horvath Creeper. His Sight drifted through the confines of the room, through the iron and brick hive of the city, and headed west to the massive wall at the edge of the city proper. Kay scanned the wall; it went all the way from the Endax in the north to the South Bazz Sea over five hundred miles distant.

Beyond the wall to the west was a great yellow plain sweltering in the heat. Farther and farther his Sight stretched, surging across the arid Gallian Plain. The plain was quite deserted, save for wild Bazz animals roaming about singularly and in famished packs.

He continued on. A compound appeared alone on the vastness of the plain.

Gallia Palace.

It was a sheer black square, turreted at the four corners in a stark, unrecognizable style, rising up out of the flat Gallian Plain like a battlement-studded fortress built for giants. It looked very out-of-place in wild Bazz, surrounded by an immense curtain wall and carpeted with landscaped grounds green and lush with pumped-in water. Kay saw the perimeter of the compound was crawling with Jones in their opera-cloaks and white shirts. Hired security, armed with an assortment of weaponry, also prowled the ramparts. Inside was a collection of stained wood and other bits of artwork and finery, unabashed in its opulence.

Kay became dimly aware of the bathroom door opening as he Sighted. Laika, slick from the shower, poked her head out and entered the room, a cloud of steam following her. She selected a shirt from the Carahil bag and sat down on the bed next to him, the bedsprings squeaking.

"What does Jarlcon see?" she asked with wonder.

"I see Gallia Palace, miles away. Many Jones there."

Kay continued his covert, long-range scan of the Jones compound. He found, beneath the structure, a great gathering place or meeting hall sheathed in polished black marble veined with rivulets of gold and burnished amber. There was a semi-human, distorted statue mounted at one end of the hall. It was made of hammered gold with acid-green eyes. The statue was displayed with reverence.

It was a monster of some kind. Could it be the Bellathauser creature Tal de Roga had mentioned in such glowing terms; the pinnacle of human perfection?

Moving on, Kay saw a honeycomb of lower levels stretching far beneath the compound, rather like Raal's Hospitaler sanctum on Hoban. Several levels below was a hydroponics garden growing thick with large, fibrous plants sporting a carpet of frosty white flowers showered with mist and vibrant artificial light.

He shuddered. The Horvath Creeper, a plant he had come to dread and whose spores waited in his head to erupt like golden grenades, was cultivated under Gallia Palace in abundance. He hoped in the coming battle he might have the opportunity to burn that garden down to the ground. If he could make the Creeper extinct on Bazz, he would do so.

Kay continued. He saw The Jones moving about here and there, along with Bazz servants and other comers and goers.

Wait!

Mixed in with The Jones at the palace were some of his house staff; he recognized their faces. They were wearing summer touristy clothing and strappy sandals, as if they were on an exotic holiday. Some were arm-in-arm with the Jones as they strolled the lavish corridors of the palace. Some were sharing their beds. He picked out about twenty of them, including Andorra, his mother's personal assistant. She was barely dressed. It was shocking to see her in such a state. Their presence would, as The Jones no doubt intended, greatly complicate matters.

Sighting further, he dreaded seeing Queen Ghome, the evil waking half of the saintly Roethaba of George, wearing Sam's face. He really didn't want to see her in such a situation—he had no idea how he would react. Would he be sad? Would he be disarmed? He had no idea how he would feel. But, in searching the palace high and low, he couldn't find any trace of her. He Sighted a lavish bedroom in one of the towers of the mansion complete with servants coming and going and continuously refreshed trays of drink and food. He saw a rumpled grand bed get made with care and fresh sheets. He saw baths drawn and tables set with scintillating feasts. He saw a boudoir of grand mirrors and marble tables fully stocked with wooden bowls filled with rare powders, brushes, combs, boxes of jewelry and other things that a wealthy woman of reverence would have, yet Kay saw no Sight of Her.

What did Roethaba say, that Ghome had access to vast arcane powers that were unique and undocumented? Perhaps she could Cloak herself from Kay's Sight, just as she had the security cameras in Castle Blanchefort. He was certain she was there, that she haunted the corridors, sat at the boudoir, bathed in the water, ate at the table and slept in the bed, and was somehow evading his Sight. He might have already passed over her, unaware of her presence. She might be sitting at the boudoir even now, looking at Sam's face reflected back at her with Sarah's eyes.

She was so much more than the humble, horribly stricken woman she had passed herself off to be at Castle Bloodstein. Though, what had Roethaba said: *"Lady Chrysania is innocent ... A lost soul drifting in their head."*

Moving on, Kay located a side building near the main house. Inside were dozens of studious-looking Jones sitting at sophisticated-looking holo-terminals. They were busy crunching data in long streams. Must be the engineers Sarah had mentioned, searching the Bazznet for traces of their passing.

Ah, there was Tal de Roga! He was standing majestic on a terrace near the top of the palace, wearing his baggy white shirt and cloak fluttering in the breeze. Kay's face stung a little, recalling the expert pounding de Roga had put on him.

His ability to zoom in with his Dark Sight and kill point blank like he was standing right there worked even at this vast distance. He had never done such a thing before—Vith honor held him. His father, Captain Davage, would do no such thing, even if he had the ability to do so, to assassinate an enemy from afar with no hope of defense or retaliation.

It was unheard of, unthinkable.

... Sam in her capsule, faceless ...

Kay squared him up, zoomed in, erasing the miles between them. To assassinate an enemy without care or fuss, Kay had always treated his enemies with fairness.

But, for Tal de Roga, a man who had desecrated his home, hypnotized his staff, attacked with full battle array, who beat him near to death, infected him with parasitic spores and injured his loved ones

...

He who was in the service of the enemy ...

Where was his gun? All he had to do was fetch it, aim, and pull the trigger and Tal de Roga would know the price for his folly.

He was ready. "Laika ..." he mumbled.

He heard an answer somewhere in the distance and felt a soft hand touch his shoulder.

"Can you get me my Poltava, please?"

The bedsprings squeaked. A few moments passed, Laika bumped about the room.

Then: "Jarlcon, pistol."

She placed it in his hand, he felt the cool familiar smoothness of his Poltava come into his grip. He cocked the hammer and aimed. Tal de Roga's death was but seconds away. But, as he attempted to zoom in and lock on, de Roga's image flickered and faded out, only to re-appear elsewhere. He couldn't lock on. Raal had told him the Creeper spores embedded in his head would foul the working of his

Gifts, and here it was, foiling his efforts.

He blinked in frustration and was back in his room at the inn. Laika was sitting next to him, damp from the shower, her long hair draped over her shoulders in wet strings. "What does Jarlcon see?" she asked.

"Tal de Roga. Miles away. I was going to shoot him dead. My Gifts are too erratic. I couldn't zero him."

"Kay!" came Sarah's voice from the main area. "Kay!" she said again, "come out here, please, now!"

Kay wearily stood and put his pistol in the pocket of his robe. "Get dressed," he said to Laika as he exited. Sarah was sitting at the table crunching data. Holo-screens whirled around her head; it was quite impressive to see.

"Did you see the palace?" Sarah asked.

"I did. And I saw Tal de Roga there as well."

Data whirled by. "I've got a silent tap into The Jones' network, and I don't like what I see."

"Why?"

She pointed at a screen. Words printed off at a high rate of speed.

WHERE ARE YOU?
WHERE ARE YOU?
WHERE ARE YOU?
WE KNOW YOU'RE HERE
WE'LL START KILLING THEM
WE'LL KILL THEM ALL

"What's this?" Sarah asked. "Who's '*Them*'?"

"Probably our staff. I saw about twenty of them in Gallia Palace dressed like they're on holiday, including chief of staff Andorra. I tried to assassinate Tal de Roga but I couldn't zero him; my Gifts are too erratic at the moment. With the staff there, they probably would have executed them if I had done so."

Sarah threw up her hands. "Great. They probably want us there on their home turf safe and sound, using our staff as human shields. They probably want you to start signing over money to them or something."

Kay puzzled over the data. "Roethaba mentioned something about that. She thinks Queen Ghome is after something besides just Sam's face."

"Well yeah," Sarah said. "She wants our stuff and our cash too. Why not take it all? Let me get with Raal, he might know something. Until then, we need to lie low and figure out a plan, got it? The Jones are probably hoping we'll just rush right in. Don't make any Coms, whatever you do."

∗　∗　∗　∗　∗

They laid low for the rest of the day. Sarah manipulated the Bazznet, carefully looking for a way out into the system without being detected by The Jones and their army of prowling network analysts. Kay dressed in his newly dried clothes and went out to get food, Laika coming with him. Disguised and Cloaked, they found a noisy market and shopped around. Laika had a healthy appetite but was surprisingly picky and tender of palate, and finding things she would eat was tough on Bazz, where everything was drowned in volatile spices and thick, pepper-laden sauces not to her liking. They bought raw meat, breads, vegetables with mild familiar spices, and took them back to their suite. Sarah was working away when they returned, making slow progress in creating a safe tap into the Bazznet.

"Damn Jones, they're mucking everything up," she complained.

"I think we should mount up, Cloak ourselves and hit them," Kay said. "We get Queen Ghome and our staff and lay havoc on The Jones in retaliation for their Castle Blanchefort escapades. The sooner the better."

"That's easier said than done," Sarah said. "We're going to be out-gunned, out-flanked and operating on their home turf. We need air support. We need something working in our favor. We have *The Ultra* and its Monties, but those automated Jones Winger ships flying around up there will shoot it down in no time—it's too slow. We need something fast and light on the helm—something like the *Goshawk*. I'm doing a low rent search on the broad waves; I'm looking for Phillip and Thomasina. Enough of the lovey-lovey stuff, they need to get their butts over here and they need to bring the damn *Goshawk* with them pronto."

Meat sizzled in the kitchen as Laika squeezed herself in and made dinner. She was eager for Kay to eat her cooking.

"Sounds good," Sarah said. "Smells good, too."

Soon, the cooking was done. Kay and Laika shared dinner while Sarah continued to struggle with the Bazznet.

"Ah—finally! I've got a tap out the Bazznet and The Jones

will never know a thing about it! I'm getting my guy Raal!" Sarah typed at blinding speed.

A few minutes later: "Oh wow! Wow! Hey, Kay, come here!"

Kay sat next to her. "What is it?"

"You won't believe it! Listen!"

Sarah brought up a low-power audio cone. A tiny wheezy voice spoke in the background, draped in waves of static. "Hey ... Kay ..."

He was elated. He put his plate aside. "Ki? Is that you?"

"Yeah ... yeah, it's me." Ki's voice sounded drawn and weary, a far cry from her usual rough and ready tone.

"Are you all right?"

There was a pensive pause. "I've been better, that's for sure. I could use a nip, but the Hospitalers won't put anything in front of me but water. It's like I'm in the bloody Marines again. Can you believe that? Tweeter's here keeping me company." They heard him happily chirp in the background. It was a comforting sound.

Ki was out of the capsule and whole again. King had succeeded in his mission to Hoban. Raal and his Hospitalers had done it. Now that Ki was out of danger, it was a load off Kay's mind. Now he could take a breath; it was one less thing for him to worry about.

She spoke again, and this time her voice was elevated and clotted with emotion. "Next time I see you, Kay ... I'm going to punch you in the face! You got that?"

"Why?"

They heard a noise through the cone. It sounded like crying. Ki's voice was bloated with tears. He had never heard her like that before, ever. "Why, you Vith bastard? Because I'm sitting here next to the capsule containing my son's body. Why didn't you tell the Hospitalers to save my son instead of me? Why? My little boy ..."

Kay didn't know what to say.

"Because," Sarah said, jumping in, "Sebastian is stable. He's doing fine. You, on the other hand, Ki, you big pain in my ass, were critical and ready go headlong into an Insanity Curve. You would not accept the RDP! Go figure you'd be the problem child in the group!"

"My son is more important than I am."

Kay composed himself and jumped in. "All right, let's not go down this path, shall we, Ki? You were going to die and that's a fact. You want your son to grow up without his mother? Do you? How can you expect us to have to stand before him some day and admit that we allowed you to perish when you could have been saved? Your son is a big old tough bat, just like his mother, and he's fine for now. You, on the other hand, needed out of that capsule in a hurry. So, you can be mad at us if you want, but we made the right decision. Look at the choice I had to make. I chose you over Sebastian, over the staff, over Sarah, and over Sam too because your need was the greatest; how do you think that made me feel? But I gladly did it because you're my friend."

"Yeah," Sarah said. "Don't forget, right now I'm just a couple rows away eating my baby paste dinner through an extruder."

There was a delay on the Com, then: "Ok, ok ... I see your point, and ... thanks. Sorry, I ... You know me."

"Forget it. Your job is to get better. Our job is to gather the things we need to get your son and everybody else out of those capsules as soon as possible. I feel better knowing you're there with Sebastian and Sam, watching over them."

"Hey Ki?" Sarah asked.

"What?"

Sarah giggled. "Watch this…"

Over the com, Kay heard a distant sound. *"Boo!"*

Sounded like Sarah's voice.

Ki gave a start. Kay heard her chair slide across the floor and tip over, as if she had suddenly stood up. "Holy Creation! Sarah, where'd you come from?"

"Hahaha! I'm a hologram, baby doll. I can be in lots of places at the same time. I'm on Bazz with Kay, and I'm right there with you in the infirmary. Nice, huh?"

Sarah was ear to ear smiling. "Listen to this, Kay."

knock ... knock ... knock.

"What was that?" Kay asked.

"That was me knocking on the side of my capsule," Sarah said with glee. "There it is, and there I am inside laid out like a loaf of bread. Isn't that creepy?"

Over the Com, Kay heard Ki pick her chair up and reseat herself. "Crazy kid, this must be right up your alley, isn't it?" she mumbled. "Anyway, it's good to see you, Sarah."

"Thanks—hey! Do you remember dreaming?"

Ki's voice was distant. "Hell yeah ... I ... remember dreaming in bright colors. Weird, my dreams are usually pretty monochromatic, I guess. I remember something about a beach, nice blue water. It was the Big Blue on Onaris, I'd know that water anywhere. I'm pretty sure I was seeing Fazo, lots of tourists, lots of pale, un-tanned skin. Lots of sunburns. I was standing there in my old Marine uniform, I think. I was the only person in sight wearing boots. Dang tourists. Phillip and Thomasina were there, at a little inn by the sea. They checked in under some weird name. I banged on their door and told them to knock off the baby-making and get dressed."

"Phillip and Thomasina were at Fazo?" Sarah asked.

"Yeah, yeah. They got married in a temple of Auld down there. I dreamt I was sitting there in the chapel by the sea, watching. There was no baton like they use in the Vith ceremonies. I passed the baton for your mother and father, and for you and Sam, Kay. I kept looking for the baton. I kind of like it."

"Phillip's never wanted to have a Vith-style wedding. He's just not showy enough, I guess," Sarah said.

Ki continued. "Afterwards, Thomasina was walking around in a beach dress with no shoes. Her hair's back to brown again—I can't stand that. Green, brown, pick a color and stick with it. Anyway, yeah, you're right, Sarah, they said they wanted to be alone, no big Vith ceremonies. I'm pretty sure she's already knocked up and all. That was fast."

"I'm going to be an aunt?" Sarah said, chuckling. She called up a floating holoscreen and input data. "Ki, do you remember the name of the inn you saw in your dream?"

"It was the Bridgewater Inn, I remember seeing the sign swinging in the sea breeze," Ki said. "I remember dreaming about it. I was having a nice cold Onaris beer sitting on the beach and I could see the sign."

Sarah pounded data fast. "Well, look at that? Here's the Datatemple for the Bridgewater Inn, on Onaris—Fazo, just like you said, and ... there's Phillip and Thomasina, checked in under the name Lord and Lady Illibuck. Phillip loves using that name as an alias; remember when we were kids and he'd call down to the village and order grog under the name 'Mr. Illibuck'? I ought to get them a truckload of pizzas sent to their room or something and hit 'em with the tab."

Ki waited a moment to respond, her voice a dry rasp. "I must have got lucky or something, right? It was just a dream, right?"

"Nope," Sarah said.

"Why not?"

"Because we Gamed you up to keep you sane, Ki. A Gaming Session is a hyper-energetic Mentralysis state achieved by introducing stenotarcin into your brain."

"What's that?" Ki asked.

"It's an acid. It puts a lot of tension on your synapses and it's really not very healthy for it to be there, but it helped protect your sanity while you were on ice. It gave you something hard to focus on. It was a risky move, but you're a risky sort of person, Ki. Gamers often have very accurate dreams of places they've never been before."

Kay jumped in. "That reminds me. Carahil's daughter, Atha, did mention to ask you for information, Ki. She told me that twice."

"Carahil's daughter?" Ki asked.

"Yep."

"Didn't know he had a daughter."

"Did you dream of anything else other than my brother and Thomasina consummating their marriage?" Sarah asked. "Any info you can give us would be great."

There was silence over the Com for a moment.

"I also dreamt of a demon," Ki said. She paused a moment. "No, wait, I dreamed of Sam."

"Sam?"

"It was Sam, but she was really creepy, and mean too. Not like the Sam we know at all. I saw her looking through the windows of the chapel while Phillip and Thomasina were getting married. I about jumped out of my chair. I thought it was a demon, but it was Sam. I could feel her looking at me. She creeped me out and I drew my gun. She fled and dragged this girl off the beach."

"What girl?" Kay asked.

"Some girl, said her name was Chrysania. Maybe it was Lady Chrysania of Bloodstein."

Kay and Sarah exchanged glances. Ki continued. "Sam dragged Chrysania into this weird underground tunnel and I went in after her. Inside was this long corridor lined with glass cases like you'd see in a museum."

"What was in the cases?"

"Stuff; treasure, I guess. It was Sam's stuff. Just stuff that she liked and kept out to look at every day as she passed by. Something important was in those cases. She didn't know what she had."

"What things?" Kay asked.

"Don't know. Just a feeling. And then the corridor ended in a large, walled-in enclosure. The sky was yellow—not on Onaris anymore."

"Where were you?"

"No clue. Not Onaris. The last thing I remember, the courtyard I was in was piled up with stolen treasure. I think it was Castle Blanchefort treasure. I think the Machine was there, piled up with the other stuff still in its Silver tech disguise. There was something in the sky flying around. Something big with wings."

"An air ship?" Kay asked.

Ki's voice was drowsy and slurred. "No, no, it was a monster of some kind. A big one. It reminded me of a Walpole."

"What's a Walpole, Ki?"

"It's a little type of dragon with two legs. You guys need to get with Onaris lingo sometime. Anyway, that's it. Don't ask me because I don't remember anymore. It's making my head hurt."

"Sounds like a heck of a dream," Kay said.

Something happening in the lab distracted Ki. She turned from the cone, her voice acquiring a distant, 'far-off' sound. "Hey, are these weird machines down here supposed to be making all these creepy breathing noises? Hey, hey! Can one of you look at this thing, please?"

"Ki, don't give the Hospitalers a hard time, all right?" Sarah said. "Just relax and get better."

"Yeah, yeah. You wanted me out, so I'm out."

"Rest easy. We'll be in touch soon." Sarah cut the connection. "Ki sounds like her old self, doesn't she?"

"It was good to hear her voice," Kay said. "Do you think we can really rely on her dreams? They sound rather fantastic to me."

"Gamers' dreams are pretty potent and almost always very accurate down to the smallest detail. I've already established that Phillip and Thomasina are getting it on in Fazo, just like Ki said, and Atha said to seek her for questions. You know what? I think that Walpole Ki saw flying around was Ghome's Bower Chest. That might prove it exists. I'm going to do a little digging. And you know what else? I think I'm feeling a little hurt; my brother goes off and gets married and he doesn't invite either of us. I'd have brought Raal as my date. It would have been nice to get him out of his Hospitaler uniform for a change."

"You're not exactly presentable right now though, are you?" Kay said.

"Sarah never presentable," Laika said as she plated up a second helping of the food she had prepared and brought it out to Kay.

"Thank you, Laika," he said, accepting the plate.

She sat down next to him and began eating. Kay finished his plate and set it aside.

"More, Jarlcon?" Laika asked.

"No, Laika, thank you. It was very good. Sarah, I'm wondering if we haven't been approaching this situation completely wrong-footed?"

"What do you mean?"

"I mean we, or perhaps I should say *I*, have been under the impression that all of this is a result of Queen Ghome's desire to wear Sam's face, steal her parts, and have at our money. I took it for granted because Sam is very beautiful, so why wouldn't Ghome wish to wear her face?"

Laika made a noise as she ate, as if to offer a dissenting opinion regarding Sam's alleged beauty.

"Sam's way hotter than you are, Toots," Sarah said. "Even with the extra poundage she's put on recently. Don't think I didn't notice."

Laika scowled.

"Roethaba told me some things while we were inbound on *The Ultra*," Kay continued. "She said that there are actually three people inside her head, not just her and Queen Ghome. Lady Chrysania is another Waking Self, subservient to Queen Ghome."

"You mean the lady we spoke to at Bloodstein wasn't Queen Ghome in disguise?"

"No, it was Lady Chrysania, and she told us what she thought was the truth."

Sarah thought about that for a moment. "You know, that sort of makes me happy. I liked Lady Chrysania, even though I got mad at her a few times."

"Lady Chrysania is sort of a go-between, and she told Roethaba that Queen Ghome loathes Monamas, had a bad experience with them once and never wanted to wear their parts again."

"So?"

"So? If she despises Monamas, why has she gone to these lengths to go after Sam in particular? Why has she gone out of her way to defile our home, to enrage me to the point of madness, ensuring I would follow her to Bazz, the bastion of her Jones followers? She's not exactly fleeing back into Xaphan space, is she? She's taking her good sweet time and left a trail for us to follow, as if she wants me to go after her."

Kay paused a moment. "It's all so clear to me now. Sam was just the bait; it's the bloody Machine she was after all along. I'm certain of it. We have been incredibly naïve, Sarah. Carahil himself said the Machine is a miracle, a one of a kind. It can do things even the gods cannot, he admitted it. With the Machine, no place past, present or future is beyond one's reach—I saved Sam through the veil of time itself with it. The bloody Wunderlucks from Remnath tried to kill us over it. I'm pretty sure Carahil uses it all the time too. How arrogant were we to believe that such immanence in our Grove would not attract infernal attention?"

Sarah, even in holographic form, fidgeted. "How did she know we had it?"

"She didn't at first—that's the whole point. She must have heard rumors that the Machine had been recovered, probably from Wilhella Cormand-Grande. After the destruction of Ethylrelda's Temple, Wilhella said she sent her Gogan Spectres out looking through the ruins for the Machine's arch and couldn't find it—because we had it. And then she started writing op-eds, stating her belief that the Machine had been recovered and put back together. Queen Ghome must have read those postings and started searching for it herself. Look at the Wunderlucks. They were strutting around their holdings in Remnath claiming to any who would listen that they had it. Clara Wunderluck even built a sham iron Machine and put it in their warehouse as proof they had it. Ghome must have caught wind of that and, using helpless Lady Chrysania to hide behind, lured them to Bloodstein to determine if they actually did have it. Remember when Tal de Roga came by and visited with you in the Firth House? He said he had toured many Great Houses, searching for information. When you told him under hypnosis about the Machine in the Grove, he reported back to his master and they set us on the quest to recover Wilhella Cormand-Grande's Perlamum pieces to see for certain if it was in our possession—to see if we would use it to collect the pieces, which we did. I am now convinced The Jones have lured us here to Bazz to capture and force us to deactivate the Silver tech protections around the Machine so they can give it to their mistress as a gift."

Sarah took in the info and it made sense to her. "So, now what are we going to do? If we attack, we're walking into a trap, but we can't let Queen Ghome escape and we can't let them have the Machine either."

"No, of course not. And Ghome still has the dust and Sam's face. They don't have the powering stone, and the Machine is still protected by its Silver tech defenses, so it must be deactivated for now. We'll probably have to hire an army to get the Machine back and keep the Sisters from being alerted. I'm not jeopardizing Sam and you and the rest."

He pushed his plate aside and closed his eyes, allowing his Dark Sight to drift ahead in the near future.

"What are you doing?" Sarah asked.

"I'm going to look into the future and see what is there to see, if anything."

Sarah watched with interest. "Ok. What do you see?"

"Quiet, Sarah!" Laika snapped.

"Will you dummy up! Kay, what do you see?"

He sighed. "It doesn't look good. The Jones know we're here on Bazz, Sarah, they just don't know where exactly. If my Creeper-addled Sight is still to be trusted, bad things are going to start happening about an hour from now. First, The Jones are going to cut you off, Sarah."

"Cut me off?"

"Don't ask me how, but they manage to lock you out of the Bazznet, leaving me and Laika here alone. Then, they take over all the city folk here, probably with a hypnosis wave. I see the locals wandering around outside like zombies, and they're all carrying Horvath Creepers. They've also got an impressive amount of Winger ships casing the planet. If we try to fly off, they're going to be all over us."

Sarah checked her data. "If they're ramping up for something big, they're hiding it pretty well. You sure?"

"As sure as possible. And then I see a huge storm blow in from the west, a big one, almost like a gale. This inn is going to be flattened and a large portion of the town is going to be flooded."

"If Queen Ghome is a Gellar, then she can control the weather. What then?"

"I see my Gifts getting swamped by the bloody Creeper again. I see something about Shadow tech …"

"Shadow tech?"

"And then I see the Machine. Tal de Roga is there, and so is Queen Ghome. By dawn, this mess is going to be decided one way or the other."

Kay became confused. He struggled with his Sight.

"What do you see?"

"I'm not sure. I saw Andorra, my mother's chief of staff, and she was holding a knife, trying to kill me with it, no doubt. And then I saw the sky full of fireballs, like a meteor shower. And that was it. Everything else is blacked out."

Kay turned to Laika. "Laika, you better suit up and get ready to move."

She took her plate back to the kitchen area and padded into her room. Kay stood and headed into his.

"Where are you going?" Sarah asked as she worked.

"I'm going to do something I was hoping to avoid."

13—A Bag of Shadow tech

Kay entered. The room was small and neat, lacy in the Bazz style; a bed in the corner with an iron-wrought headboard, a footlocker, desk and a simple holo-terminal flickering with the Inn's header.

He settled in front of the holo-terminal and hit the keys, trying to get a connection. It was locked.

"Sarah! I need a line out," he called.

She stuck her holographic head in, appearing through the wall like a ghost. "What are you doing?"

"Something I really don't want to." Kay reached into his coat pocket. Sitting there was the card Wilhella Cormand-Grande had given them at Castle Bloodstein, inviting them to her Top of the Universe restaurant in Waam. He had tried to get rid of it numerous times, but the card was stuck in his pocket like a comb of sticky honey, refusing to come out. Now, with his need great, it came out easily, black and ominous in his hand. She had said it was some sort of Whamic, just hold it up near any active terminal and it would seek her out.

Sarah's eyes widened. "Creation—you're trying to contact Wilhella Cormand-Grande! Are you insane? The woman tried to kill the lot of us."

"Who hasn't lately? Things are going to come crashing down and we're going to need all the help we can get. Do it, Sarah, give me a line. Don't worry being sly about it; the Jones are going to have us out of here before long anyway."

Sarah moved through the wall and stood near him. "Ok. You got it."

He held the card near the flickering terminal screen. The card jumped out of his hand and dove into the terminal. The data reacted and smeared about the screen in vivid sprays of color. The psychedelic dance continued for several minutes. Sarah watched with morbid fascination.

Laika re-entered wearing her armor and boots. She also had her cloth bag from Carahil's store tied to her belt. "Laika ready, Jarl-con," she said.

"Good. Sit down, will ya?" Sarah said. "Kay's about to do something really dumb."

The bed groaned with protesting springs and straining slats as

Laika got into it and curled up on her side facing the wall, her hips and ribcage rising up over the valley of her narrow waist. "Laika here to protect Jarlcon," she said from the bed, her voice groggy with sleep.

"Well, I feel safe now," Sarah said as Laika began snoring a few moments later.

The signal went out, passing through light years of empty space.

PLEASE WAIT … printed out on the cone in utilitarian Bazznet script.

Kay sat there waiting for the connection to firm up.

CONNECT …

The screen went dark to smoky black. Something jostled in the darkness and he smelled rich menthol tobacco drifting out of the terminal.

"Whamics. Wow," Sarah said. "There's lot of power in this feed."

Shadow tech formed in front of them.

A sarcastic voice crawled out of the screen: "Well, look who it is … Lord Blanchefort …" On the swirling black cone the mouth of Wilhella Cormand-Grande appeared; tapered feminine lips and a row of white, surprisingly well cared-for teeth. Kay couldn't see the rest of her, only her mouth and teeth, floating.

"How sweet … One time is never enough, is it?" she purred as the mouth detached from the cone and drifted in midair in front of Kay. It noticed Sarah with disgust. "What is this primitive automaton?"

"Primitive?" Sarah cried.

"My cousin is here via remote in case you attempt to attack," Kay said.

The mouth looked reproachful. "Attack? You called me, remember? I'll just cut the line now and be on my way … Bye, bye …"

"Wait!" Kay cried, standing. "I must treat with you!"

Wilhella's mouth was triumphant. "Then get rid of the automaton, it is fouling my connection."

"Like hell!" Sarah cried.

Kay calmed Sarah. "Sarah, go ahead and monitor for Jones activity. I'll be fine."

"All right, but don't do anything stupid."

"It might be a little late for that."

Giving the mouth a dirty look, Sarah exited the room.

The mouth smiled in an evil fashion. "Now then, you couldn't get enough of me the first time, I see."

"I have no particular interest in you or your tawdry games. I contacted you for a specific point of business."

The mouth frowned. "No, no, no, my love," it chided. "You should understand me better by now. You want something, you come and see me in Waam-Core. I've our usual table set aside. I insist ... Imagine the postings: Wilhella Cormand-Grande, the Mad Black Hat of Waam and the Queen of Gothan, versus Lord Kabyl of Blanchefort, Invernan. Who shall be victorious, I wonder? It shall make for smashing reading."

Kay swiped at the mouth and it fluttered about like a giant fly evading a swatter. "I demand that you listen to me, Black Hat!"

The mouth darted away and tittered in delight. Kay unsaddled his CARG and ran the horn through its open lips. Wilhella's Whamic mouth, like a ring on a lance, hovered for a moment and then latched onto the shaft of the CARG, as if performing a sex act upon it.

This was not working. Kay was playing into Wilhella's eternal and obvious need for attention. He decided to change his tactics. "It appears you are incapable of entertaining a promising business offer and are therefore not worth my time. I think I'll contact Jenna-Maxx of Waam instead."

The mouth was appalled. "Jenna-Maxx? What can that sniveling slut do that Wilhella Cormand-Grande cannot?"

"Much, apparently. And I intend to let League Society know what an incompetent buffoon you are. When I'm done with you, your name shall be a laughing stock here in the League."

That seemed to get her attention. "Many have died for less," the mouth said.

"Truth be told? It seems I survived your previous attentions with ease. I've had much sharper knives at my throat. Laika, it seems I have wasted my time with this bore."

"*Bore*!?!?!" The mouth grew large and pulled back into a straight, annoyed line. It got into Kay's face. "I have been called many things, but certainly never a bore. Come to me in Waam and we shall see how bored you are! I've plenty of entertainments in mind for you!"

"I told you, I am not coming to Waam."

"Then name your game and we shall play. Would you care to quest for my pieces again? I have them all re-hidden just waiting for a brave soul to fetch them."

"We'll play the 'Helping Game'. I need your help."

The mouth became quizzical and then gave a wry, wicked smile. "My help? I see ... And what can I do to help you?"

"I need a favor."

"*A favor*?" it cried with a sour note. "Not in four hundred years have I granted a favor to an Invernan, or anyone else for that matter. I do believe I admire your idiocy and raw nerve. Go on, ask your favor."

"I need Shadow tech."

"Shadow tech? Is that all?"

"Yes. I need it. Will you offer some up?"

Wilhella considered it for a moment. "What do you need Shadow tech for?"

Kay decided to hit her with the truth. "I am surrounded, out-gunned, soon to be denied use of my Gifts and facing an ancient enemy. The people are entranced and a terrible storm is about to blow in."

The mouth pulled back in thought. "Really? Sounds most distressing, you must be facing a Gellar of particularly evil note. Well, then, I never give away anything for free, Lord Blanchefort, that should be obvious. What will you give me in return for this favor, for saving you from the horrors to come with my Shadow tech?"

"I have money, as much as you want."

Wilhella's mouth didn't bother to reply. Money, what was

money to her, it seemed to imply.

"I can rescue you from the Black Abbess' Clutch. I can free you."

A wicked laugh from the mouth. "But ... I *like* being a Black Hat ..."

Kay sighed. He had hoped to avoid this but Wilhella didn't appear to be budging and the usual enticements didn't interest her. "I will pledge you my CARG."

The mouth curled into a wicked smile. "*Yesssssssss* ... Now you're bargaining, Lord Blanchefort. Imagine, a brave Vith lord from the League standing at my whim—my, my, that does sound attractive to me."

Kay protested. "I shall not be at your whim, ma'am. I shall assist you once and once only and at a time of my choosing."

The mouth compressed to a stubborn pucker. "Then we have no deal, sir. Your death awaits."

The negotiation was on in earnest. He now had an item to barter that Wilhella wanted; it was merely a matter of terms and length of service. He recalled sitting in on his mother, Countess Sygillis, negotiating a lucrative fabric deal with a group of merchants from Hoban. It went on for hours with all sorts of threats and sore feelings mixed in between; though, in this case, it wasn't fabric he was bartering but his very freedom—and possibly his soul. He glanced at Sam's doll at the head of the bed and began. "As you will be offering me one favor, then I shall assist you once. That is fair."

The mouth was resolute. "Once is not enough."

He became angry. "I need your Shadow tech!"

The mouth wasn't budging. "Once is not enough! You can rot there on Bazz for all I care."

From the bed, Laika snored quietly.

Kay thought it over. "Very well, for one favor, I shall pledge you my services for one month."

"One month?" the mouth asked. "What is one month? I ought to be insulted. I ought to cut this feed and let your enemies have at you. No, no, I shall require your absolute services before me for ten years as measured on Waam, and not a day less."

Kay disagreed. "Ten years is ridiculous! One year on Waam equals at least three Kanan years!"

From the bed, Laika mumbled: "Three years, one hundred four days ..."

"Yes, thank you, Laika. That means I would be under your

boot for well over thirty years. Unacceptable and I refuse. One favor, one year, Kanan."

"I shall need at least five years Kanan, and I shan't go a day less."

Kay wasn't finished bargaining. "We shall have half a year Gothan, that's one and a half years Kanan, and that is the most I shall go."

The mouth became perturbed. "Sir, I am not a vendor on the streets selling fruits and sundries. How dare you haggle with me! My will is absolute."

"One Gothan year, three years Kanan," Kay replied. "And, for three years of service, I shall need at least three Shadow tech uses."

The mouth considered that and weighed the possibilities. "Three years Kanan for three uses of Shadow tech, and your service to commence at a time of my choosing."

Kay sighed. "Done."

"Ah, done!" The mouth slid down the length of his CARG in a greasy fashion and detached itself. "Let us seal the terms of the deal with a kiss." Kay tried to pull away, but the mouth followed him. "I insist." The mouth came down and gave Kay a long, noisy kiss.

"See, that wasn't so bad, was it? Oh, to think what shall be said in Waam when it is discovered that I, Wilhella Cormand-Grande, have the absolute services of a Vith League lord for one Gothan year. Ohhhhhhhhhhh, what shall I do with you, hhhhhmmmmmm mmmh-hehhehehehehehehhe? I'm certain I'll think of something."

Kay had just pledged three years of his life in the service of a diabolical Black Hat from Waam. What would he be compelled to do? What would he become? However, if Sam could be saved and the Machine recovered, it would be a small price to pay.

"I have given you my pledge in exchange for three uses of your Shadow tech, and my word is my bond; however, allow me to make one thing perfectly plain to you," Kay said. "If you attempt any treachery, if you cheat me, then I shall come to Waam specifically for you."

"Is that a fact?"

"Yes indeed, and you know what I am. You know what I can do to you. I will take control of your soul and do what you most probably fear most."

"And what is that?"

"I will break the Black Abbess' Clutch and drag you off far from the bright lights and familiar bustle of Waam and compel you to live the remainder of your days in quiet, unremarkable oblivion with not a word said or a byline written. They might ask in Waam 'What happened to the Mad Black Hat Wilhella Cormand-Grande? What has become of her?', and the reply shall be 'We don't know. We've not heard from her in years'. That will be my fate for you."

The mouth considered that. "A clever cruelty, Lord Blanchefort. Very well, you wish to have Shadow tech at your command, and I shall deliver."

Soon, a sinister, slightly smoking bag made of ashy felt fell from the monitor and sat before Kay on the desk. An embroidered message on the bag read, in lurid red threads; "*To my favorite slave …*"

Kay picked up the bag. Two black medallions clattered out, shaped like smiling mouths. "To protect you and your Haitathe dog," the mouth said. "Shadow tech is very toxic, yes? Whamic Shadow tech is doubly so."

Kay took one of the medallions and put it on. Inside the swirling, misty interior of the bag were a number of tiny black kernels. "What are these?" Kay asked.

"It's Shadow tech, as you requested. Throw the bag down and you will have protection," the mouth said. "Careful, you have three uses and that is all."

Wilhella's mouth was quizzical for a moment. "Do not be shy in your use of my Shadow tech. Be imaginative, be bold, I cannot have my slave killed—that would not do at all. And, by the by, death is no release from your service to me."

With that, the mouth faded away. *"Be safe, my slave, be safe … for I shall soon be calling on you and we shall make history together …"*

Kay stared at the smoking bag. The bed squeaked and Laika stirred. She got off the bed and crawled to Kay's side.

"Bag is evil," she said, staring at it.

"Yes, it is," Kay replied.

14— The Night of Dead Birds

Kay gave Laika her Shadow tech medallion and she put it on. He took Wilhella's bag and stuffed it into his vest pocket where it jostled around with his Poltava. He exited the room. Sarah was seated next to the terminal. "So, what happened? How bad is it?"

"I have to serve Wilhella Cormand-Grande for three Kanan years."

Sarah was open-mouthed with shock. "Oh Gods, Kay. In exchange for what?"

"Shadow tech."

"Why in the name of Creation would you want that?"

"Because, in a few minutes you're going to be gone and we are going to be under siege. We need some sort of advantage to counter The Jones' next move. Shadow tech can provide that."

"What about your mom with her Silver tech?"

"What about my mother? I don't see her around anywhere and she can't Whamic it to me through the bloody screen like Wilhella can."

Laika stood near Kay with two LLAGs drawn, her Shadow tech talisman gleaming at her throat. "Laika will protect Jarlcon from Black Hat!"

Sarah glanced at her terminal and was alarmed. "Gods, Kay, you were right. There's a surge in network traffic. The Jones are setting off data bombs everywhere. The whole damn net is pinholing!" She waved her hand. A green holographic screen appeared, floating on air. "This screen will let you control the Monties on *The Ultra*. Use them if you can!"

Her image flickered. "I'm being squeezed out."

She vanished and the cones went out. They surged for a moment and Sarah reappeared in matrix.

"I'll get help ..." She flickered again and was gone, including the Monty holograph.

"Good!" Laika cried. "Good! Laika glad Sarah gone!"

A knock came at the door. Laika turned and pointed her LLAGs.

Kay Sighted through the walls. A male and female wearing inn staff uniforms were standing at the door. They knocked briskly.

They were both carrying Horvath Creepers in damp earthen pots. Kay loathed the sight of the plant and if he were able to feel fear, he would certainly be afraid.

The Creeper ...

He knew what one whiff of that plant could do to him. It was him and Laika alone, and they needed his Gifts operable for as long as possible, otherwise this night would be their end.

"Gods, I'm not losing my Gifts again!" He checked the two over in his Sight. They didn't seem like Jones, they weren't armed. They seemed like ordinary staff of the inn.

They tried the door, finding it locked.

Laika grit her teeth and cocked her LLAGs, ready to blow the two of them away. "Battle begins!" she said with a bit of Haitathe relish.

Kay allowed his Sight to slip back in time, seeing the two at the door in reverse, regressing back to the afternoon and morning, seeing them in their modest homes with their families, making noisy splattering breakfast for many noisy Bazz kids. He saw them walking to market, arguing with the merchants over prices, arguing with passersby in the streets, doing ordinary things Bazzers tended to do. These were just two innocent people caught up under The Jones' influence. As with his staff, he didn't want them hurt if possible. "Wait, Laika, don't shoot." He thought fast. Sighting into the next suite over, he found it empty. "We're going to Waft. Hold still." He put his arms around her and they Wafted away with a crash of wind. The adjacent suite was similar to their own, except it was unoccupied. Laika pulled free and aimed her LLAGs at the wall.

"No, no, wait a moment."

He Sighted through the wall. "I'd rather not fight these people if we don't have to."

Laika peered through the curtains. "Many people outside. Many people to fight!"

Kay continued to Sight. Outside, the wind was picking up and the first waves of rain were beginning to fall, soaking the ground. People milled about, unmindful of the wind and rain. Dark streaks moved through the clouds in long lines.

The future unfurled in many paths, some that were blacked out and impossible to look in on, and others that were plain to see. The plain paths brimmed with defeat.

He saw it coming; a devastating blow, the flapping of ancient wings, the flattening of the town killing many of the inhabitants, and the killing of Laika too, in the rubble of this very inn. And he would be taken and kept partially alive, whisked away across the plain to Gallia Palace and forced before the enemy, Queen Ghome. And, most importantly, he would be forced to look into Sam's face and see evil looking back at him. He would resist, he would refuse, and then she would bargain, offering the lives of his staff and Sam's face in return. Then, like a noble Vith, he would sacrifice himself, give in and let her have the Machine, unlocking its defenses and making her the master of past, present and future. For good or for ill, that's what it would be.

Things got pretty fuzzy after that.

"Laika, we've got to get out of here now. The open paths into the future that I can see lead into ruin. The only alternative I can think of is to force ourselves down a path that I can't see."

He reached into his vest pocket and pulled out the smoking bag of Shadow tech. "First and foremost, we need my Gifts. They can take their Creepers and be damned!"

"No, Jarlcon!" Laika cried. "Bag is evil."

"I've already paid with three years of my life. I intend to make certain those years will be well-spent."

Now that he had Wilhella's Shadow tech, what was he supposed to do with it? Kay wasn't certain how to use the bag. He tried squeezing it and all it did was smoke heavier.

There was a knock at the door. Laika glanced out the window through the curtains. "People, Jarlcon, with plants."

Kay was desperate; he couldn't allow his Gifts to be lost again so soon. If they were to survive this with no Sarah and no King to assist them, he had to have his Gifts. "Take care of them, quietly incapacitate them and keep those damn plants away from me." Laika strode to the foyer as Kay struggled with the bag.

How was he supposed to use it? How?

Wait! Wilhella's mouth mentioned something about throwing it down. He took the bag and cast it to the floor like a bean bag. As it hit, a cloud of soot came out and slowly swirled into the air, lingering near Kay with other-worldly heaviness.

Raw Shadow tech waiting to be formed.

He heard the sounds of a struggle from the foyer. He heard bodies being tossed about and the snap of bones breaking. An earthen pot clattered to the floor and broke.

He didn't have much time. Now what? He tried speaking aloud: "I need protection from contaminants in the air. I need a respirator and filter of some sort."

The sooty cloud of Shadow tech instantly, if somewhat methodically, reacted. It formed around him, adhering to his flesh creating a black skin-tight suit, like that of a diver. The wave of black crept up his legs and waist, moving steadily toward his head like a painted-on layer of hot tar. From the foyer he heard the crack of a gun and saw muzzle flashes. Laika was shooting. There seemed to be many people in the foyer trying to get past her, a fierce struggle in progress.

As the wave of Shadow tech approached his neck, it spread out, forming a black bubble around his head. The forming Shadow tech seemed to resemble the black spacesuit the terrible Dead Man from Mare wore during their battle in the Grove—perhaps his recollection of it unconsciously shaped the Shadow tech. As it formed around him, all the whirling and banging and shooting sounds coming from the foyer were shut out into sudden nothingness. The last thing he heard was the clear ring of a solid sword strike and the cries of people dying. The bubble around his head was black and he was plunged into pitch, humid darkness. He had a moment of extreme claustrophobia, not being able to hear or see and feeling the hot grip of the Shadow tech suit all around him like a smothering straitjacket. He felt as if he were suffocating. Regaining his composure, he Sighted through the bubble. Over his shoulder he saw two ribbed tanks form at his back and a number of organic-looking exhaust tubes twist and intertwine. He looked at his hands; they were sinewy, ribbed, clawed like the hands of a demented beast turned inside out. A dark pouch formed at his waist. Inside the pouch were his Poltava, his CARG and his bag of Shadow tech ready for two more uses. He pulled the CARG out and slung it into a bony saddle.

To his shock, the Shadow tech wasn't done. Inside the bubble, it formed a hot, flexible appendage that clapped itself to Kay's nose and mouth. Kay resisted but it throbbed and writhed and forced its way into his mouth, where it went deep down his throat. He gagged. He doubled over, trying to breathe. He was smothering.

Just relax, he heard a voice say. *Let Wilhella take care of you ... Hhhmeeehehehehehe ...*

He forced himself to be calm. He felt air flowing into his lungs.

A man appeared through the foyer, torn and bleeding. He was carrying a wilted Horvath Creeper. He saw Kay and ran to him with surprising speed. Kay unsaddled his CARG. He met the attacker, slapping the Creeper out of his hand. Spores from the plant filled the air in a pervasive yellowy cloud. It coated his suit in a golden dusting and stuck to it. Kay smelt nothing except the primal reek of Shadow tech; the suit appeared to be filtering out the dust as planned. An enraged Laika slick with gore appeared from the foyer and reached out for the man, her arm stretching. She seized him and slammed his body several times into the floor.

CARG in hand, Kay joined her in the foyer. Twenty people lay there; some badly injured, some dead, mixed into a weedy carpet of Creepers and loose soil. Laika slammed heavy furniture against the door to brace it. "Many people come, Jarlcon!" she said, her voice coming in as a synthesized whine through his Shadow tech bubble. She turned and was surprised, seeing him in the demonic black suit for the first time. She drew her swords.

"It's me, Laika, I'm all right. I used the bag to create a hermetic suit to protect me from the Creepers. It seems to work, I don't smell them. I have my Gifts still."

She reached out and tentatively touched the bubble around his head. "Jarlcon?" she asked.

"Laika, can you hear me?"

She nodded. "Jarlcon's voice strange," she said.

"I'm fine," he said. "I created this suit to protect me from the Creeper spores. It seems to be working." Kay patted her on the wrists. "Don't take off your medallion whatever you do; this stuff is toxic."

She led him to the window and they peered out into the night. Outside, unmanned Bazz Winger ships flew through the stormy skies, bathing the streets with spotlights and tongues of red scanning cone energy. Hordes of Bazzers marched about in the wet, wind-driven streets; most carrying drenched Creepers in pots, others toting weapons of various kinds.

As Kay and Laika watched, a voice came in through his bubble and crawled into his head.

Kay ... Time to come out ...

Kay recognized the voice:

Tal de Roga.

Outside, the Winger ships dropped a steady stream of small bombs all about the city proper. They went off with a muffled 'whuff', distributing a cloud of spore-laden vapor.

The Bazz Winger ships came in and fired lines of missiles into seemingly random areas of the city, battering the iron and brick buildings, destroying people's homes.

"Come out, Kay!"

More missiles. More explosions.

"Kay, come out!" de Roga ordered. *"We were hoping you'd follow us to Bazz. We figured violating your House and killing some of your staff would get you to come out. Messing with your wife was the final blow, wasn't it? Our Leader came up with that idea herself. We needed to get you out of Blanchefort. Too much Vith magic floating around in that accursed place. Here, though, you're exposed and alone. And now that we've got you, you're not going anywhere. Of course, you must know by now that She wants that bloody Machine of yours, not that Monama filth she's currently wearing on her face. She's wanted it for a long time, and now here it is; we just need to get you to deactivate all those pesky Vith traps around it."*

The Winger ships cavorted over the city on stilts of scanning energy. They fired missiles to the ground here and there, one of them detonating not far from the inn.

Tal de Roga continued. *"We know you're somewhere in this city, hiding like a scared rabbit. I suppose we're just going to have to flush you out with H-Grenadiers. So, pardon us while we blow out your windows so our hypnosis wave flows through nice and strong."*

The Winger ships pulled away and the crowds of people melted into the shadows. Outside became eerily quiet. Laika stood by the windows, her DeeDee drawn.

"Laika, get away from the windows," Kay said.

She came to his side. "Get down and stay low." She knelt down and Kay stood over her. "A storm's coming in, I see it."

The wind outside picked up, howled, and went vertical. A devastating tornado blew in, low to the ground and shapeless, its vortex churning up the earth. The ground shook as it neared. Laika took Kay into her arms and braced herself.

It hit in a deafening growl. The windows shattered and were swept away. Loose objects in the suite took flight and were sucked out. Laika was pelted front and back, but held firm as the vortex moved away. The structure of the inn had taken a severe beating and looked ready to come down around them. Laika was injured; blood trickled down one of her arms.

"Laika, you're wounded. Let me have a look."

"Laika fine," she said.

De Roga's voice came through again. *"That should do it, now for the H-wave. It won't hurt a bit, I promise."*

Laika went to the window and gazed out. She was lacerated with several small cuts on her arms; her composite armor and her rubbery Haitathe flesh had warded most of the blows aside. None of her wounds appeared to be serious. The tornado was gone, leaving a massive swathe of destruction behind and a momentary path of starry night sky in its wake. There were destroyed buildings all around, fallen masonry and pockets of fire lighting up the cloudy night. Anybody who had been out in that maelstrom was no doubt dead.

"Do you hear it, Kay, our gentle voice? Certainly you do ..."

Kay heard nothing but the stillness of his confining suit and the beat of his own heart. There was a snide, expectant sort of silence from de Roga, as if he had anticipated to have snared Kay by now.

"Laika, do you hear the H-Grenadiers?"

"Yes, Jarlcon."

"I can't, the suit is protecting me."

In his Sight, the night was livid with scanner cones coming down and overlapping from Winger ships loitering high above. If he and Laika ventured out and tripped a cone, the information would immediately be relayed to The Jones' command center back in Gallia. They were pinned down in the wreckage of their suite.

Tal de Roga's voice came back on, a bit more flustered this time. *"So, you're somehow evading our H-Wave? It isn't a problem. Time for round two, and if you're entertaining the notion that we need you alive, think again. I suppose we're simply going to have to kill every living thing in this city. We can bring your dead body to our Leader and she can reanimate it no problem. All we need is your damned Vith head. Now for it ..."*

There was a terrible silence and an uneasy pause. A buzz grew in the distance, quickly growing loud. Kay Sighted. He saw a number of black, funnellike shapes descending on the city, snaking through the streets and twisting into the alleys with fluidlike movement.

He and Laika backed away into the center part of the suite, Laika drawing her LLAGs. Moments later, a mass of flapping wings and cawing throats poured in through the windows. Birds, thousands of them of various sizes and species, moving with a singular consciousness marking their passage with a near constant rain of droppings and shed feathers. They surged around Kay and Laika. She didn't like them and reacted fiercely, swatting at them with her six arms. She drew her giant long swords and flailed away, killing dozens of birds with every stroke. Dead birds covered the floor.

Tal de Roga's triumphant voice came in. *"There you are, Kay! The Inn of the Hidden Surprise, I should have guessed! Too bad, I liked that place. Good lunch menu."*

Winger ships closed in, power-diving from above. Missiles

blasted, taking fiery chunks of stone and masonry. The structure of the inn groaned, ready to collapse. Kay had had his fill of Tal de Roga and The Jones, and their uncaring immortal leader, Queen Ghome. He glanced at the floor, covered with dead birds; some common pigeons, others rustic thrushes and rooks, and a few were delicate, colorful birds from the moist forests of Bazz, taken from their nests and compelled to die in a ruined inn that was about to be flattened. More dead left in The Jones' wake.

It was time to give The Jones back. It was time to fight! He took his bag of Shadow tech from the pouch and threw it down, leaving one use left. He picked the bag up as the wispy cloud of Shadow tech came up, awaiting his command.

Shadow tech was a wonder; with it one could create towering monsters, unbreakable weapons, and complex machines. His mother used her Silver tech to create her familiar of the *Seeker*, the old Fleet warbird she and Captain Davage sailed the heavens in before Kay was born. His mother knew nothing of ship design, of stellar mechanics or engineering, yet with Silver tech her tiny *Seeker* flew in miniature like a model airship; it banked, it soared and was utterly deadly when it needed to be.

If she could do it, so could he. Thoughts entered his head and the Shadow tech reacted, forming into a hollow bubble resting on the floor just big enough to fit two people. He crawled in and pushed himself to one side. "Laika!" he called. "Laika, get in here quick!"

She glanced at the small black Shadow tech bubble and hesitated.

"Laika, hurry!"

She dove into the bubble, her giant bulk and weapons filling it in a rubbery mass. Kay reached out and pulled Laika into him, giving her more room. She embraced him tight with her six arms, her long hair clotted with bits of dust and plaster. The bubble closed around them and they were sealed within; there was barely enough room to breathe.

Several moments later, point-blank missile shots devastated the suite. Gouts of raging fire erupted, scouring the masonry, cracking stone, melting iron. The inn came down all around, burying them deep.

"Entombed, Jarlcon," Laika said. The Shadow tech bubble seemed to be holding fast, but Laika was right, they were sunk in deep, buried under tons of burning masonry and iron. The tiny bubble they hid in was certainly not what Kay had imagined. He had imagined a great ship, fast and strong, spiderlike and brimming with dark weaponry moving as a juggernaut through the enemy.

They waited for what seemed like an eternity. Outside the bubble, fires raged.

And then the Shadow tech reacted, forming, linking into complex structures at a very slow rate. The bubble expanded and elongated, shifting the masonry around them without effort, like a large animal buried in the sand pushing its way out. Soon, Kay and Laika could sit apart. Soon, they could stand. As they watched, machinery formed around them with effortless, fluid movement. Chairs sprouted out of the floor, control panels blossomed and became solid. A great window appeared through which they could see the tightly compacted masonry dappled with fire. Kay and Laika stood together, watching the process with wonder and a bit of dread. Lights came up, systems came online. The black ship around them thrummed with steadily growing power. Laika plopped into the pilot's chair and took in the layout.

"Laika, can you fly this?" Kay asked hopefully.

"No. Not familiar with layout." She took hold of the control sticks. "What ship is this?"

"I don't know, I just dreamed it up."

"Where canards?"

"The what? I don't know, do your best," Kay said, sitting next to her.

Head on a swivel, Laika memorized the control panels and, using four arms, took the sticks and moved them.

The ship lurched a little. "Ah!" Laika cried. "Ah!"

She moved them again and the black ship trembled. Masonry shifted and fell aside. They emerged into the damp night.

"What the hell are you playing at, Kay?" came Tal de Roga's thoughts. *"Never mind, lay into him!"*

A barrage of missiles came in, exploding in a steady sparkle. The ship yawed a little under the weight of the pounding but Laika adjusted the sticks and the ship leveled.

Kay Sighted to assess the damage. Outside of the control room, the ship appeared to be solid Shadow tech. The ship seemed to be a partially living thing, resembling more a large organism rather than a piece of machinery. The missiles were having no effect, the Shadow tech shell holding fast.

"Jones' ships!" Laika cried. Kay looked up. A wave of Winger ships was coming down fast, ready to launch missiles and bathe them in neurocones.

"Weapons!" he cried. "Where are our weapons?"

As if in response, a screen came up. It was the Monty control screen Sarah had called up before she was locked out of the network. From that screen, he could commence a surface-to-surface or surface-to-air attack. The screen was rich with targets. He pressed the holographic buttons and selected targets. The screen indicated the Monties had launched and were in flight.

Outside, they heard a number of explosions, followed by the dull thud of Winger ships falling to the ground. Kay continued selecting targets, launching and eliminating them. Suddenly, the screen went blank.

"I think The Jones just took out Sarah's ship," Kay said. "What other weapons do we have? We must have more!" Sighting, he saw a number of spidery, stalklike black tentacles reach out and seize the remaining Winger ships on the move, plucking them out of the sky. The tentacles crushed some and ran-through others, knocking them about like children's kites.

Kay watched with wonder. "Laika, get us moving, west, over the wall. We're going to Gallia Palace and we're bringing a little piece of hell with us!"

The ship moved smoothly over the city. Kay saw the width of the devastation The Jones had wrought; the city flattened both by the tornado and The Jones' ordinance. In his Sight, Kay spotted a battalion of Battle Units waiting just beyond the city perimeter. He saw them scramble into position. A barrage of missiles, rockets, lasers, sonics and heat came up from the ground, hoping to stop his ship.

And he watched with satisfaction as the black Shadow tech tentacles came down and rent them into shapelessness tinged with fire. Jones operators clambered out of the wreckage of their fallen units. The tentacles hesitated, waiting for his orders. Kay hardened his heart and The Jones were killed. Other Jones took refuge in buildings and under heaps of wreckage, hoping to seek shelter. Kay dug them out and ended their lives.

The ship passed over the Gallian Wall and entered the openness of the plain.

"Storms, Jarlcon!" Laika cried.

Ahead, three tornados of terrible fury dropped out of the clouds and closed in on them. They hit the ship dead on. Kay felt the black vessel shudder. Through the glass, Kay saw nothing but churned earth and debris. Frequent lightning strikes hit the ship, coupled with continuous thuds of loose objects driven by the wind striking the hull.

The ship appeared to be holding. "How are we?" he asked Laika.

"Ship good." She moved the sticks and they continued on, ignoring the pounding maelstrom outside. Instead of slowing, the Shadow tech ship picked up speed, plowing ahead regardless of what Queen Ghome and The Jones could throw at them. Only the arcane could harm Shadow tech.

"How far are we from Gallia Palace?"

"Ten point three-two miles."

As quickly as they had come, the storms died away leaving an unnatural calm; the sky overhead vaulted with turbid clouds. There it was: Gallia Palace way off in the distance in plain sight, lit up like a pearl.

Kay saw something big coming in. "Laika, to our right!"

The ship was slammed by a holocaust of steam. Something outside was blasting the ship with steam, raking it with flashing claws. The attack was having an effect. The ship shuddered hard and lost altitude. Kay fought back, reaching with black tentacles, latching on to whatever was out there, ripping metal scales away. Giant claws tore their way into the hull of the ship.

The outer skin was breeched; Shadow tech howled in pain. A blast of steam scalded the ship a second time, the tentacles curling up and dropping off. Systems went down. Shadow tech screamed and was defeated, blasted away. Laika fought with the controls, but it was no good.

The ground came up fast. Laika reached back to protect Kay and they slammed into the earth, churning it up.

The ship crumbled around them. Digging through the ashy wreckage, they clambered out into the night. Something was in the sky, a heavy-bodied black patch darker than the darkness around it. Headlights of orange intensity cut the dark before it like a pair of lances, and a set of small gleaming eyes turned to them with disdain. Victorious, it flapped away, moving through the low-hanging clouds.

Kay got his first look at the ship from the outside. It was a horrifying collection of pulsing nodes and coiled tentacles; it looked like some sort of terrifying bug or mollusk that had been pulled from its shell and cooked over a hot fire. It quickly shriveled up and crumbled into soot. Whatever had brought them down was arcane in the extreme to defeat Shadow tech so easily.

"Not bad, Kay," came Tal de Roga's thoughts again. *"I didn't think you had it in ya. But, as you see, our leader has an answer for everything."*

"Laika, how far are we from Gallia Palace?"

"Five point six miles."

Kay looked around, seeing a horde of Jones units moving in their direction. "They're coming in."

Laika drew her DeeDee. "Let Jones come!"

"Wait!" Kay cried. "I have an idea."

Part 3

The Chadburn

1—Through the Gellartron

The *Goshawk* climbed up fast through the clear blue atmosphere of Onaris and took a hard 7:45 pm bearing toward Kana.

Phillip of Blanchefort sat at the controls as usual. His brand new wife, Lady Thomasina of Blanchefort, formerly of Waam and the 19th of her line, emerged from the rear of the ship. She had just changed out of her beachwear and back into her usual green and brown armor. She was flush and tan from their trip to the sunny beachside town of Fazo, glowing with young love. Carrying her boots and Phillip's duster, she sat in the adjacent chair and gazed at the sandy white fingernail of land jutting into the ocean far below, rapidly getting smaller and smaller as the ship sprinted away from the planet. She had loved Fazo with its huddle of whitewashed buildings and aquamarine waters; she didn't ever want to leave. They had even purchased a little property there near the beach strewn with sand and driftwood, just a quiet little place out of the League's eye they could disappear to when the mood caught them. She had heard from the locals that the giant turtles were soon to come in from the sea to bury their eggs in the sand, and that was a spectacle not to be missed. Her Bondar ship, the *Sparrow*, had departed Xandarr and returned to Waam, reporting back that the uproar Wilhella Cormand-Grande had stirred up had largely blown over. Thomasina informed her people that when she returned to Waam, she would have a husband at her side; something that hadn't happened in her line in generations. The 'Thomasinas' of Waam, progeny of the old House of Woolover, chaste prohibitionists known throughout Waam for their ferocity, never married. But she desperately loved Phillip and Waam wasn't the same without him. Times changed, and she would bring a husband home with her.

But then there was Sarah blaring in over the Com, shattering their peace, chattering nonsense, having found them in quiet Fazo despite their alias.

Her angry voice pounded down over the transponder. "I still can't believe you two up and got married and didn't invite any of us! What is that? I'm your twin sister, dude! We're supposed to be tight!"

"Sorry, Sarah," Phillip said. "It just sort of happened, you know? The time had come and we just did it. I didn't want to be without Rose any longer."

"Well, now that you're family and all, can I call you 'Rose'?" Sarah asked.

"I'll think about it," Thomasina replied. "And, if it's any consolation for you, Sarah, we raised a toast in your honor. Honestly, it's not like we haven't been married in spirit for some time now anyway. This trip just made it official."

"Thanks," Sarah said. "It's probably just as well that you did, otherwise you two would be on ice here with me on Hoban."

"What do you mean?" Phillip asked.

Sarah took some time to get them both updated on the current situation, Phillip listening intently as the *Goshawk* picked up speed and settled into its flight to Kana.

She told them that they had been deceived, that Lady Chrysania was immortal, that she, in one of her many guises, was the Xaphan tyrant Queen Ghome. And she told them what had happened to her, to Sam, to Magistrate Kilos and her son. Phillip was speechless. Thomasina rustled in her seat and looked at her tan hands.

"We must have left just before the attack commenced. So, Sarah, you're telling us that, right now, you are systolic in a capsule missing your face and other essentials?" Thomasina asked.

"Yep. Me and several others. Listen, we're ok, nobody knows what has happened. The bad one was Ki, but she's out of the bag now, grumpy as ever."

Thomasina tried to revive Sarah's humor. "So, even unconscious and without a mouth, you still speak?"

"That's right," Sarah replied. "There's no stopping me. See what you married into?"

"So, now what?" Phillip asked, a bit of guilt and worry for his family seeping into him. "What do we do, how can we help?"

"Kay needs us bad. He's down there on Bazz with The Jones all over him."

"And he's alone?" Thomasina asked.

"No, he's got a Haitathe warrior named Laika with him."

"A Haitathe warrior?" Phillip sputtered.

"Yeah, it's a long story."

"Is he safe alone with a Haitathe warrior?"

"Not really, no. And you want to know why? She's giving him a big head, she totally wants to have sex with him and she wants to kill me too. Go figure! I've let her know on repeated occasions that Sam isn't going to be having any of this 'lovesick' stuff once she's out of the capsule. The Haitathe's pretty annoyed with me, says she's going to wring my neck."

"I can't imagine why, Sarah," Thomasina replied.

"Very funny. Home is a mess right now. It's ok—the Hospitalers are there and are tending to our staff, though my library is half destroyed and I'm really pissed about it. So, here's my main issue: The Jones have me locked out of the Bazznet, so I'm not much good over there right now."

"And you're telling us that you are some sort of Networking Adept in your sleep?" Thomasina asked.

The lights in the cabin went out for a moment, the HOM scanners came on, and the Airnet cone jumped up all at once.

"Yeah," Sarah said. "The word is *'Ultra'*. I'm an Ultra in my sleep. So, here's the deal. We got taken for a ride. Queen Ghome was after the Machine all along and she played us for a bunch of chumps. All the Perlamum stuff she had us doing, all the running around and the stealing of our various body parts, it was all to get her bloody hands on the Machine."

"But how did she know we had it?"

"It's a long story and I'll tell you later."

"Weren't you aware going in that Lady Chrysania wasn't being fully truthful with you?" Thomasina asked.

"Well yeah, but we thought she was lying to cover up something embarrassing, or to do some social maneuvering—stuff like that. We didn't know she was out gunning for the Machine the whole time, and she just about killed the lot of us while you two were off rolling around in the sand. And, by the way, Lady Chrysania is innocent; it's Ghome who's the problem. She's some sort of split-personality, or something. It's complicated."

Thomasina grappled with her feelings of guilt. "You seem to have all the answers, Sarah. We are with you now, what is our next step?"

Sarah paused. "I'm thinking we talk to Ki."

"Magistrate Kilos? Why?" Phillip asked.

Sarah sounded giddy over the transponder. "Just a minute, let me get her. You'll see."

Phillip and Thomasina listened to static for a minute or two until a weary, gruff female voice filtered through.

"Hello?"

"Is that you, Ki?" Phillip asked.

"Yeah, yeah, it's me," she replied over the transponder. They heard hazy bouts of static mixed with nebulous background noises.

They heard the creaking of a chair and occasional hints of shuffling movement.

"You all right?" Phillip asked.

"Sure. I'm just sitting here in the creepy room watching the Hospitalers do whatever it is they're doing. Hey, congrats on your nuptials. You got a good man, Thomasina."

Sarah jumped in. "Phillip, I grabbed Ki here because she might be able to help us out. She had a pretty saucy Gaming Session while you two were hiding out in Fazo—she's the one who figured out where you two were and what alias you were using—that's how I fingered you. So, I thought I'd ask her to join us and let us know if she has any additional info to provide to get us pointed in the right direction. So, Ki, not to put you on the spot or nothing, but you got anything?"

Static. They heard the sounds of her chair creaking, as if Ki were rustling in her seat.

"Not really sure what you're hoping for, Sarah," she finally said. "I told you everything."

"Just whatever comes into your head. Any detail, no matter how small, could be a big help. Kay's counting on us."

"Well..." She sighed and took a drink of something; they could hear her take a sip and swallow over the cone. She mumbled something that they could just barely hear: *"Damn, my head hurts ..."*

She cleared her voice and spoke up. "Kay isn't going to be on Bazz, I can tell you that much. So, forget about Bazz. The Jones are going to get him and take him someplace off world."

"Where?" Phillip asked. "Can you tell us where?"

"No, well, I don't know. I remember something about a yellow sky. Kay's there. He was wearing a weird-looking black suit, like a spacesuit covered in bones."

"What?"

"Don't ask me, I don't know. That's what he's wearing. It sort of looked like the suit that dead guy from Mare was wearing, only creepier." Ki paused. "Wait. Something about plants, plants with a big white flower. Kay's afraid of them, the pollen or spores or whatever, so he's wearing the suit to breathe easy."

"The Horvath Creeper, is that what you mean?" Sarah asked.

"Sure, I guess."

"The Horvath Creeper will kill his Gifts, he has good cause to be wary of them. Anything else?" Phillip asked.

There was a long, scratchy pause. "Ki?"

Her voice was tentative. "Something about a dial mounted on a podium."

"A what?" Sarah asked.

Ki was tired and exasperated; it came through in her voice. "I don't know. It's one of those dials they used to have on old ships that told engineering how fast the helm wanted the ship to go."

Phillip and Thomasina exchanged glances. "You mean a 'Chadburn', right?" Phillip said. "An Engine Order Telegraph. It's a dial mounted in the bridge, so if the captain wanted to go at a certain speed, flanking speed for example, the helm would move the dial to FLANK, and a similar dial in engineering would also move to FLANK, accompanied by a bell. You sailed in space for how long and you didn't know that, Ki?"

"Hey, they didn't have one of those stupid things on the *Seeker* or the *New Faith*, ok, so how would I know?"

Sarah was impatient. "So what about it? What about this Chadburn?"

"Lady Chrysania was hiding it from Sam, and it wasn't the happy, smiling Sam we all know; it was a rotten, blaring, intense Sam. From what Sarah's told me, Queen Ghome is wearing Sam's face, so that was Ghome I was seeing. I can't tell you how creepy that was. Anyway, Chrysania was hiding the dial from Queen Ghome. It was made from enameled brass, and I think the face was ivory and the lettering sepia. It had a fancy brass handle with a bunch of dial settings. The setting I remember most was SHUTDOWN."

"Where did she hide it?" Phillip asked.

Ki thought for a silent moment. "She ... hid it in various places. I must have dreamed about her hiding it several times. The first time, she hid it in the beachside church where you two got married; the next couple of times, I saw her hiding it in a pile of treasure. I caught a glimpse of it stashed in a massive hoard of treasure. It looked sort of out of place there to me."

"Why do you think this Chadburn is important?" Thomasina asked.

"You got me. All I know is Lady Chrysania was desperate to keep it hidden from Queen Ghome, that's what I got."

Sarah piped in. "I think I know why it's important. I'm pretty certain from the reading I've been doing that the Chadburn Ki dreamed of is the control column for Queen Ghome's Bower Chest. Before you say anything, Phillip, Bower Chests exist, and Queen Ghome's got her most prized possessions stashed inside of it. There's no way Kay can stand against an ancient Bower Chest loaded with arcane treasure—he'll be obliterated. If we have the Chadburn, then we can turn the tables. We can shut the Bower Chest down, cold."

"What, in the Name of Creation, is as Bower Chest?" Thomasina asked.

"Monsters from Vith lore, Rose. I'll fill you in later. All right, Sarah, assuming what you say is true, then where is it?" Phillip asked. "Where's the Chadburn?"

Ki answered. "If you guys are expecting me to tell you from what I saw in my weird dreams, I have no idea. It's in a big room full of treasure—it think it was open to the sky, a weird sort of greenish sky. It's been there for a long time, and the handle is missing. Somebody hid it. That's all I've got."

"Do you know where this treasure room is, Ki?" Phillip asked.

"Nope. Sorry."

"What about the handle?" Phillip asked.

"It's missing; after that I got nothing."

Sarah laughed. "Ok, Ki, thanks. I guess we'll have to figure out a Plan B or something. We'll put our noses to the ground and—"

"I've got a better idea," Ki said. "Why don't you guys hook me back up and get one of those Game Sessions going again? Maybe I'll dream up more of that secret treasure room. Maybe I'll be able to tell you where it is."

"No, no Ki," Sarah said. "Gaming Sessions are too dangerous. Doing it to you once was bad enough, but twice is asking for trouble. Maybe you can get with your husband, the Professor, and—"

"There's no time. It might take forever to get him on the line, and then he'll need to perform research. He'll find the answer, he always does, but it might come too late to be of any help. We need answers now. Maybe I'll Game Up where it is and you can go snag it. It'll probably take a lot less time. Look, Kay's out there fighting for all of us and I'm just sitting here doing nothing like a useless slag. I ask for a drink and I get water, or fruit juice. The well-being of everybody here depends on the success of this operation, and Kay's going to need our help. Come on, I'm a big girl, I know what I'm getting into. Let's do this."

"What sort of danger would Ki be in if we initiated another one of these sessions?" Phillip asked.

"Plenty. Her brain could short-out or she could dip down into an Insanity Curve," Sarah replied.

"Yeah, well, I wouldn't be losing much," Ki responded. "Come on, let's get this going. I'll be fine."

✱　✱　✱　✱　✱

Hours later, the *Goshawk* plunged into Kana's atmosphere. Kana was always bumpy. Phillip gripped the sticks hard; his new bride Thomasina sitting back to watch him fly.

During the trip to Kana, they'd been in touch with Ennez and Bethrael of Moane, who were overseeing the care of the staff at Castle Blanchefort. They said the staff were fine. Many were returning to the castle from the trip to Bern that Sarah had sent them on. The Jones' hypnosis had, thankfully, worn off. Of those who had been Hypered by The Jones, most had been treated and freed from the condition. They were back on their feet and had no idea what had happened to them; which was a blessing. A few, however, were too damaged to be treated locally, so they had been Ripcared to Minz for IU care. Ennez added that his own wife, Lady Tellerran, had personally flown the staff to Minz. Under the Hospitalers care in Minz, the staff were recovering. Additionally, the Heads of Staff, with the exception of Lady Andorra, had returned to oversee the castle, along with Lady Poe and her husband. Captain Davage and Countess Sygillis, along with Kay's sister Hathaline and his brother Maser, were still out of the League with a small armada, investigating the newly rediscovered world of Eng. Kay's sister, Lady Kilos, was in Zenon attending an endurocon ball that was not scheduled to officially end anytime soon.

The castle seemed to be safe, though soon Lady Poe would be Comming, demanding to know what had happened.

As the *Goshawk* plunged into the clouds and Phillip vectored in, Sarah's voice came through. "Ok, the Gaming Session's over and Ki's in the IU having her vitals checked."

"How is she, Sarah?"

"Seems to be good. We only Gamed her up for about twenty minutes; Raal thought that would be a safe amount of time. We'll know more once she comes out of the IU."

"Keep us informed. Did we learn anything useful, Sarah?" Thomasina asked.

"Did we ever! Phillip, set a vector for Castle Bloodstein, right away."

Phillip set his course and veered to the north over the hard, mountain-tattooed landscape of Vithland.

"Our course is set. I'll have to get clearance."

"Clearance? Don't bother. Ki said it's empty except for Queen Ghome's demons, who probably won't be answering your Com."

"Demons?"

"Yep. Remember, Kay saw them in the woods. The Menks; they're creepy servants of Queen Ghome. Ki doesn't think there are any Menks on the surface, they're all underground."

Phillip brought the *Goshawk* down through the cold air, high over Vithland and its fierce mountains studded with corniced cliffs.

"So, Sarah, what will we be doing at Castle Bloodstein?" Thomasina asked. "What is our objective?"

Without missing a beat, Sarah replied, "We're after the Chadburn. According to Ki's Gaming Session, the Chadburn is the controller of Queen Ghome's Bower Chest monster, just like we figured. With the Chadburn, you can turn the Bower Chest off. She set it to AUTO-RUN centuries ago and then removed it so the Bower Chest couldn't be manually shut down by hostile forces. Ki said Ghome was going to melt the Chadburn down once and for all, but it got stolen before she had the chance. So, that's our objective: we get the Chadburn, we re-install it, and then we shut the bugger down cold. And to get the Chadburn, we're going to have to enter Queen Ghome's Gellartron."

"Her what?"

Sarah was giddy as she spoke. "Ok, so get ready for a shock. Aside from being immortal, Queen Ghome's a Gellar."

"A Gellar?" Thomasina said. "An enchantress? We used to have those in Waam before the Black Hats came."

"Don't steal my thunder, Thomasina!" Sarah cried. "A Gellar's way cooler than a boring enchantress. Gellars can do all this weird stuff; she can control the weather, she can control animals and people's minds if they're not Vith. And the cool thing of it is, *anybody* can be a Gellar; all you need is to have lots and lots of stuff. She's got the deck pretty much stacked in her favor, and she's probably letting Kay have every bit of it right now. Anyway, a Gellar like Queen Ghome gets their power from their *Gellartron.* A 'Gellartron' is basically a castle or stronghold with a hoard of treasure and arcane items. According to the laws of Acquisition Magic, the more things you have collected in one place, the tougher you get. Castle Bloodstein is a Gellartron, and, long ago, Castle Blanchefort was one too, until the Sisters butted in and deactivated it. Back in the day, all the Vith Households had a Gellartron. That must have been cool and we're going to tear Castle Blanchefort apart looking for ours once we get this sorted out.”

"And Magistrate Kilos told you all this while under the influence of mind-altering drugs?" Thomasina asked.

"Well, yeah, sort of. So if we don't deal with Ghome's Bower Chest monster, then Kay's got no chance. Thomasina, do you still have that locket my mother gave you containing two Whispers?"

"Yes, I have it in my baggage."

"Get them out, you're going to need them."

Thomasina headed into their cabin in the rear of the ship.”

Ahead, the gray domain of Five-Finger Mountain came up fast in a cobwebbing of haze and thick mottled snow; the black wart of Castle Bloodstein nestled at its center. Far to the east was the gray frozen line of Xandarr Bay. The *Goshawk* shuddered a bit in the thickening air.

"There it is," Phillip said.

"Set down in the central courtyard," Sarah said.

Phillip slowed the *Goshawk* as Thomasina returned from their cabin. She wore a silver locket given to her as a gift by Lady Poe. She clipped a furry white cloak to her back and pulled on a pair of thick gloves.

Phillip slowly brought the *Goshawk* down; the black spires of Castle Bloodstein, dark and ominous, looming over them.

2—"I am Chrysania"

Phillip shut the *Goshawk* down, the interior of the ship going dark. The northern wind knocked on the hatch door and howled across the cockpit glass, dusting it in pearls of snow.

"Keep the engines running so I can stay connected," Sarah said. "Unhook the Dash 6 transponder and take it with you. I'm going to see if I can tap into the castle's grid, if it's still operating. Give me a sec."

Phillip pulled the transponder and placed it in his duster. "Still with me, Sarah?"

"Yep," came her voice from within, slightly muffled.

He reloaded his Poltava and slipped it into his duster pocket. Thomasina stared out the glass at the dark, crablike edifice of Castle Bloodstein towering ahead, as black as the snow was white. The driving snow and lightless towers of the castle gave one the impression of fathomless isolation.

"I dislike this place intensely, Phillip. It has a dreadful feel. I feel as if we are the only people within a thousand miles."

"You probably are," Sarah replied.

Phillip draped two SAPP scarves around his neck. "It's just an old castle, just like Xandarr and Clovis. Kana has its fair share of ruins. Sarah even said it's abandoned."

"And what of Queen Ghome's demons, the Menks? What of them?"

"They're not on the surface," Sarah said from the transponder in Phillip's pocket.

"Should we release the Whispers?" Thomasina asked.

"It couldn't hurt," Sarah replied.

Thomasina opened her locket. Two Whispers, one pink, the other a soft teal, came buzzing out and slowly orbited her head in concentric spirals. "They're released," Thomasina said, catching them in the palm of her hand. "I'm very fond of these two; they were a gift from Phillip's mother. I named the pink one 'Bridgewater' and the teal 'Inn' after the place we spent our honeymoon."

"Lovely," Sarah said. "She can always make you more, you know. There are only two of them and the more Whispers you have the better they work, but these two should grant you basic sight/sound

Cloaking. Any little bit helps."

"Are you making any progress with the castle's systems?" Phillip asked.

"No," Sarah replied flatly. "Just give me a few minutes. Their systems are trash. It's like talking to a turnip."

Thomasina gasped and pointed out the glass. "Phillip, I see a light, just there. Do you see it?"

Far off through the gloom and the veils of snow, a soft orb of silver light gleamed; dim but steady and inviting.

"What's that light?" she asked.

Phillip stared at it. "I don't know. We're Whisper-locked, we're armed. Let's get this over with."

Whispers buzzing and weapons ready, Phillip opened the hatch. Freezing air and tendrils of snow barged in. They stepped out into the cold, the snow riding up their boots, spilling into the courtyard following the nebulous ball of silver light in the distance.

"What a depressing place," Thomasina said, noting the low-hanging gray skies and bare gothic stone blackened with age. She clutched her cloak around her. Phillip with his Vith stock was impervious to the cold, while Thomasina, a Xaphan of old Barrow heritage from the temperate city of Waam, was certainly not. She shivered. Water, locked in frozen channels, cracked beneath their feet. Landscaping and statuary were covered in ice.

"Sarah, you still with us?" Phillip asked.

"Yep. I'm duking it out with the castle here. I think I've got this system knocked. Just another minute or two."

"We're investigating the silver light. Seems to be located in the central courtyard."

"Be careful."

Thomasina's teeth chattered in the cold. She admitted Phillip into her cloak to warm her. "Xaphan's Beard, I miss warm Fazo. My Barrow blood does not favor this cold, and I don't like this Elderdown place one bit. History teaches us the Bloodsteins once attacked Barrow and laid waste to Saga."

"The Bloodsteins used to attack everybody," Phillip replied.

The silver light came into focus. Perched on a stone bench by a frozen pond where Lady Chrysania herself once sat was a small silver bird, glowing with warm light, fluffing his feathers. He took no notice of them.

"Is that King?" Thomasina asked.

Phillip was overjoyed. "It sure is! Sarah, it's King! He's here waiting for us! He's probably his old dour self, as always."

"What did I tell you? King's a champ! You'll need to let him into the Whisper's Veil so he can hear and see you," Sarah said. "What's the password?"

"Mr. and Mrs. Illibuck," Phillip replied.

"Really?" Sarah asked as the veil opened. She favored more 'heroic' passwords.

"King!" Phillip cried, lowering his Poltava. "It's good to see you! What are you doing here?" They turned away and King responded.

"I knew you would soon arrive, so I came from Hoban and waited."

"That's cool!" Sarah said. "Great job dropping off the chest to Raal and his boys. Did you have any trouble?"

"I did not. I visited your capsule for a bit while I was there, Lady Sarah."

"Yeah? How was I?"

"Quiet. Hairless. Faceless. Asleep."

"I must be a looker!"

"Indeed."

Thomasina curtsied to King. "Well met, Great Bird. We value and appreciate your presence."

King fluffed his feathers in response.

Thomasina rubbed her eyes, the cold making them water. "So, here we are standing in the freezing cold. What's next?"

"We're going to have to get you a Snugs or something, Thomasina," Sarah said over the transponder. "It's cold in Vithland. Better get used to it."

"Where are we supposed to go?"

Sarah answered. "Down below the surface, into the Gellartron. I'm hacking in to activate the castle's systems." There was a frustrated pause. "What the heck sort of ridiculous language are they speaking?"

"It's probably Vith, Sarah," Phillip replied.

"*Nope, Ultra Sarah can speak Vith—what do you think about that, eh?*" she replied in perfect Vith. "*Hold on.*"

As they waited, Phillip noticed a pair of delicate footprints in the ice in front of the bench; perfect, delicate feet.

"Those are Lady Chrysania's footprints," he said, nostalgic. "She sat right over there, fully repaired and glowing with good health after her trip to the Top of the Universe. How she smiled; I was so

happy for her. I was proud to have assisted in restoring her health."
He shook his head. "All of it a lie."

"You couldn't have known, Phillip," Thomasina said. "You and your cousins are good people."

"I heard that! Thanks, Thomasina!" Sarah cried.

Around them, lights came on in a soft white dash-dash glow at the perimeter of the courtyard. "I got the power going!" Sarah cried. "Ha! What'd I tell you? Ultra Sarah can-do! Follow the lights. Let's go!"

"What about Ghome's Menks?" Phillip asked.

"You're Whisper-locked, that should give you some protection, and Ki said they're not on the surface. Don't worry about them for now, but when they do show up, King knows what to do with them, right, King?"

He took flight and landed on Phillip's shoulder. He didn't reply.

They went inside the castle, seeing the ruins within, the torn cloth and rotting furniture turned over in the dark, freezing within towering runs of old stone. "What a forlorn place," Thomasina said, holding her MT CALM club. "It seems no one has lived here in centuries." She shuddered under her cloak. "It's just as freezing inside as it is out there in the snow."

"The main Bloodstein household relocated to a remote planet on the other side of the League a few centuries back, leaving the castle here pretty much abandoned," Phillip said. "The castle did look a bit more livable when we were here last. We might have been seeing a Painted Cloak; that must be the case."

A string of lights came on overhead, leading them into the dank interior of the castle. The place seemed vacant and sad, permeated with drifting shadows and old memories.

"Come on," Sarah said from Phillip's duster. "What's taking so long?"

"May we switch her off, please?" Thomasina asked.

"Don't you dare," Sarah replied. "We're family now, remember?"

They entered the area where they had seen Lady Chrysania previously; the large oaken door was heavy in its stone frame, closed tight.

"Alert!" King cried.

A robed, hooded figure leaning against the wall appeared in the fringes of King's light. King fluttered over the figure and lit it up in his cones. It was Lady Chrysania's servant, the one they had seen several times in their previous visits to the castle. The figure seemed crumpled up. It didn't move.

Phillip marched up and pulled the figure's hood back, revealing a rudimentary, vaguely human head made of contoured metal struts and tautly strung wire. Phillip stepped back in shock. "It's an Analog!" he cried, pulling the robe away from its body. Inside were an assemblage of struts, well-made pulleys and cable innards. It had a gear pack mounted in the chest area for inserting simple pre-programmed cartridge controllers. Its head consisted of nothing more than wire mesh, fiber bundles and a voice tube.

"What is this?" Thomasina asked, poking around with her MT CALM, seeing the skeletal wire and cog workings.

"It's an analog mannequin," Phillip said. "Just a simple automaton that can perform a few pre-programmed movements from a cartridge. This one has a voice tube, so a remote operator can speak for it." Phillip thought a moment. "I wonder who we were speaking to then?"

"Probably Queen Ghome herself, or one of The Jones," Sarah said. "Ok, let's move on."

Phillip pushed the Analog aside and tried the oaken door. "Lady Chrysania's gallery is through here. It's locked."

"Come on, muscles, get that door open," Sarah chided. "I'd have it opened by now."

Thomasina tried it and also couldn't budge it.

Phillip checked the mannequin for keys but found none. "Where's Sam when we need her?"

"Flat on her back on Hoban without a face just down the way from where I am, fighting pirates," Sarah replied. "All right, step back. King! Take out this door!"

Phillip and Thomasina backed up and King hovered up, scanning the door for weak areas. "Back up a bit farther," he said.

They took a few more steps back.

Satisfied, King accelerated fast, flying through the wooden door like a bullet, leaving a round splintery hole in his wake. He crashed back out a moment later, knocking the lock off. Gripping the door with his tiny feet, he swung it open.

"Great job, King. We're in," Phillip said.

"Ha, ha! Atta' boy, King!" Sarah cried, approving of the damage he could do.

Inside was a narrow corridor of inky darkness heading down

at a slight angle. King flew forward, the sweaty cavelike stone glistening in his light. Phillip added his own Sight. They moved down the corridor and came to a felt curtain draped across the threshold. Phillip pulled a SAPP from his neck, formed it into a sword and sliced it down the center. Beyond, the open gallery room was bathed in dim, humid light, dusted with frost. The gallery previously basked in total darkness, the windows and skylights blacked out, but now the windows were open, the panes swinging in the chill breeze, admitting a trickle of gray light. To the right of the threshold was the statue of a menacing dragonlike beast. King fluttered around and inspected it as a possible threat.

"That's our boy," Sarah said. "That's an image of Queen Ghome's Bower Chest, and that's what we're up against, people. If we don't put it out of action, it's going to be using Kay and the Haitathe's dead bodies as a pillow. According to Ki, it's a pretty rough customer."

Thomasina looked it over and gave it a thump with her MT CALM.

"Now, according to Ki, this next bit is going to be pretty weird."

"As if it isn't already weird," Thomasina replied.

"According to Ki, we need to look around for a message from Lady Chrysania herself," Sarah said.

"A message, from the one who lied to you?" Thomasina asked.

"That was Ghome, not Chrysania," Sarah replied. "Ghome used Chrysania to hide behind, to feed us information, to keep us in the dark and to provide a credible brainscape in case we tried to Stare her for the truth, like we did with the Occulum that third time out. So, Chrysania left us a message; let's find it."

They checked over the gallery, not quite certain what they were looking for. On the other side of the room was the grand old table where they had dined with Lady Chrysania. The floor around the table was messy with old food, discarded goblets and plates, as if they had been swept from the tabletop and allowed to clatter to the floor. The surface of the table was empty save for one thing: an odd assemblage of twisted silver and gleaming linkages sitting in the center of the table like a loaf of bread. Phillip picked it up. It was a finely crafted silver gauntlet made to fit over a slender arm, bewilderingly intricate and lightweight, yet strong and durable. At the end of the gauntlet was an automated hand studded with long, impossibly sharp-looking claws, made to kill.

Holding the gauntlet, he looked at the tabletop: old and strong, stained a deep red, probably used by the Bloodsteins for centuries. He remembered Kay had seen a bit of juvenile vandalism carved into the wood by the deplorable Wunderlucks during their previous visit. There it was, crudely scratched into the ancient surface: THE WUN-DERLUCKS WERE HERE. However, a new message was cut into the very wood of the tabletop over the top of the graffiti, carved with a fragile, delicate female script and leaving a litter of curled wood shavings across the top. Phillip brushed the curls aside.

"Rose, this must be Lady Chrysania's message," he said as Thomasina came in to look. "She didn't have hands, so she must have worn this gauntlet and carved the letters."

"Read it to me," Sarah said.

I am Chrysania.

You see what a sorry wretch I am, not only for the terrible infirmity foisted upon me, but for the gullibility and poor choices I've made over the centuries. Long ago, I was a daughter of Bloodstein. I married, had children, had grandchildren, and I watched them all live their lives and die while I continued on; my tomb forever unoc-cupied. What was wrong with me? I went to the Sisters for help, and I suffered for decades in Valenhelm—a prisoner of the Sisters. They didn't bother to lock my cell door, for I was so weak and compliant, so afraid, I simply sat there and allowed them to torture me. Simple Chrysania. Frightened Chrysania; an immortal freak and plaything of the Sisters. My House, fearing the Sisters' wrath, abandoned me as an oddity, pronouncing me dead, holding vigil over an empty tomb.

As I wept in my bed, I begged for someone to help me, to comfort me, to correct all my problems. And, from the depths of my dreams, my prayers were answered; Ghome came, speaking to me in the night, approaching across a river of sanity, promising to do all I asked. I listened, I took heart. In Valenhelm I gave her my body, and then she imprisoned me just as the Sisters had done; though, like a fool, I continued to listen to her promises.

I'm sorry I'm not stronger. I'm sorry I keep listening to lies, hoping they're the truth. When I returned from the Top of the Uni-verse, you saw me, healthy and whole, the happiest I had been in such a long time, and you shared that moment with me. I wasn't dead to you—I was alive. Afterwards, I was put back in the dark again; my beautiful new face torn away by the beasts in the dark like it was nothing, like it was worthless trash.

Just like me.

Now, before She returns to claim my blank body and decorate it in fresh travesties stolen from a tainted hearth, I wish to offer you a gift. You helped me before, and now I want to help you. The great Bower Chest; I saw what She's done to it, how She uses it to oppress, uses it to kill. The Bower Chest was a thing of wonder, a thing of riches, so patient, so strong. I was there with my brothers and sisters when our House built it. I remember how sunny and warm it was that summer, the castle so vibrant, thriving with life and possibilities, fluttering with Bloodstein banners. I remember the hammering, the shower of sparks, the smelting, the sun glittering off its brand new scales as they were lifted into place. We walked among the craftsmen, offering them water to slake their thirst as they labored. I recall the thrill we had going inside for our first ride, feeling its arcane heart beating. My father lifted me with his strong hands and I set the control column to FLY and away we went, soaring into the sky. We all laughed with joy.

How we laughed.

Now, the Bower Chest I so loved serves Her, an unkind hammer bearing stolen treasure taken from murdered hands.

And I finally understand ... The voice in my dreams was right. How long it took me to see it: that I had surrendered my soul to a monster... turning the things I loved, my family loved, to evil.

She removed the controlling column from the Bower Chest centuries ago when the Brotherhood of the Murdered Queen attempted to capture it, and set it aside to be melted down. I and my brothers and sisters helped assemble that column; it was our contribution to the Bower Chest's making and it's all I have left of them. I couldn't let it go. When She wasn't watching, some little bit of defiance rose up in me. I stole the column and hid it deep within the Gellartron. I took a piece of the column and enchanted it to serve as a lantern to guide the faithful to it. The piece is nearby; I'm hopeful, with your skills, you will locate it. It will lead you through the Gellartron to the column. Take it and be safe. Give our Bower Chest a second chance to be what it was intended; a thing of wonder—not of evil.

Perhaps, after so long and so much has been done, I finally place my faith in those worthy of it. I pray this message finds you. Know this; my face can shield you against Her creatures. Let it help you as best it can. You are my champion. Do not be killed by the things I love.

I would beg a favor, though I do not deserve it.
Bury my body.
—Chrysania, former heiress of Maug and Bloodstein. Last of my Line.

Phillip and Thomasina stood there silent. Sarah spoke over the transponder. "You know, call me a sap, but I really feel sorry for Lady Chrysania."

Phillip looked at the metal gauntlet studded with a clawed hand, a savage creation of Queen Ghome, used by a desperate woman crying out for help. He, too, pitied her.

"And you believe she can be trusted?" King asked.

Phillip answered, "I read her words and I feel her sorrow. We have to help her."

Thomasina looked around the forlorn room. "But where is it? What are we looking for? Sarah, does Ki say where to look?"

"No. But she says we need the part Chrysania hid. We won't locate the Chadburn without it."

"She mentioned the part was 'nearby'. It must be in the gallery somewhere," Phillip said.

They spread out, checking everywhere they could think of, moving furniture, searching in the dark corners, finding nothing but mold and grit.

"King, you got anything?" Phillip asked.

"I do not," he said.

Thomasina wandered over to the far side of the room, passing the Bower Chest statue. Phillip watched her and had a thought. "Rose, Lady Chrysania spent a fair amount of time talking about the Bower Chest and how it meant a great deal to her. I wonder ..."

He went to the statue of the Bower Chest placed near the entrance to the gallery. Thomasina and King joined him. He lit his Sight. "I think this might be hollow." They searched the surface.

"What are you doing?" Sarah asked. "Give me an update."

"We're checking the statue to see if it opens."

"Well, hurry it up! I should be there! I'm better at finding secret levers than you are."

They eventually located a hidden button within the statue's breastplate. The breastplate of the statue opened, moving aside to reveal a cavity. A plain brown box the size of a hatbox was situated inside. The box was manila brown in color, constructed of sturdy cardboard. Phillip pulled it out, feeling its considerable weight, and returned to the table. Inside, wrapped up in thick beige paper was an ornate brass handle splendid with engraved twisting ivy and wrought flowers. It shuddered slightly in his grasp.

"This must be the handle for the Chadburn," Phillip said. He turned it over in his hands, inspecting it closely. "I see a number of names etched into the brass. I see Feronald, Seth, Tyvonia, Mystryal, and Rantine—all names I recall from the antiquity of Bloodstein. I think Lord Feronald went on to found Planet Bloodstein. Oh, look here. I see the name Chrysania mixed in as well."

He handed it to Thomasina and she gave it a close inspection. She saw the names, all etched into the handle with an energetic hand. "Why is it moving?" she asked, feeling the handle bump about in her grasp.

"You read the note; Chrysania put a Bloodstein spell on it," Sarah said.

King landed on the rim of the box and gazed into the interior. "I am detecting organic material."

Phillip reached into the box. It was full of thick beige paper. Wait…

"Rose, this isn't paper in the box." He pulled out a limp face draped in golden hair. It was Chrysania's face that he had seen as she returned from the Top of the Universe. It was soiled with filth, as if it had been put out into the cold and left to rot. Underneath were the rest of her parts: hands, feet, etc. Phillip laid the parts out on the table in rough proper order. From top to bottom, they all appeared to be there. They stood there staring at the parts of Lady Chrysania; a grotesque, deflated un-whole amalgam; silent and desperate, crying out for help.

Phillip felt a wave of emotion course through him. He felt for this poor woman. He spoke to her disembodied face and held her unmoving hand. "We have come, Lady Chrysania. After all this time, after all that has been said and done, we have heard you at last. You are not trash, and you are not worthless." He took his SAPP and formed it into a sword, ramming the point into the floor. "We accept your charge. As you cannot walk, we will walk for you and do as you ask in the hope you may be granted some measure of peace."

Thomasina placed her hand on Phillip's. "Come, let us do what we came to do."

"That's the spirit, you two. Let's go!" Sarah said.

They placed Lady Chrysania's parts back in the box. Phillip replaced the lid and tucked the box under his arm. At the end of the room was a stair heading up to a mezzanine.

"Go up the stairs," Sarah said. King fluttered up ahead of them. In his pool-like Sight, rows of dusty rectangular machinery and vinelike runs of tangled cabling emerged, looking like the darkened skyline of a mirthless city of the damned. "These are life-support systems Queen Ghome used to use. Pretty old tech, if I say so myself. Don't trip on the cables."

A dim white light came on at the far end of the mezzanine. "Through there, keep going."

Making their way across the mezzanine, they found a modern hermetic door shut tight against the old stone. Through the window, they saw a long corridor heading down. "I think I can open it, just a moment ..." Sarah said.

"Got it!" The door opened with a hiss and slid out of the way. King flew into the corridor and they followed, the two Whispers merrily buzzing around their heads. "Where are we going, Sarah?" Thomasina asked.

"It's not far, you'll see. A word of caution; we're leaving the upper levels of Castle Bloodstein and entering the lower areas. We're getting near to the Gellartron. Ki said Ghome's Menks might be running around down there, so keep your eyes peeled, mind your Whispers, and stay out of King's way. Let him do work."

They reached the end of the corridor. A heavy stone door awaited them. Thomasina felt the surface of the door; it was stony and solid, featuring a dramatic, old-styled knocker—a leering dragon-face forged with a crooked smile and a heavy iron ring held in its teeth.

Victims approach ... the dragon knocker seemed to say.

"Must we enter?" Thomasina asked. "I don't like the feel of this."

"You'll need to pass through the door into the next chamber, and it's probably locked or rusted shut," Sarah said. "I can't help you with this one, it doesn't have a mechanism for me to access."

Phillip tried the door and, sure enough, it was stuck in place. They stood back and King went to work on the door, hitting it at high speed over and over like a jackhammer, chipping away, the knocker vibrating.

Victims, Victims, more Victims ... the knocker chided.

King eventually made a small hole in the door's stone face. Cold, musty air drifted out.

"Someone's talking in there," Thomasina said. "Do you hear?"

"I hear no talking," King replied, his feathers coated with coarse dust.

Phillip stuffed his SAPP through the hole and formed it into a stout lever. Together, he and Thomasina pulled the door open.

Shhh, shhhhh ... victims ... Come in. Join us ...

Inside was a dark, vaultlike room with a stony circular table placed at the center, taking up most of the space. Crude stone chairs draped with gangly, tubelike machinery and dangling hoses tipped with heavy barbs were arranged around the table at regular intervals.

Be seated ... and never stand again ...

Phillip and Thomasina walked in. At once, the room had a horrid feel to it, an oppressive chill, a diabolical, hopeless weight that dragged on one's soul, pulling it into the earth. Thomasina cringed.

"This place is cursed," she said, breathless, barely able to speak. "I feel the hand of the dead reaching for our throats."

The Whispers didn't seem to want to come into the room. They lingered outside the door. Phillip gently snatched them out of the air and held them in his palm. He pulled his Poltava and stepped in, protecting Thomasina. "It has a dankness about it, Rose, that's for certain. It's just RF or something, and our bodies are reacting."

"This is the Wailing Room," Sarah said, voice scratchy, the transponder popping. "This is where Queen Ghome once put her victims. She would seat them in these chairs and keep them alive with machinery. Lots of suffering. Lots of bad things happened here, lots of people going mad and the wreckage of bad dreams. I guess I sat in one of these chairs not long ago, a faceless blank; so too did Sam and Ki before we were bartered off to the Hospitalers on Hoban and my boy Raal came to get me. I wouldn't doubt if this place is haunted, cursed, whatever you want to call it. On the other side of the room is another door. Go through it. Hurry up. Be careful."

There was the door across the impossible gulf of the room. It seemed a long way off.

The room was littered with shadows. Phillip opened his Sight momentarily. Images of hunched faceless figures appeared, all sitting in the chairs under coarse, thready robes, all hooked up to the machinery, the barbs plunged into their flesh; all in incalculable suffering.

See us! See us! they cried to him.

The fact that one of these poor souls could have been Sarah, his sister, or Sam or Magistrate Kilos, all people he loved, was too much for him. He shut his Sight down. He didn't want to see.

"Rose, can you fly us across?"

She stood there, hugging herself.

"Rose?"

He took Thomasina and led her around the edge of the table toward the small door on the other side. It was difficult going. The table took up most of the available space, its rough-stony surface caught at their clothes with invisible hands, and the floor was treacherous with unseen rises and falls. The chairs themselves were vile obstructions. It was impossible to take a clean step without stumbling on something.

"There is someone sitting in that chair!" Thomasina said, pointing, an edge of panic in her voice, something unheard-of for the normally courageous woman from Waam. She fell into Phillip's embrace.

"There is nobody here but the three of us," King replied.

Machinery clinked and a set of barbed hoses slid off the tabletop to the floor, making a rude amount of noise in the process. King snapped his Sight on, illuminating nothing but rising dust.

"Sarah!" Phillip cried.

Give us your dreams ... came through the transponder.

We shall take those too!

"Phillip, we must be away from here!" Thomasina said.

Phillip pressed on, moving past the table. He nearly tripped on something bunched up on the floor. He kicked it aside; it was an empty, rather shapeless robe made of rough threads carelessly loomed together.

Sarah wore that robe ...

They arrived at the door. Phillip fumbled with the latch, struggling to get it open.

Another set of hoses slid to the floor. Machinery hissed. Rough fabric rustled.

He got the door open, quickly shuffling Thomasina and himself through, eager to be gone. King followed them.

Your dreams ... came an ephemeral voice from the transponder.

"Sarah?" Phillip asked.

"What?" came her usual voice.

"We're out. Thank Creation we're out."

Phillip shut the door. As soon as it closed, the latch moved as if something on the other side was trying to open the door. He held it shut, the latch shaking.

Soon, it faded, the latch settling to stillness.

3—The Blood Box

On the other side was a spacious antechamber, thankfully free of the oppressive heaviness of the Wailing Room. Phillip and Thomasina took a moment to catch their breath and thank their maker for their deliverance. On the far wall was a simple door with an old-looking palm lock to the left of the frame. Phillip opened his hand and released the Whispers; they too seemed relieved to be out of the Wailing Room.

"Ok, welcome to the Gellartron," Sarah said. "This is the place the Sisters deactivated centuries ago, only to have Queen Ghome return in secret and reactivate it later. She's got some moxie, you gotta hand it to her. You're seeing a door, right?"

"We are."

"Good. Phillip, open the door and tell me what you see."

With King and Thomasina covering him, Phillip tentatively opened the door. It opened easily, squeaking slightly on its old hinges. Behind the door was a continuation of the stone wall.

"It's a dead end," Phillip said.

"No, no," Sarah said. "This is the Gellar door. If you don't know how to work the arcane combination lock, a solid wall is all you'll come up with. You could blast through the wall and find nothing but more wall. But, if you know what you're doing and you put in the correct combination, then you'll gain entrance to the Gellartron and, depending on what combination you use, you'll end up in different areas of the Gellartron. Without the knowledge Ki derived from her Gaming Session, our journey would end right here at the Gellar door. It sounds pretty cool and I wish I could see it for myself. Check Lady Chrysania's handle. What's it doing?"

Thomasina looked at the brass handle gleaming in her hand. "It's not doing anything."

"Place it on the floor."

Thomasina placed the handle on the floor. Moments later it began moving, scratching on the stone, picking up speed until it was spinning like a top.

"Is it spinning?" Sarah asked.

"Yes."

"Good. That's what Ki said it would do. Now we hit the Gellartron. There's a complex combination lock to the left of the door. When we manipulate the lock and open the door to the correct area of the Gellartron, the handle will stop spinning and start pointing. Ki said we're looking for a 'blood box'. I guess the Chadburn will be inside of it. Got it? Look around; you should see the lock near the left-hand side of the door."

To the left of the door was an odd palm lock carved into the rock, where one could place one's hand.

"I see it. There are five depressions where I can, presumably, place my fingertips," Phillip said.

Sarah was elated. "Ki's right on the money! Place your left hand in the slot and situate your fingers. Moving your fingers in various ways will alter the lock and the Gellar door will open into different areas in the Gellartron, if you've moved it correctly. Now, here's the thing; Ki couldn't tell us which area holds the Chadburn, so it's going to be trial and error until we hit it. It's going to be in that 'blood box' thing, ok? Let's go, and be on the lookout for Ghome's Menks. First, put your hand on the lock; next, lift your pinky, lower your thumb and then move the lock to your right. Be careful—if you mess it up, even just a little, the Gellar door will open up into a trap. Queen Ghome has protected her hoard well."

"What kind of trap?" Thomasina asked.

"Ki didn't say. She just said 'trap', so let's assume it's a deadly trap—therefore, Phillip, don't mess it up."

Phillip did as Sarah instructed. He carefully situated his fingers and then slid the lock to the right while Thomasina and King covered the door. Poltava drawn, Phillip carefully swung the door open.

Beyond the door was a vast darkened room piled high with boxes and draped sheets. At first glance there did not appear to be anywhere to walk in the room; it was a disorganized mountain of clutter piled at least fifty feet high, taking up every possible inch of floor space. King fluttered in and rose up into the heights, looking for guards or traps.

"See anything?" Thomasina asked.

King panned around with his Sight. "It's difficult to tell. The room is packed full of hoard."

"Is it a trap?" Thomasina asked.

King poked around amid the boxes, sheets and crates. "It does not appear to be."

"Is the handle still spinning?" Sarah asked.

"It is," Phillip said.

"Fine then—wrong hoard. Before you close the door, we're going to de-fang Queen Ghome a little and burn it."

"Why?" Thomasina asked.

"Queen Ghome gets her Gellar powers from all her hoards. Her sheer volume of stuff gives her power. If we destroy as much of her hoard as we can, she'll weaken. If we take out enough, she might lose her ability to get into people's heads and control the weather. So, get in there, start a nice hot fire, and get out."

King fluttered back through the door. "Alert!" he cried. "Menks!"

Crawling about on the walls of the hoard room with a disquieting 'clacking' sound were a number of horrific, somewhat elongated creatures. Like the blank vision of Lady Chrysania, these creatures had no discernible facial features; they were motile blanks. Attached to their mannequin-like heads were elaborate crowns of interlocking metal tubing and circuitry. Tubes trailed away from the crowns and plunged into their flesh under their chins and behind where their ears

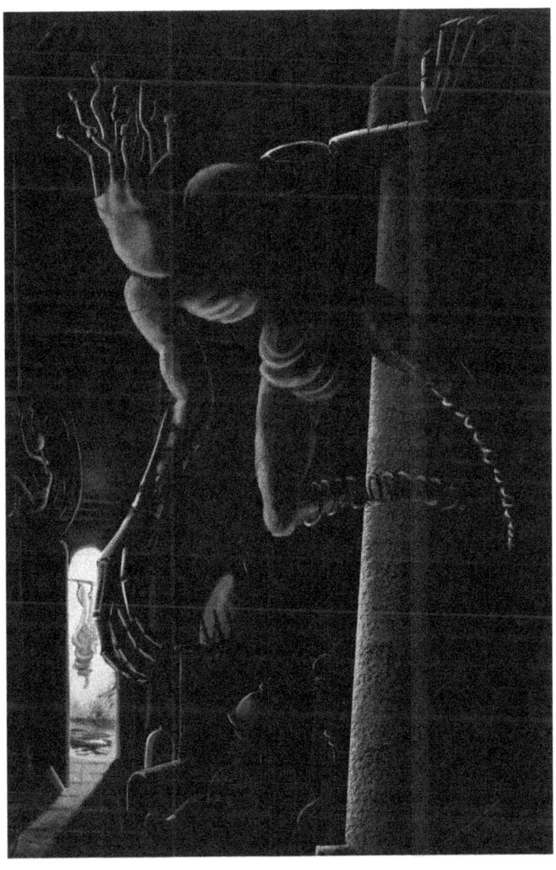

would normally be. Hornlike exhaust tubes of rusty metal respirated lazy jets of humid air with a machinelike 'whoosh, whoosh' sound. The limbs and torsos of these creatures were impossibly thin and elastic in appearance. Shoulderless, hipless, jointless, it was as if they were made of soft puttylike flesh and had no bones under their skin.

It was impossible to assign a gender to their vaguely human forms. Their flesh was dotted with festive painted-on circles of pink, blue, yellow and green. They appeared to have no hands or feet; instead they were fitted with glittering delicate silver gauntlets tipped with articulated fingers crafted in gothic finery—the same type of gauntlet Lady Chrysania had used to scratch her message into the table. The fingers were tipped with sturdy, daggerlike claws of a particularly sharp note. They also wore odd metal harnesses on their legs that wound around their calves like stout springs.

Sightless and deaf, these creatures clattered about the walls like giant-sized geckos, forever guarding Queen Ghome's treasure.

"Menks," Phillip said, Poltava at the ready. "Guarding the hoard."

"How many?" Sarah asked.

"A lot."

King fluttered up, ready to attack. Thomasina drifted into the air behind Phillip, her MT CALM club poised in her hand. "Can they detect us?" she whispered.

Before Phillip could respond, one of the creatures scurried in their direction, its metal fingers sparking on the walls. It clattered through the Gellar door, bold and aggressive, its metal hands raised in a fearsome fashion, but confused and somewhat apprehensive at the same time. It appeared to know Phillip, Thomasina and King were there, but could not pin-point them due to the arcane power of the Whispers' Veil. It moved its clawed hands about and waggled its head from side to side, metal tubes swishing through the air, collecting information.

"It can't," Phillip said.

The Menk moved about the room. It placed one of its metal claws on the wall and made a series of clacking sounds. A host of return clacks came from the hoard room.

"Alert!" King cried. "Menks are converging!"

"Phillip! Shut the door!" Thomasina cried. "Hurry!"

Before he could get it closed, a second Menk came through, slinking across the stony face of the walls and bounding across the floor like a dire rabbit.

They attacked!

Chaos!

Confusion!

The room was too small to create any sort of battle front. Though there were only two Menks, they were fast and savage, and the battle quickly became a horrendous free-for-all. Straight away, the Menks targeted the two Whispers—Bridgewater and Inn, as Thomasina had named them. Despite their lack of eyes, they flung their metal gauntlets at the Whispers with great accuracy, skewering both of them, their metal claws digging deep into the wall.

"No!" Thomasina cried, seeing them killed.

With the Whispers destroyed, Phillip, Thomasina and King fell out of Cloak. Their quarry exposed, the Menks chattered in excitement.

Phillip took aim and fired at the nearest Menk.

POW! POW!

The shots slammed into its body, the pressure waves of each shot deforming its flesh in a grotesque fashion as blood erupted from the wound in a meaty geyser. Both hits were on-target and quite mortal, but despite the blows, the Menk pressed on, attacking with blinding speed as if nothing had happened. Phillip raised his SAPP and formed it into a shield to ward it off. The Menk drove into the shield, clawing at it, bleeding all over it, trying to get around into Phillip. He pumped shots through the SAPP and into the Menk.

POW! POW! POW! POW!

At last, the faceless monster fell, spewing blood in vast quantities. Six shots! Phillip boggled on it. A Poltava, though small, was powerful enough to drop a large man with one shot, much less six. All to the torso. All deadly, and the Menk just kept going.

Nearby, Thomasina was in a desperate situation. The second Menk had closed in, trying to rake her with its metal claws. She had no room to maneuver, to fly, and all she was armed with was her MT CALM club, which did nothing but drive the Menk into a frenzy. King fluttered overhead, trying to get into position to strike the Menk, but it was in too close with Thomasina—attacking it would probably kill her as well.

It swiped at Thomasina, missing time and time again. It flung its claws, hoping to impale her against the wall but she was too quick, evading the claws as they bit into stone, leaving the Menk with rounded stumps. The Menk slapped at her with its stumps. She ducked again and the Menk's stump hit the wall.

BOOOOOOOOM! came a thunderous explosion, shattering rock, stunning Thomasina, knocking her back, nearly bursting her eardrums.

The Menk came at her, stumps raised.

POW! POW! POW! POW!

Phillip came to her aid, firing his Poltava, moving the Menk away from her. Huge holes opened in its flesh. Buckets of blood poured out. Undaunted, the Menk pressed on.

King came. A cloud of light, and the Menk fell. Phillip and Thomasina stood there panting, gazing at the elongated dead bodies with horror and hard-won respect. His Poltava smoked.

Sarah spoke up through the transponder. "What happened? Is everybody ok? Somebody say something!"

Phillip regained his wits. "We were attacked by Queen Ghome's Menks, Sarah! It was terrible! It takes half a clip to bring down just one and there's a whole bunch more waiting for us in the hoard room."

There was confused silence from Sarah over the transponder. "All right, wait a sec," she said.

While they waited, Phillip checked over Thomasina. She was kneeling, holding the silvery remains of the two Whispers destroyed by the Menks.

"Rose, are you all right?"

Thomasina was shaken. "The Whispers are gone. I promised your mother I'd take care of them. They were a gift."

"She can make more. There's only one of you."

She stood. King perched on her shoulder. "You fought well, Lady Blanchefort," he said.

"Marilith's praise for you, Great Bird," she said. "Phillip, how are we going to do this? We have King, and he was magnificent, but just two of them were almost too much for us. What if they manage to destroy King, as they did Bridgewater and Inn? We will be overwhelmed."

"I will not allow them to damage me," King replied.

Sarah came back on the line. "Ok guys, I think I might have messed up what Ki said. Sorry, you can get even with me later. She mentioned a 'blood box'. I assumed it was literally a box somewhere in the hoard where the Chadburn might be kept. I re-reviewed Ki's Gaming Session and cross-referenced various bits of Menk lore. It's a little cryptic, but I now think the blood box is actually a room somewhere in the hoard. That's the thing with Menks; they always have a hidden room somewhere where they keep things very important to them. What they keep in these rooms, these Blood Boxes, makes them vulnerable. You find it, you go in, and I think you should be able to neutralize the Menks there."

"Can we confirm this with Ki so we can make certain there

are no mistakes this time?" Phillip asked.

"Hey, give me a break, will you? And, no, we can't ask Ki, she's still out in the IU."

King fluttered into the air. "I will go. Re-enter the combination, let me in and close the door after me. I will discover this Blood Box and see what's there."

"We cannot lose you, King," Thomasina said.

"I will not be lost."

Phillip situated his fingers in the lock and moved the pads to the correct position. "I'm ready. Rose, open the door and let him in. King, five minutes and we'll re-open the door. Are you ready? Don't try to be a hero, King, avoid contact as only you can."

King fluttered into the air. "Ready. Open the door. Close it behind me."

"Auld go with you," Thomasina said. She opened the door to an uneasy, skittering darkness. Tapping. Sparks on the walls. Menks moving around unseen. King zipped in and she closed the door.

Phillip re-loaded his Poltava. "Sarah. Keep the time. Five minutes, and we're going in."

"Right!"

Thomasina was miserable with worry, staring at the Gellar door. "What is happening to him right now?"

"King can handle himself," Sarah said.

They waited for what felt like an eternity. Phillip, curious, opened the Gellar door a crack; stone wall, King far away.

"Ok, that's five minutes," Sarah said. "Get in there and be careful."

"All right. Rose, I'm going to give you my Poltava and a spare clip. When we open the door, soar up into the heights where the Menks can't get to you. I'll try illuminating the Menks with my Sight. You take them out. There are fifteen shots per clip; make them count."

Thomasina took the Poltava and the clip. She kissed him for luck and readied herself. Phillip set the lock and swung the Gellar door open. Poltava at the ready, Thomasina soared in. Phillip put the box containing Lady Chrysania's parts aside and followed her.

Inside was the hoard room, packed solid with a giant mountain of crates and boxes, all tenuously piled upward. Phillip lit his Sight, casting strong silvery cones of light to pierce the darkness. It was difficult going for him as there was little if any level floor space for him to traverse without having to climb on crates.

It was deep silent in the hoard room.

"King!" he cried out.

No answer, just silence.

The room seemed to be built as a cube about a hundred feet square and possibly a hundred feet high, capped by a flat ceiling of ominous stone. Overhead, Thomasina floated in the center of room above the summit of the hoard.

"King!" she called out.

Phillip climbed up onto some crates, feeling them shudder and shift under his weight. A Menk appeared in his Sight, huddled against the wall, veiny and deathly pale, its silver claws sparkling and dug in.

Thomasina saw it, took aim and fired.

POW!

It shuddered under the weight of the shot and dropped off the wall, huddled up like a dead insect, leaving its claws embedded. They discovered several more clinging to the walls; each was dispatched with a single shot.

"I see many more!" Thomasina said, whirling about. "Scattered about all over, either dead or very near to it!"

Phillip tried to climb higher, but the hoard was too unsteady, ready to give way and come down around him.

"Phillip, let me help you," she said as she came down and lifted him into the heights. The hoard was like an artificial mountain rising up in an unsteady cone, bathed in total darkness save for Phillip's Sight.

"Where is King?" he asked as he reclaimed his Poltava.

As if in response, the hoard rumbled. A white light burst through the clutter, rising into the heights.

King.

"Good Creation, King, we feared for you!" Phillip said.

He presented himself before them. "My apologies. The Menks attacked, fast and savage as I entered. I took several down, but there were so many. I took refuge in the depths of the hoard, making my way through the small spaces where the Menks could not easily follow. I discovered, at the far end, buried deep under the hoard, a doorway, which I smashed through. The doorway led to a long chamber. There, I found a place of horror and pestilence which I believe to be Lady Sarah's Blood Box. I saw hundreds of collections of living organs: lungs, hearts, kidneys, whole systems, suspended individually from hooks and bathed in vile red liquid. I believe what I saw were the vital organs of the Menks, removed from their bodies yet somehow maintained in a living condition, furnishing them with life from afar. I destroyed the organs, I destroyed them all, and the Menks fell. I heard the dull thuds of their bodies dropping onto the hoard."

Phillip patted him on the crest. "Well done, King. Sarah, did you get all that?"

She did not reply. Static snaked from the transponder. "Wherever we are now must be far from Castle Bloodstein, the transponder is out-of-range. Let's get back through the Gellar door." He took a bullet from his Poltava. "King, take this bullet and burn the hoard as Sarah said to do."

King took the bullet and winged away. Thomasina carried Phillip down toward the open Gellar door, a pool of orange light spilling out amid the darkness. As they exited, Sarah's voice popped back over the transponder.

"What happened?" she yelled, concern heavy in her voice. They told her how King had discovered the Blood Box.

"Buried deep like that at the bottom of the hoard, if we hadn't had King with us, we'd never have gotten to it. The Menks would have crushed us."

"Yep," Sarah said. "Old Queen Ghome doesn't have an answer for King, does she?"

Through the door came a loud 'POP', followed by an eerie flickering of orange light. King rejoined them as Phillip poked his head into the room. A small but rapidly growing fire danced at the base of the hoard; several crates were already completely ablaze. Smoke reached upwards.

"Again, well done, King," he said as they quickly closed the door and turned the lock. Phillip opened the door again and the stone wall had returned.

"Atta' boy, King! If only my mother properly appreciated how bad you are!" Sarah said. "Now, we're going to continue infiltrating Ghome's hoard, we're going to let King kill the Menks and then we're going to burn each hoard until we come up with the Chadburn. Each one of these hoards we burn, Ghome's going to get a little weaker. Let's do it!"

As Sarah advised, they repeated the process at least ten times, Phillip manipulating the lock with his fingers per her instructions, the Gellartron door opening to a massive hoard of treasures, the spinning handle on the floor, releasing King into the hoard and slamming the door behind him, and then, once it was all done and the Menks were dead, King setting fire to the hoard using a bullet from Phillip's Poltava. Knowing their weakness and being able to reach the Blood Box made it fairly simple.

Still there was no sign of the Chadburn; just piles of hoarded treasure and the blind, deaf monsters defending it.

4—A Familiar Prisoner

"We're getting toward the end," Sarah said. "The next hoard is going to be a lot different from the previous ones, so listen up! The hoards we've seen so far have all been indoors; the next one though will be outside in a place Ki called 'Queen Ghome's Playroom'. Ki was a little fuzzy on the details, and we didn't have time to drill down and press her for more, but she says the 'playroom' is located on some backwards, sparsely populated world out there in the universe, somewhere where she terrorizes the locals and periodically raids them for slaves. Don't ask me where the Playroom's located, Ki didn't say. It's built atop a very high plateau that's at least a couple thousand feet high, and she's excavated the heck out of it. She uses this area as her private 'back door' and personal escape route should she need to make use of it. Get ready for lots and lots of Menks, ok, and they're going to be flying as well as jumping around on the ground. Ki says there are a ton of them guarding the Playroom, ok?"

Phillip and Thomasina both cringed at the thought.

Sarah went on. "According to Ki, the Playroom is also where Queen Ghome keeps her junk. You're going to see a central causeway that goes on for a long way down the center of the plateau. On either side of the causeway will be a number of giant-sized holes dug into the ground where Ghome keeps her junk hoards. Ki said there should be six of them. Let's hope the Chadburn is in one of them, as we're running out of hoards to check. Be aware, as we keep destroying these various hoards, the Gellartron is going to start malfunctioning. The power of the Gellartron at Castle Bloodstein depends on the amount and well-being of Queen Ghome's hoards so, as we burn more and more hoards, it's going to falter and behave erratically, which is great as that'll help Kay out. But you don't want to get stuck in there, so don't burn anything until we locate the Chadburn. Ok? Also, don't forget when you step through you'll be cut off from my signal. Get in and get out, then we can move on to the Bower Chest itself. Once we infiltrate the Bower Chest, we're installing the Chadburn and shutting it down!"

Phillip and Thomasina readied themselves. Sarah instructed Phillip and he turned the Gellar door lock. The door opened, King went in, and Thomasina shut the door behind him. Several minutes later, they opened the Gellar door again. King returned.

"Alert! The area is as Lady Sarah described; a large plateau 6,452 feet in height that has been heavily excavated into several levels cut into the top. There are a number of Menks present; however, they are concentrated at the far end of the plateau. There are no Menks currently patrolling the hoard area beyond."

"No Menks?"

"None. I also could not locate a Blood Box. It is not where the previous ones were located."

"All right. We'll go in and accomplish our tasks as quickly as possible and then retreat. Are we ready?"

Thomasina reluctantly nodded.

"Don't forget," Sarah said, "no burning until we're done."

Phillip opened the door again. As promised, the Gellar door swung open to a vast outdoor setting bathed in weak moonlight from three quartered moons hanging in a vast olive sky streaked with thin clouds. The whole scene was quite a departure from the close-in total pitch darkness they had become accustomed to in the previous hoards. A long dusty causeway about twelve feet wide ran ahead into the somber distance. The spinning handle on the floor came to an abrupt halt, pointing straight through the open doorway.

"Sarah, the handle is pointing," Phillip said.

"Is it? Good! About damn time! Get in there and hurry it up. Watch the Menks."

They went in; King first, with Thomasina rising up and Phillip trailing with the box and the handle. The first thing Phillip noticed as he stepped through was the thin, unsatisfying air; it was difficult to draw in a decent lungful. Thomasina was feeling it too, wheezing and taking deep breaths to fill her lungs. The altitude was telling.

"Rose, are you all right in this altitude?" Phillip was used to the altitude at Castle Blanchefort, but Thomasina came from Waam, which was pretty much at sea level.

"I'll manage," she wheezed, struggling to maintain her flight.

"Go back through the Gellar door and wait for us."

Thomasina wasn't budging. "Let's do what we came to do and be done with it, Phillip."

Ahead, at the distant end of the plateau, was a rolling expanse of reasonably flat land marked at various intervals by dramatic rises in sudden elevation and abyssal falls. Stairways, leveled platforms and various structures were cut into the rock like dark scrimshaw highlighted with dim dots of orange lantern light. Black specks like floating cinders occasionally rose into the sky and drifted down.

"Phillip," Thomasina gasped. "Do you see those specks off in the distance? Are those Menks?"

"Affirmative," King said. "Winged Menks, 4.5 miles distant."

Behind them, the Gellar door they had emerged through was built into a small mound of piled up stones placed at the end of the causeway; past the stones was sheer emptiness. Phillip peered over the edge; the plateau ended in a sheer cliff wall going down thousands of feet to a cauldron of clouds far below.

"We are at the eastern edge of the plateau," King said.

"How high are we, again?" Phillip asked.

"6,452 feet, or 1,966.569 meters."

Following Lady Chrysania's handle, they moved inland away from the Gellar door. There were six treasure hoards situated around the central causeway. They were dug into the ground in perfect cubes roughly one hundred feet long and one hundred feet deep, divided by a ten foot partition. All of them were open to the elements. Thomasina looked down into the hoards.

"Phillip, what is this?" she asked. "It's a bit dark to see in the night air, but it looks like these hoards are full of junk. I see bits and pieces of furniture. I see toppled over crates and torn fabrics. I can smell mold."

"Sarah said something about these hoards containing mostly junk. Apparently, she was correct."

As they moved farther in, the handle nudged slightly in Phillip's hand. He placed it on the causeway. It wobbled and slid through the grit to the right.

He picked it back up and they continued, concentrating on the hoards to the right of the causeway. When they passed the forth hoard cube, the handle turned abruptly in his hand.

"Here. This one," he said. They peered over the edge of the causeway, looking down into the hoard room. It was piled deep with boxes, crates, racks and all manner of loose items of varying sizes. The galling smell of mold and dead things drifting upwards was thick; it troubled them. Thomasina covered her nose. Loose items were piled in a ratty, torn heap filling the entire room with no obvious place to walk or stand, and with no obvious entrance or exit other than going up.

"This is the correct one?" Thomasina asked, covering her mouth.

"The handle indicates so. I suppose we're going to have to go down and dig the Chadburn out."

"Down there? There's no flat place to stand. You'll break your ankle or worse. King and I will do it. Cover us, please, Phillip. Watch for Menks."

He gave her the handle. She and King drifted down to the summit of hoarded things, floating over its spectacularly unsafe surface, Thomasina poking and testing the mountain of boxes to see how stable they were. Crates shifted and boxes toppled, spilling out seedy contents. With Phillip covering, Thomasina and King set to work, following the handle. They moved to the far corner of the hoard and dug down into the pile, tossing things aside.

Phillip stood on the causeway holding the box containing Lady Chrysania's parts and his Poltava. "Sarah?" he asked. He got nothing back but static through the transponder. He wondered where they were. He looked at the moons hanging overhead; Phillip was an amateur selenologist and was familiar with most moons in the League. He didn't recognize any of these three; they couldn't be in the League. Perhaps Xaphan space? He looked back, seeing the edge of the plateau and the little pile of stones where the open Gellar door was located, centered in a rectangle of orange light like a lone breakwater against a sea of darkness. He could see the dank stony interior of Castle Bloodstein through the door; their lifeline home.

Down below, Thomasina and King rattled around.

"How goes it?" he asked, holding the box tightly, eager to be gone from this place. They didn't hear him. "Rose!" he said, raising his voice to be heard.

"Who's there?" came a voice carrying on the night air.

Startled, Phillip set the box down and raised his Poltava. In the distance, he caught hints of noise; voices and indistinct banging interspersed with uneasy silence. As King and Thomasina were still hard at it, he wandered farther down the causeway to investigate, walking quite a distance from the Gellar door which he didn't really want to leave, but he also didn't want to be ambushed by hostile forces. He would investigate the noises and then return as soon as he was satisfied they were secure. Just beyond the end of the hoard chambers was a small cluster of darkened shacks situated in a ramshackle fashion around the causeway. Their size and shape reminded him of the lovely, windblown shacks by the sea in Fazo that he and Thomasina had loved so much, had consummated their marriage in. However, there was nothing festive or romantic about these buildings; they were dark and forlorn, places one would wish to flee from, not visit for a vacation. As he got nearer, he saw stout metal bars on the windows, like those from a jail cell.

"Is somebody there?" came a frantic voice from one of the cells. Phillip saw a slender form gazing at him hopefully through bars. A pair of hands held the bars and rattled them.

"Hey, hey, please. Can you help me? Can you get me out?" the voice asked. Phillip analyzed the voice. It seemed to be female, though it was flecked with fear and a bit of mania, making it difficult to determine gender. It could be the voice of a high-pitched man, or a contralto woman. Phillip also thought he detected hints of an accent—South League, possibly Zenon or Remnath.

Poltava readied, Phillip stepped forward. "Identify yourself."

The figure behind the bars hesitated. "Me? I'm just a slave, that's all. If you get me out, I can cook for you and tend to your clothes. I'll work real hard. You won't know what you did without me. Please, don't leave me here!"

Phillip felt pity for the prisoner; his natural inclination was to help but he had to stop himself. Look where he was, look what they were here to do. Danger was everywhere and the Menks, floating in the sky miles away, could possibly detect him and attack at any moment. Without knowing the location of their Blood Box, they would be unstoppable. He came to the barred door. "I'm sorry," he said. "I cannot help you. I wish I could."

He turned to walk away.

"DON'T LEAVE ME!" came the voice again, hysterical this time, shouting.

Phillip hardened his heart and continued.

"They hurt me," the voice whined pitifully. "I'm hurt. I'm *dying* ... I need medical attention or I'm going to die. What will become of my soul in this Elder-down place?"

Phillip stopped. The voice seemed to belong to a League citizen from the accent and the words used. Phillip was Vith, and despite the situation, he had to help if he could. If it was a trick, then it was a trick and he had his Poltava. He approached the cell—his conscience would give him no rest if he didn't. "Back away," he said.

The figure meekly complied and spoke in a hopeful voice, this time clearly female. "Ok, ok. I'll just stand back here. Thank you. Thank you for not leaving me." She scooted to the back of the cell and waited.

Phillip inspected the door. It had a barred window over a metal ledge that stuck out about a foot. Beneath the ledge was a complicated handle—the ledge preventing the cell's occupant from reaching it. He tried the handle. With a few turns he was able to open the door, swinging it wide with a rusty clank.

"Come out of there," he ordered.

The figure came out of the cell. It was a tall woman, pale of features, dirty, wearing a threadbare gray sack that billowed about her thin body, arms and legs bare, sliding off her shoulders, hanging on by a thread. Crazed, somewhat windblown with a mess of silvery-brown hair, she came toward Phillip, hands held up as if seeking an embrace.

"Gods, yes!" she cried.

"You don't look injured to me," Phillip said.

"Oh, I'm fine; I just didn't want you to leave me here. Thanks, mister, you won't regret this. Look at you, you're so handsome and ..." she took a good hard look at Phillip and stopped dead in her tracks. "Oh Fimbul Wolf!" she cried. "It's you!"

Phillip recognized the woman. It was Clara Wunderluck, of the Jocanda clan. He hadn't seen her since the ordeal with the Dead Man in the Grove where all of her brothers had been killed. The Wunderlucks had been treacherous, lying scalawags, with Clara Wunderluck being the worst of the lot. "You!" he yelled, aiming his Poltava at her head. "I thought you imprisoned in our village jail!"

She balled her hands up into little fists. "I was jailed in your village with no Barr and crappy food—thanks a lot for that! And then this guy came in to see me—I thought he was a Barr or something! I thought he was going to get me out, but instead he brought in this woman with red eyes and horns. Horns! She fricken' took me out of the cell to Atrajak knows where, tore my clothes off and interrogated me for days. I thought I was dead for sure!"

"And did you talk? Did you give away our secrets?"

Clara slapped her forehead. "Well, yeah! I was trying to stay alive, you know, you Blanchefort Frag-Wagon! I was scared to death! I told her all about the Machine, where it was and the defenses around it!"

"I ought to shoot you right now!" Phillip roared.

Clara stared at Phillip, the wheels turning, assessing the situation. Phillip had been told that Clara Wunderluck was a crafty customer, nothing to trifle with. She seemed to sense weakness in him, that he was a civilized gentleman and that she was in no danger of getting shot by him no matter what she did. She smiled and came at him boldly, going for his gun. "Oh yeah, go ahead, shoot!" she said. "Shoot me! Can't do it, can you? Can you? Too much of a gentleman to shoot a lady, aren't you? Admit it!"

Grinning, she reached out and touched the barrel of his Poltava; Phillip slapped her hand away.

"Give me the gun," she purred. "Come on, give it to mc. Are we going to have to have a girl versus boy wrestling match for it? Oh, and by the way, I believe I've kicked your blue-haired sister's butt on several occasions; maybe I could kick yours too." She tried to trip him with a leg sweep, using some sort of formal fighting technique that she had used on Sarah several times, but Phillip knew techniques of his own and countered her move, pushing her down into the dirt. She smiled up at him like a hawk. He knew Clara was an unabashed opportunist; shamelessly testing every angle no matter how improbable to improve her situation.

Clara re-assessed, altering her approach. She stood, giggling and flirting, trying to charm the gun out of him. "Oh, come on, give me the gun. Give me the gun, you handsome fellow, you. I'm going to start tickling in a moment. I will! Give me the gun and I'll give you a nice wet kiss ..."

Clara was wrenched away and spun around. Thomasina's fist crashed into her chin, knocking her down flat. Wheezing, Thomasina stood over Clara, her Xaphan blood boiling.

"For the love of Auld, who is this person who has presumed to lay her hands on my husband?" she said, voice shaking. She was holding an intricate column of brass and enameled steel five feet long. An ivory-faced dial sat atop the column, bold and ornate. On the dial face were a number of words written in flowing black script: FORWARD, BACKWARD, LEFT, RIGHT, and so on. Some of the lettering was too small to read. Thomasina had attached Lady Chrysania's brass handle to the dial face. It was currently placed over the FREE RUN setting, moved there long ago by Queen Ghome. King was perched on the dial, watching the situation unfold.

"We located the Chadburn, Phillip," Thomasina said. Her eyes widened as she recognized Clara. "In Marilith's name—it's that insane Wunderluck woman again. I'd hoped we'd seen the last of her."

"Phillip said he was taking me with you," Clara said, rubbing her jaw. "He promised me!"

"You're going nowhere with us, you filthy Wunderluck trollop."

"Who's a trollop?" Clara shot back.

Phillip pointed at the cell where Clara had been held. "She was locked in that cell over there, Rose. She called out for help, said she was wounded. I didn't know it was her."

Thomasina picked up Clara by the scruff of the neck. "Well then, we'll simply put her back where we found her and take our leave." Thomasina dragged Clara through the dirt back to her cell.

Clara struggled. She kicked and clawed. "Wait, you can't leave me here! I don't even know where here is! Her naked minions make me do all their filthy wet work for them: scrubbing their tanks, fishing their cisterns. All the time! Grunge work! I'm no mechanic. I don't know what I'm doing, I hurt myself and I don't get any help! They're working me to death! They feed me scraps of unnamable food and putrid water, and they'll probably kill me or steal my face once I stop pulling my weight!"

"Then you'll have something to look forward to, won't you?" Thomasina chucked Clara into the cell and closed the door. "There you are, back where you belong."

Clara wailed. "For the Love of Firth, Lord Blanchefort, take me with you! Have a damn heart! Hey! HEY!" She picked up a metal bowl and banged on the bars, making a fearful racket.

PANG! PANG! PANG!

"Get me out of here!" she screeched.

King hopped off the Chadburn dial and rose into the air a bit. "Alert! Menk!" he hissed.

Phillip plucked King of out the air and hid him inside his duster to douse his light. They threw themselves into the shadows, hoping to hide from the Menk.

"We cannot be discovered. Without knowing the location of the Blood Box, the Menks will overwhelm us," Phillip said.

As they watched, a winged Menk glittering with metal claws passed about fifty feet overhead, its wings knuckled and batlike, its claws glittering in the olive light. It continued on down the causeway heading east until it reached the pile of rocks at the edge of the plateau, and the open Gellar door.

"Gods, Phillip, what's it doing?" Thomasina asked.

The Menk came down on all fours, raking its claws on the stony ground. It noticed the Gellar door was open and went to it, inspecting the frame, its rail-thin body catching the light. Before they could react, the Menk swung the Gellar door closed, shutting it. The Menk then took flight and winged away to the north.

Alarmed, Thomasina stood. "I'm going to check the door." She took flight and soared down the causeway at great speed.

"Your chick can fly?" Clara asked.

Phillip didn't answer her. He watched Thomasina arrive at the pile of rocks and frantically feel about with her hands. She soon resumed flight and returned, huffing and puffing, red in the face.

"It's gone, Phillip, the door is gone!" she said in misery. "It's just a pile of rocks now, and it's all this little slut's fault for attracting the Menk!"

Thomasina marched up to Clara's cell. "You've stranded us here!"

Clara was jubilant. "Ah, so you're stuck here, right? How's it feel? Stinks, doesn't it, you stupid Frag-Licking Leg-Wagon!"

Thomasina wheeled around. "Hold this," she said, handing Phillip the Chadburn.

"What are you going to do?" Clara asked.

"I'm going to beat you until you meet your end!"

"Bring it to me, babe! I'm all here for ya!"

Thomasina rattled the metal door in its frame, trying to get it open.

"So, you need some help, right?" Clara said as Thomasina fumbled with the door. "I know how to get out of here. I can get us to Bazz. She's got this weird flying machine. She lives in it with her army of naked ladies, and she's got treasure all over the place."

"The Bower Chest?" Phillip asked.

"The what? I caught a glimpse out a porthole once and I saw wings flapping, like a dragon or something. That's where they make me work for her. They often go to this place in a desert where they worship her like a goddess. Up in the mountains is a door that goes to Bazz. I've seen it. I've been through it, but I couldn't get away. I can take you there."

Phillip came up. "Rose, wait!" She was shaking with rage. "Just a moment. So, you claim to know a place where we can access Queen Ghome's Bower Chest?" he asked.

Clara gave him a toothy smile. "Sure. It's not far. I've been in it lots of times. Pretty confusing to get there. You need a guide."

"She's lying!" Thomasina said. "Let me teach her a lesson!"

Clara laughed. "Well, love, if I get taught a hard lesson, I just might forget where it is and you all will be stuck right here with me," she said in a sly voice.

Phillip pulled Thomasina away from the door. "King, do you know where we are?" he asked.

"I have no point of reference at this time," he replied. "Perhaps, as I gather celestial information, I might be able to determine our location."

"Ha! Even your demon's stumped!" Clara cried.

Phillip thought a moment. "And, Lady Wunderluck, you'll take us to the Bower Chest straight away?"

"The dragon, right? Sure. I can get you there, and then I'm going to Bazz and going home. What are we waiting for?"

Seeing little other choice, Phillip opened the door. Thomasina dragged Clara out and pushed her forward down the causeway.

"Don't touch me!" Clara warned.

"Lead the way," Thomasina said, pushing her again. "And do not annoy me, I warn you."

"Wait a moment," Phillip said. "I need to get the box." He ran down the length of the causeway and retrieved the box. He checked it again, making sure all of Lady Chrysania was in there, and returned, thankful he'd had the foresight it bring it with him.

"What's in the box?" Clara asked.

"Nothing that concerns you," Thomasina said. "Let's go!"

Moving down the causeway, Clara admired King. "I remember your silver demon from before. He is pretty awesome, I'll give you all that. How much for him? I still got money out there somewhere, I think. Hey! Hey!" she yelled, trying to get King's attention. He ignored her.

"He's not a demon and he's not for sale. His name is King and he's a Silver tech familiar," Phillip said. "My mother created him."

"Yeah?" Clara said. "Hey, come here, buddy, I want to have a look at you."

King glared at Clara and stayed where he was.

"I think he's probably still a little sore from where you tried to enslave him in the Telmus Grove and then force him to kill Kay. Remember that?" Phillip said.

Clara laughed, as if reveling in a warm memory. "Oh yeah, with the Finger of Zahuti. I remember. That would have worked, too."

"Are you always so casual with your treachery?" Phillip asked.

"I was trying to better my family. Listen, you do what you have to do for your family, right? I'm really not a bad person, you know." She glanced at the box Phillip was carrying. "Are you going to tell me what's in the box or not?"

"No," he replied.

"Oh come on, you can tell me."

Thomasina yanked Clara by the hem of her sacklike garment. "Stop talking and show us the way before I lose my temper and beat you to death with this device."

"Ok, ok!" Clara muttered under her breath: *"Gods, woman, how I'd love to put my foot up your mud thumper ..."*

Clara led them down the causeway for a long distance, eventually coming upon a sudden rise in elevation. A series of buildings was cut into the cliffside, stacked up several levels high, pagoda-style. Staircases went up and down in all directions in a bewildering tangle. Clara scratched her head, confused for a moment.

"This way," she said, heading up a staircase.

Phillip stopped her. "Wait. I see Menks floating around all over the place up there."

"Her guards, the ones with the claws, right? The ones that shut the door on you?"

"The very ones."

"There's a lot of them. They jump around on the walls. They fly. I wouldn't want to mess with them," she added. "That's on you three Frag-Wagons! You're here to protect me. Deal with them!"

Phillip, Thomasina and King huddled for a moment to consider their response, their respect for the Menks considerable.

"Well, are we going to the flying dragon or not?" Clara demanded, impatient.

"Just a moment. King, scout the area ahead," Phillip said.

King fluttered off. Several minutes later, he returned.

"Alert! The area is profuse with Menks! One hundred, plus."

"We'll never make it through a hundred Menks," Phillip said. "There must be a Blood Box around somewhere. King, did you see it?"

"I did not."

Clara scratched her head. "What's a Blood Box?"

"The Menks' internal organs have been removed from their bodies, making them extremely difficult to bring down. If we can get where they keep their organs, the Blood Box, we can take them right out."

Clara thought about it a moment. "Keep their organs? Oh! Oh, you mean that nasty room with all the guts hanging from the ceiling? Yeah, I've seen that. Is that what it's for? I was wondering."

"Show us," Phillip said.

A sly look crossed Clara's face. "Yeah, sure, I can show you where it is, no problem. First, though, you're going to give me the box you're carrying, right, *Phillip*?"

Thomasina was livid. "We are not negotiating with you, Wunderluck! King, fly this person out to the Menks and drop her amid them. Let them rend her to paste!"

"Wait! This demon can't lift my weight, can he?"

King seized Clara by the hem of her garment and easily lifted her into the air. She kicked and thrashed. "Ok, ok! Boy, you people have no sense of humor, do you! I'll show you where it is! Put me down!"

"King, put her down," Phillip said.

He set Clara down. She was impressed. "Wow! This demon just keeps getting better and better. What can't he do? Come on, let's go. It's not far." Clara led them down several flights of steps to a leveled area cut into the rock. Ahead awaited a long, rectangular building with a single door under a portico of four massive columns. There didn't appear to be any Menks in the area. Two fierce dragonlike statues guarded either side of the entrance. Four brass lanterns hung from golden chains between the columns. Clara motioned for them to stop.

"Here it is—there's nasty stuff on the other side of that door. Those statues, see them there? They come to life when She's around. They snort and snap their teeth and She pets their scaly heads like they're dogs or something. About bit my head off once. When she leaves, they turn back to statues again. That's actually pretty cool; I'd love to know how she does that."

Despite himself, Clara's spirit reminded Phillip of Sarah.

The two of them, in many ways, were more similar than Sarah would probably want to admit. "I think that's Queen Ghome's Gellar powers at work," he said. "King, go on and scout ahead."

King went ahead, flying toward the building. As he moved near the statues, the lanterns hanging from the eaves lit up in strong yellow light. Inside each lantern a shaved female head appeared, light pouring from their garish open mouths. Bathed in the light from the lanterns, the statues came to life, stone melting to living flesh, the soft bluish streaks of marble on their carved bodies intensifying into lurid reds, livid greens, shiny blacks and oily blues. The heads inside the lanterns then commenced a dire howl thundering into the sky that near burst their collective eardrums.

"An alarm!" Thomasina cried. "The Menks are surely coming!"

The fully animated statues swatted at King, trying to bat him out of the air. Phillip and Thomasina burst from their hiding spot. Clara remained where she was, cringing. Unconsciously, Phillip still carried the box containing Lady Chrysania's parts, and Thomasina carried the Chadburn.

"The lanterns, Rose, get the lanterns!" Phillip cried. One of the statues, a horror of twitching muscle encased in clashing vivid colors, came at Phillip. He pumped several shots into it, momentarily slowing it down as Thomasina took flight. The beast snarled and continued its attack. King reversed his flight and headed in Phillip's direction, trying to assist. In a lightning move, the beast opened its jaws and swallowed King whole, its jaws slamming shut, teeth interlocking.

Phillip was moments away from being devoured himself.

My face can shield you against Her creatures, he recalled from Lady Chrysania's note.

He opened the box and pulled out Lady Chrysania's face, holding it before him. The beast skidded to a stop and gazed at the limp face draped with golden hair. It seemed to recognize that its master, if only for a little while, had worn this face, and some of her residual power remained in it. The second beast, the one with King in its belly, also seemed entranced by the face. They snarled and scraped at the ground, eyes fixed on it.

"The lanterns, Rose!" Phillip shouted as he held the beasts at bay, moments away from being devoured, the face dangling in his hand. Thomasina crashed into the lanterns, smashing them with her MT CALM. The lanterns resisted, the glass cracking at a slow rate.

The two beasts roared in fury, shambled around Phillip and came after her, covering the distance in only a few muscle-laden bounds.

"Rose!"

The first beast arrived, ready to gut Thomasina. Instinctively, she swung the Chadburn as it had much greater reach than her MT CALM club.

Surprisingly, the Chadburn didn't dent or break with the force of the blow; instead, it smashed into the beast, flattening its head, knocking it down as it shed buckets of blood. She turned to the lanterns, sweeping all four into wreckage with a deadly swipe. The heads within, all beautiful, all flawless, fell to the ground and rolled about like legs of beef, continuing their fearful screeching. Thomasina trampled them, flattening their skulls with the Chadburn, which was proving to be a weapon of immense power.

Thomasina extinguished the last head just as the final beast arrived. As the light from the heads went out, it reverted to marble, teeth bared, gullet open, claws extended. Frozen solid, just as it prepared to rip Thomasina to shreds.

The beast rumbled from within and shattered into small bits.

King emerged, rising into the air.

Phillip ran to Thomasina's side, embracing her. "Rose, are you all right?"

"I'm fine. During the fight I used the Chadburn as a weapon. I hope I haven't damaged it."

They inspected the Chadburn. It was straight as ever, gleaming and unmarred. But ...

"Oh, Phillip, look at it," Thomasina cried in dismay. "The dial face and the handle are gone, broken out! I've destroyed the Chadburn."

King landed on the dial. "I do not believe this device is damaged. I am detecting a great deal of energy coursing through it."

As they inspected it further, the dial face was not gone; instead, it was covered up with a stout metal shutter, midnight blue like the pole. Phillip tinkered with the dial and the shutter retracted, revealing the clean, undamaged dial face and the brass handle beneath it. Thomasina breathed a sigh of relief.

"Oh, thank Creation! Well then, this Chadburn is a very powerful weapon. That's good to know."

Just then, Clara came running toward them, her eyes wide with fear.

"They're coming! The guards! The Menks! Whatever!! A whole bunch of them!"

King fluttered into the air to get a better vantage point. "Confirmed! Many Menks en route from the pagoda area above!"

Phillip tried the door to the Blood Box.

Locked.

"King, get us in there!" he said.

King turned to the door. "The door is protected by an energy field."

Thomasina lifted the Chadburn and the armored shutter snapped back into position. "Stand back!"

She swung the Chadburn into the door hoping to smash it, but it bounced off, the door undamaged.

Clara panted with fear.

Dozens of Menks came bounding in, leaping down the steps, clattering into the open area before the building, their silver gauntlets gleaming, ready to draw blood. Winged Menks clogged the sky like a plague of locusts, coming down fast.

Clara dove toward the lock. "Let me in there! Move!" she yelled, pushing Thomasina aside. She knelt and began moving the components of the lock this way and that with her nimble fingers.

Phillip and King went out to face the charging Menks. As before, Phillip raised the face of Lady Chrysania, showing it to them. As with the stone beasts, the Menks hesitated, crawling about on all fours, their claws clacking on the stone, sensing their master before them.

King attacked, devastating them, staining the ground with their blood. More and more Menks came. One darted in fast and knocked Phillip to the ground.

POW! POW! POW!

He pumped bullets into it. The Menk would not be stopped. It took Lady Chrysania's face from Phillip's grasp and the box as well and was away, protecting the face and the box, taking hits as it departed, bleeding profusely but still functional. The Menks regrouped and readied an all-out assault from the front and from above.

King charged in, destroying Menks in a cloud of light, moving too fast to be seen. Others came at Phillip, meeting his Poltava. He pumped shot after shot into them, taking many shots to stop just one. He reloaded and fired again. Soon, they would have him.

King returned to his side. "Alert! Menks are down."

Phillip took a breath. He heard no more clattering, saw no more movement. Fallen bodies and twisted limbs lay before him. Dead Menks tumbled from the sky, splattering into the ground like giant-sized grenades.

"Phillip!" cried Thomasina. She came to his side, her armor and the Chadburn covered in sticky blood. Looking back, the door to the Blood Box was open, Clara Wunderluck standing there.

"She got the door open, I'll give her that," Thomasina said. "Inside, oh Phillip, inside was a charnel house of hanging bodies. No skin, no muscle, just pulsing organs, beating hearts! I uttered a prayer to Auld and went in! I ripped them down, stomping on them, covered in gore!"

"It's over, Rose, it's over. Well done! Well done all, even Lady Wunderluck. We all have each other to thank for our deliverance."

They approached the Blood Box. Clara was standing by the door, leaning against the wall. She looked rather proud of herself. "You're welcome," she said. "Yeah, I've seen them work that lock enough to know the combination. Looks like I saved the lot of you."

Phillip glanced into the building: gore everywhere, dripping blood, destroyed tissue, and the strong smell of innards. "Yes, well, thank you. Very smart work."

Clara rolled her tongue across her lips and got in close with Phillip. *"How do you like me now, Phillip? You married the wrong girl ..."*

Thomasina recovered from the horror of the Blood Box and pushed Clara away. "Yes, and in assisting us, you saved yourself. Those Menks would have killed you just the same. You may thank me and Phillip and King for saving you."

Heading back the way they had come was a terror trove of huddled Menk bodies lying on the ground; all dead.

Mostly dead, though some still had a flicker of life. Phillip and King finished them off as they moved along.

"Rose, I lost the box. The Menks took it from me," he said.

"Oh, yeah, I saw that," Clara said. "What was in it?"

"Something very precious," Phillip replied. "Something I intend to get back."

They moved up the stairs, checking every Menk they passed, Phillip and King killing the ones still struggling for life.

Clara watched them work. "You're just an all-around nice guy, aren't you, Lord Blanchefort? May I call you Phillip? I've been calling you that, but I hadn't asked permission. It's not something we do in Remnath."

Thomasina reacted. "You may not! Xaphan's Beard, do not test me, woman!"

Clara ignored Thomasina and mused to herself. "Hmmm, Blanchefort, Blanchefort, *Clara of Blanchefort*. I like the sound of that. I'm sort of a freelancer now ... And ... "

Clara raised her voice and spoke to Phillip. "You have a brother, right?"

Phillip was sweating and under duress as he attended to the grim task of checking and killing the Menks with King. He wiped his brow, horror etched into his face. "What? A brother? Yes, I have an older brother."

"What's his name?"

Thomasina gave Clara a shove. "What's it to you, you Wunderluck vermin? Any good will you created with us at the Blood Box is now gone. Are you seeking to somehow ingratiate yourself with us? Should you manage to survive this situation, you're simply heading right back to the jail in Blanchefort Village to await arraignment, which, if I correctly understand Vith law, could take years, possibly decades, where you emerge from the jail cell a withered scarecrow. And, by the by, Phillip's brother is far too studious and intelligent to be seduced or taken in by the likes of you, a refugee from a dead Household looking to better her situation by any means necessary."

Clara rubbed a careless finger along her lip. "Yeah, yeah. Ok *... we'll see ...*"

They reached the causeway. Dead Menks lay strewn about everywhere. One of them, still clinging to life, held the box containing Lady Chrysania's parts. Phillip came to reclaim the box, and the Menk raised a dying claw to protect it. Moments later, the Menk was dead. Inside the box, all the parts were present.

"Ah, you got the box back?" Clara said. "You going to tell me what's in it?"

"No."

"Eh, I'll find out sooner or later. Come on, this way."

Clara led them up a long flight of steps to the pagodas at the top. She pointed to a corridor covered with an elaborate mural.

"Down there is the door leading to the dragon. It's normally crawling with demons, but thanks to me, they're all gone."

King landed on Phillip's shoulder. "Before we enter, I wish to burn the hoards as Lady Sarah suggested. While in the area, I will check on the Gellar door. Perhaps it has returned."

Phillip gave King several bullets and he fluttered off. "Be careful."

While they waited for King to return, they examined the vast mural painted on the corridor wall.

"This is fascinating, Rose. This mural here, it tells the story of Lady Chrysania, from her birth at Castle Bloodstein during the Splendor of the Vith, and her young adulthood with her siblings. I see her taking journeys with her family to a far-away place through the Gellartron. I see a stronghold and treasure and a great beast, a Bower Chest treasure vault, where they kept it all in a secret place they called 'Edamathrombo'. She was wed to a handsome Vith lord and she seemed perfectly happy. And then, her husband and family died and she lived on. Look at her here in the mural, bewildered, lost at the gravesite of her husband and children. I think she either contemplated suicide or actually attempted it and failed. She married again, and here as well, and here. More tombs, more dead kin. Here, look, she went to the Sisters in Valenhelm for help, and instead of helping her, they appear to have imprisoned her there for a long time. They experimented on her. She fell into despair. And look here, here's a representation of Queen Ghome coming to Lady Chrysania out of the ether of her own troubled thoughts, soothing her, promising to get her out of Valenhelm, and taking control. As per this mural and Lady Chrysania's message on the table, Queen Ghome appears to be a separate, dominant personality created during her years of anguish in the Sisters' capture, strong and ruthless. Chrysania couldn't escape the Sisters, so she inadvertently created a personality of someone who could. She escaped Valenhelm, engaging in arson, body-snatching and brute force. The Sisters chased after her, but Ghome was clever enough to elude them across Vithland. They deactivated the Bloodstein's Gellartron, cutting Ghome off from Edamathrombo and the Bower Chest that was hidden there. It looked to the skies, waiting for her to return. And here, as a fugitive, she moved on and married into other Households to cover her tracks."

Phillip stared at the mural. He sucked in his breath. "By Creation, Rose, she married into our House! Queen bloody Ghome, and Lady Chrysania, are our direct ancient ancestors!"

Clara laughed. "Awesome! That's awesome! Ha, ha!"

Phillip composed himself and continued.

"Rose, remember the Professor had us go out to the Grove and investigate a hole in the ground at the base of Dead Hill that turned out to be a tunnel leading up into a confined rectangular open space? Given all of this, I think the open space we discovered was the inside of her tomb. She must have had a tunnel built in secret so that she could fake her death at a time of her choosing and then escape to her next assumed identity. If she can escape from Valenhelm under the eye of the Sisters, then she can certainly escape from Dead Hill."

Phillip pondered the notion. Thomasina examined the mural. "And then, she seems to have abandoned the standard life of a Vith heiress and began the rootless life of a vagabond, rolling from one place to the next, collecting treasure and stockpiling it. Over several generations, she gathered enough treasure and other items that she was successful in secretly re-activating the Gellartron at Castle Bloodstein and went through to Edamathrombo, reuniting with the Bower Chest that was waiting for her there and filling it up afresh, increasing its power."

Thomasina tapped at the mural. "Phillip, look at these foreboding drawings here. I see figures in black accepting from Queen Ghome gifts of treasure, weapons, slaves, whores and other fealties. I see the figures in black desecrating the dead and placing them into the sky … Look there!"

Thomasina and Phillip both went white at the same time. "Rose, the hidden Vith world of Edamathrombo in the mural; it's Mare, the place where we ran afoul of the Dead Men while questing for Wilhella's Perlamum pieces," Phillip said. "The old Vith put their dead into the sky to protect the world from the Sisters who were trying to take their power from them—it must be. Therefore, if Ki's Gaming Session continues to be accurate, then Kay has been taken by Queen Ghome to Mare where the Dead Men float in the sky."

They both stared at the mural in horror, remembering the ferocity of just one Dead Man. Clara got impatient. She came up and gave Phillip a slight tap on the ear lobe. "Enough admiring the artwork. Come on, this way."

The corridor ended in a door. A lock similar to the one at the Blood Box was built into the wall to the right of the door. Soft light spilled through under the crack. They gathered by it.

"All right," Clara said. "On the other side of this door is the dragon. The first room we enter is Queen Ghome's bedroom. Are you ready? There's a lot of treasure on the other side, and a lot of naked ladies too. You better be ready to take them down because they are some mean Hussie-Whumpers, the lot of them. Think of them like Menks, only cuter."

King returned. "The hoards are ablaze. The Gellar door has not returned."

"All right," Phillip said. "We've done all we can here, and with luck we've struck a blow against Queen Ghome. Let's be gone from this place."

Clara worked the lock. "Hey, I need some light." King settled on her shoulder and provided light for Clara to see. "You're just all kinds of useful. I like, I like."

She manipulated the lock with a deft hand. "Door's ready."

King flapped up, ready to destroy anything that might be waiting on the other side. Phillip opened the door and they peered in.

5—Ghome's Bedroom

Inside was what appeared to be a small but opulent bedchamber. The walls were hammered brass, sloping up to a convex ceiling of lapis and beryl, studded with gleaming jewels arranged to resemble a starry night sky. The grand bed was spread with the finest silks, the posts made of the rarest of woods. The hardwood floor was pebbled with fitted smooth blue, red and green gemstones like inviting candy. On a nightstand, scented candles peacefully floated in golden bowls of clean water. Soft incense smoke drifted out of jade burners. By the bed, light from a splendid lantern created a warm halo. A muted throbbing, like the workings of great machinery, pulsed with a reliable beat throughout the room. It was a surprisingly serene and tranquil place where an immortal tyrant slept safe from Roethaba of George and her Mentralysis waves.

The room felt slightly unsteady under their feet, as if they were floating on water, or possibly flying through the air.

A door creaked open and light spilled across the floor. A thin, partially-clad woman glistening with oil and scented powders emerged from an adjacent chamber, bearing an armload of folded linens. She stopped and looked about in surprise.

"What are you doing in here?" she said to Clara in an ugly tone.

"I got my buddies with me this time," Clara said as Phillip covered her with his Poltava. "Guess I won't be working on the fraggin' cistern again today, will I, you wretched nudibug?"

The woman saw Thomasina carrying the bloody Chadburn and Phillip with his drawn Poltava. "Please," she stammered, still holding the linens, "I don't know who you are or what this woman has told you. I am simply a servant of the great Queen Ghome. I am Alona, her body servant. I have served her all my life."

"She's a rotten, bossy mankin' bitch!" Clara roared. "Let's knock her out!"

Phillip waved Clara off. He lowered his gun and spoke kindly to Alona. "Come, put your things down, please. You needn't fear, we shall not harm you. However, we must, unfortunately, inconvenience you for several hours at least."

Clara rolled her eyes. "Oh come on! You're too nice! A real

Fudgin' you are, Phillip! Let's take this bitch down! She's dangerous, and I owe her one right across the chops!"

"Please be quiet," Phillip responded.

Eyes wide, Alona nodded. "Yes, yes, I'll do whatever you ask."

"You could do us the courtesy of putting some clothing on," Thomasina said, noting her oiled body covered with only a few scant swatches of light fabric.

Alona tried to cover herself. "I am sorry, this is how we all dress. It is Her will to deter us from stealing. I will cover myself." She put her linens down on the bed and pulled one off the top, unfolding it.

"How many servants of Ghome are nearby?" Phillip asked as Alona unfolded the linen.

Without warning, she dropped the linen and sprang at Phillip, hands raised, her palms glittering with small, painted-on circles of colorful powder. "We are many!" she roared with sudden ferocity. King rose up to attack.

Clara seized a golden bowl from the nightstand, scattering water and candles, and swung, hitting Alona across the bridge of the nose.

PANG!

Alona fell.

Clara was ecstatic. She threw the bowl down. "Hell yeah! Gods, I've been wanting to do that to one of these naked Frag-Wagons for awhile now! How do you like me now, babe? Ha! Guess you ain't pretty no more, huh!"

Phillip and Thomasina stood there staring at the fallen woman. "Creation, she had me fooled," he said.

Thomasina scolded her husband. "You must be more calculating, Phillip, I was suspecting treachery from the beginning. Never trust a strange naked woman, of all things."

"Told you, she's a bitch!" Clara said, standing over Alona's body. "And guess what, Phillip? I just saved your life right now."

"I'm certain I could have safely restrained her."

Clara raised one of Alona's hands. Her palms and knuckles were coated with dots of festive color. "Oh yeah? See this? This is Aboleth. It's an explosive powder Queen Ghome invented from those magnificent plants she cultivates. It's pretty awesome stuff. Queen Ghome and her attendants paint themselves with it all the time, and they aren't afraid to cut loose when they need to. You think they're all cute and naked, totally disarmed, right? Oh, no, no, you don't want to get hit with this stuff, Phillip."

Phillip was puzzled. Alona's body was covered in festive dots and swirls of various colors. "How so?"

"This stuff explodes. Just a little bit and they can blow your head off, without injuring themselves in the process. I kept trying to steal some to blow off the door to my cell, but this naked Dead Rita here always made me wash off."

"We've seen explosions from the Menks before as we made our way through the Gellartron," Thomasina said. "It was coming from this dust?"

"Yep." Clara pointed at the door Alona had emerged from. "She's got some in there if you want to see it."

Phillip looked about the room. "Wait a moment. What about Queen Ghome? Where can we expect to encounter her? This is her bedchamber, correct?"

"Yep," Clara said. "I'm pretty certain she's not around right now. If she was here, we'd know it—there'd be tons of these naked ladies running around all over the place. She doesn't do anything for herself—the naked ladies do it all. I'm amazed they don't chew her food for her."

Phillip nodded. "All right. I suppose we're fortunate she's not here. Show us this powder. I'll take care of the girl." He lifted her off the floor, blood dripping from a deep gash over her nose.

Clara led them through the door to a vast bathing area. It was like that wonderful spa they had enjoyed in Fazo after they were wed. A colossal mosaic of Queen Ghome sitting on a golden throne being worshipped by a throng of people and served by a host of naked females loomed over a number of wading pools. There were heated pools wreathed in feathery steam, mineral baths, bubbling pools, colored tincture waters and cool pools of clear water to wash off the water from the previous pools. The whole place smelled of aqua chemicals, clean water and minerals. A grand boudoir with a dizzying collection of pots and jewel-encrusted urns full of powders, salves, oils, perfumes and other accessories was situated in an alcove before a full-length mirror. Thomasina took a moment to wash off the gore from the Blood Box, dipping into a pool and cleaning both herself and the Chadburn. Clara selected several golden pots and set them aside.

"Better wash that Slut-o-Matic off to get rid of the Aboleth in case she wakes up," Clara said.

Phillip took Alona to a pool and dipped her in. The swirls and dots of color quickly dissolved in the water.

"So," Clara said. "This first pot here is the actual Aboleth itself." She removed the lid. Inside was a pinkish crystalline powder that looked like fine sea salt. Clara removed the lids from the other pots, revealing pigments of various shades and a thick, gel-like substance.

"These here are dyes, to shade the Aboleth however you like. Once you have it the color you want, you mix it with this gel, paint it onto your body, and there you go. Or, you can leave it un-dyed and just brush it onto your skin. You can't see it, it becomes like body armor. If somebody tries to grab hold of you—BOOM! The force of the explosion is directed outward away from the person wearing it, so the wearer isn't hurt at all. It's actually pretty cool to witness."

Thomasina returned from the pools and dipped her damp fingertips into the powder, examining it closely. "And, this is stable?" she asked, rubbing her thumb and fingers together.

"Oh yeah. I guess it takes a little practice to determine how much force is required to set it off, but it's stable enough that they don't accidentally blow themselves up; not that I've seen anyway. Cool, huh? I'm planning on copying this stuff and producing it myself when I get home. I'll make a fortune with this shit."

"Oh, from your jail cell, is that what you're going to do?" Thomasina asked. Clara seated herself next to Thomasina and grabbed a brush, eager to put some powder on.

"King," Thomasina asked, "will you please take this woman and dunk her in the water? I want to make certain she's not wearing any of this powder."

"What?" Clara squealed. "Why can't I have powder?"

"Because we don't trust you."

King came up and lifted Clara off her feet. "Hey, wait a minute! Let me go! You're not still sore about the Finger of Zahuti thing, are you?" King said nothing. He carried Clara out over a pool and dunked her several times. She splashed and coughed. While Clara was getting dunked, Phillip took the opportunity to attend to Alona. He tore up several linens and treated her wound, dabbing away the blood. With the rest of the linens he tied her up. He was pretty good at it, having plenty of practice tying Sarah up when they were younger to see if she could free herself. He got to the point where even the unrestrainable Sarah couldn't escape. He finished and pushed her into a corner.

King dumped Clara onto the floor soaking wet; the sack she

was wearing was bloated with water. She miserably coughed. "I lost my shoes," she sputtered.

"King, please retrieve Clara's shoes," Phillip said. King went out over the pools and dove in. Phillip found a towel for her to dry herself. She took it and winked at him.

"*Thanks*," she purred. King returned and dropped her soaked shoes on top of her.

Thomasina stood. She had filled a small chest with Aboleth powder. "It sounds interesting. We'll take some to analyze later," she said. "Phillip, do you have room in your duster for this?" She held the chest out.

"Certainly." He took the chest, ensured the lid was tightly closed, and placed it inside his coat.

Clara was furious. "So, I can't have any Aboleth?"

"No," Thomasina said.

They exited the bathing room, Clara still sopping wet and muttering to herself. At the far end of the bedchamber was an untried wooden door.

"What is on the other side of this door?" Thomasina demanded.

Clara refused to speak to her. She turned to Phillip instead. "There's a bunch of rooms outside. To the left is the treasure hoard; to the right is a service area housing a lot of filthy machinery. I think we're in the air right now. Up a ways to the right is a hangar that opens up to the outside. She keeps a big floating skiff where she puts all her potions and nasty stuff, sort of like a big trunk you take with you on vacation. Wherever she goes, it goes. So, if the skiff is gone, then she's not here."

"What about the Menks?" Phillip asked.

"I've never seen any of them in here, but she's got this hideous robot out there. It just sort of wanders around checking the hoard and the machinery. That's all it does. I've never seen it do anything else. It gives me the chills, though."

"Is it dangerous?" Thomasina asked.

"Probably. I don't know."

"King, go out and have a look. Be careful," Phillip said. Cautiously, they opened the door and King fluttered out. They waited for him to return.

"So, how much am I getting paid for this help?" Clara asked as they waited.

"Paid? You get to live," Thomasina replied.

"I get to live anyways. Your man isn't going to kill me, and I'm pretty sure he's not going to let you kill me either. So, what am I getting paid? I'll want the silver bird, he's pretty useful. I've got a little workshop back home where I reverse-engineer arcane items and reproduce them. I'm actually pretty good at it. That Finger of Zahuti I was using to dominate your demon's will—I replicated that myself. My goal is to replicate the other nine fingers as well when I get my hands on them. And I'll take a pot full of Aboleth. That stuff's going to make me and what's left of my House a lot of money."

Phillip spoke up. "We're not killers, and we appreciate what you did getting the door to the Blood Box open. You're not going to be killed; however, you're not going to be paid either, Lady Wunderluck. You're going back to Magistrate Kilos' cell to await trial. Maybe, once everything's said and done, I'll do what I can to get you a speedy trial and testify on your behalf."

"My name is 'Clara', *Phillip*!" she said, defiant.

"Phillip, are you forgetting this woman and her foul brothers tried to murder Sam and Sarah, and, she is personally responsible for us getting stuck here in the first place?" Thomasina said.

"I get the feeling you don't like me," Clara replied. "You like me, right, Phillip?"

"I do not, and I'm not going to allow you to mislead my husband either," Thomasina said.

"Gah!" she hissed in frustration. Clara crossed her arms and moped.

King returned. "Alert," he said. "Outside is a plush hallway lined with chambers filled with treasure, including a botanical area and a hoard of live animals. A throne room is situated at the end of the hallway. To the right is a maintenance area and power plant. I encountered no one outside. No servants or Menks present. Queen Ghome is also not present. The skiff Lady Wunderluck mentioned appears to be housed in a small hanger with an armored door leading to the outside. Neither skiff nor trunk are currently present in the hangar."

"Told you," Clara said.

"What about that robot she mentioned?" Phillip asked.

"I did not see a robot," King replied.

"Where'd it go?" Clara asked.

They opened the door and went out. Outside was a hallway padded in light blue silks and encased in gold. A thick carpet woven with golden threads ran the length of the corridor.

"I hate this carpet," Clara said. "They always made me take

my shoes off and wash my feet before stepping on it. I'm gonna get it good and dirty." She rubbed her heels into the pile. She whispered into Phillip's ear: "*I got pretty feet, Phillip.*"

Phillip smiled. She never quit. She was still fishing for an opportunity, searching for an angle and a card to play. He whispered back into her ear: "*Sorry, Rose's are prettier…*"

They crept out into the corridor. The sound of machinery at work was markedly pronounced, much more so than in the bedroom; the whisperlike breathing of a great steam engine hissed all around them. They felt the floor beneath them trembling. To the left was a line of finely-crafted doors; to the right was a dark, smoky service area.

"I would assume the Chadburn will go out in the service area somewhere," Phillip said.

"I think I know where it goes," Clara said. "This way." They headed to the right. The carpeted hallway ended and a hard bare-metal floor began. A fairly spacious hangar area opened up to the left. It was clean and well-organized with space to house a vehicle fifty feet in length. The floor space where the vehicle would go was conspicuously empty. Past the hangar was a vast, dirty mechanical area. A basin filled with clean water to wash one's feet was placed off to the side. Past the basin, iron steps went down into a central gantry passing over a hot, dark region covered in rust and soot. There were pipes ducted every which way. Giant riveted tanks strapped to the walls sloshed with uncountable gallons of water stored within. Before them was a grand industrial dance; machinery and linkages, gears meshed together, spinning flywheels, pistons rising and falling in regular puffs of steam moving massive armatures in precise order. Giant furnaces blazing hot were lined up like massive pills, and steam chests wheezed steadily, filling the open space with an oppressive humidity laced with smoke. The rusty gantry they stood on snaked precariously through the center of the machinery; to fall off the gantry would mean certain death chewed up in the teeth of turning gears or scalded in cones of steam.

Phillip took it all in. "Who maintains all of this? I would think a setup this size would require an army of craftsmen performing constant maintenance."

"I've never seen anybody working on this equipment. It runs itself. Don't be fooled by all the rust, it covers up an arcane heart. I'd know it anywhere," Clara said. "The only thing I've ever seen out here is the robot."

"Are you certain?" Phillip asked.

"It's always been out here or back in the hoard," she replied.

Thomasina looked around. "I don't see anything. Describe it. What should we be looking for?"

Clara scratched her head. "It's weird. It's fifteen or twenty feet long. It's shaped sort of like a bowling pin—you know, bowling, that game you Vith love so much but won't admit to. It moves about on rails, and it can move fast when it wants to. I can't ever tell if it has a back end or a front end—it sort of slides around in any direction it wants. And it makes this Fog-Bottom mumbling sound that gives me the chills, though it's too noisy in here to pick out the sound. It's also covered in rust, so I guess it blends in pretty well."

They looked around the vast area again, Phillip and King lighting their Sight. They saw nothing. The robot could be hiding anywhere.

"King?" Phillip asked. "Can you take a look from the heights and tell us what you see? Be careful."

King flapped up toward the lofty metal ceiling, panning about, the cones of his Sight cutting through the steamy haze.

"Anything?" Phillip called up.

"I see …"

Something happened. One moment King was there, the next he was snatched out of mid-air and gone at withering speed.

"King!"

Thomasina soared into the steamy heights with the Chadburn at the ready, hoping to come to his aid. At that moment, a great red shape came sliding down from between ribs of machinery. It approached in a fast, somewhat predatory fashion, moving along the walls, shooting past Thomasina. She took a broad, whooshing swing at it but missed.

"That's it!" Clara shouted. "That's the robot!"

It was ruddy and quite plain to look at with red jewels encrusted in the center of its body at four equidistant points. It was attached to the walls from the front and the back via sturdy jointed legs sliding on rails, and, as Clara had noted, it did look much like a bowling pin. It made a disquieting, mumbling sort of sound coming from deep within. Red and black streaks of rust and soot crusted on the construction's capsule stood out in bold stratalike hues. As it approached the plush carpeted area, it passed through a tube. The rusty capsule around it was left behind in the tube, revealing a gleaming clean shell of blue metal. The robot then proceeded past them out of the service area and entered the carpeted hallway, sliding on a central rail built into the ceiling.

Clara watched it depart. "I'll bet it thinks your demon is a piece of hoard trying to escape."

"We must get him back! Come on!" Phillip said as Thomasina rejoined them. They turned and followed the robot. Despite her bravado, Clara took a moment to wash her feet in the basin before stepping on the carpet. "Habit," she said.

Down the hallway was an impossible collection of treasure. There were chambers filled with piles of gold, with platinum of ghostly luster, with silver, with antimony, cadmium and other precious metals struck into coins, shaped into bars and melted into nuggets of extraordinary size. Crystal vases overflowed with sparkling jewels of mouthwatering color. There were rooms stacked high with rare fabrics made on forgotten looms, while fabulous jewelry in indescribable configurations peeked out of open drawers. Each chamber contained more jaw-dropping wealth than the last. There wasn't a central lighting system in the chambers; the treasure generated its own ephemeral light. And then there were collections of rare items wrought in exquisite beauty. There were scrolls of golden parchment, wands, glyphs, brooches, robes, gowns, armor, shields, swords, innumerable types of guns and other firearms, bits of arcane technology, and wondrous machines; the wealth collected over centuries was mind-boggling. There were stacks of paintings created by nameless masters and sculptures of pure perfection. Menageries of rare and extinct beasts pacing in cages went on for as far as the eye could see. Water and fire seemed to be created by the hoard in endless quantities, pumped and ducted away to fuel the machinery at the front of the Bower Chest.

Phillip and Thomasina took in everything in silence.

The robot turned and entered a chamber housing a host of arcane creatures: big ones, little ones, two-legged, three legged, four-legged and more; tiny people with gossamer wings confined in tiny cages, horned toads, fiery salamanders, and pacing tigers. The collection seemed endless.

The robot stopped in the center of the room. A panel in its capsule opened. Out came a hinged metal arm. It selected an empty silver cage from a shelf and took the cage into itself. A few moments later, the cage was brought back out, only this time King was confined within it. The robot gently placed the cage back on a shelf.

"We're going to get you out of there, King," Phillip said.

The robot seemed to go dead. It sat motionless on the ceiling.

Thomasina puzzled. "Well, what's it—"

Before she could finish her sentence, the robot moved. In a blur, panels opened and metal arms shot out. The robot plucked the box out of Phillip's hands and the Chadburn from Thomasina's, securing both items within its capsule before they could react. It turned to Phillip and Thomasina; though it had no eyes, it glared at them, aggressively moving fast in their direction. The mumbling within its body rose in pitch to a terrifying scream. An arm emerged, tipped with a whirling blade, whipping the air in frenzy.

It went for Phillip, he dove aside, the blades missing. He raised his Poltava and fired.

POW! POW!

No effect. The robot advanced on them fast, brandishing its whirling blades.

"Free me from this cage!" King said.

The robot was between them and the imprisoned King. It went for Phillip again.

Missed! Thomasina wrenched Phillip by the shoulders and dragged him across the floor, taking flight. She flew into the hallway. "Phillip, we've no room and nothing to fight with!"

Moments later the robot was there, gleaming, sliding on its rail, blades turning. Flying as fast as she could, Thomasina soared down the hallway with Phillip in her arms. The robot came after them and was quickly gaining. Panels opened, more arms came out and more deadly blades whirled.

Casually, Clara, forgotten and unnoticed by the robot, came striding out of the chamber moments later. She held the cage containing King over her head.

"Betrayed!" King said from his cage. "You have been betrayed!"

Clara was jubilant. "You're all mine now, baby doll," she said to King. "Sorry, suckers! Looks like I'm not heading back to the crappy cell in your crappy village, am I, you bunch of Rumble-Pumps! Have fun with the Vith Stickin' robot!" She turned and fled in the opposite direction.

Phillip fired at the robot until his Poltava emptied. The robot was undamaged. "Why is it after us?" Thomasina cried.

Clara had said Ghome's robot attacked those attempting to steal from the hoard, and that it ignored all others. Phillip had a thought and slapped at his duster pockets. Sure enough, several platinum coins jangled about in his duster, placed there on the sly by the treacherous Clara Wunderluck. He pulled the coins out and threw them aside. The robot immediately stopped, opened panels, and retrieved the coins.

At last they reached the end of the hallway and entered the great throne room of Queen Ghome, shaped from pure gold, her molten throne unoccupied. Overhead, lanterns hung from chains of brilliant luster. Exotic plants in all colors drank up pure water from channels that emptied into clear shallow pools. Lily pads floated on the water. Large white flowers with golden stalks jutted up out of the pools. Nearby in a prominent place were two earthen footers atop an elevated platform.

Thomasina soared across the room, looking for an exit and finding none. "Phillip, we're trapped and defenseless!"

She had a thought and touched ground. "Give me the chest of Aboleth!"

Phillip pulled it from his duster. "We have no idea what this substance will do."

Thomasina took it and opened the lid. "No time like now to find out." She pulled her gloves off and dipped her hands in.

The robot burst into the throne room a few moments later. More panels opened in its chest; the robot reached into the hollow and pulled out two female heads disembodied at the neck. The heads moved and throbbed with a hideous unlife. Their mouths opened and closed, emitting cold yellow light. They murmured in dead sorrow. Two more arms emerged from the robot's body. The arms ended in lengths of wire like a cat-o-nine tails. The robot spun the wire around, picking up speed until it whirled about like a deadly buzzsaw. The robot held the heads aloft and came at Thomasina and Phillip. Phillip pulled his remaining SAPP and formed it into a shield, protecting Thomasina as she applied the powder to her hands.

The blades and serrated wire slammed into the SAPP shield, Phillip straining to hold them back.

"Hurry, Rose!" he cried, feeling the blades cutting through his shield.

Her hands covered in Aboleth powder, Thomasina launched herself into the air. "For Auld and my husband!" she yelled as she spiraled toward the robot.

Thomasina attacked. The robot's arms created a barrage of razors and deadly wire, all whipping this way and that. At full speed, she dove past the cloud of wire toward the robot's body. It flailed about, fishing through the air, hoping to hit her. Her life depended on Queen Ghome's Aboleth powder; if it failed, she would die. She reached the disembodied heads having no idea how effective the powder would be, if at all. She punched out with her hands.

BOOM! BOOM!

The Aboleth coating her fists functioned marvelously. The explosions blasted the heads into bloody nothingness in an orange-green flash of fire. She turned her attention to the robot itself. Phillip's Poltava had proved useless against the robot's capsule, but the power of the Aboleth bit through like a cutting torch, blasting large holes in its metal shell with each hit. With just a few blows, Thomasina worked her way into its inner, unarmored mechanisms. A few more hits, more flashes and smoke, and she blew the guts out of the robot. It went still, hanging lifeless from the ceiling. The wire clattered to a stop.

"Rose!" Phillip said as he approached, still holding his tattered SAPP shield. She crawled out of the ruined metal remains and embraced him. "Are you hurt?" he asked.

"I'm fine." She looked at her hands. "I must admit, this Aboleth powder is stunning. Absolutely stunning! It's potent and energetic, it cuts through armor like it's not even there and all the while my hands are undamaged."

Phillip dug through the remains of the robot, going deep inside its ruined body. He found the box containing Lady Chrysania's parts. The box and the parts within were slightly scorched from the Aboleth blasts, but still intact. Further back was the Chadburn, its armored shutter closed. He dug it out and gave it to Thomasina.

"Let's go get King!" he said, holding the box.

They exited the room, moving fast down the corridor. "Rose, I think Queen Ghome intends to place the Machine in her throne room back there. I saw two hard points, footings made of earth, just like it sits upon earth in the Grove, and they're the correct distance apart and the right size. Like Sarah said, she wants the Machine in her throne room available for her easy use. We cannot let her have it!"

They passed a closed chamber to their left. Glancing inside through a small window, Thomasina saw that the room within was empty save for a copper bowl placed on a pedestal. The bowl overflowed with alluring golden dust piled up like a snow cone. The dust was scintillating, glinting with power and untold possibilities, generating its own light like the first rays of dawn. Of all the treasure hoarded here, none seemed greater than this bowlful of dust.

"Phillip, look. What is that?" She tried the door; it was

locked. "We tell stories of the Urn of Life in Waam. The urn of a goddess taken by force of arms and lost. Could this be it?"

"We'll come back for it, Rose," Phillip said. "First, we recover King."

They continued on. Ahead, a door on the right side of the corridor swung ajar. There was the posh interior of Queen Ghome's bedroom again. They heard a commotion going on in the washing area. Inside was Clara Wunderluck. She stood there before Queen Ghome's boudoir biting her lip, big-eyed and somewhat sheepish. A cloth bag stuffed full of pots of Aboleth powder lay at her feet. She blushed.

"I ... uh ... Yeah, I was just collecting some powder, and ..."

King was sitting on her left shoulder, his gleaming beak poised at her neck. On the tiled floor were the twisted remains of the silver cage he had been confined in.

"Naturally, I escaped," King said.

Thomasina charged forward. "You're going to die right now, Wunderluck!" she roared.

Clara held her hands out in a defensive manner. "Oh, no, no ... wait!"

Thomasina plowed into her, knocking Clara down, rousting King from his perch.

"Owww! No, no, please. I'm sorry!" Clara cried. Her eyes grew wide. "Hey! Do you have Aboleth on your hands? Don't hit me, it'll blow!"

"That's the whole idea, you little scoundrel! Be silent and face your death with a bit of dignity!" Thomasina roared.

Clara struggled and crawled around. She pleaded to Phillip, as he seemed to be the only one around slightly sympathetic to her cause. "Wait! Phillip, please! I'm sorry! What did you expect me to do? You said I was going back to the jail to stay there until I'm an old hag. Why would I want to do that? Wouldn't you do the same? You would! You wouldn't let yourself get hauled off to jail! I figured you'd beat the robot! I just wanted to get away, that's all! Stop!"

Thomasina was trying to prop Clara up into a kneeling position so she could blow her head off with the powder, but Clara was having none of it. She managed to get hold of Thomasina's leg and pulled her down, the two momentarily struggling on the floor. As Sarah had previously found out, Clara was much tougher than she looked and wasn't going down without a fierce struggle.

King fluttered up to Phillip's shoulder. "Shall I dispatch her?" he asked.

Phillip waded in and grabbed Clara by the neck, pulling her up. "Enough!" Clara gasped and sputtered for breath. Wide-eyed, she stared up at him.

"I really don't know why, but I'm going to let you live," he said.

"Phillip, no!" Thomasina cried, standing.

"We are not cold-blooded killers, Rose, and nor are we executioners." He locked eyes with Clara. "Lady Wunderluck, allow me to pay you a compliment. You've shown quite a bit of spirit, a good pair of hands and a never-quit attitude, and I admire that. I suppose I see a little bit of my sister in you, despite the fact that you are also a shameless opportunist who would say or do anything the moment required to better your situation. You are a fanatic, a casual murderer, a liar and an unprincipled, untrustworthy bore. As you determined, I have been taught the whole of my days to value the life of a lady, even if she does not value mine or that of my wife."

"No, no, that's not what I was doing, Phillip, I helped you, I …"

Phillip shushed her. "Quiet. Do not confuse our compassion with weakness, for that would be a deadly mistake. Now then, you are going to lead us to the control area. You shall do so promptly, without diversion and, you shall not utter another word until we say you may speak again. If you say anything, or if you make any unwise moves, King shall pierce you through the heart. Do you understand?"

She opened her mouth to speak.

"No, no," Phillip said. "No talking. Do you understand?"

She nodded vigorously.

"Excellent. Whether you live or die depends entirely on you. Now then, lead the way."

Thomasina shook her head. "Gods, Phillip, you're showing much more charity than I would have, but that's one of the reasons I love you."

King perched on Clara's shoulder, ready to run her through. Thomasina applied more Aboleth powder to her hands. She then filled the chest to the lid and took it with her.

6—Valley of Forgotten Dreams

They re-entered the corridor and continued on past the chambers of treasure into the much darker, much dirtier machinelike area. Clara led them off the central gantry into the maze of pipes to an elevated platform at the far left-side of the room that emitted strong yellowy daylight. It was partially hidden behind a network of water tanks. They made their way to it.

The platform was hexagonal and built into a recessed blister of faceted glass that stuck out, allowing clear views of the outside to the front, side and rear. A rusted rail stood over five of six sides on the platform. There was an array of disused levers arranged in an organlike pattern surrounded by a cluster of voice tubes. They were connected to complicated nodes of grimy ribbed cabling that rose up along the contours of the wall to the ceiling. Through the glass, they saw a vivid arid landscape under a yellowish sky. They were high in the air, gently floating over the craggy landscape. Looking back, they saw the surreal and somewhat frightening line of a great articulated metal wing slowly flexing and flapping up and down. The wing moved in time with a pair of great flywheels driven by pistons. Hints of hammered scales and brilliant stained metals caught the sunlight with each stroke. Far away past the wing was a long black tail ridged with shining brass plates swishing through clouds of white steam. To the front was the great dark blue mass of the main body, and, farther ahead, they caught occasional hints of a long articulated neck and a great dark blue reptilian head.

"This must be the control platform," Phillip said. "We have starboard-side views to the front, side and back for steering. Look at the dust and grime. It doesn't seem to have been used in a great while."

Thomasina and Clara stepped up onto the platform. Thomasina pointed at the Chadburn. "Where does this device go?"

Clara tapped Phillip on the shoulder and pointed at a plate bolted to the floor. Phillip examined it. "Here?" The bolts were rusted tight. King fluttered off and found a rusty wrench that would fit. He resumed his perch on Clara's shoulder.

"Get this plate off and be quick about it," Thomasina ordered, thrusting the wrench into Clara's hand.

Exasperated, Clara got down on her knees, instantly getting filthy. She set to work, struggling with the bolts, using the wrench in a clumsy fashion. King perched on the railing and watched her intently.

Thomasina went out into the glass blister and looked about. "Look there, Phillip. Far below, I see our shadow passing across the hills. See that, wings, long neck and a tail. We are indeed inside a mechanical dragon."

Down below, the dragon's shadow passed over a vast valley pocked with canyons and dry riverbeds. The valley was littered with ruined structures, with toppled columns and partially buried monuments all knocked about in various directions. In the canyons, relief carvings large enough to be easily seen from the air were cut into the yellowy rock. Here and there, great mechanical beasts of assorted types lay scattered about, covered in dust, some partially buried like fossils heaped together in a forgotten junkyard. Through one of the canyon arches, a beaked, birdlike head peeked out, looking hopefully skyward.

Phillip wondered; were these the great Bower Chests of ages past, left here beyond the Sisters' reach by the old Vith and forgotten on Edamathrombo?

Edamathrombo, the place he thought could be Mare with its ring of dead bodies. Phillip looked upwards. "Rose, look to the sky. Do you see it, just there, above the clouds?"

Thomasina squinted. "What am I looking at?"

"I see hints of a ring. It's difficult to make out in the daylight, but it's there. This planet has a very thin, moderately reflective ring." He thought a moment. "Rose, I think we're on planet Mare. Right now."

Her eyes widened in apprehension. "Mare? The planet with the ring of dead bodies?"

"I think so. The mural we examined depicted Queen Ghome's Bower Chest sequestered in a secret place of Edamathrombo far from the gaze of the Sisters and protected by the dead placed in the sky. Mare is the old Vith world of Edamathrombo and we are now on it under a sky full of dead men."

Metal groaned and rang out. "Ahhhhhh!" Clara suddenly cried. She was sitting up holding her hand, the wrench cast aside, tears streaming down her face. Her clothes were covered with red soot. "Ahhhhh ..."

"Continue working," Thomasina said.

She sat there holding her left hand, her mouth drawn back in pain. Phillip felt genuine pity for her.

"Let me see your hand," he said. She held up her hand and he enabled his Sight. Clara's hand, though dirty from the wrench, was pale and soft. "You've broken two of your fingers. Clearly, you're no mechanic. Stand over there by the glass; I'll do it. King, watch her, please."

Clara moved silently into the blister and nursed her hand. King took up position near her. Phillip took the wrench and went to work on the bolts. They were on good and tight, possibly machine tightened or simply rusted into place with age. Thomasina tried to help and got nowhere.

"King, can you get these bolts off?" Phillip asked.

"No need," Thomasina said. "King, continue to watch that Wunderluck miscreant. Stand back." She pushed up the sleeves of her leather armor.

BOOM! BOOM! BOOM! BOOM! Thomasina slapped at the bolts with the palms of her hands. The Aboleth coating her palms went off and cut through the rusty metal. She kicked at the plate. "I'm nearly through. A few more hits and we'll have it."

As Thomasina worked, Clara tapped on Phillip's shoulder. She pointed out the glass. Down below, a square structure made of ochre stones with a three-sided wall and two spired turrets appeared at the base of a dusty mountain range, growing large as the beast neared it. It had a wide central courtyard open to the sky; Phillip could see the ground within the courtyard was painted with a colorful speckling of white and dark green; tiles, or possibly flowers. Through the open end of the courtyard, a disused road wound its way out and up into the mountains. Situated between the two spires was a large tunnel-like archway that went down into the ground.

The machinery quickened their pace. Steam built up. The Bower Chest banked hard and they had to hang onto the railing or topple over the side. The structure below came up fast. Phillip saw a sprinkling of people scattered about in the enclosure, some wearing dark uniforms, others either lightly dressed or possibly not dressed at all. Intricate clawed feet enameled in midnight blue extended from below the Chest. An armored shutter came down over the glass, covering their view.

"We're landing. Hurry, Rose!"

She slapped at the plate: BOOM! BOOM!

"Got it!" she said in triumph. Thomasina stood and kicked the plate aside, revealing a deep hole.

"Well done, darling. The shaped explosions of the Aboleth are amazingly efficient," Phillip remarked. He checked Thomasina's hands. Not a scratch on her skin, and only slightly heated from the blasts. "Quite amazing."

Phillip took the Chadburn and slid the pole into the hole. It went down several feet and clanked to a stop. "There's some sort of linkage down there. I can't get it to properly insert." He turned the pole this way and that. "I think it has to go in just right and engage the linkages."

They felt an earthquakelike shudder as the beast landed and came to a halt. Steam built up for a terrifying moment. Valves hissed, pipes clanked, flywheels turned.

"Hurry, Phillip," Thomasina said.

The glow of the furnaces went from a dull orange to radiant white. Water boiled, and steam shuddered in the pipes. There was a great exhalation coming from the front of the beast. They heard high-pressure steam rush out in a terrible fury.

"Gods, what did it do? Did it just belch fire?" Thomasina asked.

Phillip struggled with the Chadburn. He felt the pole working its way into the machinery below. "I think it's almost there."

The boilers stoked up to white hot again. Water flowed, the pistons rattled. Armatures cranked. The metal beast readied for another exhalation.

Phillip worked the pole in deep. It dropped down significantly and engaged. "I got it, I got it!" Dust-covered lights came on around the platform in a rusty halo. The armored shutter covering the Chadburn dial retracted, revealing the ivory face and the handle.

He gripped the handle and cycled it one way, then the other. DING! DING! DING!

Bells sounded inside the dial as the handle passed over the various settings. Switches clicked. The levers mounted over the rail changed positions with a sooty fuss as he cycled the handle. Phillip moved the handle to the SHUTDOWN position, feeling it ratchet across every setting as he did so.

DING! DING! DING! DING!

The effect was immediate. Valves snapped open. Steam gushed and pressure was released. Fumes filled the air. The noise was deafening. The air became so humid and laced with noxious exhaust it was difficult to breathe. All three of them covered their mouths, trying to get a clear breath of air.

"Alert!" King said over the din. "I am detecting dangerous levels of industrial fumes, including sulfur dioxide, ozone, nitrogen oxide and various particulate materials. I do not recommend inhaling these fumes for a protracted period of time."

Phillip tried to dissent but couldn't speak. He coughed and gagged.

The lights overhead and around the platform went out. They hacked in the dark.

Clara toppled over, passing out. Clinging to each other, Thomasina and Phillip both fell victim to the fumes.

＊　＊　＊　＊　＊

Later, Phillip awoke, along with Thomasina. Clara lay on the platform, unmoving. Steam still vented, but not nearly as much. The fumes also seemed to have lessened greatly. King was perched on the Chadburn, watching them, his silver light allowing them to see.

"King, what happened?" Phillip gasped, his head pounding.

"You, Lady Blanchefort and Lady Wunderluck succumbed to the fumes. I fanned my wings, hoping to direct away the gasses. They have greatly diminished and been vented outside. I monitored your vitals while you were unconscious."

"How long were we out?"

"Twenty-five minutes."

Thomasina stirred. "Rose, you all right?" Phillip asked.

"I'll live. Have we succeeded?"

"The Bower Chest has not moved since the Chadburn handle was cycled to the SHUTDOWN position," King said.

They waited in the dark for a few minutes. "Well, we've accomplished what we came to do. I think we should find an exit and determine a method to get off this planet," Phillip said. "Clara said something about a doorway to Bazz, possibly another Gellar door. We should find it at once."

PANG! Something hit the outer hull of the Bower Chest, making a terrible racket, dislodging bits of rust from above.

Clara stirred and sat up. "What in the Poppintoff was that?" she asked. She put her hand over her mouth. "Oh Creation, I forgot, I'm not supposed to speak. You're not going to let the bird kill me, are you?"

PANG!

Another hit, like an artillery shell. And then another. It was like a great hailstorm rattling the sides of the Bower Chest.

King came up. "Alert!" he cried.

Far away, a small hatch opened in a notch in the machinery, admitting a shaft of yellow daylight from outside.

Two people entered, one staggering, carrying the second. The second figure seemed quite unresponsive, as if asleep or unconscious.

"Kay, is that you?" Phillip called out over the noise of the hissing steam. "Kay!"

Thomasina flew up shakily to get a better look, though she had trouble managing the clouds of steam.

"What do you see?" Phillip shouted.

"Dead," Thomasina cried. "He's dead!"

7—Queen Ghome

The Jones came in fast, ready to shoot it out. They found a terrible crash site on the Gallian Plain, a badly wounded Kay next to the dead mangled body of Laika amid a field of strewn wreckage. They put a few rockets into Laika's giant body just to be certain she was dead, leaving her in flaming pieces, and then they took her head off for good measure.

The Jones cautiously collected Kay's body, still encased in its hideous black Shadow tech suit. They attempted to get him out of his sinister suit, but found it quite impervious to their efforts. Wary of it, detecting massive levels of Shadow tech toxicity, they attached him by his neck to a chain and dragged him along the scrubby ground behind their land vehicle.

There was Gallia Palace and all that waited within. It rose up straight and tall in gothic majesty against the flat Bazz plains, its conical battlements speckled with slits of dim orange lights from openings in the stone. Atop the high walls, spotlights panned about in slow whitish arcs, lighting up the night; an island of glitz in the darkened plain. A drawbridge came down and Kay was dragged into a darkened central courtyard.

A gaggle of twenty people aimlessly milled about. They saw Kay being dragged in and came at a crazed, ghoul-like run. "Lord Blanchefort! Lord Blanchefort!" they cried as they neared, drawing knives from their clothing.

It was his House staff, fully under the control of The Jones. There was Andorra, his mother's personal assistant, always stately and proper in accordance with her important position in the Household: oiled, brown hair teased like a harlot, barely dressed, everything falling out, fingering a poisoned knife. They fell on Kay, pulling on his tanks, prodding with their knives, probing for weak points in the Shadow tech, all the while asking if they could make him breakfast and turn his linens. They were like ants trying to pry apart a doomed crab.

"Pick him up, please," came a soft voice. Kay was hauled up by his arms. Standing there casually was Tal de Roga in his cloak and white shirt, his trim blonde hair neat and tidy. He studied Kay's rather horrid-looking Shadow tech suit.

"Well, this is an interesting turn of events. Shadow tech, and it's pretty hideous as well; you're full of surprises. That is you in there, right, Kay?" He glanced at the staff. "Come on, girls, let's take him where he needs to go." The gibbering, half-naked staff hauled him off by his arms.

They turned and moved north through the courtyard. The staff, their bare skin in direct contact with Kay's toxic Shadow tech suit, were quickly sickened by it. They coughed and sweated. Their skin erupted in blazing red rashes that broke open and oozed. Soon they were spitting, gasping for air. Nevertheless, fully mesmerized, they enthusiastically followed de Roga's commands, dragging Kay along with glee.

Tal de Roga spoke in a cheerful manner as they neared the Palace entrance. "Once again, I'm sorry about all of this, Kay, I really am. You killed a great many of my brothers and sisters this evening, but it's not like we didn't have it coming to us. Let's make a pact. If you behave from here on out and do the right thing, then I'll do what I can to ensure your Ne-Countess is restored. You have my word."

They reached an iron door sweaty in the night air. Tal de Roga opened it. The staff dragged Kay through. The interior of the Palace was opulent: fine rugs, rich paneling and luxurious appointments from top to bottom. "We're taking you to see our Leader. She's not here on Bazz, if that's what you were thinking. We've always understood the Vith are arcane and full of tricks. There's something to be said for the old Acquisition Magic the Vith used to employ, you know; the more cool stuff you have, the more powerful you become. Our Leader is living proof of that, and so are you. We knew we couldn't beat you out in Blanchefort; your holdings and all the arcane things your House hoards gives you power. Just when it looked like you were done, a demon shows up and saves you—the Vith always have a trick or two up their sleeve. This palace was an old outpost of the Sorranders before they got kicked off the planet. We've stockpiled arcane items here at our Leader's command and transformed it into something the old-timers used to call a Gellartron; it's a sort of amplifier that allows our Leader to travel great distances, to control things like animals, the people, even the weather—you saw all of it this evening. Amazing what you Vith used to be able to do until you allowed the Sisters to water your Houses down."

They twisted and turned through the complicated interior of the palace, many of the staff becoming sick with Shadow tech poisoning. They got so sick, they began retching.

"Yes, you need to clean that up," Tal de Roga said, pointing. One of the staff, her body covered with rashes, stopped to clean up the mess. She was so weak, she dropped her knife and fell face-first into the pool of sick. She did not move after that.

They continued on, Tal de Roga making certain to remain several feet away from Kay at all times.

"Once our Leader gives us Bellathauser, we can truly serve mankind. We can put all this darkness behind us and celebrate a new day. Good will come from what was done tonight. I truly believe that."

At the end of a dark paneled hallway they came to a closed doorway. "Here it is, a wonder from the age of the Vith; the Gellartron. The great beast that knocked you out of the sky passed through this very door. It can become small, or walk on two legs and be just as human as we are; a true wonder."

Tal de Roga unlatched the door and swung it open. Yellowish bright light came through, as if from a fully-lit summer's day. He stepped through, followed by the staff, who dragged Kay with them.

They emerged into a dusty, rather hot landscape dotted with lazy hills baked hard in the sun under a thin sky.

"Come along," de Roga ordered as the staff pulled Kay down a gentle mountain path. They had lost some of their giddy verve along the way. They labored with him, grunting, crying, as they were poisoned by Kay's suit. And then, they succumbed, falling out, trembling on the dusty ground, leaving a little trail of colorful clothing and akimbo limbs of the fallen marking their passage. As the staff fell out, others joyously came in to replace them.

Overhead was a tepid sky painted with hazy clouds. An ominous storm brewed in the distance. The shadow of a thin planetary ring climbed skyward like a pair of opened scissors.

"Know where you are, Kay?" de Roga asked. "This planet has many names. It's an old scion of the Vith, a place of refuge safe from the growing power of the Sisters. They knew what was coming, of the hand that was to descend upon them, and here they staked their claim … and put the Dead in the sky above to defend it."

Kay glanced up to the indistinct ring high overhead.

"This is Edamathrombo, the fastness of the Vith as they were in their splendid pagan glory ages ago, a place no Sister or anyone else has ever set foot, the Dead have seen to that. The Xaphans call it Mare, I believe."

De Roga took a deep breath and looked around. "The Old Vith hid their sacred objects here to protect them from the Sisters.

They're still where the Vith left them; several hundred miles to the west. Most are deactivated, covered in dust. I'd imagine your family has something stashed here somewhere, all the old Vith Houses do. Sometimes I wish I was a Vith and not a crap Bazzer with a mongrel history. Such a pity."

Waiting for them at the end of the trail was a Vith-style keep surrounded on three sides by an ancient wall and adjacent ridge. Tall temperate shrubs reached up polelike into the arid air. Two spires guarded the western end of the enclosure. There seemed to be no central structure or edifice present on the surface, though a tunnel entrance built into the northern wall indicated structures hidden beneath the surface. Ochre sandstone of the finest quality lined the walls. A gallery of flawless white marble statues in both human and monstrous forms some ten feet tall lined the center pass. Jones Battle Units waited in the wings, covering Kay with their Man-to-Man rockets, polka-dotting him in targeting lasers. Armed snipers sat on their shoulders and hung from the towers like rotten fruit, covering him with their rifles.

Heaped up near the tunnel entrance was a veritable mountain of piled treasure in the form of coins, paintings, weapons and other valuables. It was unmistakable; all swag taken from Castle Blanchefort. In front of the pile was an odd sight: a large oak tree sitting askew, complete with wilting leaves and a mangled root ball.

It was the Machine hidden behind its Silver tech disguise, ripped from the ground in the Telmus Grove and stolen along with the rest.

The remaining staff dropped Kay in the dust and backed away, all of them spitting and vomiting all over the rich clothes The Jones had dressed them in, turning green, sick with Shadow tech. Kay landed face-down, his Shadow tech tanks clanking. A host of scanning cones instantly locked onto him. The ground ahead down the center pass was littered with a leafy carpet of fresh Horvath Creepers, their vivid white petals wilting in the sun and their spores lacing the air in a perfumy haze.

"End of the line, Lord Blanchefort," Tal de Roga said in a cheerful fashion. "If you wish to revenge yourself upon me as a ghost, I really wouldn't blame you."

A storm cloud came in from the west and settled over the courtyard. From the open southern end, a mechanical procession appeared bearing a massive litter of gold and carbuncle. Twelve Jones Battle Units, painted black and adorned with decorative metal horns, marched in; the elite forces had arrived. In the center of the litter they carried was a throne of bronze, moltenlike and shining, mixed with resplendent titanium. A luxurious robed figure of pale visage sat on the throne, carrying a large black scepter. The Jones bowed in reverence as the litter passed them. Tal de Roga roughly kicked Kay to the ground.

"Bow! Bow before our mistress, she who will lead us to Bellathauser!"

The procession reached the center of the courtyard, followed closely by the storm clouds darkening the sky.

Lightning struck. Thunder cried out her name:

GHOME!!!!!

The Battle Units lowered the litter to the ground and took their respective places at its side. The pale figure seated on the throne lightly stepped off, coming forward, crushing the white Creeper flowers underfoot kicking up a glittering cloud of even more golden pollen. Kay caught glimpses of pale feet appearing through the hem of the robe and the swishing of pampered legs. As the figure passed the gallery of monstrous statues placed in the center of the clearing, they came to writhing, snarling life, complete with scaly texture and vivid oily colors from a demented nightmare; the figure petted them with a clawed passing hand as if they were mere pets. When the figure departed and created some distance, the creatures returned to white smooth statues locked into place. The figure selected two of her favorites, two snakelike wyrms lurid with reds and blues and long flicking tongues. The newly animated beasts padded along at her side. Beyond the perimeter of the enclosure, rain came down in sheets, creating a ghostly black curtain hanging from the sky and a chorus of solemn thunderclaps. Along the perimeter of the storm clouds, Jones Winger ships orbited the sky in lazy turns.

The figure neared Kay and stopped. "Pick him up," a stern, mirthless voice said.

The wyrms thundered up, taking Kay into their stinking, tooth-lined maws, tugging on him like two dogs fighting over a piece of meat, almost but not quite tearing him apart. Their teeth and claws bit into the Shadow tech.

The figure stood before Kay wearing a coarse white robe with a sash wrapped around her face. The figure removed the sash and let fall the robe. There, standing before Kay in jeweled veils was the enemy, an ageless woman of a thousand names and faces: Lady Chrysania of Bloodstein, Queen Ghome, and a host of others long forgotten. Here she was at long last, the Immortal, the last of the old Bloodsteins, the evil waking self of Roethaba of George.

She was a terrible sight. She wore Sam's face, her hair, her hands, her feet, her breasts, everything. Kay recognized them easily, though her expression and bearing were completely alien and uncaring, unlike the inviting, hugging, full of life Sam.

This woman was quite a bit taller than Sam, shorter waisted and thicker in the hips, built like a typical Bloodstein. She had a belly button which Sam did not have, and her skin complexion was that of a Vith; pale, but much more heavily pigmented than the bone-white Sam. Her pigmentation had somehow leeched into Sam's parts, darkening them a few shades. Her eyes were not Sam's. They were bright blue, Vith blue: Sarah's eyes. Kay knew ahead of time that Queen Ghome was wearing Sarah's eyes, as Sam's were in the cryochest on Hoban, but seeing it in person was heartbreaking. Her hands bore ten clawlike fingernails, sharp enough to slice metal; typical Monama claws. She had allowed them to grow out much longer than Sam did even in her Monama heyday. Aimlessly, she clinked her claws together.

"So, Lord Blanchefort," she said in a sneering voice, raising her arms. "We meet again. What think you? Am I not beautiful?" Kay noted her scepter was studded with stout spikes.

Kay did not reply. She swung her scepter down in a whistling arc, burying it into Kay's helmet. Skewered, she hauled him up. "Well?" she demanded.

Kay said nothing. Queen Ghome spat in disgust. "Pah! What has happened to the Vith? Look what the ages have done! Made you soft, made you pathetic!" She looked at her pale Monama hands studded with claws.

"Look at the filth with which you pollute your bloodlines. No Vith of old would admit a Monama to his bed, not even for a night's pleasure. They are not Vith, they are not human. What of your Household? What young will come of that? The true Vith are dead, and here is the proof!"

She raised her stolen hand, making a 'come here' motion with her fingers. Through the open end of the enclosure, a long black sledgelike vehicle twelve feet high and fifty feet long came in floating on a hovercone, kicking up the Creeper spores, holding them in gridlike patterns of force. Riding on the vehicle were a dozen, possibly more, lithe females; all beautiful, all oiled and nude, covered with colorful festive dots and swirls of paint. The sledge came to a halt in the cen-

ter of the enclosure. The females bounded down in a well-practiced ballet and presented themselves to Queen Ghome, bowing before her with nimble grace. She touched them all gently on the top of the head and said their names; Alifair, Concenta, Vim, Melazarr, Tentha, and on and on until she had greeted them all. Panels opened along the sides of the black vehicle, sliding back with a sinister hermetic hiss.

Cold fog rolled out, revealing the sledge to be a giant trunk of sorts, containing innumerable shelves, drawers, pots, vases, jugs, and tankards full of vast quantities of water. In the center of the vehicle, dozens upon dozens of bodies hung on hooks, swaying slightly, nudging against each other.

The females, attendants of Ghome, brought out jugs and vases and small golden chests, awaiting their master's command.

Ghome scowled at Kay. "What did you think; that I simply had to have your pretty Monama wife's face? Is that what you thought? I couldn't care less about your bloody Countess' face, or any other of her filthy Monama parts for that matter. I've been wearing pretty faces for centuries; your wife does not rate in the top ten thousand! See, watch ..."

She raised her claws and effortlessly sliced Sam's face to ribbons. Blood poured out, staining her garments. With her thumbs, she poked Sarah's eyes out and cut off Sam's ears, throwing the ruined bits at Kay.

Overhead, the rain stopped and the clouds parted. Swatches of sunlight passed through.

"*I suppose she's not so pretty any longer, is she?*" Queen Ghome gibbered in ghoul-like fashion, blood foaming from her wounds, staining her linen garments. The attendants came forward. They brought forth a wooden bowl overflowing with glittering golden dust and a jug from which they poured clear water.

The water ... That dust ...

They took the water from the jug and washed Queen Ghome; the blood from her destroyed face bubbled out, mixing with the water and dripping to the ground. They painted on a coating of dust. In one smooth motion, the attendants pulled what was left of Sam's face and Sarah's eyes from her head as if peeling an orange. She stood there, her head hairless and blank. Two attendants came forward, holding a set of golden chests. They opened the chests. In one was a pair of lurid red eyes, like the eyes of a demon. In the other was a mouth sporting a long tongue and a sharpened set of teeth like that of a shark. Like children decorating a snowman, the attendants applied the eyes and mouth to Ghome's blank face, splashing water and dabbing golden dust. The red eyes blinked, taking on an evil depth, and she took in a long, deep breath through the mouth, allowing her tongue to pass over her sharp teeth.

In a long procession, the remaining attendants brought forth bodies from the trunk, presenting them to Queen Ghome, allowing her to pick and choose what she wanted. They washed Queen Ghome again, powdered her with more dust, and on came a face, stolen from some doomed maiden. It was so beautiful it was hideous, so perfect it was formless. Her red eyes emerged through the eyelids like a set of angry moons appearing through breaks in the clouds. The selection process continued at a casual pace, Ghome discarding Sam's parts and casting them into the dirt in exchange for select parts from the various bodies brought in for her inspection. The attendants also carried lengths of variously shaded hair as if dressing for a grand evening on the town. She selected a head of whitish gray hair, the locks slightly curled. The attendants pulled off her feet, adding perfect replacements from the trunk. In a moment, all of Sam—except for her clawed hands, which Ghome kept—lay discarded in a heap on the ground like a pile of soiled laundry. Queen Ghome stood tall, dripping wet, rebuilt as a smoky demoness with red eyes and pointed teeth. With brushes and pots of paint, the attendants decorated her in swirling dots and streaks of color.

A final touch came out of the trunk: a pair of long mottled horns which the attendants placed on the sides of her head with dotted hands. They draped her hair around in loose swirls. Now the picture was complete.

"Now, I can relax," she said, her voice now completely different. "Pardon my horns, I do love them so."

She pointed at the Machine. "And now ..."

Tal de Roga came up. He spoke to Kay in a calm reasonable voice. "The arcane defenses around the Machine are quite formidable; we weren't expecting such a thing. Several of your staff died attempting to breach it for us. Can you take care of these defenses, please? I know what you're thinking. You're thinking, 'why should I?' and I fully understand. If you do this for us, all these girls in your service who still live will be set free and sent home. I promise. We shall also attend to those requiring treatment for Shadow tech poisoning. They can all walk away from this and I know you care for them, went to your grave protecting them. You can still be a hero, Kay, just let her have the Machine. Who's to care what she does with it? You and I and nobody else shall ever know the difference, then we shall locate Bellathauser and all the suffering of man shall be forgotten. You can be the father of all of that."

Kay slowly stood, the staff hovering around him, fingering their knives. They came up and moved him toward the Machine, gripping him by the shoulders, their knives clutched in their hands. Andorra prodded his neck with her knife, looking for a weak spot. As Kay neared, the Silver tech disguise around the Machine moved aside in response to his presence. There it was, the Machine revealed at last, the great arch like two silver trees welded together.

"So, this is it? Your cousin and the Wunderluck woman were right," Tal de Roga said, standing next to Kay like an old friend. "Such a seemingly innocuous thing for all this fuss, wouldn't you say?" Scanning cones from the Jones focused on it, greedily bouncing off its contours in a dance hall display of light. They tabulated data.

"Are they removed, Kay? Are the defenses gone?"

Kay said nothing.

"We're going to find out right now." De Roga motioned to the staff and they noisily surged to the Machine. They passed through the perimeter of the Silver tech disguise. They touched it with their hands and sauntered through the arch unharmed. Tal de Roga watched them carefully and then tentatively touched it himself. Satisfied that the defenses around the Machine were disabled, several Jones Battle Units approached. They lifted the Machine and pulled it out of the hollow interior of the tree. Setting it down to stand on its own, it gleamed untarnished and goldlike in the yellowy sunlight. They scanned it with hand-held equipment.

"Inert," they said.

Queen Ghome walked across the courtyard flanked by her beasts given life by her presence. She stood under the Machine's arch, her breast rising and falling in excitement. She reached up and passed her fingers across the round depression where the powering stone went. "And where is the powering stone?" she asked.

Kay said nothing.

She thundered up to Kay and lifted him off the ground. "Where is it?"

"Not here," he replied in a strained voice. "It's gone. I don't know where it is."

"WHHHHAAAAATTT!!!" she screeched, dropping him. One of the animated beasts at her side came at Kay, ramming its clawed foot into his chest, pinning him to the ground. Ghome snapped her fingers. Several of her attendants went to the great trunk in the center of the enclosure, opening more panels. They lugged out a large wooden chest inlaid with brass.

"Do you really think hiding the stone shall prevent me its use? Do you?" she asked, her lip curling, sharpened teeth gleaming. The beast flexed its reptilian foot, its claws digging into Shadow tech.

Kay struggled, unable to move.

"Oh, the Vith through the ages, still the same ... Why do you think I left the miserable League in the first place?" Ghome spat.

The Jones in attendance mumbled in agreement; her attendants clapped.

"Silence!" she thundered. The attendants came over the carpet of Creeper plants and set the chest down. Queen Ghome padded across the Creepers, the dark green leaves and white flowers crushing underfoot. The great beast looming over Kay reverted to marble as she moved away, its stone claws lodged in his chest.

Ghome pushed the attendants aside and opened the chest that had been brought out. Inside was a shining collection of large round jewels of immense carat size. They glistened in deep greens, swirling reds, amber yellows and glinting blues, like a trove of flawless, sparkling candy. Ghome selected a purple stone from the chest and thundered toward Kay, holding it aloft. As she neared, the creature holding Kay to the ground reverted back to life, but more slowly this time, its vivid colors mottled with stone slowly receding. The rain had stopped. The clouds overhead were nearly gone. Queen Ghome took no notice. "Look, take a look! Did you think hiding the powering stone would stop me? I have dozens of them! I was there when this Machine was constructed! I soothed Lord Want. I slept in his bed. He even asked me what color it should be—I favored purple back then."

Tal de Roga took the stone from her and inserted it into the Machine's arch. It clicked into place.

"Ah, see, now it is ready," Ghome said. She glanced at Kay. "The places one can go with this Machine. I wondered if I'd ever see it again. I was there, wrapped around Lord Want as his submissive pet. I can be rather fetching when I wish, when I want something, and I wanted this Machine. How I've lusted after it. After centuries, I shall put it to proper use and in a proper place."

Ghome flushed up in anger. "One might think after centuries that patience would be one of my assets. Live for centuries and the first thing to leave your soul is patience. You think I'm evil ... you think I'm cruel? There is no good or evil in immortality; there is no right or wrong as you wait for the days to fade into centuries. The only thing keeping one sane in the sea of time is wanting things and allowing nothing to get in your way. And I want the Machine. I want it! It belongs to me! It hasn't left my thoughts in centuries. There are things I would undo. There are things I haven't forgotten, and the passing of centuries does not make that any less. I heard all about the Machine's resurrection after centuries. Wilhella Cormand-Grande wouldn't stop talking about it in those silly posts she writes. She is a fool, of course, yet she seemed to be onto something. It was possible the Machine had been restored to wholeness at last. I heard nothing in Xaphan space; surely some warlord or Xaphan prince would have come forward and said something had they possessed it. I sat in my Bower Chest gazing at the earthen spot I'd long prepared for it and guessed that if the Machine truly were out there, it would be somewhere in League space.

"So, I decided to go hunting for it in a passive fashion. There are several people inhabiting my body with me. There's the sniveling little girl who needed me to get her out of the Sisters' capture, and there's that 'soft voice' from my dreams. I've known about her for centuries; the one who won't stay quiet. The one who won't do what I tell her to do. My conscience, I've been told. What an inconvenience, to have a conscience, and it seems she has her minions listening for her worrisome voice in the dark. I have learned to sleep in a protected place within my Bower Chest to keep her from communicating with her followers. Such a simple matter to deal with my conscience. However, the woman in my head has her uses. It occurred to me that I could use her hand-wringing antics to help me discover the Machine. I've used her before. I've heard she is a genius, but she doesn't seem all that intelligent to me. All I need do is sleep outside my Bower Chest and she comes to life, worshipped by her followers on Hoban. After that, it's a simple matter for my Jones friends to spy on them over the networks, listening for minute chatter and other such tidbits that filter through. I heard tell of the Wunderlucks from Remnath as they claimed to possess a number of old items from across antiquity; including the Machine. They showed something that they claimed to be the Machine to my attendants, but I had my doubts, so I decided to test them. I let poor, fragile Lady Chrysania out. The Wunderlucks Stared her, seeing not me but that weak little girl in my head, figuring her for an easy mark—playing right into my hands. Using Chrysania, I set the Wunderlucks to collecting Wilhella Cormand-Grande's Perlamum set she loves to tantalize heroes with. I assumed that had the Wunderlucks actually possessed the Machine, they would have used it to collect the pieces. Unfortunately, they turned out to be frauds. Frauds with an ugly piece of homemade artwork they claimed was the Machine! My blood was up. I was so close. I had to have it! I sent out notes to many Houses fishing for clues, for information. Most of my notes went unanswered.

"And then, there you were, visiting old Castle Bloodstein wishing to help poor helpless Lady Chrysania, listening to her babble about lost love. The House of Blanchefort, so bold and adventurous. I should have known those of *my line* would have *my* Machine."

Ghome glared at Kay. "Yes, my blood flows through your veins. Castle Blanchefort was once my home. I, in a sense, created you, and therefore I cannot stand you! I sent my Jones to you to dredge up information. Your cousin, the little blue-haired girl, said much, and there it was, out in the Telmus Grove in the oak trees that I helped plant ages prior. But, of course, it was protected by powerful magic, magic even I couldn't get through. That bloody silver disguise. So, I needed you, here, in my place of power, to be rid of it, and here you are at my feet."

Ghome sneered. "Or, should I say, your wife's feet?"

Tal de Roga came up beside her in subservient fashion. "And what shall we do with Lord Blanchefort?"

She sneered again and thought a moment. "What shall we do with my great, great, great grandson? His task is done, the Machine is free. First, let us get him out of his suit." She pointed with Sam's claws to an attendant. "Get me some dust!"

An attendant bowed and presented the bowl of golden dust to her. She held up the bowl; Queen Ghome plunged her clawed hand in deep, withdrawing a handful of glittering dust that trickled through her fingers in golden streams. She thundered up to Kay, smearing the dust roughly into his black bubble helmet. It instantly reacted to the Shadow tech, steaming, hissing, eating through it.

"I just wasted a whole handful of dust on you, enough for a hundred years' use. Why? Because I never run out. I have enough dust for a thousand immortalities."

The golden dust and the Shadow tech roiled about, bubbling, dripping off in boiling blobs. Kay's helmet was quickly eaten through, revealing his face. The grotesque parts stuffed down his throat melted away and he coughed up black slime. His hideous black suit dropped off in sluglike patches. Ghome scoffed, seeing Kay on his knees.

"Look at the state of my progeny." She thought a moment, considering what his fate would be.

"Ah, I know. I shall give you a death the Old Vith, the real Vith, would have been proud of. As you are my kin, it's the least I can do."

She pointed off to the east. "Behold! See what your ancestors wrought in defiance of the Sisters! See what you have squandered!"

From the lonely passes of the hills to the east, something cried out, its shrill roar echoing in the solitude, rolling over the land. A black winged form crested the hills and struck a pose there like a gargoyle, a silhouette in broad daylight.

A demonic face pinpricked by two orange eyes turned to the courtyard. Kay was locked in its crawling gaze. It gave off a drifting pall of smoke, framing itself in a veil of hell. Then it took flight, winging its slow way down with heavy wing beats to the flats, snorting a trail of super-heated gases from its nostrils. As it neared, it came into clear focus: it was some sort of dragonlike creature made of hammered brass and fitted steel, all enameled to a dark midnight blue. Its head and neck were about fifty feet long, its articulated pear-shaped body about two hundred, and its long segmented tail about a thousand.

It seemed to be wearing some sort of armored breastplate bearing the Bloodstein crest forged in resplendent notchless brass against dark blue. It had two round windows or portholes cut into the breastplate at either shoulder. Fierce orange light came out of the windows, as if a great fire burned within. It had a muscular, bird-like set of brass legs tipped with ringed claws which it kept tucked up into its chest as it flew. It appeared to have no front legs. Exhaust ports lined the complex hammered ridges of its back, exuding great belches of super-hot steam and coal black smoke in regular cloudy pulsations, leaving a trail of churning clouds as is passed.

Ki, while Gamed Up, had dreamt of this monstrosity. Here was the Bower Chest of Queen Ghome; a carry-over from her Bloodstein roots. This was the creature that had destroyed Kay's Shadow tech ship with its arcane claws and its scalding steam. The beast of old from the days of the Splendor of the Vith was before him at last.

It made a slow, somewhat predatory circle of the keep, snorting steam, churning the air with steam and burning fumes. It extended its claws and came to an earth-shaking perch on the northern wall, accompanied by a blast of steam and smoke. It fanned its wings and gave those in the courtyard a great wing flap, kicking up a cyclone of gravel and Creepers.

Queen Ghome raised her arms in welcome and the beast acknowledged her, lowering its head to the ground. She came up and lovingly caressed its metal skin.

"This is what my family, the Old Bloodsteins, hid here on Edamathrombo. These walls are its home. I have fed it! This is an old Vith Bower Chest, mystical constructs of an age now forgotten in the

Sisters' drunken, moribund League. All the old Households had one roaming the castle grounds in all shapes and colors, darkening the skies, making the ground tremble in their majesty. Inside the Bower Chest, we keep our most sacred and powerful objects, and they, in turn, give it life. Inside my Bower Chest, under constant vigilance, is where I keep the things of great importance I have collected over the centuries. Here is where the Machine shall go and I, from the safety within, shall have dominion over the universe itself."

Queen Ghome pointed at the fallen Kay. Everyone backed away.

"Kill him!" she said to the Bower Chest. "I give you the honor."

Without hesitation or delay, the great metal creature curled its neck, breathed in and shot forward, exhaling a withering blast of steam. Kay wilted under the attack and the last few bits of his Shadow tech suit were blasted off. He was scalded beet red and then consumed totally, flesh and bone melting away, leaving little more than a discolored patch on the ground. Gone in an instant.

The Jones cheered. The hypnotized staff giggled. The attendants, apparently used to this sort of spectacle, remained quiet, ready to carry out Queen Ghome's next command.

Ghome curled her lip and glanced at the Blanchefort staff capering about, all teetering, sick with Shadow tech. "These people are his sniveling servants, is that right?"

"Yes, my queen," Tal de Roga said.

"Collect them in the center."

He hesitated. "I promised Lord Blanchefort I would send them home."

"I will send them home," she said. "I will certainly do that! Collect them in the center along with the Monama's disgusting parts."

Tal de Roga herded the staff girls into the center of the courtyard. "Where's Lord Blanchefort?" they asked as they fingered their poisoned knives. "We miss him," Andorra said, so badly poisoned her teeth were coming out by their roots in horrid strings.

"You'll see him in a moment," de Roga said, backing away. "I'm sorry. Where are Lady Sammidoran's parts?"

Two attendants looked about. "We do not see them."

Queen Ghome turned to the great metal beast. "Enough. We shall find the parts later. Kill them!"

The metal beast lifted its head and took in a great expansion of air in a rushing vortex, ready to exhale a second jet of deadly steam and scald the staff into oblivion.

Just as it was ready to let fly, it seemed to hesitate and diminish in size. It tucked in and curled up, folding its wings, placing its head on the ground. Valves snapped open and clouds of pure white steam vented from its pipes, climbing into the sky like churning geysers. The light in its furnace grew dim and cold and then went out entirely. Sooty smoke belched out from its sides. It seemed to be asleep.

Ghome watched with sputtering fury. "STOP! WHAT HAPPENED?" she screeched.

Her attendants looked on in confusion. "It has been shut down, my queen," one of them stammered.

"HOW? HOW IS THAT POSSIBLE?"

"My queen, we don't know."

Chaos came down on the enclosure. Powerful explosions ripped through The Jones' ranks, felling one Jones Battle Unit after the next. For the first time, Queen Ghome and Tal de Roga appeared confused and unsure of themselves.

"Queen Ghome!" came a voice leaden with fury. "Your conscience is about to have her day; her voice is about to be heard! She is eager to make right what you have done! Your time has come at last!"

Queen Ghome looked around. "Who is speaking?" she demanded. "WHO IS SPEAKING?"

The voice answered in a calm manner. "The man you've stolen from. The man whose beloved wife you have mutilated."

Ghome threw back her head and laughed. "Ah, grandson! Hiding behind a Cloak. Still have a little bit of Vith cunning in you after all. I must admit to a bit of pride in my kin having the audacity to attempt to stand against me. Perhaps there's a bit of my blood in you after all."

"That was a Shadow tech simulacrum you ordered killed! A spineless fake for you to have your fun with. I had a final use in the bag and it served me well, did it not?"

"I will strike you down with rain and lightning."

"I see no clouds."

Ghome looked skyward, seeing a clear sky. Confusion crossed her face.

The remaining Jones Battle Units adjusted their lines and saturated the courtyard with scanning cones and a dusting of No-Cloak powder, trying to locate Kay's Cloaked form.

"You spoke of the Vith," came Kay's voice. "See the Vith, and see the face of your doom!"

Kay appeared several feet away, wearing a hideous black suit and holding his glowing CARG.

"Lord Blanchefort! Lord Blanchefort!" the staff cried, approaching him at a run, lifting their knives. They ran into his CARG. They were so weak from their Shadow tech poisoning that they fell with only slight, non-cutting blows.

Targeting cones saturated him from The Jones, ready to fire. Man-to-Man rockets leapt out of their tubes and headed in fast. Kay vanished at the last second, the rockets exploding on nothing. Overhead, Winger ships orbited, dropping No-Cloak powder bombs and saturating the courtyard in high-energy scanning cones.

"You want truth, Queen Ghome," came Kay's voice, "here is truth ..."

A Jones Winger ship was knocked out of the sky, followed by a second. A Battle Unit was hit and shredded, and then another. An H-Grenadier was blown off its feet; a mangled operator dying at the controls.

Kay appeared before them again. He held up a pale Monama face with long black hair. "Behold, as you destroyed with malice, I repaired with love using your own water and dust right under your nose. For the love of my wife and my kin, I am ending this, now!" He placed Sam's face back into his pouch.

With Ghome's Bower Chest asleep and the storm clouds gone, her vast power seemed to be greatly diminished. Her faithful Jones servants seemed a little less in her thrall; some hesitating at their controls, some even abandoning their Battle Units and other equipment and fleeing into the desert. The marble beasts were sluggish and slow to come to life. One, partially transformed, exploded in a cloud of guts and crushed marble. A second beast reached Kay and was impaled on his CARG. He lengthened the shaft, lifting the beast over his head. It fell out of Ghome's sphere of influence and reverted to a statue. Kay rammed it into the ground, shattering it. A third was lifted into the air by an invisible hand and thrown a considerable distance away. A giant six-armed Haitathe form briefly appeared in a fading scanning cone and then disappeared.

"We are so close!" Tal de Roga roared and came at a run, yelling, speaking hypnotic words, trying to bring Kay under his control. The Shadow tech suit shut out his voice and blurred his image. This time, there would be no hypnosis, no Jones' tricks. This time, with room to move and full use of his CARG, Kay met Tal de Roga in battle. He first wounded his right arm, then his left. Kay ran him through, intentionally missing all the vitals, flicking the blood off his CARG. He battered him, he knocked him about, inflicting a multitude of searing cuts, turning the man who caught bullets in Castle Blanchefort into a nearly helpless bleeding mass. Sniper fire came down from the walls, hoping to take Kay down; he casually Sighted the bullets coming in and Wafted away to avoid them, spinning de Roga around. Bleeding, in agony, de Roga fought on unarmed, trying but unable to pierce Kay's defenses. Tired of the game, Kay swept him down and ran him through the chest.

"So ... close ... " he gurgled.

Kay then turned his attention on Queen Ghome.

She spat and raised her scepter to brain him with it. He countered with his CARG.

CLANG!

"You are not walking away from this," Kay said. Grinning, she engaged, whirling her scepter, their weapons clashing.

CLANG!

One of the few remaining on-duty Battle Units came to cover Queen Ghome. As it moved into position it was split down the center like a tin can, the operator ripped from his seat by an invisible hand.

Another Battle Unit exploded into flaming wreckage. A sniper went down, and then another, and another. Most of The Jones were now either deceased or had fled.

Victory was at hand. Kay met Queen Ghome's scepter and turned his CARG, cutting through it down the center in a shower of sparks. Kay reached out to take her at last.

Queen Ghome threw her useless weapon down and lunged at Kay, throwing her arms around him.

BOOM!!!

Kay was rocked back by a tremendous explosion and thrown to the ground. As he lay there, dazed, Ghome kicked him twice with gut-wrenching effect.

BOOM!

BOOM!

Satisfied that Kay had been dealt a mortal blow, she turned to her grand prize: the Machine, gleaming in the sun, splashed with droplets of The Jones blood. But as she approached, the great Silver tech tree created by Lady Poe of Blanchefort that had hidden it in the Telmus Grove came to life. With flowing silver tendrils, it lifted the Machine off the ground and retracted, returning it to the hollow of its trunk where the silver flowed back around it. A moment later, the entire length of the tree became studded with savage thorns dripping with deadly Nyke poisons, daring Queen Ghome to come closer and be destroyed.

SHING! came the sound of the thorns unsheathing.

From knotholes along its length, a legion of tiny silver StTs paraded out, moving into position, defending the tree and the Machine within like a colony of enraged ants, jaws open, ready to kill.

Deterred by the deadly display, she sprinted away, pushing through the crowd of staff and attendants. She ran into the tunnel at the far end of the enclosure and disappeared, her attendants following.

Kay shakily got up on one knee, trying to regain his wits and assess what damage he had sustained. The Shadow tech suit had held, the killing blows she had inflicted upon him had been warded off. The giant form of Laika fell out of Cloak and came to his side, helping him up. She was lusty with battle, her DeeDee rifle still smoking, her swords dripping with crazy streams of hydraulic fluid and blood. Kay had heard stories that Haitathe, when in the heat of battle, tended to grow in size, and Laika had grown from her usual ten feet to a whopping sixteen feet tall. Her composite armor strained to hold her in.

"Hail, Jarlcon!" she yelled lustily, her voice thundering. "Shadow tech from bag worked well! Laika kill many Jones!"

"Well done! Come, Laika, we can't let her get away!"

Together, they tore off in pursuit. Every bit of Kay's body hurt. "What in the Name of Creation did she hit me with?"

"Aboleth!" Laika cried. "Explosive powder. Mother tells Laika Ghome wears Aboleth!"

Kay's guts were ablaze with agony. "Confirmed. Thanks for the heads up!" he wheezed.

They reached the end of the enclosure. There was the tunnellike archway cut into the stone leading underground. Ten nude attendants, oiled and dotted, stood before it hefting spears at the ready position, blocking the entrance. None of them looked like they were in a particular mindset to fight.

Laika rose up to full height and covered the attendants with her DeeDee, three LLAGs and two swords still fresh with Jones blood. She was itching to pull her triggers, battle lust filling her. Several attendants dropped their spears and fell to the ground, praying for mercy.

"Step aside, please, this needn't concern you," Kay said, and the attendants promptly moved aside.

"Cover them, Laika. GHOME!" Kay roared as he entered the

passage. He thundered forward brandishing his CARG, ready to take his prize.

Within was a dimly lit corridor heading down into the sub-levels beneath the surface enclosure. Marking the walls of the passage at regular intervals was a series of glass display cases all lit up in warm orange light. Inside the cases were golden artifacts and precious stones arranged in a museumlike set-up. One after the other, reminders of past theft, past conquests. Ghome had so much, she could afford to leave some out.

Ki's words from the Inn of the Hidden Surprise filtered into his thoughts.

She's got these cases all lined up. Just stuff she liked but didn't really think about too much. What you're looking for is in there. She didn't know what she had ...

Didn't know what she had? Was Ki referring to the Artifacts of Vehelm? Kay had assumed the Artifacts of Vehelm must have been among her most closely guarded treasures, kept safe in the belly of her Bower Chest. But what if she didn't know or properly understand what those artifacts did? What if she thought they were simply beautiful trinkets and left them out in the open in a display of other pretty but otherwise unimportant pieces of treasure?

If that was the case, then she had made a colossal blunder.

What had Raal said: *"... she thought Vehelm of Waam had Maliked her into a protracted sleep."*

She didn't know he had used the necklace and the headset to bind her.

Didn't know what she had ...

Eyes wide behind his Shadow tech bubble, Kay examined every case down the line. Full of treasure, each splendid, each full of lost weapons and plundered armor, rare trinkets and jewelry for the gods; all perfect, just a fringe of her massive hoard. And there, somewhere down the line, was a case laid out with random bits of gorgeous swag. A wondrous necklace of twisting golden finery was laid out on the upper shelf, and on a lower shelf, a headset of red brass and flawless copper; striking colors. The workmanship and genius of design stood out and caught his eye.

Here they were, the long lost Artifacts of Vehelm of Waam set out in a display of things that Queen Ghome 'liked', thought pretty enough to display but didn't think important enough to protect in her Bower Chest. The Cult of Roethaba had kept their secret hidden all this time. He crashed into the case with his CARG and removed the necklace and the headset, holding them in his hands, marveling at their construction. He opened his Shadow tech bag and placed them inside atop all the parts of Sam he had so lovingly collected out of the dust above and repaired under Queen Ghome's nose.

Victory for Sam was in his grasp! He continued down the corridor.

A bit farther down, the corridor ended in a circular room featuring a pair of pools of shallow water and a great wooden door that Queen Ghome was opening with a palm lock. Her attendants stood with raised spears, defending her. A bowl of golden Noberry dust and a jug of overturned water lay discarded nearby.

Pools of water! Before Kay could stop himself, the Creeper in his head spoke. Not in control of his own body, he plunged into one of the pools and sank to the bottom. Moments later, a torrent of spears penetrated the water, the attendants stabbing him again and again, plunging their weapons into him over a dozen times top to bottom. Thinking him dead, they returned to Queen Ghome's side. The Shadow tech suit had protected him from the spears, turning them back, and it also furnished him with oxygen. As he lay there unharmed, undrowned, the Creeper voice in his head that was compelling him to drown himself, thwarted and denied a victim, lessened over a few minutes until he had control of his wits. He Sighted from the pool's bottom to assess the situation.

Queen Ghome had opened the door. A torrent of black fumes gushed out, filling the room with dense, choking smoke. Through the door was a chamber full of treasure items piled to impossible heights, all burning in a horrendous inferno of fire and smoke. The door seemed to be an escape route she had hoped to make use of, to pass through and be away. This door must be an arcane portal Sarah had called the Gellar door. How many times in the past had Queen Ghome faced destruction, faced defeat, only to slip away through a door just like this one and left, to vanish without trace? Just like at the Battle of the Tomb on Trimble; cornered, defeated, and then gone to rise again somewhere else. However, this time her escape was not to be. This time the fires of Hell itself waited for her on the other side of the door. The smoke quickly incapacitated Ghome and her attendants. She crouched on one knee, hacking, struggling for breath.

Kay rose from the pool, clambered out, and seized her by the horns. He roughly plunged her into the pool, washing off her deadly Aboleth dots before she could devastate him with them again. She coughed and sputtered. Her voice rang out with the Dirge. "Die! Fall upon your own CARG!" she ordered.

Kay felt the stinging touch of her Dirge, but it was too weak to sway him. He dunked her again, making certain the Aboleth was gone. She looked like a drenched horned rat.

"Do as I command!" she screeched, spitting water, a hint of desperation in her voice.

Kay drew the necklace from his bag. Ghome saw the piece and struggled. "What are you doing with that? That item belongs to me!"

"Yes it does, and I intend to give it to you!"

She made a final attempt to break loose and flee, but Kay held her down. She slapped at him with her hands, but the Aboleth was gone. Her palms turned a blazing shade of red, the beginnings of Shadow tech poisoning. She screamed with fury as Kay slipped the necklace over her head and around her neck, past the horns and draped gray hair. The effect was immediate. She gasped, fell silent and went into a deep sleep, one from which she could not awaken until the necklace was removed.

With Ghome out of the way, he could deal with the attendants. They were in no shape to fight or mount a defense, the smoke from the open door was overwhelming them. Kay shut the door, cutting off the smoke. One by one, he dragged them to the pool and dunked them, washing away the powder.

"Out!" he barked as he finished the final one. "Everybody out!" Naked and dripping, they meekly followed his commands; all of them hacking and struggling for breath as the smoke from the fire cleared. Kay followed, carrying Queen Ghome.

Outside in the bright sunlight, Laika terrorized the remaining attendants, had them cowering on the ground by the wall. The four attendants came out and sprawled to the dirt, thankful for a breath of clean air.

"Laika, fetch some water!" Kay yelled. Laika marched away, soon returning carrying an impressively large tankard of water the size of a bathtub taken from the open trunk in the center of the enclosure.

"Dunk all of these attendants, please. We want to make certain all of that Aboleth powder is gone."

Laika was overjoyed. "Get in water, attendants! Do not anger Laika! Move! You first! Get in!" The attendants meekly stepped into the tankard one at a time and Laika roughly dunked them by the hair.

Kay laid Queen Ghome down on the ground. The Necklace of Vehelm was doing its job—she was out cold, her breathing shallow, but steady. He then pulled the Headset of Vehelm from his pouch. It comprised a number of copper fingers and gentle pads meant to rest against the base of the skull behind the ear. He fitted it over her ears, situating it around her horns, which was no easy task and took  some doing. The antennas came up like a pair of alien feelers glinting in the sunlight. It seemed to be properly installed. With the headset in place, Roethaba of George should awaken at long last.

"Attendants washed, Jarlcon!" Laika proudly announced. They huddled on the ground, hair stringy, all of them wet and miserable.

Kay and Laika stood over the silent demonic form of Queen Ghome, waiting for a new woman to stir.

8—The Dead Fall from the Sky

Laika gazed down on Queen Ghome, her ferocity gone. "Mother?" she asked tenderly, shaking her gently on the shoulder.

Ghome lay on the ground, her breathing shallow, eyes shut in cloudy slits, mouth flaccid, sharp teeth glinting in the sun. She was unresponsive.

"Mother does not stir," Laika said.

Kay was puzzled. "I think I recall Jana del Lavi telling me that it will take a little while before she awakens." He felt her pulse; it was steady. Her breast rose and fell. "Let's give her some time. When she awakes, Roethaba should be with us." Laika knelt and adjusted her body into a comfortable position on the ground.

"The first thing we should do when she awakes is to get rid of these horns and these teeth, and do her up in something more becoming," Kay said.

As they waited for Roethaba to rise, Kay took stock of the situation. The enclosure was a mess, full of destroyed, smashed, and in some cases, burning Jones equipment, trampled Creeper plants, dead bodies and shattered statue beasts. Tal de Roga lay in the center of the compound, while Ghome's sleeping Bower Chest took up a healthy portion of the eastern section, its head resting on the ground. It vented towers of steam. Ghome's trunk floated in the center; open, full of chill hanging vapor and beautiful stolen faces. The Silver tech tree remained cactuslike in its defense. It glittered with the subtle movements of the deadly StTs roaming its surface.

Kay pointed. "Laika, I see three of Ghome's attendants fleeing on foot to the south. Will you go get them, please? Don't harm them if possible."

With relish, Laika tore off to the south, hurtling the compound wall with hardly a single bound.

Kay desperately wanted out of his sweatbox of a suit; it was galling to wear and claustrophobic in the extreme, but there were Creepers everywhere, he could see the hazy cloud of their dreaded spores hanging in the air just waiting to disrupt his Gifts. He would have to remain in the suit for the time being. Kay turned his attention to Ghome's attendants. There were fourteen of them, all slender and beautiful, all nude, glistening from their bath, their colorful dots and swirls of Aboleth thankfully gone. All were abased on the ground and seemed submissive.

And then there was the Blanchefort staff, rolling about the enclosure like horrid zombies holding their knives, all poisoned with Shadow tech, seeing demented phantoms before them, occasionally stabbing out at nothing; the ghostly drone of *"Lord Blanchefort"* issuing from their near dead mouths. Some were down on all fours, retching. A few lay on the ground not moving at all.

Laika returned with a flourish, scaling the walls with a six-armed load of attendants and staff who had fallen by the wayside. She set the staff down and terrorized the attendants, herding them into a corner, dunking the three she had caught in the water and adding them to the group. She loomed over them. "Quiet, attendants! Quiet!" she roared.

With Laika covering Ghome's attendants, Kay could focus on the staff. He could not bear to see the staff—people who had served his family loyally for years, some of whom had helped care for him as a child—slowly dying of Shadow tech poisoning. He had to do something for them. He saw the wooden bowl the attendants had brought out earlier full of dust. It was lying face down on the ground, the remnants of Noberry dust, as Atha had called it, slowly blowing away.

He had a thought.

He fetched the bowl, scooping up as much dust as he could; the dust was fine and flighty. It took flight in even the smallest of breezes, drifting all over the courtyard and covering everything in a fine layer.

Gone, it was all gone.

He went to the giant trunk, the staff limply stabbing at him as he passed. He searched the shelves within. More, she had to have more dust here—the staff needed it.

It didn't take him long to find more Noberry. There were chests full of it, along with a score of pouches crammed full. The pouches, when squeezed or patted, emitted a small measured amount of dust; they seemed perfect for his needs. He placed several pouches into his bag.

He had the Noberry dust; now he needed the water. Near the chest was the jug from which the attendants had washed Queen Ghome. He inspected it. It was nearly empty, containing a mere few cups of rich clear water. This must be water from Salonmae that Atha had shared with him in Carahil's store. He needed more, much more. There were several bathtub-sized tankards lined up inside Ghome's floating trunk, all filled with vast quantities of the water. One tankard was missing—Laika had taken it to douse Queen Ghome and the attendants.

He felt a tug from within. He felt the urge to jump into the tankards and go to the bottom. The damn spores in his head, whispering to him once again. He forced himself to concentrate.

Kay filled the jug with water. He recalled from his time with Atha how good the water had smelled, so clean and cold, though he couldn't smell it now through his helmet. Armed with the jug of water and the pouches full of Noberry dust, he found the staff member he thought was in the worst shape. It was clearly Andorra, his mother's personal assistant. She was wearing a flimsy and revealing set of clothes slung low and cut high; something very out-of-character for the starched, upright, covered-up Cyan lady he had known the whole of his life; the one who had lectured him on the virtues of promptness, cleanliness, courtesy and etiquette, whose skills in calligraphy had taught him proper penmanship, the lady who had full license to paddle him when he fell out of line—a license she exercised on several occasions. She was near death; her skin a sickly green, her eyes melted into dripping wax and her teeth falling out by wretched strings. She was barely sensate. Her poisoned knife lay forgotten on the ground nearby.

"Andorra, can you hear me?"

She mumbled something in response and feebly reached for her knife.

"No, stop!" Kay commanded. "I am your lord and you will listen to me! Wake up! Andorra, wake up!"

She hesitated; Tal de Roga's hypnotic spell lessening in her head. "My … lord …" she rasped.

He needed to lay his hands on and heal her, but it was the toxic nature of his Shadow tech suit that had done the damage in the first place and to touch Andorra again might just send her over the edge and kill her. He tried to remove his gloves, but the Shadow tech wasn't budging. He recalled how the Noberry had eaten through the simulacrum's suit. He took a pouch from his bag and vigorously patted his hands and forearms, coating the Shadow tech with a fine layer of Noberry. Very quickly, the Shadow tech reacted with the dust and bubbled away, revealing his bare hands and forearms, his skin red and sweaty from being confined in the hot suit.

Now he could help her. Tipping the jug, Kay washed Andorra, singing into what was left of her ear, careful not to touch her with any part of him but his hands. He dabbed the pouch onto her skin. The dust began working moments later. It bubbled and seethed. It drew the Shadow tech out of her in a sooty cloud. He wondered what he could do about her teeth and her eyes. He tried patting her eyes gently with it. She blinked, and with every blink her eyes plumped back up, becoming whole again. Feeling better, sitting up, she opened her mouth, allowing Kay to work on her teeth, dousing her with water, coaxing new teeth from the holes left by the missing ones. He repaired her ears. Soon, she seemed fully healed.

"How are you, Andorra?" he asked.

Shy, grateful, she nodded, taking his hands and holding them against her heart. She noticed the drenched, revealing clothing she was wearing and tried to cover up. "I feel much better. Thank you. Thank you, my lord. I apologize for my dress."

"You are part of our family, and you have our love and protection as best we can give it. There are many in need of assistance. Will you please help me triage those needing help most?"

"Yes, yes, of course." She stood and ran to the nearest staff member. Andorra triaged the staff with a practiced, critical eye, quickly organizing them into the center of the compound. Methodically, assisted by Andorra, Kay treated them with water and gentle pats of Noberry dust, one after the next. He took a head count: 24 staff. All were present, including the ones who had fallen by the wayside. Sighting, he could see no more scattered about. That was one less thing to worry over. Many had been dreadfully poisoned, but the Noberry dust and the cleansing water coupled with Kay's ever more skillful use of it was up to the job, and they were soon resting comfortably, free of the Shadow tech poisoning and de Roga's hypnosis. Some even stood and assisted Andorra, working together refilling the jug and getting anything Kay needed. Always hard-working and industrious, the staff.

Laika called out. "Jarlcon, Mother awakens!"

At last, Queen Ghome, wearing the artifacts, stirred, raising her hand to her horned head, her necklace and headset gleaming.

Kay went to her side. "Roethaba? Lady George?" he asked with excitement. "Can you hear me?"

Laika came over and leaned down. "Mother?" she asked, shaking her slightly. "Mother?"

Ghome sat up and blinked at Laika, her red eyes tentative. "Who are you?" She seemed frightened seeing the giant Laika leaning over her. She kicked at the dirt, trying to stand and get away. "W-what sort of monster are you?" she said in a terrified voice. She touched the great horns sticking out of her head, and probed her sharpened teeth with the tip of her tongue. "*What have you done to me*?" she cried in despair.

She didn't know who Laika was. It was understandable that she didn't recognize Kay in his horrendous Shadow tech suit, but Laika? Roethaba loved Laika.

"*I think of her as my daughter,*" she said once.

"Mother?" Laika said, her voice shaking with sadness. "Remember Laika!"

Ghome squirmed in fear. "G-get away from me, p-please! Someone help me!"

Kay was horrified. The truth came upon him.

This woman is not Queen Ghome.

"Laika, this isn't her, it can't be her. She must have changed parts with one of her attendants when she ran into the passageway! She had a few minutes to do so! That's what must have happened." He glanced at the group of attendants by the wall, all wet and glistening. "One of them! She must be hiding as one of them!"

Laika stomped into the gaggle of attendants and drew her swords. "You attendants! Where is Ghome?" They crawled on the ground in terror.

Kay removed the artifacts and the woman wearing Ghome's face collapsed into unconsciousness. He approached the attendants. "Well played, Queen Ghome. Well played, indeed. Unfortunately for you, we have discovered your deception and determined that you are hiding behind the face of one of your attendants. If you think that's going to stop us discovering you, think again."

The attendants were frightened. "What are you going to do with us?" one of them managed to stammer.

Laika hoisted her swords. "Talk, attendants, who is Ghome? Answer Laika!"

"We don't know!"

She stomped into their midst, scattering them. "Liars!"

Kay had to step in and save the attendants. "Laika, Laika, let's be calm for a moment. We're not going to hurt these people. We could place the artifacts on each until we discover the correct one, but that is too slow a process. I think I know how we can get this figured out much faster."

He released his Sight and wound it back in time, hoping to see the process in action and determine which one was Ghome. The tunnel leading to the sub-levels was blacked out. His Sight would not assist him in this case. Kay looked over the attendants. It must be one of the four who had been in the underground room with Ghome, but which was which? Soaking wet and crawling on the ground, they all looked rather the same. He would have to test them all. Hiding in their midst, certainly, was the crafty Queen Ghome.

Kay wandered out into the central compound and rummaged through the wreckage. The staff, hard-working as always, had already begun the process of organizing the dead Jones into neat groups and had the marble bits of Ghome's beasts heaped into a pile. He soon found what he was looking for: the severed head of one of Ghome's marble beasts, blown to bits by Laika's rifle.

"Andorra," he said. "We'll be leaving soon. Please make certain everyone is fit to travel. We've a mile or two to walk." She nodded and gathered the staff.

He picked up the marble head and returned. Kay selected an attendant from the group and motioned for her to come forward. Fearful, naked, dirty from crawling on the ground, she stepped out from the group toward Kay and bowed.

"What is your name, please?" Kay asked.

"Tentha Seamanie. I-I'm from Midas. I've served Queen Ghome since I was a little girl."

"I see. You must be very loyal to her then."

"I ..." She saw Laika nearby holding her giant swords and fell silent. Kay held out the marble head. He was waiting to see if it turned to flesh as it had done so previously in Ghome's presence. If so, then Ghome was nearby.

Nothing happened. Kay recalled Ghome's Gellar powers seemed to be waning as the battle unfolded, the clouds parting and the beasts transforming much slower.

"Place your hands on the marble, please," Kay said. Tentha stood there in fear. She placed her small hands on the marble head, taking it by the horns.

Nothing happened.

"Thank you," Kay said. "Please rejoin the others."

"What is to become of us?" Tentha asked.

"I don't really know at this point. I won't harm you, you may rest assured of that, but that doesn't mean I won't exile you here in this Elder-down place either. Please, rejoin the others. I thank you for your cooperation."

Tentha stepped back and Kay went through the process of

testing the rest. Each was shy and repentant. One tried to offer her body to Kay in exchange for her safety. He politely declined and sent her back to the group. So far, none had given life to the marble head.

Three left. He pointed at a black-haired girl and motioned for her to come forward and be tested.

She held back and refused.

Laika spat. "Come forward and be tested!" she roared, seizing the girl by the arm.

BOOM!

A fiery explosion ripped through Laika's hand, destroying it. Before Kay could react, the girl sprang and slapped him across the face with the palm of her hand. There was a pinkish glob of Aboleth smeared in her palm. He just managed to catch a glimpse of it before …

BOOM!

The force of the explosion shattered Kay's Shadow tech helmet, throwing him back. She took a handful of Creeper and stuffed it into the shattered bubble. He could smell the perfumy spores and his Gifts went dark.

His Gifts were gone!

She leapt away, sprinting toward the Bower Chest.

The attendants burst into action. It was as if the gods had flipped a switch; one moment the attendants were cowering and compliant, the next they were attacking with ruthless skill and coordination. While feigning compliance, the attendants had been passing around a small pot full of Aboleth they had hidden from him. They were almost fully re-armed with it. They swarmed Laika, pelting her with their hands and feet, punching her, kicking her, headbutting her, each blow creating a powerful explosion.

BOOM! BOOM! BOOM!

They were overwhelming Laika. She fell, bleeding, dropping her weapons, one leg and two arms blown off.

The bulk of the attendants sprinted away to defend Queen Ghome, while three stayed behind to deal with Kay. They held up their hands, pinkish powder rubbed onto their palms, and attacked. Kay was still somewhat bleary from Queen Ghome's attack and his Sight was gone thanks to the Creeper.

The attendants were skilled and fast. One came in and slapped him in the chest.

BOOM!

Kay was rocked, but the Shadow tech suit again held; moments later the attendant was dead, pierced to the belly by his CARG.

A savage kick blasted him in the back.

BOOM!

Kay fell to his knees. The explosive power of the Aboleth was devastating. His Shadow tech suit was failing.

Just as the attendants were ready to finish him off, they were met with a surge of fists and scraping knives. The staff had come to Kay's aid, overwhelming the attendants, fighting village style, binding the attendants' arms and hauling them down, stabbing them in the guts. Moments later, after a fierce struggle, the two attendants were dead.

"Lord Blanchefort, are you all right?" Andorra asked, panting, helping him up, careful not to touch the Shadow tech.

Kay checked himself over. His Shadow tech suit was mangled, but it seemed to have shielded him from the brunt of the Aboleth blasts. He glanced at the fallen attendants. One of them was the previously demure Tentha Seamanie, pierced to the belly.

Nearby, Laika lay in the dirt, badly wounded.

"Andorra, I want you to take Laika and go into the passageway at the north end of the enclosure. Be careful, it might still be a little smoky in there." He handed her a pouch of Noberry dust. "Take the jug of water and the dust from the pouch and heal her with it. You watched me, you can do it. Help her and do not come out unless I say it's safe to do so."

Working together, the staff quickly bore the fallen Laika away and disappeared through the archway into the lower levels.

Alone and Giftless, Kay shed what was left of his suit except for his Shadow tech bag and took two of Laika's LLAGs. He made his way across the compound in pursuit of Ghome.

The attendants had set up a defensive perimeter in front of the dormant Bower Chest. They had two panels open and were manually turning cranks. Slowly, one crank at a time, the Bower Chest's breastplate was opening like a clamshell, revealing a dark, smoky interior. They were trying to get inside and take refuge, possibly to try restarting it. Kay could not allow that to happen. With her Bower Chest operating, Queen Ghome would surely escape and obliterate himself, his staff, and Laika in the process.

There was Queen Ghome, wearing the face of one of her attendants, protected by them.

"Ghome! By Creation, this is your end!" Kay yelled, trying to sound bold.

The attendants sprang forward to meet him, their hands, legs, feet and hips shimmering with deadly Aboleth. Kay cut loose with Laika's LLAGs, the workmanlike hammers tapping out a steady dose of lead. The attendants fell like ten-pins; occasionally a bullet would hit a spot of Aboleth, touching off a fiery explosion. They tried to spring aside, leap away and get to him, but there was just too much lead flying. Soon, every one of them lay bullet-riddled on the ground.

Now, it was just Queen Ghome and Kay. He pulled Vehelm's artifacts from his bag. "And now, you're going to put these on even if I have to break your neck doing so!"

She gritted her teeth and charged Kay, her hands raised to slap him with Aboleth. Without his suit, one slap would be the death of him. He lurched aside, but instead of trying to hit him, she sprinted past, heading toward the trunk. He sprinted after her—she was so fast. She reached the trunk, throwing open a number of drawers. As Kay arrived, she climbed up to the top of the trunk, holding a small controller in her hand. "We shall see who lives to see the sunset and who does not … grandson!" She pressed the button.

Nothing happened. She pressed it again and again—still nothing. She threw the controller at Kay and dove at him, hands extended. Kay caught her by the wrists, driving her hands into the ground. There was an explosion that created a deep crater, displaced earth raining down bits of debris on the both of them. He wrenched her head back, trying to slip on the necklace of Vehelm. She sputtered like an enraged cat, trying to reach back to hit him. Kay wrestled the necklace over her head at last. Before she could utter another word, she fell unconscious.

Kay wasn't going to be fooled a second time. He carried her to the pile of stone the staff had made and selected a piece of one of her marble beasts, slipping it into her limp hand. He wanted to make certain there were no tricks. Sure enough, with marked slowness, the piece transformed from disembodied marble to an oily reptilian bit of flesh stinking of blood.

Finally, here was Queen Ghome, asleep; when she awoke, she would be a new woman.

Roethaba of George. Saint and genius given lease in the waking world.

He knelt down and carefully placed the headset, moving the feelers into position at the base of her skull. The going was much easier without the horns. The antennas jutted up through her wet mass of brown hair.

"Now, she just needs to wake up."

A fear-filled cry came from the other end of the enclosure. "Lord Blanchefort!" Peeking out of the archway was the brown-headed crop of Andorra. Without his Sight, he had to squint to see her clearly.

She was pointing up at the sky. Kay glanced skyward. A blinding fireball, like a second sun trailing a messy streak of smoke and condensation, hurtled through the clouds, getting larger by the moment. It seemed to be headed right for the compound.

"Andorra, get yourself and the others deep underground and do not come out!" Kay shouted.

A few moments later, the fireball came through the far wall in a calamity of smoke and shattered stone, taking a healthy bite out of the western enclosure. It slammed into the sleeping side of the Bower Chest, bounced off and dug deep into the ground. A tower of earth was thrown into the air. Kay tried to protect the prone Queen Ghome from falling debris. The Bower Chest, aside from being roughly displaced by the impact, appeared undamaged.

As the soot cleared, something stood in the heart of the crater; something that roared. A giant figure came out, smoldering, stinking of ozone and scorched composites, encased in a black suit with a fishbowl helmet.

It was one of the Dead Men of Mare from the ring high above. Queen Ghome had used her controller and brought one down like a summoned commando. His crooked antenna flashed red, his tanks issued brownish smoke. The smushed dead face inside the helmet turned a milky shade of blue as caustic fluids were pumped in. He grimaced and gnashed his teeth. With grating slowness, he turned his head, seeing the scene around him, determining what chaos to create and whose bones to rend first.

He locked onto Kay and Queen Ghome and tottered in their direction.

Kay had hoped not to see another Dead Man from Mare ever again, not after the debacle in the Grove, but here one was, his dead eyes focused on Kay. He remembered these Dead Men with dread—how just one took the combined efforts of himself, Ennez and his Monama wife Tellerran, as well as King and Ki with her SK pistol to bring down. How it seemed unstoppable. How it was much stronger than a Monama like Tellerran, and radiated bone-chilling cold. And, most importantly, he'd had his Gifts to battle it previously—now he was alone, with his Gifts Creepered into silence.

But he had learned much since that first horrendous encounter. He had learned that the tanks at their backs and the caustic fluids contained within gave the Dead Men a great deal of their power; remove the tanks, deny them the fluids, and they were vulnerable, they were beatable. Therefore, the tanks would be vigorously targeted. With nothing else available to him, he would use his knowledge to fight this dead horror.

They squared off, Kay trying to stay between the Dead Man and the helpless Queen Ghome. The Dead Man was at least nine feet tall. He reached out with his gloved hands. Kay swiped them aside with his CARG, trying to slice them off. As before, the rubbery body warded off Kay's attack. He knew that when the Dead Man's face became a blue shade, his body would be practically indestructible. Scrambling to the ground, Kay crawled though his legs and got behind him.

There were his tanks and cluster of tubes and hoses circulating the caustic fluids that gave him life. Saddling his CARG, Kay drew Laika's LLAGs and opened up with a long burst. Bullets bounced off the Dead Man's tanks, doing little damage. Before Kay could blink, the Dead Man was on him. It seized and rammed him into the ground, its grip impossibly strong and frigid in the extreme.

There was nothing Kay could do. The Dead Man picked him up and hoisted him off the ground. Kay dropped the LLAGs and drew his CARG. He aimed and loosed a blast of Silver tech. The blast passed through the Dead Man's chest and went out the other side, destroying his tanks. A choking cloud of brown smoke burst out, temporarily obscuring the daylight. Kay held his breath, knowing it would sicken him if he breathed it. When the cloud dissipated, the Dead Man had lost his bluish hue and turned a dull gray. Now he was vulnerable. Kay slashed with his CARG, taking a chunk out of his leg. Without his fluids, the Dead Man was no longer impervious to damage. Kay lashed out and hacked off the Dead Man's arm. Denied his main source of power, the Dead Man's system went into back-up mode. Emergency fluids were pumped in and he turned a vivid shade of pink. He became like a crazed berserker. He saw Queen Ghome lying there on the ground and he went to take her and do Creation knows what to her flesh.

Kay was on him, slashing, stabbing with his CARG. Kay took the Dead Man's knees out and then chopped off his head, his flesh bright pink like candy.

The Dead Man was done. Alone, Kay had fought the Dead

Man much more efficiently this second time around and was victorious.

A whistling sound caught his attention. Another fireball came crashing into the courtyard at the south end. And then another.

And another.

The sky was full of fireballs screeching in from all directions with a crosshatch of fiery contrails painting the sky. Craters blossomed all over, churned earth and crushed stone.

The Dead were everywhere. Many were giants in both male and female configurations, while others were tiny, barely a tenth of Kay's size, like miniature people. The giants were slow and lumbering; the little ones, however, buzzed about like demons flying with rockets strapped to their backs. They swarmed in on Kay and though they were tiny, they were surprisingly strong. They latched on, grabbed at his clothes, poked at his eyes, went for his neck and sought to trip him up and hold him still; their dead, shrunken faces jeering through their helmets. One of them got his CARG and flew off with it. Meanwhile, the giant-sized Dead Men were busy reviving the slain Jones and the attendants, pumping fluids into them, shrinking them down into vile animated dolls all converging on him and Queen Ghome with glee.

He saw only one chance. Nearby was Queen Ghome's trunk, still open, still spewing chill vapor, sporting a host of parts for her to try on and wear. He recalled the attendants bringing out several bowls, one full of Noberry dust, and the other a bowl of pinkish powder that she dipped her hands into.

Dust that explodes. Aboleth! That's what Laika had called it. If it worked for Ghome and her attendants, it would work for him too.

He sprinted to the chest, laboring with the tiny dead that buzzed around tormenting him. He found several shelves full of urns containing various oils and powders. There was a jade one full of fine pink powder. Eagerly, he thrust his hands into it, coating them, and then he set to the Dead.

BOOM! BOOM!

Kay slapped at them and punched. He saw the tongues of orange and green fire erupt from his hands, he felt the rush of compressed air and a slight moment of heat, but that was all. To the tiny Dead, Aboleth powder was devastating. It bit through their suits and destroyed their tanks, sending them shooting off in crazy directions. They went down in mangled heaps of mutilated flesh. One slap was enough to bisect them. The Aboleth had intense power to direct the force of the explosion, to cut with precision. He slapped one in the face and shattered its miniature helmet. He saw the tiny dead face, the glittering doll-like eyes. He slapped it again and its head was gone. He punched another, blowing its arms and legs off.

More Aboleth! More powder!

He took grim satisfaction in dispatching the rest; watching them struggle, listening to them scream and go still. Elsewhere, the tiny reanimated attendants of Ghome were doing the same thing, pulling pots of Aboleth from the shelves within the trunk, diving into it, coating themselves top to bottom and coming at him like little naked missiles, piping obscenities from their tiny mouths. He targeted them with Laika's LLAGs, their tiny bodies going off like grenades with each hit; doing enough damage to be extremely dangerous.

Through all the killing, he saw a figure pick up Queen Ghome and carry her away toward the Bower Chest.

It was Tal de Roga—not dead! He was crippled, bloodied, near death, but still alive. He was working the crank, trying to get inside the Bower Chest and steal away with Queen Ghome. He leaned against its metal body, cranking with all the strength he had left. The doors to its chest slowly parted.

Kay could not let him get away. He covered himself in Aboleth, pouring the urn over his head and letting it coat him. Then he sprinted to get to Tal de Roga.

A line of ten giant Dead stood before him and more still were coming down, adding their number to the battle.

Charging, Kay picked the clearest path and threw himself into a giant male.

BOOOOOOOM!

A terrific explosion shredded the male's black spacesuit and blew the clear bubble helmet off his head. The force of the blow sent him down to the ground. Kay got behind him and went to work.

BOOM! BOOM! BOOM!

Kay destroyed his tanks and also took several large chunks out of the Dead Man himself. Dark brown fumes erupted from his destroyed tanks, instantly sickening Kay. The Dead Man fell lifeless.

A female Dead, ten feet tall, seized Kay, her howling dead face and matted white hair pushed up inside her fishbowl helmet.

BOOM! BOOM! BOOM!

Kay punched and kicked, the Aboleth sawing through her arm and chest like a fiery torch. He pressed on, but the Dead were all around him. Too strong. Too many to contend with. The smoke, the fumes getting into his lungs made him see stars. Too many to fight.

He watched with dismay as Tal de Roga disappeared inside the Bower Chest with Ghome's limp body, the doors closing behind them.

That was it. It was over.

Exhaustion set in. The fumes were overcoming him. Kay fell to one knee. The Dead towered over him. Explosions and craters. More Dead arriving. Tiny dead attendants cavorting toward him, ready to lay into him with Aboleth.

A hand came down and plucked Kay from the ground just as the Dead closed in.

"Laika!" he cried.

Fully repaired and wielding her swords and DeeDee rifle, Laika perched on the wall like a great spider.

"Laika take Jarlcon below!"

She quickly made her way back to the archway, firing her DeeDee, knocking the Dead down, though they got right back up again. She targeted a Jones Battle Unit manned by a dozen tiny dead Jones and obliterated it.

"Laika! Ghome's ... escaped!" Kay rasped. His body was roiling from the fumes. He wanted nothing more than to pass out.

"Get Ghome another day! Jarlcon fights well! Jarlcon comes below to escape with Laika!"

She fired off one dart after the next, creating catastrophic damage, though the Dead were beyond catastrophic. She was unable to target their tanks, and there was no stopping them.

Laika arrived at the archway and dashed in. They took up defensive positions, Laika pelting away with her DeeDee, picking off tiny Dead as they flew in, their bodies erupting in Aboleth flashes.

Kay could barely stand.

More Dead than he could count headed their way in a giant line of black spacesuits and blinking red lights. It was only a matter of time.

Through the din of battle, Kay heard something: the slow, steady, ever-growing sound of turbines and hissing steam. Metal grated and linkages engaged. Kay watched with horror as the massive Bower Chest shuddered, lifted its head and neck and uttered a roar of ancient fury. Fire appeared in the boiler windows and glowed strong from dull red to vibrant orange to bright yellow. Towers of steam belched from its pipes. It had been restarted, with Queen Ghome and Tal de Roga safe inside.

It stood up on its two clawed legs and took in the scene around it. Looming over the Dead, it locked onto Kay and Laika with its tiny orange eyes.

The ground trembled. The Bower Chest took in a great expanse of air.

"Laika, it's going to blast us! It'll scour us right out of this passage."

"Then Laika dies with Jarlcon!"

The Bower Chest let fly with a scalding wave of steam.

Dead Men flash-boiled into nothingness, their tanks exploding, their gases consumed. As Kay and Laika watched, the Bower Chest waded into the courtyard and trampled on the Dead, its wings sweeping them high into the air. It dealt with them as if they were nothing. Deadly smoke rose as giant bodies were trampled.

The Dead Men turned and attacked the Bower Chest. Tiny dead buzzed around it like a swarm of bees. They pounded its haunches and climbed up its sides. Aboleth explosions glittered off its scales. Working together, the Dead got hold of its head and held it down. They piled on, pulling off metal scales. Nothing could stop the Dead.

The Bower Chest shuddered, held fast by the Dead. Overwhelmed.

WWWHHHHHHHHHHHUUUUUUUMMMM!!!

Two great geysers of steam clawed their way out of the Bower Chest along with a thundering foghorn of fury that shook the ground. Dead Men were tossed aside as the Bower Chest spun up to full power, the fire in its windows ramping up to white hot. The beast rose up with maximum fury, stomping and flapping, belching steam, throwing the Dead Men off, scalding them to nothing.

More steam, more vanished Dead Men, the Bower Chest sweeping them from the enclosure. Soon, Kay and Laika and a few stragglers were all that was left.

The great metal beast, victorious, thundered forward and turned to face them. Its fire lessened and its doors opened once again. Out came a silver ball of light flying high, contesting with the swarm of tiny Dead not yet destroyed.

Kay squinted to see. Was the silver ball of light King? It looked like him.

Out came four people; a man and a woman assisting a third. The third was female, hunched over, wearing a man's coat. The fourth person was a female in rags, lagging behind the rest.

Kay and Laika emerged from the archway. "Phillip? Thomasina?" Kay asked. "Is that you?"

"Aye, Kay, it's us!" Phillip said, waving to him. "Aren't you a sight! You all right?"

Phillip and Thomasina were carrying Queen Ghome, her arms thrown over their shoulders. She wore Phillip's duster. The fourth person looked to be Clara Wunderluck—what was she doing here?

They met them in the center. Kay was overjoyed. "What happened to Tal de Roga?"

"The Jones fellow, you mean?" Phillip asked. "We saw him come in carrying this woman, and then he died. His wounds were too great."

The woman. She looked up at Kay and Laika. She blinked in confusion, her headset sticking up through her hair.

"Laika?" she asked, smiling, her voice filled with wonder. "Lord Blanchefort? It is so good to see you both. It is so good to finally see you …"

"Lady Roethaba?" Kay asked.

"Mother?" Laika said.

She smiled and nodded. "It is I."

"She asked us to restart the Bower Chest, said that, going forward, it would help us, that it would do as she commanded," Phillip said. He blushed a little. "We couldn't say no, though it was pretty complicated getting it going again."

The Bower Chest flapped up and perched on the western wall. It turned to Roethaba and bowed its head in reverence, acknowledging her is its master.

"You need never fear it again," Roethaba said, trying to stand.

Kay wobbled. The Dead Men's gases took their toll, and he fell to the ground.

"Jarlcon?" Laika said, picking him up. "Jarlcon!"

"Kay, what's wrong?" Phillip asked.

"Poisoned …"

They came around Kay, desperately trying to assist him. As he lay there, the enclosure spinning, he watched Clara Wunderluck running away as fast as she could to the south. He chuckled to himself, watching her run away as everything went dark.

She could run pretty fast …

9— Awake

"Kay?"

When Kay opened his eyes, he was in a bed in a sterile white room, the lights all dimmed. Machines bleeped all around him.

Sam was sitting by his bedside holding his hand. Her face was haggard with care; her black eyes cloudy and exhausted. Kay saw a number of fine scars marring her skin. A plate of cold food sat on a nearby table, uneaten.

"Sam!" Kay cried, sitting up.

She gently but firmly moved him back down to his pillow.

"Sam, are you all right? Where are we? When did—"

"*Sala* ..." she said in Anuie, meaning: "shhhh."

"We're on Hoban," she said in a tired voice, gently pressing her fingers to his lips. "You're safe. "*Sala, Arin-Dan...*"

Kay noticed her beautiful hands were bruised, knuckles skinned.

"Sam, what happened to your hands?"

"I'm fine, darling. Don't worry about me. I've been waiting for you to wake up. I've not left your side since I returned. I've not eaten or slept. I would not leave you."

She stood. She was wearing odd clothing; a black leather suit stitched together with metal plates. She had on a tunic of similar construction, along with a pair of stout boots.

"Are you wearing armor, Sam?" he asked. Kay also noticed a few streaks of gray hair mixed into her mane of coal black.

"Just some clothes they gave me to wear."

Sam went to a nearby door and peered outside. Someone huge was standing there in the hallway. Sam opened it a crack.

"Jarlcon?" came a soft voice from outside.

"It's all right," Sam replied. "You may go. I want to be alone with my husband." Sam shut the door and locked it.

She returned to the bed and began undressing. She shed her boots and set them aside. She undid the complicated straps and fasteners and removed her leather tunic.

"Sam!" Kay cried. "Your back ..."

Her pale body was covered with welts and bruises. "It's nothing, darling; the Hospitalers said I might be bruised up for a while."

She stepped out of her pants and folded them on a chair. She slid into bed with Kay, nude. She took him into her arms; it was like paradise feeling the warmth and strength of her body next to his.

"Oh, how I've longed to hold you again, my love," she whispered. He felt tears stream down her cheek. Her warm body spasmed a bit. Sam was weeping.

"I'm fine, Sam. How long have I been out? Did the Hospitalers take care of the Creeper spores?"

Sam answered in Anuie, but she used words he wasn't familiar with. "Sam?"

"*The Hospitalers fixed you. They fixed you,*" she said.

10—On Hoban

Kay and Sam entered the recovery room lined with sterile beds. Occupying the beds were several staff girls from the kitchens they had rescued from their faceless slumber. The Noberry dust used to put them back together was truly remarkable. They all rested as if nothing had happened to them. According to the Hospitalers, Sam was the most difficult to repair; her Monama physiology making the repair tough.

At the end of the row was Sarah, a bandage covering her eyes. The Hospitalers had learned much regarding Noberry and its proper use. They had rebuilt Sarah's destroyed eyes with delicate care, and she seemed to be responding well. However, her demeanor as a recovering patient was not good. She brooded in her bed, was surly and looking for people to feel sorry for her. Raal had come to visit her many times, but she wanted nothing to do with him. Towering over her bedside, Laika was conflicted and struggling with something internally. She eventually pulled Kay and Sam aside and announced: "Laika will not pound Sarah until Sarah can see."

"That's very kind of you," Kay replied. "Sarah will appreciate that. One thing to consider though before you pound her—it's not Sarah you've beef with, it's *Ultra Sarah*, the Sleeping Sarah. The awake Sarah's done nothing to you—yet."

Laika frowned and grappled with the thought.

As for Kay himself, he was out of danger, the Creeper spores gone from his head, but the ordeal he had been through had done considerable damage to his Gifts. He could still Waft and Cloak as always, and he could see far with his Dark Sight, but his ability to see into the past and the future was greatly reduced. He could only Sight a few seconds into the future and a few minutes into the past, just like his father, Captain Davage. He also could no longer interact with objects in the past or future. Raal thought the damage would heal in time. Perhaps he would get those abilities back someday, perhaps with therapy. For now, his Dark Sight was greatly diminished.

One of the staff girls stirred. Hospitalers gathered around her bed to tend to her.

Raal and Jana del Lavi came in. "Lord Blanchefort? Ne-Countess?"

"Yes?"

"Could you please come with us?"

Kay and Sam came away with them out into the hallway. "Everyone seems to be doing well," he remarked.

"Yes," Raal said. "We are most pleased."

"How's Sarah?"

"Repaired and healing, though, with her MC deviation, her WS seems to be a much angrier, less sophisticated person than her Ultra SS."

Kay laughed. "You might be correct. Where's the urn?"

"Safe here with us, where it will receive proper study. We are hopeful it will lead to great things."

They led Kay and Sam down the hallway past several doors. "Through here, please, sir," Jana motioned. Kay went in.

Inside was a quiet IU tended by several Hospitalers. In one bed littered with scanners was the tiny form of Ki's son, Sebastian, fully re-assembled. He was kicking and squirming a little under his knitted blanket. The scanners indicated a strong heartbeat and good lungs. Ki's son was going to grow into a strong young man. In the next bed surrounded by a host of blinking screens and hissing machines was Ki. Tweeter sat by her head. Kay came up and leaned over her. She seemed whole, but somewhat deflated. Tubes were thrust down her throat. The Hospitalers, not knowing her tomboyish nature, had painted her fingernails a cheery red color. They had also curled her windblown hair, creating a tangled nest of frizzy brown hair around her face. It was surreal seeing her with red fingernails and curled hair. She would not be happy when she woke up. That should be something to see.

Tweeter seemed uncharacteristically quiet and dour. He was normally a little bundle of energy.

"Did you reattach everything with the dust?" Kay asked.

"We did," Jana answered. "But ..."

"But what?"

Raal spoke. "She didn't wake up, Lord Blanchefort. The second Gaming Session was too much—it would have been too much for anybody. As I said, she ..." Raal began some sort of "I told you so" speech, but silenced himself. What was the point?

Sam covered her mouth. Kay stared down in horror at the machines and Ki's beautiful, curly-haired face. "What are you saying?"

Jana swallowed and nervously adjusted the folds of her Jones dress. "Her readings are flat, Lord Blanchefort. She's gone; it's merely the machines keeping her alive. She has no brain function."

Kay glanced at the nearby squirming form of Ki's son, and then at the bulk of his mother's vacant body next to him, lit partially in Tweeter's dim light. What would he say to his father and mother when they returned to the League, that their dear friend of over thirty years was dead? He envisioned a brief glimpse of himself and Sam standing before Sebastian in the Grove one day, having to explain to him what had happened to his mother, trying to make him understand how brave she had been and why she was gone.

Jana held out a slip of paper. "She was holding this in her hand. She must have written it before the Gaming Session was started."

Kay took the paper.

Tell my son what his mother did for him without hesitation.

Kay closed his eyes. Sam's hand closed with his. He felt silent loss; for her son who would never know his mother, and for himself who had just lost a mentor and a friend. Ever since he was a little boy, there was Ki, sitting at the table, arguing with his mother, playing with him in the Grove, teaching him how to drink and fight dirty His first childhood crush.

Dead ...

He looked ahead to the future with his damaged Sight and saw nothing. His eyes stung; he wiped them. Sam embraced him, gently cooing in his ear, knowing the pain he was in.

"I should never have allowed her to do this," he said. "I should have told you not to do it."

Raal answered. "But then, Ghome would have escaped, all would still be in their capsules, faceless, locked in an RDP. Magistrate Kilos knew what she was doing, and she accepted it."

Jana tried to rationalize it away. "She was a very brave woman."

Kay pulled up a chair and seated himself next to her, while Sam stood over him. He took Ki's flaccid hand. So soft, so yielding with painted fingernails—nothing like Ki in the least.

He remembered those same hands balled up into fists, bouncing off his face in the village. What a memory—fighting Ki in a bar, slugging her in the face; rolling around with her on the floor. And then, dancing around the fire that night on Onaris.

And ...

So many memories. His entire life with Ki now just a memory.

"We have contacted her husband," Jana said. "He is on his way. When he arrives, we shall go over with him what has happened, and he shall decide what is to be done with her. We can continue her care for as long as he likes, or ... we can end it and give her peace. Her bravery and her contribution to our leader's rebirth shall not be forgotten here on the Gold Coast. Hers shall be an honored memory."

"Thank you," Kay said. "I would like to sit with her for a bit. Say my piece."

Raal and Jana backed away. "Of course. The others will sleep through the night. In the morning, they shall rise and remember nothing. I'm certain you'll wish to be there for that," Raal said.

"Yes, yes ... Thank you." Kay wished they would go. He wanted to be alone with Ki.

They walked out and the door swung shut.

Sam whispered in his ear. "Are you all right, love?"

"No, Sam ..."

Kay and Sam sat with her all night, listening to the hiss of the machines and the occasional gurgle from her son sleeping nearby. Tweeter didn't move. Kay wondered about Pendar Tower, at the empty rooms and her vacant office in the village, and the Cat God pub, her bar. He wondered what the place would be like without her. Kay absently rubbed Tweeter's beak. He hopped into Kay's hand.

"You ok, brother?" Kay asked.

Tweeter was in mourning. He seemed to understand that Ki was gone.

* * * * *

Kay and Sam strolled the grounds around the Hospitaler sanctum. They both had quickly regained their strength. Her bruises were fading. Her scarring also was disappearing a little bit more every day. The Hospitalers filed her nails down and even cut her hair to a Vith length, ending at the small of her back. It was odd seeing her without her hair spilling down to her ankles. They both were eager to return to Kana, finish their jar, and have their first batch of children. Children, new vibrant life, would, symbolically, put an end to this episode. But the Hospitalers wanted to continue examining them both for a few more days, just to make certain their conditions were stable. So far, they appeared to be so.

Phillip and Thomasina were gone, off to Waam for Phillip to acclimatize to his new home. Sarah was still mad at them for eloping. Sarah went on and on about the Gellartron at Castle Blanchefort, how she wanted to locate and reactivate it and create a gateway to Waam so Phillip and Thomasina could come and go as they pleased. Sarah was not willing to let go of her brother. Kay, though, wanted nothing to do with Waam and Wilhella Cormand-Grande, to whom he owed his allegiance, though without her Shadow tech, he and Laika would never have survived. He dreaded when she would come calling.

Sarah felt like walking today to test out her improving vision. She wore a pair of goggles to blot out the strong Hoban sun. "These are kind of cool," she said to Sam, the gears within clicking. She knew nothing of the impressive feats 'Ultra Sarah' had accomplished while she was asleep. The Hospitalers advised against telling her for the time being, might be too much of a shock. Give her some time. Certainly, there would be no living with her once she knew. King sat on Sarah's shoulder, quietly protective of her.

However, Ultra Sarah was not gone. Kay and Sam saw her hologram every night, gliding about the Hospitalers' sanctum when Sarah was asleep. As soon as the lights went out, there was Ultra Sarah wanting to be sociable. "Hey you guys, you asleep or something? Let's get a game going!" Sam loved Ultra Sarah, found her to be fun, yet classy and sophisticated. She soon preferred Ultra Sarah over Awake Sarah. One evening Kay saw her knocking on Raal's door. The door opened, she winked at him, and went in.

"So, that Raal guy asked if I'd like to have dinner with him this evening," Sarah said, fiddling with her goggles.

"And what did you say, Sarah?" Sam asked.

"I said 'get bent'. Why in the Name of Creation would I want to have dinner with a creepy Hospitaler who just got done putting my face back together? The guy finger-paints in body fluids."

"Well, who knows, Sarah. You might like him," Kay said.

"No fraggin' way."

They rounded the bend, Sarah chattering on about nothing as usual, playing with her goggles. There, sitting in the field on a flower-strewn dais surrounded by Hospitalers was Roethaba, wearing a fiery jeweled gown. The golden necklace created by Vehelm of Waam hung from her neck, the headset sat on her head of regal honey blonde hair.

No more hologram, a real flesh and blood woman sat there. The Hospitalers had made use of the parts of Lady Chrysania that Phillip had carried and protected through the Gellartron, re-attaching them to her body. She was very beautiful, a warm, smiling woman restored to how she was thousands of years ago. Her followers from all over came to sit in attendance with her every day.

Standing at her side was Laika, armor gone, wearing a comfortable tunic, a single long sword and the DeeDee rifle Kay had given her holstered at her back. Laika gave Kay plenty of distance now that Sam was back, spending most of her time with Roethaba, and her inscrutable face betrayed nothing of what she was feeling within; though, occasionally, Kay caught her gazing at him from afar. Kay tried to include her in their daily activities. He went out of his way to make her feel welcome, but she seemed shy and distant, content to stand at her mother's side. One evening, Kay wrote a long letter to Laika and gave it to King to deliver to her. Using his Sight, he saw her sitting in her room, wearing a shirt from Carahil's store, reading it. The next night, when all were asleep, Kay met her out in the fields and finally made good on his promise to wrestle with her. They wrestled all night long.

Sarah wanted to run over and say hello to Roethaba, but she kept trying to cut the line ahead of all the other people waiting to see her.

"Cutting in line is quite rude, Lady Sarah," King said.

"Oh, come off it," she said. "She's our buddy!"

Kay laughed. "Come on, Sarah, clear her some space, will you?"

"Let's go see Sebastian!" Sarah cried. "King, where's Sebastian?"

"Around the bend."

"Let's go!"

Bursting with smiles, they rounded another corner of the sanctum. There, under a shade tree was Sebastian, playing rough with one of the staff girls on a blanket. Several people sat in the shade, watching.

They came up. "So, how you doing, you old git?" Sarah asked in her loud voice. She adjusted her goggles a little in the shade.

"Who's an old git?" came an answer.

Sitting near the edge of the blanket was the Professor. He had shed his usual scholarly aloofness, watching his son with pride. Sitting next to him in a robe and slippers was Ki, a little heavy-lidded and weary, but very much sound and alive. Tweeter, back to his old self, bounced at her shoulder, surging with energy. She was wearing a weighty necklace, it stuck out through the folds of her robe, and a headset similar to Roethaba's; the antenna rising up through the brownish-blonde mass of her curled hair, though it was constructed in a much more utilitarian Hospitaler style; it wasn't 'pretty' like the one hanging around Roethaba's neck. The Professor had the holo-plans for it sitting in front of him. He had been going over every circuit and sub-system, pasting it into his brain. He fussed with the headset every so often, re-situating it on her head. He already had various ideas on how to improve the design, to minimize it, possibly to internalize it and add redundancy. Redundancy was crucial. Still a crab-head, Ki pushed his hands away when she got tired of him. "Lemme be, will ya?" she'd say.

*　*　*　*　*

They had all gathered around Ki's bed, watching the monitors, seeing her grow thin and pale in the sterile light of her room. When the Professor arrived, he was beside himself. After contemplation, he decided to remove Ki from the machines, let her pass, and then take her home to wild Onaris, where she could be buried in her family plot in the sun by the sea; but, as they unhooked the machines and wheeled them away, Raal made a critical discovery. While her Waking Self had died due to the rigors of the second Gaming Session, her Sleeping Self still lived; faint, barely readable on the scanners, but present nonetheless. They brought in the latest Mentralysis Deck, hooked her up and there she was—Ki's Sleeping Self, her voice loud and grumpy. The Hospitalers copied Vehelm's necklace and headset from the originals and created a second set. When they placed the device on her head, she opened her eyes and lived again. The first thing she did was bitch about her painted nails and throw a fit over her curled hair. She was ready to fight somebody.

It was good to have her back.

Elated, the Professor began preparations to wire Castle Blanchefort and the village for Ki's use and the best Mentralysis Decks were to be sent there without delay, installed by Raal's team.

After analysis, the Hospitalers determined Ki was an MC, or Moderate Change Archetype, which was one of the more mild types and no differences in her personality could be readily detected; she was still the same loud, crabby person—which was just what they all needed. They would have Ki no other way. She was just too ornery to die.

*　*　*　*　*

"I can't get these damn curls out of my hair," Ki said, pawing at her curly locks with disgust. "If my sisters saw this, they'd give me no peace. I'd have to fight every one of them. I'm probably going to have to cut them off or something. Who told the Hospitalers to curl my hair?"

"Nobody, they did it on their own," Kay said. "They thought it made you look pretty. When we get home, see Lady Kilos and she might be able to tease the curls out without you having to chop your hair off. She is a sorceress when it comes to hair."

"I swore she'd never get me in that ruddy chair of hers. We'll just bob this mess down and be done with it," Ki said. "It'll grow back; in fact, we all used to sell our hair for money when I was a kid. Somebody was buying, don't know who, but somebody did. Did I ever tell you that?"

"No, Ki," Kay said.

She laughed. "Oh, you know what? The Hospitalers said they named this condition after me; they're calling it the 'Kilos Syndrome'." She gave the Professor a sharp elbow. "Hear that, hon? They named a horrible brain condition after me. How about that?"

She stood up and stretched. "Ok, Sebastian, you ready for your mom?" She stepped out of her slippers and got down on the blanket with her son, roughly rolling around with him. Sebastian had his mother's pugnacious spirit. He grabbed her around the neck, her Mentralysis headset went ajar as they wrestled.

They all watched with nervous anticipation, ready to dive in and save her should she need it. "Hey, Ki," Sarah said, removing her duster and goggles. "Look, you should rest. I'll fight with him, ok?"

"Will you people relax?" she said, re-situating the headset. "I can feel the tension with you guys; it's going to be ok, I promise. Look, if I can't sit in the sun with my husband, if I can't enjoy the company of my friends, and if I can't wrestle around with my son, then I'd rather be dead. If I'm going to live, then I'm going to live."

They seated themselves and watched Ki for the rest of the afternoon. The technology keeping her alive seemed sound and durable. For Kay, seeing Ki as a doting mother, Sam whole, Sarah whole and well, brought this ordeal to an end.

11—The Tower of One Hundred Spires

Kay honestly had no idea what to do with Clara Wunderluck. Vith law gave the local lord great powers when dealing with criminals and other assorted law-breakers. With his parents still out of the League and given the old laws, he could, essentially, do with her what he wished. He could have her hauled off and executed on the old Blockman's Stump near the bay; he could have her beaten out of the village into exile and certain death in the mountains; or he could hand her over to the Sisters. An old Maserfeld classic was known as a *Jockanar*, to launch a criminal into space from the old rail tube without benefit of suit or oxygen and allow them to expire. Or, he could simply hold Clara without trial forever.

The problem with Kay was that he was no tyrant or executioner; he couldn't simply have people killed or *Jockanar*ed into space like his great grandfather once did, and he couldn't simply make people 'disappear' in the night, or have them sent off to the Sisters. From what Phillip had told him, despite her treachery, Clara had shown skill and level-headedness and had contributed to their safe passage through the Gellartron at Castle Bloodstein. Kay admired those things and found them worthy. His plan was to simply keep Clara in Ki's jail until Captain Davage and Countess Sygillis returned to the League from distant Eng. At that time, he could brief them on what had happened and they could decide on what to do with her.

The problem with Clara: she was a sly little fox. With plenty of time on her hands, Clara did some research from her jail cell and discovered an old proviso in Vith law that compelled the local lord to immediately respond to a longhand letter marked URGENT.

Clara pummeled Kay with letters. She sent them all day long, she sent them while Kay was taking his meals, while he was having a soak in the bath house; they came in the middle of the night while he was sleeping, and sometimes while he was making love to Sam. Once, Clara sent Kay sixty letters in one day. Running out of paper, she soldiered on and sent them on napkins, towels, scraps of clothing, toilet tissue—anything she could write on.

In all cases, Kay was compelled, by law, to stop what he was doing and respond to her letters immediately. Her letters varied wildly in tone; some making threats and issuing outlandish demands regarding her care and release. She demanded entertainments, authentic Remnath foods, and scheduled furloughs from the jail cell, including visits to her home in Remnath. In one letter she demanded a conjugal visit, and had further demanded that Kay himself, or Phillip, or both of them at once, perform the servicing. Some letters were more tentative in nature, seeking to open some sort of dialogue between their two 'great' Houses. She bemoaned her fate; in others she resorted to out and out harlotry to entice Kay to free her—if Sam had seen those, she would have marched down to the jail and throttled Clara to death. Sometimes, Kay had a mind to allow her to do just that. In all the letters, though, Clara maintained a fair amount of wit and charm, and Kay sometimes found himself laughing out loud as he read them. He found himself, at least in a small way, enjoying the hand-written joust. As he had with Laika, Kay found he admired Clara's spirit.

Still, from his own recollections, and from what Phillip and Thomasina had told him, Clara Wunderluck could not be trusted. She was a relentless opportunist, an anarchist, a thief, casual murderer and a liar supreme who wasn't afraid to get her hands dirty.

And, worst of all, she knew they had the Machine and was obsessed to get her hands on it. The best place for her was behind bars in Blanchefort Village until his father and mother returned to the League, then they could determine what to do with her.

The Professor, though, came up with a solution to the relentless letter-writing.

"If the letters are an issue, you can simply change the law. Do you not know your own laws? Use of arbitrary powers was a highlight of your great-grandfather's rule. Shall I show you the statutes? The text is fairly clear," he chided.

The next day, Kay made a proclamation and the letters from Clara stopped. For now, she was silenced.

✶ ✶ ✶ ✶ ✶

Kay and Sam found Sarah in the Mystery Library. She had been laboring for days, getting it back into order, the two of them helping her however they could. She had books and papers spread all over the Durst table, meticulously putting them back exactly where they had gone before the Jones attack. King sat on the table. He was busy separating a bowl of red and blue colored grains of sand into two individual bowls, one grain at a time.

"Wow, Sarah, you've done some work here, haven't you?" Kay said, admiring what she had accomplished so far.

"Thanks, still got a ways to go." She fussed about. "Grab a seat, keep me company while I work. Don't touch anything! I've got a system going. Sam, I'm going to need you to help me lift some stuff soon. Is that ok?"

Sam seated herself. "Certainly, Sarah."

"Great!"

Kay smiled. It was so good being home with the people he loved.

"Hey, I've got something here for you, Sarah," Kay said, holding out a stack of leather-bound books. "These just came in to-day."

Sarah stopped what she was doing. "What are these?"

"A present from your friend, Lord Raal of Niles," he responded.

Sarah rolled her eyes. "Oh, not him again! Creation, he must have gotten his thrills peeking at my blank naked body or something while I was in the bag on Hoban. How many times am I supposed to tell this guy to get lost?"

"Don't know. Have you ever considered, Sarah, that deep down, you might fancy Lord Raal after all?" Kay said.

"No. Why would I?"

"Just a thought." Kay pushed the books across the table toward Sarah. "Might as well have a look."

Sarah looked them over. They were tales of ghost stories and mysterious happenings on Hoban, subject matter Sarah loved. She seated herself and opened them, fascinated. "Well, maybe he's not so bad," she said, flipping through the pages. "Maybe I'll invite him to the Firth House sometime to say thanks for these. As soon as I read them, I'll get them shelved."

As she looked through the books, King finished his tedious work with the sand; all the red grains were in one bowl, all the blue in the other. He fluttered toward the exit. "Hey, where you going?" Sarah asked as she mixed the grains of sand back together again in a common bowl, undoing all he had done. "Get your butt back over here. You're not finished yet—these grains still aren't separated. Get back to work."

Silently, King returned to his spot on the table and began separating the grains of sand once again.

"Why are you making him perform this pointless work?" Kay asked.

"Because I'm afraid he's going to kill himself. I'm trying to keep him busy."

King patiently moved the grains of sand around with his beak, saying nothing.

"Kill himself?" Kay asked. He turned to King. "King, is this true?"

They all looked away and King spoke. "It is my Creator's wish," he said.

"My mother," Sarah yelled, "snuck some sort of suicidal programming into King's brain—probably because I kept hiding them and Mother didn't like that. Once all his tasks are complete, the death programming will kick in and he'll fly out to the servant's graveyard in the grove, thereby destroying himself."

"King," Sam said. "There's no need for you to do such a thing. Do you want to destroy yourself?"

King methodically worked the sand. "My wants are irrelevant. I hear my Creator's call, and I must obey."

Kay laughed. "Well then, King, who says your tasks have come to an end? Forget this sand business; your task is to protect this castle and all those within. That task is ongoing. We need you here with us."

King responded, bits of sand clinging to his beak. "My life force is derived from yours, from all present during my summoning. I would not rob you of your life to sustain my own."

"If you need a small bit of our lives to exist, then it is well-given," Kay said. "Protect us from evil, King, that is your task. Are you up to it?"

King blinked. "Evil is a concept. There is no being rid of evil, for it is a by-product of good."

"Then, I guess you'll be busy with all this evil floating about," Kay said.

Sarah was elated. "Good one, Kay!" She collected the bowls and threw the sand into a bin. "You're not going anywhere, right, King?" she asked.

King fluttered up to his favorite perch and fluffed his feathers. "Apparently not."

＊　＊　＊　＊　＊

The bulk of the items stolen from Castle Blanchefort came back slowly over the next few weeks, hauled in through the Gellartron at Gallia Palace, now patrolled by a company of Raal's Hospitalers. They made many expeditions to Ghome's bastion at Edamathrombo, slowly going through and reclaiming the taken items. The Gellar-tron at Castle Bloodstein appeared to be dead, deactivated by Phillip, Thomasina and King. With that, Castle Bloodstein fell in upon itself and collapsed. The last remnant of the Bloodsteins on Kana was a snow-covered pile of blackened stones haunted by faceless ghosts with metal hands lurking in the woods.

The great Bower Chest was gone. They saw no trace of it soaring in the skies of Edamathrombo. Kay was certain it was near Roethaba on Hoban, much smaller, having passed through the Gellar door at Gallia Palace. One evening, he was certain he had seen it sitting out in the moonlight near Roethaba's chambers.

They managed to reclaim most everything taken, including the Machine and the Mallus Mirror. After all that had happened, they were keen to take the Machine apart and melt down the components. It was too potent and too tempting to keep intact. Who would be coming for it next?

The problem was the Machine refused to be taken part. They had had issues with the Machine in the past where the internal joints and linkages proved devilishly difficult to take apart, but now, it seemed impossible. Even the Professor wasn't much help.

Destroying it also seemed fruitless. They tried melting it, blasting it, hammering it: nothing. The Machine truly seemed invincible. So, what to do with it? Queen Ghome and the Wunderlucks had proven that there were many who would risk extinction itself to possess it. The Wunderlucks were all but gone, with the exception of a few hangers-on in Remnath and Clara Wunderluck, returned to her cell in Blanchefort Village; her trial indefinitely 'pending.'

They decided their only course of action was to hide the Machine and stand guard over it in perpetuity as sentinels. Leaving it on the surface in the Grove was out of the question. It had to be hidden somewhere deep. Phillip proposed hiding it in one of the many caverns under the castle, which seemed like a good idea, but the caverns were far from impregnable. There were many ways in and out and it was impossible to seal or guard them all. They were certain that people would come looking for the Machine. The rumor mills across Kana were turning and tales were already being spun in the various social circles in the League. Kay's sister Lady Kilos had Commed up from her endurocon ball, quite concerned. She had heard that 'something weird' had occurred at Blanchefort. She had assured her friends at the ball that nothing had happened, but she was keen to know for herself. Kay told her and she was horrified.

Certainly, there would be the casual curious. Certainly the Sisters would come, drinking tea, asking questions, Staring them for information. The Machine had to be in an unreachable, unseeable, unStareable place. The caverns were out.

Sarah wanted to put the Machine out on Dead Hill in the vaults of the dead. She reasoned the spirits of their Blanchefort ancestors would both scare off interlopers and help defend it. The issue was, the spirits of the dead might try to use the Machine for their own ends. Dead Hill was out as well.

They needed a place that was out of the open, that had only one way in and out, and that was perfectly hidden. The optimal place would be someplace that existed in Castle Blanchefort but was not in Castle Blanchefort at the same time, in case the Sisters came and made a thorough search, which was sure to happen soon.

Then Kay had an idea. He recalled passing through the Mystery Library and discovering the extra-dimensional node connecting all of the various places associated with Carahil. There was Carahil's wondrous store, where they had taken refuge after The Jones' attack (a subsequent, highly anticipated trip with Sam and Sarah to show them the store ended in failure. A CLOSED sign and gate barred their entry. Sarah was hair-pulling disappointed). There was also the dark Cathedral of Bone and Wire where King had simmered in frustration and which Kay had avoided. The final node was a little patch of ground by an unknown sea under a cheery sky: Carahil's Porch, as King had called it. Searching it, the Porch proved to be a tiny pocket node of reality with only one entrance and was uninhabited. It seemed a perfect place to hide the Machine.

They hauled in the Machine. Lady Poe, back from the south, created a giant Silver tech fortress by the sea with a hundred towers and Whisper-locked the entire place, with a million Whispers floating about powered by a grand autopyle to sustain them. In each tower she created a perfect Silver tech facsimile of the Machine and guarded it with a Bark sentinel dog. If an invader wished to take the Machine, they would first have to penetrate the Mystery Library, find their way into the correct node, get past the million Whispers and locate the correct Machine in one of the hundred towers while being observed the entire time by the Barks.

And there they left it, hidden in its tower overlooking the sea in Carahil's Porch. The Machine seemed to favor its new home.

✳   ✳   ✳   ✳   ✳

"Hello, Carahil," Kay said. "We wanted to come out and have a word with you."

Leafy sunshine filtered down to the cobbles of the Grove. Sam was there with him, wearing a pretty blue dress. She seated herself on the wall as Kay spoke. Her belly stuck out just a tiny bit. She placed her hand on it.

Kay stood before the great statue of Carahil in the Greyson Courtyard, 'Carahil's Walk' as it was known. The statue was placed at the western side of the courtyard, set up in a landscaped nook complete with a pedestal and a number of accent lights illuminating the statue from below. The statue had been donated by the House of Xandarr to mark the place where the benevolent cosmic spirit Carahil had been born. Members of the Xandarr 44 often made pilgrimage to this spot to pray and curry his favor.

Kay continued, looking up into Carahil's peaceful face. "So, I had the opportunity to meet your daughter, Atha, recently. She's very pretty. Looks a lot like her grandmother, Lady Poe. I wonder why she wears those goggles all the time? I'm certain, with her face uncovered, she would be a rare beauty."

He paused. "An arrangement was made with Atha during this whole Queen Ghome affair. She never specified what she wanted, but I believe I know what it is. She wants to use the Machine, to do with it what she will. We have hidden the Machine with the intent of it not being used any further, by us or anybody else. The temptation is simply too great. I need to make it perfectly plain that Atha came through on her end of the bargain. She did everything she promised she would and more. Many people might be dead today were it not for her help. Where my concern lies is that Atha is not you, Carahil. You give of yourself without hesitation, and I see much of you in your daughter. Were you to use the Machine, I have no doubt you would do so responsibly; however, I do not know what Atha would do. Per our agreement, when Sam and I finish our jar, then Atha will come to collect, and I expect she will want to be given access to the Machine. I do not know Atha. She has much of your light, but there is also a little bit of darkness in her that I cannot fathom, and that gives me pause. So, I suppose what I'm saying—"

"What Kay is trying to say, Carahil, is that we are pregnant," Sam said, jumping in. "New life grows in my belly. Our jar is but a few cosmetic touches away from being completed."

"Yes, and we beseech your wisdom," Kay said. "If you believe that your daughter Atha is trustworthy and will use the Machine responsibly, as you would, then we will take her to it and disarm the defenses we have put in place. I don't mean to be a snitch or a tattle-teller and inform you of things said in private, but this is a matter of grave importance, and thus we have come to you, essentially to 'tattle' on Atha."

The silent statue of Carahil smiled down on Kay from its landscaped nook.

"Do you think he heard us?" Sam asked after a minute or two.

"Of course he did."

Sam rustled. "I hope he gives us some sort of answer soon. Will you take me back to our tower, Kay? I'm feeling rather tired."

"How many children do you think are in there?" Kay asked.

"Maybe ten or twelve. Hard to say."

Kay turned to help Sam up and stroll back with her to the castle. He immediately fell face-first to the cobbles, landing on his hands. His boots had been laced together with a festive silver ribbon. Sam shot up to help him, first checking her own feet to see if they had been laced together as well. Carahil was a known jokester. Fortunately, Sam's feet were ribbon-free.

As Sam helped untangle Kay, she noticed a small note attached to the ribbon. It read:

Finish your jar without worry. I'll have a talk with my daughter.
I am very proud of her, yet she is her own person.
Teach your children well. You will see us often.
-C

Kay and Sam returned to the castle. They had their jar to finish and their children to prepare for.

Fin:
RDG April 2017

ABOUT THE AUTHOR

Ren Garcia, the author of the League of Elder Series, graduated from the Ohio State University with a degree in literature. He enjoys playing volleyball, urban exploration, taking pictures of clouds, and ice hockey. He lives in Columbus, Ohio, with his wife and their four vivacious little wiener dogs. You can visit Ren's website/ on-line glossary at:

http://www.thetempleoftheexplodinghead.com

THE DEMON KILLED THE MERTHIG

The Universe is on the brink of destruction. The Gods task Lord A-Ram and Lady Alesta to pick a replacement for the lost Merthig. From thousands of candidates, they must pick one, just one, and they better choose well, or the Universe might see its end

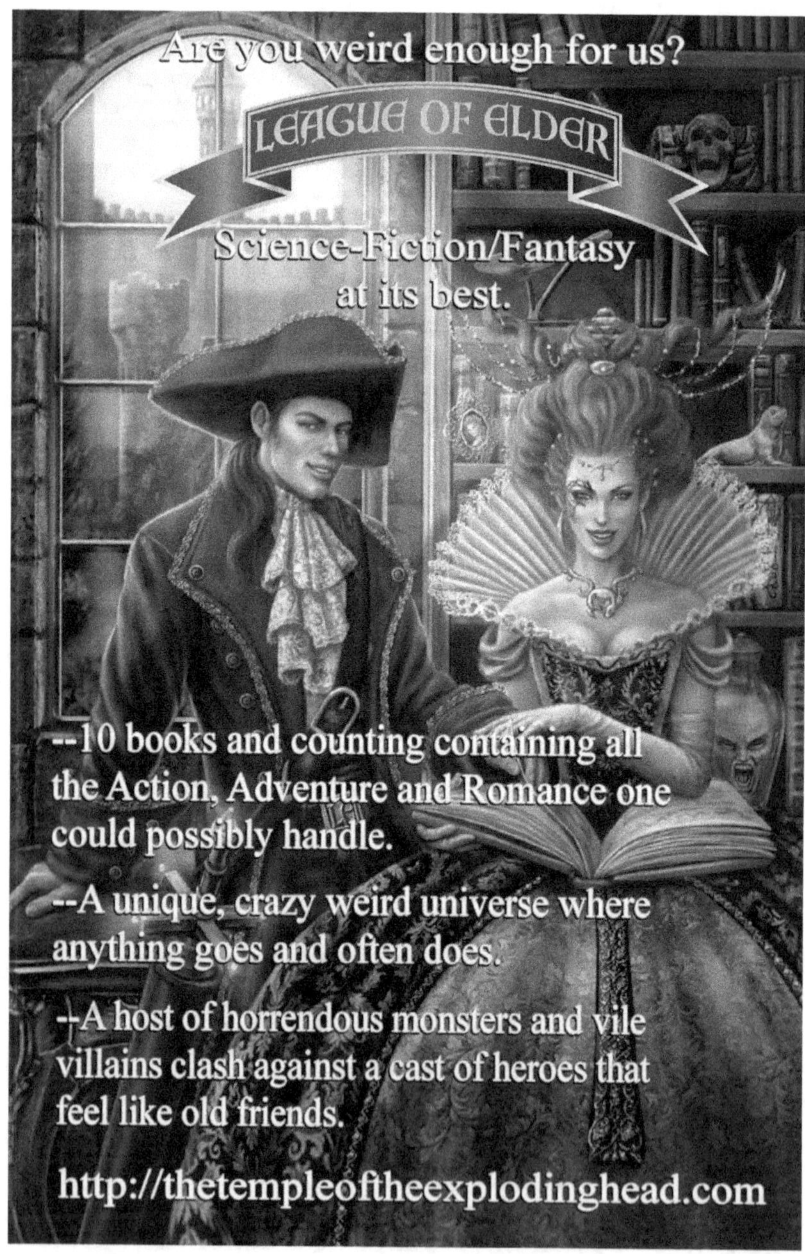

VISIT THE ON-LINE LEAGUE OF ELDER GLOSSARY

https://leagucofelderglossary.com